BY THE RIVERS OF BABYLON

BY THE RIVERS OF BABYLON

CINDY BROWN AUSTIN

SBI

STREBOR BOOKS

NEW YORK LONDON TORONTO SYDNEY

Strebor Books
P.O. Box 6505
Largo, MD 20792
http://www.streborbooks.com

ISBN-13 978-1-59309-117-0
ISBN-10   1-59309-117-6
LCCN 2006938900

First Strebor Books trade paperback edition April 2007

Cover design: www.mariondesigns.com

10 9 8 7 6 5 4 3 2 1

Manufactured in the United States of America

For information regarding special discounts for bulk purchases,
please contact Simon & Schuster Special Sales at 1-800-456-6798
or business@simonandschuster.com

DEDICATION

For My Lord & Saviour Jesus Christ, whose unfathomable love
drew me from the waters, and for the victims and survivors of
Hartford, Connecticut's Charter Oak Terrace housing project.

ACKNOWLEDGMENTS

The effort of giving birth to a new creation is an exhausting and momentous undertaking. I would not have accomplished this task without the assistance of numerous midwives who stayed with me through this long and arduous process:

For my husband, David Jeffery, whose constant love and hard work made it possible for me to dream and to reach for the stars. For my coaches and corner men, Pastor Rufus & Sister Delores Shepard Jr., who labored for years on their knees for me and fought for my vision even when I had lost it. For my amazing mother, Judith T. Ryans, who instinctively put the first book in my hand and demanded I read it, and for my three strong and virtuous sisters, Joy Brown (I miss you so much), Jackie Hawkins (my Other-Mother) and Robin Chapman (my Baby-Sis), who refused to let me give up. For Tahari, Torria, Tianna, and Tiffani, my four daughters, who patiently allowed me to sacrifice their time for the writing process; for Lary Bloom, my literary father, who took the time to love and to train me; for Reginald Callway, who believed in me; for John T. Brooks, who inspired me; for Lee Paquette, my editor and friend, who found me; for Steve Courtney, Stan Simpson, Jenifer Franks and Jeff Rivers, who taught me; for Julie North and Stephanie Summers, my kindred sisters, who dreamed with me; for John Motley, who remembered me; for Dr. Dennis Barone, who interceded for me; for Kay "Sweet" Jerome, who loved me; for Maggie Claud, who loved me; for my agent, Sara Camilli, who fought for me; for Zane, who remembered me; for

Saint Joseph College and *The Hartford Courant*, who cultivated me; for my new son-in-law, Tyron Dotson and his family, who respected me; for my father-in-law, Joe Frank Claud (and Margaret) who cheered me on. For The Church of Jesus Knows Best Inc. and the soldiers of our Women of Prayer: Cynthia T. Henderson, Erma Thompson, Terraine Perry, Andrea Williams, Saundra Mindrell, Brandi Ricks, Tashiana Henderson, Ankara Shepard & Cassandra Shepard.

For my very best friends, Beverly Mann, Darlene Lundy, Geneva Billy, Angela Herndon, Kathleen Barnett, Carol Walters, Diana Martin, Melvinia Parker, Kendra Teal, Cheryl Pressey, Dorthula Green, Sharon Claud and Vicky Alston. For my brothers, Frank "Gerond" Claud, Jerome Hawkins Sr., Ronnie Chapman, Reggie Battles, Robert Cottingham, Theodore Johnson (and Lynn), Lorenzo (and Valerie) Bouier, Dennis Henderson Sr., Mark Jocko, Troy Holt, Kenneth J. Hicks, Duane Fernandez Sr., Jonathan Mumby, Zachary Bridges, Tyrone Canino, Malcolm Tanksley, Kenneth Barnett, Gayland, Mark, Gregory and Courtney Alston. For Wayne, Valerie, Meredith, Karen, Byron, Belinda, and all of their families, for the seeds that remain; Tonya, Shannon and Tisa Claud, Deneisha Austin, Ashon Austin, Rashar Brown, Sharonne Hawkins, Jason Bush, Jacob Hawkins, Kristin Brown, Jerome Hawkins Jr., Dana Hawkins, Jason Ryans, Cherelle Cottingham, Quinneisha Austin, Jakari Austin, Amber Chapman, D'azia Austin, Julian Ryans and Jaden Austin.

For Bishop Arlonzo Boswell and the Greater Refuge Church of Christ, for Elder Willie Walker and Greater Refuge Church of Christ #2, for Bishop John Thomas and Bethesda Apostolic Church, for Bishop Marion Shaw, and New Hope Pentecostal Church, for Elder Anthony Cole and Body of Christ Apostolic Church, for Bishop Andrew Clancy and Christ Church of Deliverance, for Bishop Winfred Hamlet and the Gospel Lighthouse Apostolic Church, for Elder Lamar Belcher and the Anointed Tabernacle, for Bishop Terry Stringer and the Greater Bibleway Temple of Praise, for Bishop Eddie Cooper and the Pentecostal Church of Faith, for Bishop Theodore Brooks and Beulah Heights, for Elder Frederick

Jackson and Greater Grace Apostolic Church, for Bishop Clifton Jones and the Jerusalem Temple, for Dr. Eugene Lundy and the Church of Christ of the Apostolic Faith, for Dr. Edgar Posey and the Living Faith Apostolic Church, for Bishop James Tyson & Elder C. Shawn Tyson and Christ Church, for Bishop Noel Jones and the City of Refuge, Bishop Arthur Brazier and the Apostolic Church of God, Bishop Horace Smith and Apostolic Faith Church, Bishop Charles Ellis and Greater Grace Temple, for the ministries of the Pentecostal Assemblies of the World and the United Pentecostal Church, and to all my brothers and sisters of the Apostolic Faith world-wide.

And in memory of Lucille Lee, Regina Phillips, Ronald Bush, Diane Claud, Betty Manley, Janet Austin, Joy D. Brown, Elizabeth Shepard, Doreen Lee, Henry Mckelvey, Austin L. Dyson, Christina Bass.

Finally, for all of those who KNOW I love them, but whose names just would not fit on this page… Thank you for understanding. Please charge it to my head, not to my heart.

"By the Rivers of Babylon, there we sat down;
we wept when we remembered Zion..."
—PSALMS 137:1

Once upon an ancient time, in a world inhabited by the invisible powers of the world to come, there was a complex and volatile civilization called Babylon.

Magnificent in splendor, and situated in the river basins of the Euphrates and Tigris water courses, the city was known for its mysticism and wonder, its seductive enticement and imaginative entertainment. Above all, it was a holding place for demons and for the thousands of warring nations that had been subdued and captured by the Babylonian army. The citizens of this nation, as numerous as dust and as brilliant as stars, built their fortunes with the knowledge that they were at the mercies of dozens of miniature gods they believed dwelled in those fertile, low-laying basins all around the great Nile River. These demi-gods required their flesh and their souls for their depths of manifestation and the citizens of Babylon were willing accomplices.

It was the river god, though, the great Nile, that they worshipped most of all. It was he, they thought, the River-god, as he was called, who determined whether they lived or died. Or so they thought...

CHAPTER ONE

"For there they that carried us away captive required of us a song..."
—PSALMS 137:3

A barefoot woman in a torn dress was running along a cratered path between buildings. Her long hair, matted and wind-tousled, but silky as the inside of a coffin, flapped like ravens' wings against her shoulders. Her burnished arms, cross-hatched with scars, held the hands of two little boys who could barely keep up with her, moving so fast their feet were a blur.

The taller of the boys, dressed only in pajama pants, was sobbing uncontrollably. The face of the smaller boy, who had managed to put on one of his sneakers and only the top of his pajamas, was shut as hard as a door. Above them, the sky, clotted with stars, was as purple as a bruise.

Shades jerked as they ran past two more high-rises, past faces pressed curiously against windowpanes and hallways spilling over with junkies and teenagers. Laughter tittered behind them. A yellow dog, tied with frayed rope to an iron railing, lunged in vain. They ran on, breaths heaving, and a woman collecting cans from a driveway paused knowingly, pointed toward the last tenement's open hallway door.

"Come on," she beckoned, but they ran on. It was a typical Friday night and the odor of burning dumpsters filled the air.

At the end of the last tenement, the makeshift path suddenly curved downward into high grasses filled with rats' nests and discarded trash. She dragged them on still, crushing through debris to the mesh fencing that separated the tenements from the river bottom. The shorter boy lost his sneaker here, but held tightly to her hand, refusing to cry.

The woman groped blindly until she found it, a hole, like a slit in the mesh. She pushed the shortest boy through first, angled herself through and dragged the sobbing boy in behind her.

"Shhh now…" She smacked him so hard he bit his lip.

The shouts of a running man silenced the cicadas. The woman looked fearfully toward the sound. Behind them, the mesh quivered and they knew, drunk as he was, he had found the breach.

Moving deftly in the darkness, they huddled at last under the familiar canopy of thick willow that had become, by now, more sanctuary than shelter. She held them close, her eyes closed, lips moving like a prayer in the darkness. They knew the routine. Sometimes she dragged them here and they stayed for days, living off wild blueberries or leeks or whatever else they could find. Other times, when he appeared suddenly at the door, she sent them there alone, shoving them out the back door and into the dark hallway where they stumbled all the way down the stairs and to the river.

Now, in the grainy darkness, the smallest boy's eyes glowed like a cat's. He could smell the rich, dark riverbank soil, hear the suck of water as it slapped and lapped along the water's edge. *He* was the cause of all of this inconvenience and the reason the left side of their mother's pretty face was beginning to blacken and swell. One day *he* might mistakenly stumble through the bramble and actually find their secret place, find the three of them crouched there, huddled there as always, praying for their lives. Hatred gleamed and welled up inside of him now, the shiny blackness filling him so completely that it tangled and caught in his throat, made it difficult to breathe. He swallowed hard, tried coughing into his fist, but it refused to move. Looking up in the darkness at his mother, he saw the wetness sliding from her eyes, the bruised skin swelling like a hill along her left temple. She began her humming as usual, tonguing the words of the song he knew by heart now. Loving her was too risky he decided right then, and was relieved to hear the soft patter of rain echoing around them. Soon they'd all be drenched and the river would swell near its borders, but it was alright. The rain, like any water, was a brilliant distraction. Water, he thought, looking again toward the murky river that seemed to lord over everything, was the only constant thing worth depending on.

OCTOBER, 1993

It had rained all day and the fat heavy drops mucked up the riverbank closest to the water's edge. Lincoln Duvall was squatting, rocking back and forth on his heels, watching the surface of the water as it broke to swallow the last rock he'd cast into its center. Water was like life, he thought. Swallowed you up so fast it was like you'd never existed at all.

He knew it before it happened. Saw it in his mind's eye first, the heavy dark boots plunging and plowing through the mud and down the bank toward him. He'd be tall and wiry and pale as an egg. His arms would be held out to balance his body against the weight of gravity pulling him down. He'd be wearing black jeans and a brown hoodie under his leather jacket. He'd be carrying a striped umbrella that made walking in the mud even more difficult. He wouldn't be able to manage it and would fall on his behind. He'd jump up cursing everything then.

"What's up, Man? You coming?" The words shouted against the wind slapped him full in the face. "Look at you. I knew I'd find you here. Tripping at the river as usual…"

Linc looked up knowingly and saw he was right as usual. It *was* Ghost in the expected attire.. He held the striped umbrella forward like an offering, his words slurring into the rain. "It's late, Man. We gonna miss 'em if we don't get up to The Boulevard now."

"I'm coming."

"Now?" Ghost pressed.

"I *said* I was coming." Linc turned back to watch the last ripple. He loved the relentless violence of the rain, loved how it punctured the water's surface like a thousand daggers.

"C'mon if you coming. Don't see why you always gotta do this anyway." Ghost kissed his teeth, annoyed at the prospect of having to wedge his six-foot-four body through the fence again, to wade through all that brush and mud. He turned to start back toward the wards and slid backward easily, the umbrella flying out of his hand. Linc watched as he clamored to his feet cursing and sputtering mud.

"See. You need to learn what your momma shoulda taught you a long time ago."

"What's that?"

"Mind your business."

Linc cast a warning gaze on him and Ghost felt the heat and raised his chin. A chill swept through him. Linc probably made him fall, he thought. Linc was good for that. Was good for casting his will on innocent people and making them prey. One look into his predator eyes and you knew it was possible. Dark, hypnotic, menacing eyes like that weren't human. Eyes that could whip you without putting a hand on you, and regardless of how tough a man was in The Street, eyes like that were impossible to stare into for long. So Ghost caved in like he always did. He averted his own eyes quickly. There was no point in wondering how Lincoln had stood out in the rain all that time without an umbrella and still not managed to get wet. Nothing about Linc Duvall ever made sense.

"I never capped nobody in the rain," said Ghost. "I got a feeling there's gonna be something different about this time."

Sensing fear, Linc scowled his disgust, but said nothing.

"I guess it shouldn't be no different than all the others. Just the way I feel somehow."

Again Linc didn't respond. They stood there quietly, looking out over the restless water.

"*Capping*. What does it mean anyway? Decapitation? Taking off somebody's head?"

Lincoln glanced at his Rolex and frowned. "I hope so," he said finally. He edged forward then, as close as he could get, and hacked into the river.

Ghost shivered in the raw dampness. The wind was blowing ferociously, threatening to snatch his umbrella or at least blow it inside out. He struggled to close it as Lincoln looked up and pointed a finger toward the sky.

The wind seemed to hiccup and then lie still. An eerie calm suddenly hung over the edge of the river. Ghost sneezed twice and hurried to get out of the pelting rain. The wind had not held but the day was still miserable and bleak, fading into growing darkness. It was a day void of life and beauty, Ghost thought, a most ugly day to die.

✝✝✝

"Gabby? Hey you. Hankerson wants to see you in his office. 'Pronto,' he says."

Slumped forward at her desk with both hands clutching her forehead, she didn't move. Not because she hoped he'd go away, but because she *couldn't* move and it looked to the short man in the Brooks Brothers suit leaning half of his body into her cubicle, that she was crying.

"Hey you..." He drummed the foam partition with his stubby fingers and waited. "Gabriella?" he called softly, readjusting the newspaper folded under his arm. "I heard the call about the shooting in the second ward this morning and I knew it was yours. Are you okay? Were you hurt out there?"

Gabriella Sinclaire sighed at last and sat up. Raking tired fingers through her tousled hair, she looked over her shoulder into the denim-colored eyes. Her cheeks were wet, her lashes thickened by the salty water. She wore a gray skirt and a white blouse with a Peter Pan collar. On the front of the snowy blouse, a red blotch the size of a cabbage, bloomed like a rose.

She breathed deeply, fingered the stained collar. "I can't do this anymore, Joe. I just can't. It's just not fair."

He put down the paper and crouching beside her chair, pressed a warning finger against his lips. He watched a single tear slide down the bridge of her nose. He reeked of coffee and tobacco and the tuna baguette he'd had for lunch. Joe was a senior editor who had been with *The Heartford Chronicle* for close to thirty years. He'd be retiring soon, and once he was gone, Gabriella wasn't sure how she'd survive the newsroom's cutthroat climate. Joe was more than a boss. He was a comrade-in-arms.

Now, the police radio dangling from his hip crackled with static. Another call was coming in. Two more cruisers were being dispatched to the first of the three wards to solve yet another domestic dispute. They looked at each other and this time it was Joe who sighed. "Do you want to talk about it?" he asked.

She pressed a tissue against her eyelids and held it there. "Do you know what it's like to get called to a crime scene and find a sixteen-year-old with his chest blown open?"

Remembering his own stint in Vietnam, Joe looked at the floor. She could see his balding crown easily then, the gray wire threaded around his temples. "No. I hope I never find out," he said.

"Well, I just did, Joe, and it wasn't pretty at all." His hairy hand rested on her shoulder. She nodded, acknowledging the gesture. "You can see a hundred homicides and they never affect you the same. You get there all set to gather the facts and you realize once again that you're the only minority woman reporter on the scene. Sure there are other black reporters, but all of them, of course, are men. That's because it's like a war zone out there, what with the armed crowds and emotions flying high…

"You're armed with only a pen and paper and you really think you're ready to handle anything. Then you see the face of a kid lying there on the ground and he looks exactly like someone you used to love. Some old boyfriend you had a serious crush on in high school or some boy who had sat behind you in the sixth grade. You realize that the child is probably his son." She paused to gather the fragments of herself.

"While you're trying to process what you *think* you're seeing, the child's mother breaks through the police barricade screaming hysterically. She's trying to pick up her child's mangled body and the police have to tackle her to calm her down. They want us to report all that, Joe, write it all down. They want us to *find* a way, while this woman is experiencing the shock of her life, to ask her where she lives, what her son's name is, how old he is, just so you we can do a great write-up for tomorrow's headlines."

Gabriella shook her head, let her hands fall into her lap. "Do you know how inhumane that is?"

"Yes," said Joe, his voice very soft.

"And if that isn't enough, you look into the face of the mother and you realize you *know* her. Had gone to school with her all the way up through elementary and into high school. You can see that she's deranged with shock and suddenly, she notices you. She grabs on to you because she can't stop crying and because the shock is too great for her mind to accept. There's no way she can process what's happened to her only son and so she holds on to you until the blood of her baby is transferred from her body to yours. So much blood it messes up your clothes; becomes a terrible stain to always remind you that..." She stopped, unwilling to go on.

"Someone has to do it, Gabriella. It has to be done."

"Why me, though? Why do *I* have to keep seeing it and reporting it and reliving it over and over again?"

Joe shrugged. "Why not you? No one here cares the way you do. You know that. I know that. And *he* knows that." Joe pointed toward the closed office on the other side of the wide corridor. "You're a journalist. An exceptionally good one, which means you'd better go wash your face and get in there. He's waiting, and an audience with Miles Hankerson doesn't happen too often to any of us."

She brushed a loose wave of tawny hair back from her forehead and anchored it behind her ear with a bobby pin. Her hair color matched her eyes and both were only a few shades lighter than her skin. When she stood up to shrug into her suit jacket, her jutting buttocks made it undeniable.

"Good luck," Joe said.

"Luck has nothing to do with it. I know what he wants—a dangerous exposé about all those dealers being murdered in the wards in the last six months and nobody else wants to take it."

"And you will?"

"Have I ever had a choice?"

✝✝✝

The black Escalade rode high and plush above the bustle of the wet street, its dark windows and reinforced steel doors as formidable as a tank's.

In the driver's seat, Linc's face was lit with a sinister glow that made his countenance distorted and unreadable in the dark. He was pursuing the white car furiously, braking hard through obstacle courses of wide trucks, couriers on bikes, umbrella-wielding pedestrians scurrying to get out of the rain.

In the passenger seat beside him, Ghost touched his lighter to a thick joint he'd pulled from a silver cigar case. Fire bloomed, and the top-grade weed sent an immediate rush to his head. He held it out, and wasn't insulted when Linc ignored his offer to share in his pleasure.

"You gonna need it," Ghost insisted. "Need to calm yourself first, take it down a notch. With you, it's always business before pleasure."

"Business? Not to me. This is pleasure," Linc said and Ghost grimaced. Because he'd been pronounced dead more times than anybody cared to count, "Ghost" had seemed the only viable nickname. Shot eight times on four separate occasions, Ghost was living with one kidney (a drive-by), and had a steel plate in his head (a crow bar). He was always walking a tight rope between life and death, and on occasions like this one, he was trying to prepare himself for what could turn out to be yet another out-of-body experience.

Compared to Linc though, he was still more sidekick than equal. Linc was fire and he was ice. Ice, like arctic glaciers, was clumsy and cold, lingering harmlessly, temporarily, wherever it wanted to, in unlikely places. But fire was spontaneous, uncontrollable and deadly. Anything could set it off and cause it to kill at random, leaving charred remains as a witness to its anger. Thick-limbed and muscular, Linc was precisely that, spontaneously dangerous. He had broad shoulders, arms gnarled with muscle, and stood close to six feet tall. His skin was as dark and smooth as semi-sweet chocolate; his hair, wispy as corn-silk around his temples and sideburns, was kept braided into neat furrows traveling away from his face and touching his shoulders. His pupils, like his hair, were black as tar, and although his brows and lashes were luxuriously thick and long, almost girlish in profile, his orbs, like the rest of him, were as hard as granite.

Linc's panther-like physique was an odd contrast to Ghost's pillowy torso, his sprawling gut soft from daily quarts of beer. Thick waves of sandy hair dipped back from a high forehead, and his cool green eyes and thin lips gave away his mixed ancestry. When he brought the joint to his mouth, his teeth, reflecting years of wearing braces, were unnaturally perfect. From the neck up, inside the Escalade, he easily looked Latino. Few in the wards would believe his Italian heritage, his rich grandparents and the summers spent in New Hampshire cottages. There'd been private boarding schools before his stints with Linc at Juvie Hall, and educated nannies with names like Genevieve. But he'd had an odd proclivity for inciting violence, and after the last time he'd attacked his parents with a carjack, his ivy-league father had decided that state institutions were the best place for him. Now though, he was nearing thirty, and the wards had won him over. Now when he spoke on a phone, his thick ghetto patois was as distinct as his Heartford-born mother's.

Sure, he was unusually violent. "Maniacal," the psychologists' reports had described him. But today was different somehow. Today he just wasn't in the mood for committing a homicide. Linc leaned forward and hit his CD changer to pump up his hunting music and Ghost knew, ready or not, it was too late. Linc was rocking his shoulders to Busta Rhymes and the cascade of guns were loaded on the seat between them.

They'd been trailing Spain's white Mercedes on the boulevard for just over half an hour and already he was tired. That was impossible of course, because these runs, completed only after months of careful surveillance, were special and Linc never trusted any of his subordinates to handle this level of business. Spain was notoriously dangerous and taking him out required more than stealth. It required a willingness to die and to die hard at that.

Up ahead now, Spain's driver slowed suddenly and took a sharp right. Linc turned too from a distance. The Mercedes picked up speed, traveling above the 15 mph limit down the narrow, one-way street and Linc lingered back behind two old trucks, following cautiously. They watched the Mercedes go through a stop sign and enter the heavy traffic of Main Street, still on the north side of Heartford, still a ways from the wards.

"You think he's on to us?" asked Ghost.

"Nawl..I think he's behind schedule and wants to dump all that money at the bank before somebody takes it from him." Linc reached down and stroked his Mac 10's sleek veneer.

Spain and his men had tried to maintain a careful vigilance for the past three months, what with all of the wards' dealers getting robbed and smoked and shoved off the tops of their tiers lately. Of the top five operations in the wards, just three were left now, one of which was Spain's, and traveling with an entourage to come and go in the streets was an inconvenience all the big bosses were having to get used to. All except for Lincoln, that is. He trusted no one to know his immediate whereabouts, preferred to keep his soldiers anchored around home base.

The oldest among the five bosses, Spain had been slipping for the past month though, and today, as if scripted, was the worst of all. He'd gone from a five-car security routine down to two cars in the last three weeks, and today, it was just him and his top three boys traveling in one vehicle, the white customized Mercedes that everyone in the wards recognized.

He was just stupid, thought Linc. This would be like taking candy from a baby, and he chuckled to himself, shaking his head. Ghost looked up, frowning.

"What's so funny, Man? Why you always do that? Start laughing at a serious time like this? I mean, I'll do the job, but I ain't exactly feeling it. But you? You just insane. You'd rather smoke a fool than have sex."

"And?"

"And, you ain't nothing but a ghetto serial killer. Just admit it."

Lincoln thought this was funny. Reaching inside his leather jacket and pulling his magnum from its holster, he turned to Ghost and kissed it spitefully. "Quit hating 'cause I'm good at what I do. Yeah. You right. I get great pleasure out of capping fools that need to be capped, and if anybody needs to, it's this one. This fool don't deserve to rule. All that money he's carrying and only three men to guard it? He *deserves* to be robbed. It's an accident waiting to happen."

"I'll just be glad when it's over. Still can't believe we spent three months following this fool."

"Well, don't blink, 'cause you might miss it. This one promises to be as easy as..."

A tan Acura appeared suddenly from out of nowhere as if on cue. It cut in front of them and started traveling unbelievably slowly, so slow the Mercedes, weaving and bobbing through traffic up ahead, was rapidly slipping away from them.

Lincoln growled, leaning hard on the horn; he flicked his lights and tried hard to get around it. Oncoming traffic made it impossible. The Acura was taking up two lanes now, moving even slower as if to protest. It paused to allow a delivery van to enter traffic from a left side street and Lincoln went ballistic. The Mercedes had vanished. Nothing there now but a slow tan car still driving like it owned the road.

Linc slapped the dashboard so hard the CD skipped. Overhead, the sky had darkened from pale cobalt to deep azure, lightning winking like jagged rips in the fabric of sky.

Ghost sighed, let his head loll back against the leather headrest. "I know what you thinking, Man, and it ain't they fault. They just happened to show up in the wrong place at the wrong time. Obviously hitting Spain wasn't meant to be today, so just let it go. It ain't worth what you thinking. We can try again next week."

"*Next week?*" Linc snatched up his mag and shook it hard, pointing it at the windshield. "Whoever's driving that car just cost me fifty-thousand dollars and they gone die for it. Deep is calling unto deep and I'm 'bout to answer it. You can't hang? Close your eyes."

"I'm not closing nothing but this truck door, so pull over and let me out. I ain't trying to catch another case, and shooting some square for taking the wrong turn ain't worth me doing ten to twenty for accessory."

He could see it now: yellow crime scene tape dancing like streamers, static emanating from the radios of the milling dark-coated officers. He and Linc sitting forward in handcuffs again in the back of separate squad cars, heads raised at jaunty angles while crowds stood around gawking. The details of going to jail never changed. There would always be mottled gray cell walls, narrow cots alive with bed bugs. There'd be hours of waiting even after they'd called their lawyers, and he'd be retching into the filthy cell toilet while Linc sat calm as a flea on the rim of his bunk, eyes staring ahead at nothing, nostrils flared against the swarming stink. Prison cells, squad cars, it didn't matter. Linc adapted to any environment like a chameleon. Now he was in a killing mood and nothing Ghost said would persuade him otherwise. Ghost already knew. They'd been partners so long it felt like a marriage.

After years of riding shotgun on these kinds of escapades, Ghost was hardly squeamish, but killing an innocent person who just happened to cut you off in traffic was totally unnecessary.

"Pull over and let me out," he repeated.

"Quit whining like a female. You act like you scared."

"It ain't no act. I'm terrified. You ain't pretty as I am. You ain't got to fight off twenty young fools that been locked down so long they seeing mirages, thinking you they baby's momma."

Linc sputtered with laughter, shoulders heaving as he clutched the steering wheel hard, his body leaning into the curving road.

"Linc, Man. Let it go. Ain't no cause for this."

"Consider it justifiable homicide," Linc said, his heart ticking like a bomb now, like it always did just before he pressed his lips together and concentrated on squeezing the trigger. It's the kind of mood that inspired him to paint; an oil print this time, done in shimmering grays and stark blacks with splashes of random reds like slashes on the canvas. The kind of painting he could hang over the pool table in his rec room. He'd title it simply, "Man with Gun Before He Murders." The very thought soothed him.

The audacity of the driver convinced Linc that he was a male, probably some young cat chilling with his girl and slumped low in his seat while he rapped what was to be his last game. Yeah. By the looks of the late-model car, it was probably some wealthy little college kid who didn't even belong on this side of Heartford and had never been anywhere near the wards. Some kid that would learn the hard way that disrespect on this side of the world was the ultimate insult, payable by death.

Still pouting, Ghost grunted his disapproval and flicked what was left of the joint out the window. Linc ignored him and focused instead on where he would aim. The Mag would make a crater-like chasm in the body, and on a rain-soaked night like this, without any milling witnesses, the effect of so much drama would be totally wasted. Magnums were for making statements, for declaring one's weight and omnipotence. He'd give in to Ghost somewhat and take the merciful route—a small, neat hole behind the ear or just above the temple would make it easier on the bereaved's family. The undertaker's task would be minimal. More cosmetic than reconstruction.

He reached into his jacket and pulled out a pistol so small it barely looked real. It would be perfect for this up-close-and-personal task, but when he checked the chamber, he realized it wasn't loaded. There was plenty of ammo in the Escalade's cargo space, but there was no time to pull over and get it. Just the larger guns were up front with him and Ghost now, guns with the kind of firepower strong enough to tear through steel and take out windshields.

Linc lifted the Magnum from his lap again, stroking its mannish, undeniable strength. The first bullet would do the job.

"You sure?" Ghost looked ill, his face flushed.

Just ahead, the Acura lurched suddenly and swerved right toward the curb, its bronze finish sparkling under the torrential downpour like a goldfish under water.

Linc swerved right behind it, narrowly missing a transit bus in the process. Horns blared, rain pounded like war drums against the Escalade's tinted glass.

The Acura was parking behind a large delivery van that blocked the view of oncoming cars. In the foreground, the spire of a wide brick church pointed hard at the weeping sky.

"Linc." Ghost grabbed at his wrist, fingers slipping against the buttery leather cuffs of his jacket. "It ain't worth it, Baby. C'mon. Get back in the car."

Linc shrugged him off and stepped out into the rain with the Magnum in open view. He walked deftly up to the Acura, snatched open the driver's side door, and what he saw almost made him drop the gun. What he smelled made him speechless.

The calf-length suede skirt was hiked above exquisitely sculpted legs. The lioness eyes were spitting fire, and beneath the luminous skin, as smooth and flawless as raw honey, a strange light flickered.

"Oh...," she said, "...you've come to kill me?"

CHAPTER TWO

Gabriella

H
e had the prettiest eyes I'd ever seen in a black man's face, but why he wanted to blow me away with that big angry gun was a mystery only God knew the answer to.

I had to admit though, his bodacious intrusion into my personal space went perfectly well with the rest of the day I was having. So when he snatched open my car door like he had lost his natural mind, looking for all the world like a very crazed, *very* fine, hip-hop grim reaper, I wasn't a bit surprised.

But even that didn't go over easy.

Had he stopped to ask how I was doing before he'd shoved that pistol all up in my face, I'd have told him just how bad that day had been. How one of my oldest friends had lost her son today in the wards and I'd had the privilege of standing there when she found out. I'd have told him how I'd gone back to work with the boy's blood still on my clothes and sat through a condescending lecture by our editor-in-chief who wanted to personally commend me for all of my hard work while assigning me to yet another ward story that could easily get me killed, provided the Lord allowed it.

I'd have told him how I left work early, went home to change my blouse, called the salon to get my hair done and then sat in the shop for three more hours waiting to be permed, washed and styled according to Miss Imani's "CPT" schedule.

†††

Imani's easily one of *the* best stylists in Heartford, and her hands were legendary for being able to grow anybody's hair, but Imani never hurried. Not even for her own momma.

Three hours at Imani's and I'd still been crazy enough afterward to brave those monstrous lines down at the state's Motor Vehicle Department, a major problem when you're in the throes of ovulation and standing on six-inch heels.

An hour into my wait, and standing behind the license renewal processor's desk, I realized I hadn't brought the right paperwork with me to renew my license and would have to come back and repeat the same agonizing process all over again. I hadn't eaten a thing all day, and my stomach was pitching a serious fit when I'd finally whipped into late-day traffic and "bogarted" my Acura all the way through to Zion Apostolic Church for our Thursday night choir rehearsal.

Famished, bloated and thoroughly aggravated, I was totally tired by then. Tired of watching black folks in the wards kill themselves over nothing, tired of playing Lois Lane for a publication who could care less about my safety and nothing at all about the welfare of my people. I was tired of being lonely, tired of waiting on the promises of a man who was afraid to commit to anybody, and most of all, more than all of that, I was *too* tired to be dealing with a water-logged hoodlum with a gun. But he was standing there anyway as if he owned the world. Standing there with the strangest, orneriest look on his face, and it was then that I'd decided this was one intrusion I was *not* going to put up with.

"So you've come to *kill* me?" I demanded, shocked that after a day like mine, anybody in their right mind had the nerve to not only think they could actually bypass my great big Daddy to hurt me, but had the *nerve* to open *my* car door.

"Beg your pardon?" Brother-Thug was stammering and aiming that gun and looking so confused, I almost slapped him. It looked like it was up to me to finish what Home-boy had started.

"Look," I said, looking at my watch. "Are you gonna shoot me or what?"

"Excuse me?" He licked those pretty lips, his breathing hard and heavy.

"My point exactly. You *need* to be excused, because I'm already late for rehearsal, and Sister Emmaline Franklin, who weighs three-hundred pounds and is six feet two *without* her wig, ain't having it again this week, okay? This means that you need to do what you plan to do in a hot hurry, because to be honest, I really don't have time to die tonight."

He was not hearing me though. He was too busy staring at my fresh hairdo, like he wanted to touch it, and then, of course, when he saw them, started gawking at my legs that were trying to get out of the car. He was tripping hard now, got really fidgety with his gun. He looked at my face, at my hair, at my face, and then back at my legs again. It was always the legs. They're the first thing men always seem to notice about me, which is why I wear my dresses so long.

The fruity smell of Imani's old-fashioned hair pomade, the kind she rubs into everybody's scalp to seal her styles and heighten the hair's natural shine, filled the car. Bad boy must have smelled it too, because he seemed to be inhaling deeply. Standing there with his eyes half-closed, sniffing like he'd forgotten where he was and what he was supposed to be doing because the smell had overpowered him somehow. He looked at my face again and shifted from one foot to the other. Looked at the gun in his hand and then at me with the saddest little boy eyes.

"No offense, aiight?" he told me, "...but I *gotta* shoot you, Baby."

"For?"

"For costing me fifty-thousand dollars," he said, looking at my legs, then at the gun again, stroking the trigger as if he was thinking of what an awful waste it would be, losing those legs.

"*I* cost you fifty-thousand dollars?"

"That's what I said. You owe me fifty-thousand dollars."

"I don't know you from Adam, Sir. And if you're looking for some money, well, my credit card is maxed and I don't have a dime on me right now, so..."

"So?"

Behind us, a car door slammed, but it was too late. We were already transfixed, caught up in the heat of the moment.

My mind raced, thought, *if this is really how I'm going to die, I hope it won't be too messy.* The poor man didn't seem capable of remembering his own name, so how in the world could he accomplish killing me?

"So…," I finished, reaching for my umbrella, determined not to waste another second with this foolishness. "It looks like you're gonna have to put that fifty-thousand dollars on my tab. I've got a date to sing for Jesus tonight, and quiet as it's kept, He doesn't like it when I'm late."

I made my move then. Cutting the engine, I reached for my purse and got out of my car, wielding that umbrella like a club.

Capone just stood there staring at me and shaking his head like he was dimwitted. His lips were pressed together hard, and his nose was open so wide he could almost drown in all this rain.

A mulatto-looking man with hard hazel eyes came up from behind him and tapped his shoulder. Capone balked, obviously angered by the interruption. The pale man's smile was cinematic, but not to be trusted. He whistled long and soft at me, winked. But I turned and walked away from both of them. Pale-boy cursed deep in his throat, blew an airborne kiss. Capone just stood there in the rain like a clubbed mackerel as I opened my umbrella and strutted toward the well-lit canopy over the church marquee that proclaimed, "ZION IS CALLING!"

Horns blared. Men in passing cars motioned at me behind rolled-up windows.

Hoodlum was still stuck on stupid as I climbed the steep steps toward the wide doors of the church. Topping the landing at last, I couldn't help myself. I turned and looked back and saw that *he was* still standing there, holding that gun and looking for all the world like he was dreaming on his feet.

Trevis Cooper looked much taller than he actually was, standing there just inside the doorway of Zion Apostolic Church as if holding it in place. A sneer played about his lips as he watched me saunter out of the rain and up the cobbled steps of the church.

"Who was that?"

"I don't know, Trevis."

"What did he want with you and what was he doing in front of our church?"

"I don't know, Trevis. Why didn't you ask him?"

Nerves flinched in his temples but he pulled his mind back somehow. His eyes shifted from mine to the two men getting into the Escalade as it screeched away from the curb and back toward the wards.

"What's wrong with you?"

"Nothing," he said, but I didn't believe him at all. "You work in the wards and you didn't know who that was?"

"Just because I'm from the wards doesn't mean I have to know every Thug, Dick and Harry that comes out of there. Why does everyone think I'm the official wards' press agent?"

I shook excess rain from her umbrella as he opened the doors to the vestibule and helped me out of my wet coat. "It's hard to believe you down there all the time covering stories and didn't know *him*. Either of them for that matter."

"Well, I didn't, Trevis. Does it matter?"

"Maybe."

"There you go again..."

"What?"

"A man stands too close to me and you start tripping. Wanting to arrest him."

"What he want with *you* anyway?"

"Who knows? To rob me maybe? Except that I think he forgot how."

"You saying he tried to *rob* you, Gabriella?"

"Don't start, Preacher. It didn't actually go down that way."

"So he *was* giving you trouble then? Did he touch you? Was he carrying a concealed weapon?"

Trev was so cute when he looked like that. Concerned, paternal, like my daddy used to when I took too long walking home from school and he swore I'd hooked up with some little ward boys who'd try to make me pregnant. That was long ago though. Long before he'd up and left us for his other *woman*; that white, rocky stuff that last I'd heard, still had his nose wide open.

"Trev... Don't start, okay?"

"Did he try to rob you? That's all I want to know." But he was already reaching for his cell phone, already speed dialing.

"What are you doing?"

"Calling headquarters, to have him run in."

"Uh-uh." I snatched the phone and turned it off, holding it away from his grasping hand. "Not this time, okay? No more drama tonight."

"I was just trying to protect you, Sis. You know how you get."

It was the wrong answer. He grabbed my back. "Bunny," he said, using my nickname from the wards. "I just left the morgue and I'm hurting. One of my old college boys from way back got smoked and I still can't believe it. Joker Red. Remember me telling you about him? We were boys back in the day. Did two years of college together, playing ball, until he dropped out and started slinging. He was from Georgia originally. The A.T.L.

"He got chased out of Heartford ten years ago and it was his first time back since. He was in town last week to see his kid. Was rolling up on people, asking around for his baby's momma. Couldn't find her anywhere, so he shoulda stayed gone. Looks like somebody got the wrong idea and shot him and his cousin point-blank. They found them in his car with half of their faces blown off. More drive-by than robbery. A .357 did the job."

"Wow. I'm sorry, Trev. Really."

"Me too."

He wanted more than sympathy but I wasn't up for it. He had a way with words and could put together a sermon with master precision. He wrote speeches for politicians to earn his way through college, but I knew his weakness and wasn't impressed by any of it. Not his title. Not his clothes. Not his promises of marriage and children and full-time commitment.

At the precinct where he worked the graveyard shift, Trev was one of the few black detectives on Heartford's police force and the only officer from the city's Third Ward. He kept an ear to the pulse of the underground and it was rumored that he was only a preacher some of the time, but a rogue cop 24-7 with national alliances to frat brothers who were notorious gangsters. Trev denied all of it, of course, and downplayed the fact that Heartford's up-and-coming criminals hated him with a vengeance, nicknamed him "Super Cooper," because he was known to shoot first and pray afterward. Tonight though in his detective's sport coat and crepe soled shoes, the khaki slacks with the handcuffs dangling from his side pocket, he looked as harmless as Barney Fife.

Ahead, through the wide arched doors, the soft strains of a sanctuary piano nudged us into a semblance of order.

"I guess we better go in now. You know how Emmaline gets."

"Gabriella. Forgive me, okay? I didn't mean to take it out on you. I wasn't saying that you were..."

"I understand, Trev," I answered and cutting him off, I handed back his phone, and moved through the sanctuary doors into the flow of tinkling music.

CHAPTER THREE

Chinere

It be late Thursday night, right after "check day" in the wards, which means my shop is so filled with nappy heads, there ain't one empty chair left in the whole place. Every day seems like there's more customers than I ever imagined, back when I was still a shampoo girl working for Miss Cheryl over at Radiance. Linc always said it would happen one day if I just kept at it, kept working myself like a dog the way I do.

Ward women is sitting everywhere now, laughing and gossiping from the wait-area to the shampoo sinks, and most of these is my customers, Me and Imani's, that is.

Everywhere is mommas and toddlers eating Chinese food out of paper cartons. Teenagers draped over stools with braids and weaves and partially rolled hair spilling across their shoulders while they talk about they little boy friends to each other. The shop's phone been ringing off the hook since I opened up at 6:30 this morning, and Linc ain't called once.

I ain't seen him since he crawled out my bed two nights ago, and even then, he was anxious to get back out on Da Block, as they calls it. Boy can't rest for The Street calling him, cuz hustling's what he loves and everybody knows he's good at it. You'da think with all the money he already got, that he'd be satisfied by now. Even Ghost take a break and get him some R&R. Will find some trifling female who can cook, get the best bottle of wine, and kick back with her for a few days.

But Lincoln? He ain't never satisfied. He living tomorrow 'fore it even get here, and don't wanna know nothing about what happened yesterday.

"Past gotta lot to do with how you spend your future, Boo," I always be trying to tell him. "Past tell you who you are. Clue you in on what God be trying to do with you now," I say, but he only get madder then, when I start up about the past and about God especially. So I keeps it to myself mostly, and just let him run The Street, hoping he get tired. So far, he still at it, and in the meantime, he always know where to find me. Right here, doing these heads as always.

I named it, "Dark and Lovely," and my shop's the biggest salon in all three wards now. It ain't nothing like all these other lil' hole in the walls they got lined up from here to The Boulevard, and I has Linc to thank for that. All the money he's put into this place; buying this old building, hiring contractors to knock out walls, open spaces, lay carpet and hang the wallpaper I picked out.

He'd wanted to surprise me for my birthday four years ago, called and told me to meet him an hour earlier than I usually come in. By the time I got here that morning, there's a big crew of Italians tearing the place apart like they ill, stringing lights, painting walls, installing plumbing in places that used to be closets. When they was done, I had me leather styling chairs, shag carpet, mirrored walls, central air, an intercom/sound system, and the shiniest wash basins and dryers Third Ward ever seen. Everything was done up in black and purple, Linc's favorite colors, and he said afterward, "Just don't go up on the prices, Chinere. Keep it real. Keep it reasonable."

So I didn't. Which is why on a day like today you can hardly get in the door.

This building's worth three times what he paid for it, and I got eight stylists altogether, two shampoo girls and two girls that do facials and eyebrows and nails and feet.

On Saturdays, I lay out a nice brunch with coffee and pastry and the women flock in here like birds. So much money coming in now that Linc had to hire me an accountant, and he's even talking about expanding, about opening a "Dark and Lovely II, III and IV" in other parts of the ward. With all this money coming in, he keeps his "watchers" outside, providing security just in case some crackhead gets an idea about thieving. The other stylists think it's more than that. Think it's just Linc's way of keeping tabs on me, of staying in control.

But why would I wanna step out on a man that treats me this good? Sure he has a temper, like most men in the wards, and there has been times when he's gone too far. Much too far. At least that's what they always be telling me at the clinic when I goes to get stitched up.

"No," I keep telling 'em. "I don't want none of those protect-orders. No, I don't wanna call the police on him."

If they just knowed Linc, they'd know that things is nowhere as bad as they seem. I know Lincoln loves me, even though he has never been able to say those three little words. I remind myself of that sometimes when I get to thinking about how different my life is turning out than what I'd expected, what with me having been raised up in the church and then leaving it all behind. And I do miss that sometimes—the high drama of all that good preaching and singing and shouting. I get to remembering Momma and my aunties and all them sisters in they fancy bonnets, sweating and waving lace hankies and slipping us butterscotch when the ushers wasn't watching.

But now it's like it never even happened, cause Linc has a fit when I even think about going back to visit Morning Glory or any other church. Sometimes I think it's cause it reminds him so much of his momma, and other times I think it's cause he ain't happy with me doing nothing that don't include him. And since Linc ain't hardly about to go sit up in no church and listen to no preacher, that means I ain't about to either. Not now at least. One day though. Maybe. When we both be ready.

The phone rings again, and Imani Brooks, one of my hardest-working stylists who does most of those "churchified" Apostolic women, reaches for it. She's just finishing another retouch, and she looks over at me and giggles, sensing my preoccupation. "Chinere, telephone, Sweetie. And, no, it ain't him."

I handle the phone call and go back to spraying sheen on Aretha-Faye's hair. Spraying sheen and thinking how Linc's like the mayor of Harlem in these parts. A lot of my best customers come in just cause they like to see him up close. A rich black man in the wards is about as rare as a unicorn, so I can't blame them for being curious. The fact that he be fine only makes it harder, cuz some lil' hoochie is always trying to push up on him, promising him favors, wanting to have his child.

Not that there ain't been plenty rumors. They's always rumors about Linc and some woman or other who claims to have his baby stashed away somewhere. He ain't never admitted any of it, so as long as he finds his way back to me at the end of the week, then I ain't got a thing to worry about. At least that's what he always tells me.

"I'm here, Baby. That's all you need to know."

I've got three customers that I'm trying to get to before Linc comes to lock the place up in a couple hours, and Mrs. Drusilla Hammond cuts her eyes at me like she can't wait another minute. Gets here half an hour late and thinks she supposed to climb over the others that been waiting an hour or more to get done. She sho expecting a lot, especially the way she tips, but like Linc says, customers like her still remember when this shop wasn't nothing but a hole in the wall the city was threatening to condemn.

That was seven years ago, back when I opened these doors for the first time with one extra chair, two sinks, two dryers and a family of mice who swore I was invading their territory. I was just twenty then and cute as I wanted to be. Hair to my shoulders, fresh out of beauty school and still leading the devotionals up at Morning Glory, the biggest holiness church on the South Side then.

Up until then, I'd been renting a booth over at Myrna's House of Beauty, and didn't have nary a plan when that $3,000 tax refund check arrived from Uncle Sam. It was about that time that Miss Myrna decided she was upping my rental booth by $75 a month, so taking that money and investing in a little shop of my own seemed the perfect way to get even with that old hag. The more I thought about it, the more it made sense. So I did it. Opened up that storefront and was happy doing those six heads a day until Lincoln came and perched his fine self right at the top of my street corner.

He was driving a beat-up black Ford back then, selling "product" out of his coat pockets right across the street from my shop. He'd be sitting right there on that fire hydrant, with Ghost hustling at the other end of the street, and neither me or my customers could get off the citybus good and walk past without him serenading us.

Cute as he was though, my customers was only pretending to complain, and it became a game of sorts. Linc flirting with them, and them pretending to be insulted.

Eventually he started teasing me about the Bible I was always carrying and began coming into my shop, taking out my trash without asking, bringing in my mail, and pestering me to "touch up his fade." He started leaving tips that cost more than his haircut. Brought me six-packs of ice-cold Pepsi in the worst heat of summer. But I still didn't see it coming. I wasn't hardly trying to fall in love with a hoodlum like Linc Duvall. Not when I was professing to be "saved" and Lincoln was a known drug dealer who carried pistols and flirted with every female with a big behind that walked past his corner.

It wasn't until he brought his best friend, Ghost, into the shop to meet me that I began to understand that his plans for our friendship were far greater than anything I had expected.

"C'mon to the sink, Miz Loretta," I say now, and signal to the tall woman with orange finger waves who's flipping through a *Jet* magazine. I'm into her third rinse when the bell on the front door chimes, and the row of necks sitting under the dryers turn simultaneously, craning, as if they already know who's coming in.

Speak of the devil, I almost say aloud, and can't help smirking, because it's Linc looking as fine as he wants to. He's wearing all black as usual; ankle-cut boots, Armani jeans and a cashmere turtleneck under that leather bomber. He walks up in here with that bowlegged swagger, Ghost trailing close behind, and it don't take a fool to see that he's rattled about something.

I'm wrist deep in Miss Loretta's suds, but I don't miss how the teenagers in the foyer part to let them through. He and Ghost move as easy together as twins as they pass through the gauntlet of nosey females that are doing everything but throwing their panties on the floor.

Ghost is loving the commotion, dispensing hugs, reciting pet names, doling out cheek-kisses like some kind of ghetto Don Juan. But Linc don't see nobody but me, and he don't care whose watching. He struts up to the sink and slaps my behind like it's his, bought and paid for. "S'up, Baby?"

Even Miss Loretta, whose as old as my momma, goes to blushing, but Linc ain't got no shame. He slobs me down hard right there in front of her, and when he's done, he goes and sits in my chair and pulls out his cell, waiting for me to get her conditioned.

I look at how strong and powerful and handsome he looks sitting there, and I think it ain't fitting not to pass all that beauty down. Think, another month gonna be here soon and I gotta find a way to tell him somehow.

I gotta let him know that our lives gonna be changing real soon, and this time, no matter how hard he trips, I ain't gonna let him stop it. This is my body. This time it is gonna be my choice.

Ghost is busy making his rounds, flirting from booth to booth with my stylists, and after I condition Miss Loretta and rinse her out again, I throw a nylon cape around Linc's neck and hug him up from behind. He's too cool to smile like he likes it, so he keeps talking into his cell, and I trace my fingers carefully around all that soft baby hair that's edging his face.

"What you gonna have today, Boo?" I ask, smelling his Armani, although I wanna say, "Where you been for three days, Boy? You know I was worried..."

"Whatever," he tells me, like he's mad with the world, just as two young boys who look enough alike to be twins, except that one is obviously older, come walking into the shop. They're turning their heads, looking around for Lincoln, and the girls in the lobby go to prancing and preening, competing for their attention.

Dressed in heavy denim jackets and pants, Kyere and Kylo are brothers that can't be more than ten and thirteen years old. They're the oldest of their momma's nine kids, so Linc is always finding a way to put some money into their hands. Now their faces are shining with a triumph that makes Linc suddenly end his call, beckoning them closer with two fingers.

"Y'all handle that?" Linc asks, and they both nod, cheesing at each other.

Linc's turning his head to let me size up his long sculpted sideburns, but it's Ghost who goes into his pocket and comes out with a wad of hundreds that could choke a hog. Lincoln puts up four fingers, and Ghost gives each boy four c-notes. It's obviously more than they expected, cuz they go to cheesing again.

"Aiight now. I'll holler," Linc tells them, and they nod as he touches his nose to let them know, not now. Later, they'll talk. The boys walk out of the shop as Imani goes to the sink and dries her hands on a towel. Linc stands up like he's going toward the back store room and I call out to him to bring me back a couple jars of Dudley's perm. He disappears for a few minutes before I hear him calling me from the supply room.

"What chu need, Boo?" I ask, coming into the supply room, wiping my hands with a towel, but he just grabs my arm hard, pushes me against the wall and thrusts the plastic kit in my face.

"What's this, 'Nere?"

"What, Lincoln? Ouch, you're hurting me, Baby."

"You trying it again, huhn? You hoping to get...?"

"No, Lincoln. I ain't trying again on purpose."

"So what's up with this kit? You tripping again?"

"No, Lincoln," I lie.

"I'ma ask you again. Are you pregnant, Chinere? Are you trying to have my baby again?"

"No," I tell him, and the tears are sliding down my face. He grabs my chin between his hands and I lower my eyes quick, cuz looking into his face when all that rage is riding him is a terrifying thing to behold. It's like he ain't even human then, like he some kinda animal out of control.

He draws back his hand, palm wide open, and I close my eyes and flinch, don't wanna see it coming. The stinging pain be so familiar now I can take it without crying, like I did that last time when he dislocated my jaw. This time though he don't hit me at all. Just stares at me like I've lost my mind and then pushes me away from him like I got the plague. He picks up the plastic pregnancy tester-kit and slams it so hard against the wall it shatters. Now he's stalking off, so mad he's blind with anger.

I'm crying like a baby, the front of my smock wet with snot, but it makes no sense at all, cuz I know eventually I'll have to tell him the truth, that the doctors at the clinic say I'm going into my third month already, and there's no telling what he'll do to me then.

He and Ghost have built themselves an office, hidden away downstairs in the basement of my shop and Linc goes down there now, fuming like a madman and slamming doors along the way. I won't see him again for another couple hours when he comes up to lock up the shop and bring me home. Maybe I should just tell him then, when Ghost will be around to pull him off me.

I dry my face as best I can and go back out there to my customers. Imani cuts her eyes at me like she knows something, like she thinks I'm a complete fool, but I look away from her too. Ain't no secret she's got a thing for Linc, so every time he trips on me, she swears it's her opportunity to steal him away. Last year one of my customers swore she saw Linc leaving Imani's apartment one morning, but of course she denied it. And Linc? He didn't bother to dignify my question with an answer.

I pick up my blow dryer and fixing my face, call Miss Loretta to my chair.

VISITOR

It's almost midnight by the time Gabriella stumbles out of the elevator of her high-rise condo and slides her key into the front door. If her feet had lips, they'd be screaming by now. As it is, they're molded into the shape of the brown suede slingbacks she kicks off in the middle of the living room.

Yearning, wide and deep as any ocean, suddenly overwhelms her and she acknowledges its presence quietly. "Yes, Lord, I know and I'm coming… My soul needs to *pray*."

She drapes her trench over the velvet settee, tosses the manila work-folder onto the coffee table with the rest of her mail. The red light from her answering machine pulses with fresh messages that at this hour, feel like an intrusion.

Telemarketers. Bill collectors. Trish Weitzman, *Heartford Chronicle's* city-desk editor, checking to see if she'd had a chance to sort through the file they'd put together for her. Just thinking about the story makes her nauseous and she drops into the nearest chair.

Her living room is spacious and sparsely furnished, the walls a soft orange-pink like the inside of a mouth. The big bow window across from her 65-inch television screen is deliberately unencumbered by drapes, permits a spectacular view of downtown Heartford's skyline. The street lamps overlooking her building's parking lot are so bright, there's no need for her to reach across the coffee table and snap on a lamp. Her day is finally winding down. Her breathing finally slows as the answering machine whirs, clicks one last time.

"Gabriella?"

She opens her eyes in the soothing darkness. Trev's tenor voice this time, calm, and so intimate it's almost sexy, explaining that he needs to see her before he starts his grave-yard shift at the precinct. He's on his way there now, he says; he needs to repay the fifty dollars he'd borrowed from her the week before when they were out for lunch and he'd forgotten his wallet. Gabriella buries her head beneath plump brocade pillows. It's just like Trev to call when it's convenient for *him*.

All that overtime-practicing they'd done tonight at choir rehearsal in preparation for their winter concert and he hadn't uttered a word about it. It was too late to talk him out of it now. The insistence in his voice is undeniable. He'd be buzzing her intercom in minutes and she knew what was on his mind.

She gets up and pads to the kitchen on stockinged feet, tosses a carton of chicken-broccoli into the microwave. Watching the revolving carousel spin around and around she thinks it's just like her and Trev, just like the emotions he's constantly stirring up inside of her.

She's padding into the living room with her plate when the buzzer sounds. "Who?" she yawns into the voice-box, although she can easily see Trevis' chesire teeth, grinning into the lobby cameras.

"It's me. Let me up."

"Trevis. I'm tired. Whatever you need can wait until tomorrow."

"Gabriella. Don't make me beg. I've got the money right here and I'm not leaving until I give it to you."

"It's midnight, Trevis. Why didn't you give it to me when you saw me earlier tonight?"

"And be subject to the eyes of the entire Zion Chorale wondering why I'm handing *you* money?"

"Go away."

"Bunny. *Please*. I won't be five minutes. It's important to me."

"I'd rather you wouldn't..." She yawns, but he comes up anyway. Knocks once and opens the door like he lives there. She smells the freshly applied Issey Miyake and ignores it, refuses to dignify his intrusion with a response. He drops onto the leather loveseat across from her without an invitation and she knows without looking at him that he's dressed in his form-fitting departmental sweats, muscles defined, big idle hands resting tentatively on his knees. She sits calmly watching a rerun of *Sanford and Son* on Nick at Nite, chewing broccoli, pretending she's alone as always.

Simulated life blinks neon colors across her face, and she can sense when his head turns from the screen, can feel his eyes, studying her, waiting for an opening. She reaches for the remote and turns the volume up too high on purpose; can't bear to hear the velvet in his voice, the words that always end with silent questions.

"What are you watching?" he asks at last.

"What does it look like?" The softness of his lips are engraved into her mind from memory, and she doesn't dare trust herself to look at him just yet, especially on a night like this, when her stress level, like her nature, is peaking and both are demanding to be released. Somehow he always knows.

"Gosh, Gurl... You don't ever cook anymore, do you?" Trevis leans back against the cool leather, crosses an ankle over his knee.

"Don't start, Trev. I mean it."

"Who? I'm not starting..." He invites himself to a handful of chocolate kisses from the coffee table in front of him, unfolds her money from his pocket and lays it flat. "I'm just saying..."

"Well, say it quickly and get to stepping."

"What's wrong, Baby? You ovulating again or something?"

"Don't call me that."

"What?"

"'Baby.' I told you that."

"Why not, Sweetie?"

"Cuz."

"Cuz what?"

"My name's not Sweetie."

"Since when?"

"I rebuke you, Satan."

He giggles then, and she can't help it. She joins in reluctantly. She starts to cough and needs a glass of water, which he is quick to fetch. "See, don't you feel better already?" He squats beside the couch, watching her drink, admiring the damp sheen of wetness on her lips.

"Feel better? Who said I was…?"

"I was just wondering why you were so tense tonight."

"Tense? When?"

"All during rehearsal. Like you had something, or maybe it was *somebody* on your mind."

"You smoking crack?"

"Not at all. I just saw that look on your face after you talked to *him*."

"What look? Him who?"

"You know. That 'I'm so turned on I can't help myself' look."

"Go home, Trevis."

"I was just wondering if you needed me to give you one of my massages? Ease some of that stress and anxiety…" He's smiling. It's a poor joke and they both know it.

"Touch me and I'll shoot you with your own gun. I mean it."

"You walked into rehearsal tonight looking like the weight of the world was on your pretty shoulders. It looked like the kind of burden you needed a strong man to help you carry…"

"I'll be laying it all down before Him tonight as soon as you leave, trust me."

"Good. But I just thought…"

"You thought wrong."

"Well, is it the job?"

"It's always the job…" She leans back and closes her eyes against the tension throbbing behind her temples. Bumping her head against that glass ceiling always gave her the worst headaches.

"Let me guess. The sports editor made a pass at you again?"

"Nothing that dramatic. Just corporate politics as usual."

"You wanna talk about it?"

She sighs. He was always so understanding at the wrong times.

"You know I'll always get the Boys N The Hood assignments while the other writers get to go to Ireland, to Europe, to Japan to report on exotic flowers. It's the same ol' stuff, and I'm just wondering why the press seems to think that the only way to understand black folks is to pity them. Can't they relate to us on any other human level?"

"Maybe not. What's the subject this time?"

"Third Ward drug dealers."

"It figures."

"They want me to get inside their psyches, break down the details of their operations from head man to street Joe. How in the world am I supposed to do that? Act like I'm gonna buy some crack and then ask the dealer to tell me his life story?"

"I guess so."

"They want to know whose going around smoking rival dealers, and they're looking to *me*, not Heartford's Finest, to track down the perpetrators. The last big-time dealer that was murdered? The tall, ugly brotha they called 'Skyy'? Well, they want the dirt *and* the mud. It's one of those mission-impossible assignments that could catapult my career to an editorial position, earn me a promotion that's been five years in coming. At least that's the hook they're using to get me to bite this time."

"And you believed them again?"

"Don't I always?"

"That *is* your job though, ain't it? To get all up in business that doesn't belong to you?"

"Wrong, Officer. That's *your* job. My name's not Matlock."

"You coulda fooled me. That last article you wrote about street lotteries was juicer than anything *The Enquirer* could ever come up with." He shrugs. "Face it, Bunny. You're good at those stories, Gurl. You've got *divine* protection *and* insight. You still speak the guttural, I mean, cultural language. Everybody knows you still got one foot in the hood. We can't even drive down the street together without somebody hollering, 'Bunnay!' S'up, Baby'!"

"How'd you get to be a vice detective and still be so dumb?"

"That's not nice, Sister." Trevis reaches over and nudges her knee playfully. "When are *you* gonna learn to relax and enjoy your blessings?"

"Look. Don't come over here touching me."

"Why not?"

"Cuz."

"Cuz what?"

"Cuz celibate folk don't need to be touching."

"If you c'mon and marry me like you supposed to, we wouldn't need to be celibate. We could be right here, right now, hugging, kissing, rejoicing in our matrimony..."

As if on cue, *Sanford and Son* goes off, and Gabriella thankfully stands up. "Thanks for the money, brotha-preacher. And a blessed night to you too." She takes his elbow, then carefully guides him toward the door.

He's pretending to follow, then stops cold near the threshold, fumbling around for his keys, as if he really doesn't feel them in his front pocket. "Bunny?" he says, his voice like his eyes, softer now, probing.

"What, Trev?" Her hand is on the door knob.

"Pastor Starks called me last night at work. He told me to get myself together because he wants to ordain me, to make me an elder, get me ready to pastor..."

"*You*? Start your own church?"

"Why not me?"

She's speechless for a moment, remembering. "That's great, Trev. Really. I'm happy for you."

"Thank you. But he said something else too."

"Do I need to hear this?"

"He said I needed to leave the force while I still had time to enjoy my life. He said I needed to go ahead and give up this gun, that I needed to settle down with a good woman and start myself a real family. Commit myself to ministry for real."

"Oh, Lawd."

"I'm serious. He said I needed to 'give myself *totally* to that special woman and stop playing games.' That I needed to make her mine *permanently*." He sweeps a stray curl off her forehead, watching her eyes.

"Trevis. Don't. Not this time. Not if you really care about me."

"You know I care. And you know how good we are together. You *know*…" He touches her chin, bends low, kisses her forehead softly, hesitantly. The question is there, looming between them. The past flickers like a slow burning candle. At least in *that* area they were totally compatible; the memories, like the pleasure, were always unforgettable. And then there was that *other thing* that had almost happened. The frightening thing that neither of them could even bear to talk about now.

"Gabriella…?" His voice brings her back and she stares at the reality of her bare hand. "You know I *love* you. You know I *want* you."

There they were. Those two words again. It was always this way with him—love and lust. They always showed up together. Did he even know the difference between the two?

She shakes her head, pushes her palms against his chest. "I can't, Trevis. I can't play this game again."

"What game? I want to kiss you. That isn't a sin, is it? It surely isn't a crime…"

"Saved single folk don't kiss. Not *this* way. One kiss is all it takes. You know that, *Preacher*. Nobody knows that more than you."

"But we're together, Bunny. Look at us. There's nobody else. We'll be married soon. I don't see why we can't…"

"Good night, Officer. *Minister* Cooper."

He looks upset but she steels herself away from the disappointment that lurks in those eyes. He moves through the doorway and she closes the door and locks it as quickly as she can. Locks it against herself, against the lurking deceptions of her own heart.

CHAPTER FOUR

A night of memories it was turning out to be, Lincoln thought, and for the first time ever, he hated the velvet sootiness of nightfall, wished for the glaring strokes of sunlight instead. Sitting in the Escalade under the pool of a Third Ward street lamp, waiting for Chinere and Ghost to finish up inside the shop, he didn't fool himself, knew that this time, daybreak would be a long time coming. And it's all because of *her*, he thought. It had been over twenty years since he'd smelled that smell, although he remembered it like it was just yesterday.

He couldn't begin to figure out what it all meant. He just knew that seeing the strange woman with the fire in her eyes had provoked him to memories he'd spent a lifetime trying to forget. He was angry at what he deemed a personal violation, because now, he couldn't help seeing the dancing images again, couldn't help hearing his momma's words, ringing in his ears.

"He's coming! He's coming!"

Linc hit a switch and flooded the Escalade with bumping street music. He cranked the volume up as loud as he could stand it, waited for Nate Dog and Warren G to summon his mind back, transport his soul all the way to Cali where sunshine rules, and bikini-clad women, riding in shiny convertibles, aren't interested in commandeering a hustler's heart.

The music worked for a minute or two, slowed his pulse, quieted the beating of his heart, until his momma's face loomed again, overriding the carefully assembled barrier he had fenced around his mind.

"He's coming! He's coming!"

His momma's broken voice hovering high above the hot stale air of their ram-shackle Third Ward apartment, rousing him, as always, from a fitful sleep.

"He's coming! He's coming!"

He was no more than eight, cracking his eyes into slits and thinking he saw her propped against their bedroom doorway, a pretty brown face wreathed in hair like a halo, one hand pressed against her heart. The creaking of tenement steps like the breaking of air when a batter makes connection with the round ball, and now he was paralyzed with fear, squeezed his eyes shut and fought to imagine himself out-side of himself and away from what was coming.

He imagined himself that way—a tight ball of vinyl flying high above anything that could hurt them. The only way he could take himself out of what he was about to hear. The only way he could escape it. In reality though, it was never a vinyl baseball but her skin. His momma's amber flesh that he would swing on with all of his might. The creaking of the stairs served as an alarm they'd come to trust after so many times, because he only walked hard like that when he was filled with drink. A walk like a stomp, like he would fall straight through the rotten wood to the tenth floor below, because the weight of all that liquor was too much for his legs to nav-igate unless he stepped down hard on those rickety steps and pushed himself back up.

"He's coming! He's coming!"

"Lincoln Alexander? Runt? Quick! We gotta get down to the river!"

He didn't understand but dared not question her about it. How Runt was older than him but his momma always calling Linc's name first. Called his first and middle names together—"Lincoln-Alexander," she said, like Ms. Sykes, his third-grade teacher did. She called him like he was the one who understood, like he was the one who could do something to stop it. But he couldn't. Not when he was so much bigger, stronger, meaner than he and Runt and Momma put together.

Clink and clatter of silverware. The clank of cabinet drawers being snatched open and slammed closed again. It was 12:46 a.m. and their momma was flitting around the kitchen in that white sleep-gown like a trapped moth trying to find its way out of a screened window. Her voice was sleep-tinged, her hair soft and mussed and curled under against her shoulders.

She was humming that same song that was part hymn and part prayer, her hands moving like conveyors as she snatched up knives, heavy forks, scissors, machetes, anything with sharp edges, and carried them back to their bedroom.

"*Lincoln Alexander? You and Runt...*" *His momma's voice sharp now, full of resignation and foreboding, like she was too tired to run and too scared not to.*

He was afraid not to move. Knew if he didn't get going, she'd just snatch him up anyhow out of the bed where he was sprawled next to Runt with only his pajama bottoms on, 'cause it was much too hot for anything else. He watched as she carried the sharp, cutting utensils into their bedroom and dropped them into the top dresser drawer, replacing their underwear and knots of tube-socks, spreading them out again so they looked undisturbed.

"*Lincoln Alexander.*"

Always Lincoln she wakes first. Always his full name while Runt heard just a nickname; "Runt," 'cause it seemed his brain wasn't growing fast enough to catch up with the rest of him. At least that's what the doctors at the Children's Hospital had told her.

"He's coming! He's coming!"

"*Get your brother and come on. You hear me, Lincoln?*"

"*Yes, Ma'am.*"

His momma's troubled eyes looking toward the hallway stairs and yes, there it was, the hard jangle of keys in the door.

"*Lincoln Alexander, we going out through the back. You got Runt?*"

"*We coming, Momma.*"

"*Hurry up now!*"

Runt was still curled like a spoon against him, breathing and sweating with his mouth hung open and one leg up. Linc dragged him off the sunken mattress. "Get up, Fool. Hurry up. He back!"

Some days though, his momma didn't make it out in time and that's when she sent them across the hall to old Miss Cassie, Runt cursing under his breath all the time, promising what he planned to do to him someday and how this time, he ain't gonna be the one to knock first cuz he's "sick of Miss Cassie's liver lips always fussing" about "being woke up behind foolishness."

Ain't no use in Runt complaining though, cuz they both know it's Linc who has to do it all. Linc that their momma wakes first. Linc that has to pound Miss Cassie's door and Linc that has to pretend he don't hear the terrible things she say about their momma. It seems a lifetime passes before Miss Cassie answers the door at last, dressed in that flowered tent dress without her brassiere and looking like she's been sleeping under a bridge. Miss Cassie's steady fussing, 'cause she been woke up in the middle of a dream where she coulda got herself a good number to play, and don't they know? Her own children don't break up her sleep. She's ranting like always and pointing them toward that old sunken couch, like they haven't done this same thing fifty times already.

"One day he gonna kill her," she's fussing, but he ain't trying to hear that then, not then, although he knows. They all know. Even Runt.

✝✝✝

Now, under the soft cascade of streetlight, Lincoln's aura was brooding, ominous. He hadn't thought about his momma in that purple dress, about those nights at Miss Cassie's, in years.

"Linc? S'up, Playa? You been tripping hard all night. You gonna get out and lock the doors or what?"

Ghost and Chinere were standing in the rain on the landing of Chinere's salon. Chinere was clutching her purse and frowning under the soft spray of downpour. Ghost, thoroughly inebriated by now, had the duffel bag in his hand and was signaling for him to hurry up and bring the keys, because it was raining on both of their heads.

Linc snatched the keys out of the Escalade and held them up to the light. There were more keys on this one ring than he'd ever expected to own in one lifetime—keys to Chinere's beauty parlor, her supply cabinets, her apartment, her car. Keys to his cars, his house, his safety deposit boxes, and all those apartments in the wards where he makes his money. So it took him a little time to sift through the ring until he found the right ones. And when he finally stalked up the steps and clicked both deadbolts, it was then that he realized where he'd recognized that smell.

He'd been trying to figure it out all night. Had racked his brain trying to decipher the origin of the fragrance that had reminded him so much of his momma that it had knocked his thoughts off-center. He'd turned the last key hard and it dawned on him. It wasn't perfume at all. Was nothing like anything Chinere kept lined up at home on her dresser in those dainty little teal and rose-colored glass bottles.

"You alright, Linc?" Chinere was behind him, touching his back, but he waved her away. "Get in the car. I'm coming," he said, re-arranging the discovery in his head.

Yeah. That's what it was. Not perfume, but hair oil that had stopped him dead in his tracks—that sweet, fruity-smelling pomade their momma always reeked of, especially when she dragged them off to church on those hateful Sunday mornings, her bruised eyes hid behind long and curving bangs.

Ghost honked from the front passenger's seat, and he and Chinere looked at each other knowingly before stumbling up into the Escalade. Chinere climbed into the back seat directly behind him as always. She hated to be seen when he and Ghost were making their night tallies, hated how the young "busters" were always propositioning her with their eyes, drooling down their chins if she so much as crossed her legs. And there was always the possibility of random gunfire, especially since Linc was the Third Ward's favorite moving target.

Sitting directly in back of him was just as dangerous as sitting beside him, Linc often told her, but it was a risk she'd been willing to take. Loving him was in itself, the biggest risk of all, and compared to that, braving bullets was easy.

Linc gave the hand-signal to the four men sitting by twos in two separate cars in the lot across the street, and they signaled back as he pulled away from the curb. Ghost unzipped the duffel, coughed hard as they headed west toward the usual drop-off point.

"You done tallying?" Linc turned to ask Ghost, and he nodded, pale hands counting furiously once more, classifying and re-counting the stacks of fifties and twenties and tens and fives that he'd separated into thousands and bound with rubber bands.

Had Ghost been a Wall Street broker like he'd talked about back before they'd grown their first moustaches, he'd probably be running the stock exchange by now. Nobody in the wards could add as fast as Ghost, and he never ran out of grand schemes to triple their investments. Their last venture, though terrifically dangerous, had brought them each close to two hundred thousand dollars, and Linc was thinking that maybe it was time to change course for awhile. Get out while the getting was good and invest in something legal for a change. Providing Ghost held up.

"Why you so quiet tonight, Dog? You ain't happy lest you shooting Niggas, huh?" Ghost grinned at Benjamin Franklin and Linc scowled. "Just don't miscount my money, Fool, or I'ma have to recommend an early retirement."

From the back seat, Chinere passed up a lit joint, its tip stained from her wine-colored lipstick. Her nails were talons, an intricate design of tiny beads and pearlized cross hatchings. Her layered hair was cut close, smoothed flat against her head, and her peach-sized breasts jutted against the lycra fabric of her jumpsuit.

She was the favorite of his women so far, smart, chocolate to the bone, with a good head for business. If he lived to become old and gray, he would possibly consider marrying her, raising up a heap of lil' "Linc-ettes." They'd buy a house together in the "'burbs" where he'd spend his spare time reading the *Wall Street Journal* and investing in stocks and mutual funds.

At least that's what her fantasy was and the reason she still put up with his madness. For now, she was content to hang up under him while he handled his business, figured it was better her than some chickenhead who'd trade her soul just to be seen with Lincoln. Tonight, though, was taking longer than she'd expected.

"When you taking me home, Lincoln? I got three heads to do first thing in the morning and a wedding party at noon."

It was almost 1:00 a.m., and she was beginning to pout. He could hear it in her voice.

"At least turn the music up then," she insisted, meaning the Mary J. Blige song Ghost was humming. Lincoln leaned forward, upped the volume, until her voice faded into the lull of synthesizers.

✝✝✝

At the drop-off point, the street-level dealers were already lined up by twos to pay their cash tallies and restock their bundles of supply. They handed their cash to Ghost, waited as Linc checked off his book counts and handed them their neat foil-wrapped packages, already weighed and labeled, their names printed in slanting red marker. It had taken all of forty-five minutes and Nacho, their biggest drop-off, had still not arrived. Linc looked at his Rolex and frowned. Late again for the third time in a month was proof that a change needed to be made. Time was money, and no matter how big his receipts were, any salesman negligent enough to waste their time didn't deserve to share profits in such a well-oiled enterprise.

Ghost looked up from the money. "This his third time?"

"You know it."

"He's done then. I'll give him his papers?"

"Yeah." Lincoln stabbed what was left of the joint into an ashtray. "You think that was all her hair?"

"Whose hair?" Ghost looked puzzled.

In the back seat, Chinere slowed her singing, was watching his profile. On the third floor of a dilapidated tenement, a shade was being pulled low. The street seemed deceptively quiet, like the calm before a storm.

"Whose hair?" Chinere repeated.

"You know how females be sewing in pieces and stuff?" Linc said, as if he hadn't heard Chinere, as if she was talking behind a wall of soundproof glass. "You can't tell what they mommas gave 'em from what was made in Taiwan. Her stuff looked real though. That trick had a whole lotta hair."

"What trick in particular?" Chinere pressed and Ghost smirked.

"Nobody, Baby," Lincoln lied. "Ey," he looked at Ghost, changing the subject, "make sure it's all there. I'd hate to shoot one of these lil' fools for nothing."

"How long I been doing this, Yo?"

"Years."

"Why you wanna insult me then?"

It was Linc's turn to grin, and he let down his driver's side window, waited for Rudder, the corner lookout, and one of the widest brothas in the wards, to give him the signal.

A stray mutt crossed the deserted intersection past Celo's Pawnshop, slipping into a side alley, and Lincoln shook his head. "Guess it's the night for female dogs."

Ghost looked up at him, raising his eyebrow. Had it not been for the trench and those bad kicks, she'd been an almost old-timey-looking thing, what with that long skirt and prissy blouse. But she *was* fine, and her skin was bright, like it had a candle lit underneath it. She had pretty teeth too. The kind of woman who lived uptown, far away from the wards. The kind who, unlike Chinere, didn't believe in women's-lib, and baked a mean sweet potato pie.

But it was all that nerve she'd had that had left him so unsettled. Only that nerve and that sassy mouth that had kept him from smoking her first thing, and she hadn't even bothered to thank him, practically knocked him out of her way with that big behind of hers. He shuddered just thinking about it. Life outside the Third Ward was becoming a frightening place when he was getting chumped by females. He glanced around uneasily. Something felt off-kilter. What was it?

"Where's Nacho, Linc? I'm ready to go." Chinere yawned and this time he agreed. "Aiight, Baby. We 'bout to roll up outta here, 'cause this air ain't feeling right."

Across the street near the alley, young heads were hanging out on the stoops and in the hallways of the dilapidated houses, ready at any moment to prove that old-school was out and new-school was smarter, slicker and definitely more dangerous. They stood watching the Escalade slide by and winked at each other. Every night when it parked in its usual spot and waited for them to tally up their night's receipts, they complimented his clothes, flirted with the pretty women he sometimes ferried around. But Lincoln knew they were all just biding their time as he too had once.

Luckie, Mook, Big Black, Too Sweet, the biggest dealers Linc had grown up seeing in the wards, were all dead now. Luckie had died in a prison infirmary, but the others had all been gunned down before their thirtieth birthdays. Now, both he and Ghost were well into their late twenties, well into the age of extinction, and the new-school members were simply biding their time.

Ghost stopped counting to let his gaze wander the quiet block. "You heard what Rudder said tonight. Five-O been tripping down here lately like they do every year around election time, and ain't no telling when they might spring."

"Don't take a fool to see that. Ain't no chickenheads or busters out nowhere. It's quiet as a grave out here." Linc checked his rearview carefully, scanning both sides of the street. Years before, he could check on the whereabouts of his drops on his cell phone, but Five-O was smarter now and scanned the airwaves heavily these days. They'd know his voice, his codes, his plans, in an instant.

"After tonight, we'll have to change up. Find us a new spot and be gone by the time they decide to 'break.' In the meantime, Nacho's history. That fool's too busy running behind them lil' chicas to worry about making money."

"Ain't that him now?" Chinere was pointing, her eyelids heavy with sleep, and Lincoln sighed his relief. She was right. The late-model Beemer was rounding the corner. Rudder caught the red gleam of the low-riding sedan and threw an arm up. All was clear. There were no secret caravans lying in ambush behind him. No detectives in plain clothes pretending to be taxi drivers. Nacho was alone as always. Linc flashed his headlights and Rudder disappeared back inside the stoop.

Nacho was a short Latino with rimless specs and a curly ponytail like a sprig of broccoli at the top of his head. He swung up beside them and got out. "Yo, *Papi*; *hace calor*," he said, thrusting his paper bag quickly to Ghost. The last package of coke that Linc pulled from under his seat and passed to Ghost to give him was packed solid as sugar. Nacho nodded without looking at it and shoved it into his jacket.

"Yo, Esse. You messing up. Looks like I'ma have to make some changes." Linc's gaze was hard, but Nacho backed away from the car, his hands held out in a pleading gesture.

"You don't wanna do that, *Hijo*. *Por favor*. We have *poco* problems but we work 'em out, no? I calla you," he promised. "We have *comida*; we talk… "

"You said that last time," Ghost observed, but Linc said nothing, watched as Nacho got into his car, swung a left and was swallowed up by a mall of darkness. Checking his rearview carefully, Linc started the engine and rolled off in the opposite direction. Fine bumps rose on the back of his neck and he looked to his left, saw the flash of silver-emblem hidden carefully behind a dumpster. A cruiser with two officers, their faces turned away toward the opposite end of the street, sat idling. He could see their mouths open, engrossed in talk. They hadn't seen him yet and he was relieved, hoped it was Mahoney and Burgess. Anybody but that weak-wristed "Super Cooper." He was a preacher, they said, and one of the few officers they hadn't been able to bribe. The only cop who'd shoot you in cold blood, then kneel to say a prayer over your bleeding body.

"Ghost," Linc hissed, gesturing with a jerk of his head, and Ghost, following the direction of his eyes, saw the gilded doors, the low beamed headlights like lion's eyes in the dark. "Hurry up, Baby."

"I got it. It's all good." Ghost zipped the duffel and tossed it back to Chinere who caught it and snatched up the floor mat, loosening the hatch up under her feet. The custom-built compartment slid open quietly and she stuffed the duffel in quickly, replacing the mat and leaning back into her seat with her arms folded. .

Linc was fumbling under the seat, looking for the .357 to toss her when one of the officers looked up, nudging his partner. Linc swore quietly under his breath. The nudge was all the sign he needed. At least one of the cops wasn't an ally. He was much too suspicious, his gaze lingering on the Escalade longer than it should have.

The gun was still there, the iron pressing hard against his boots, and he felt the urge to swing the car around, to hit a sudden U-turn, but they'd chase him down for sure then. Pull their pistols. Look for a reason to harass or, if that were Coop in the cruiser, to make an arrest. The trick was to play it cool. Pretend they were out chilling as usual, leaving an "after-hours." Enjoying Blige.

"Linc, they coming this way," Chinere whispered and he smiled without flinching. Eyes forward, the wheel sliding easily between his hands.

"Just be cool, Baby," he sang to the beat of Blige, slowing the car to let the cruiser sidle up beside him.

The glare of a flashlight hit him squarely in the face, blinding him temporarily, stirring his rage. He stopped the car totally, waited for the game of humiliation to run its course.

"S'up, Homes?" The officer fished and Ghost groaned under his breath. It was Cooper alright, and in one of his righteous moods.

"You, Cuz." Linc spoke through clenched teeth, staring straight ahead.

"Y'all out here kinda late, ain't you?" The question dropped hard, like a dime, and Lincoln forced a grin.

"Ain't no law against chillin', right? And that's all we doing."

"At this hour of the night?" Cooper was smiling too now, unhitching his seat belt.

"Yeah. We just left The Hideout. Was over there with Big Mac and 'nem, getting our groove on. You don't believe me, ride over there and ask him."

"Like Mac won't cover for you. Again."

"Big Man's legit. He ain't got no priors."

"But y'all do. So throw this thing in park and get your hands on the hood. Both of y'all."

"You tripping, Cuz." Linc's dander was rising, the blood bubbling like oil in his veins.

"Did I stutter, Man? And I ain't your relative."

"Nawl, but…"

"Y'all hiding something?"

"Nawl."

"Then get out the car," said Cooper as he and his partner, a redhead named Brady with greedy hands and a mouth that could be bought for $500 a week, both disembarked.

"Linc. Chill, man." Ghost tossed the warning over his shoulder, eased out of the passenger seat with his hands in front of him and automatically assumed the position.

Lincoln followed reluctantly, glaring past the sienna skin into Cooper's coppery eyes. He bit down hard on his bottom lip to endure the frisking, the skilled hands rummaging between his thighs. Brady feigned indifference, only pretended to search Ghost. But Cooper had found Lincoln's ankle holster and removed the tiny pistol.

"You got a permit for this, Criminal?" he said, holding it up.

"Yeah," Linc lied.

"Where is it?"

"Your momma got it. It fell out my pants last night when I was taking 'em off in her bedroom."

Cooper was laughing and fighting the urge to strike him as he pulled out his cuffs, snapped them easily around Linc's wrists. Shoving him away from the car, he peered into the back seat.

"My, my, my… What do we have here?"

"I'm not doing anything wrong, Officer," Chinere pleaded.

"So you won't mind stepping from the vehicle, will you, Miss Lady?"

"Niggaz get shot up quick harassing another man's woman," Lincoln offered, and Ghost sighed, shook his head, spit hard at the ground. It was going to be a long, uncomfortable night.

Cooper helped Chinere carefully from the car. "You threatening me, Duvall?"

But Lincoln was smiling and looking hard at the stars, wondering how many he could hit if he took aim with his eyes closed.

NEGOTIATIONS

It was close to 5:00 a.m. when Cooper dialed her condo and she picked up groggily on the third ring.

"This better be Jesus," she gasped into the phone. "No, Baby. Just His next best thing."

"Trevis?"

"Gabriella. Listen."

"What did I tell you about calling me that? I'm nobody's…" She was barely coherent but fussing already, so he lowered his voice, practically cooed into the phone. "Hush, Woman. You gonna want to marry me tomorrow when I tell you what I did for you."

"Oh, Lawd. Why do I feel scared all of a sudden?"

"Bunny, listen. That story? The one your editors are pressuring you to write?"

"About the dealers? What about it?"

"I got somebody for you to interview."

"Trevis. It's five in the morning. Have you lost your mind? You couldn't have called me at eight to tell me this?"

"Gabriella, when you see who he is, you'll thank me; I'm sure of it."

"*Thank* you?"

"This brotha's the real thing. He knows everything about what's happening in the wards. He's undisputedly one of the biggest, if not *the* biggest, dealers down there. And he knows something about those last murders; I just know it."

"Trev?"

"Ma'am?"

"You'd better not be playing with me."

"Have I ever woken you up at five a.m. to play a game?"

"Well…" She groaned deep in her throat. "Who is this man and where'd you find him?" She was up now, groping for the pen and pad she kept on her nightstand table.

"According to his rap sheet, which is as long as my car, he's Alexander L. Duvall, but on the Street, among other names, they call him Lincoln."

"Lincoln?"

"Something about him being in charge of slaves. Whatever that means."

"Uh-huhn."

"You know the brotha that tried to jack you yesterday?"

"Oh Lawd, Trev, you didn't?"

"I did… I uh… I arrested him for you."

"For *me?*"

"Yeah. But that ain't for you to worry your pretty head about."

"Merciful. Jesus."

"I'm just calling to tell you that I can get you in to see him now if you'd like. He's already made bail, and we won't be able to hold him much longer."

"Trevis. This is totally crazy. That man is a lunatic. Wasn't there anybody else you could have picked?"

"I figured this may be your last and only opportunity to get it live from the horse's mouth. It could easily be the kind of story to earn you that promotion you're always dreaming about."

She sighed, fell back against the pillows again. "But it's five in the morning, Trev."

"Five-sixteen, and I can't promise this animal's gonna live until six, seeing I'm releasing him back into the wild in a few hours."

"Lawd."

"So, do you want this story or not?"

"You know I do. But I just have one thing to say about your crazy tactics."

"What's that, Sweetie?"

"Only you, my brotha. Only you."

CHAPTER FIVE

Bluecoat Rodgers stood awkwardly in front of the cell holding the luke-warm Styrofoam cup of jailhouse coffee and a stale bagel spread with margarine. A fearful expression played about his lips as he fought hard to maintain direct eye contact with the man inside the cage. A man who had been growling like a rabid dog for the past hour, a man whose very glare threatened to consume him.

In the end, Rodgers lost the contest, and looked away from those bottomless eyes, found a crack in the ancient plaster spread behind the rancid toilet to concentrate on instead.

It was bad luck, he'd heard, to stare into the face of the devil, and this man, if not Satan himself, was certainly the next best thing. He was a monster if Rodgers ever saw one. A man who possessed the persona of some kind of wild beast, and since precinct wasn't in the habit of keeping raw meat on hand, he didn't know what he'd do if the animal genuinely became hungry and decided to tear through their iron bars.

The caged man's arrogance wasn't hard to understand; the coffee and bagel Rodgers was holding out to him now were downright insulting.

There wasn't an officer on late watch who hadn't heard of Duvall's after-midnight arrest, and Rodgers, like all the other bluecoats on duty now, wanted no parts of this spectacle.

Was he smiling back there or baring his teeth? Rodgers couldn't tell. All he knew was that even behind more than 1,000 pounds of reinforced steel, the man's evil emanated, was stronger than King Kong. Rodgers thought that hatred, when it came alive like that, when it hovered around him like an aura so thick it was palpable, had to be purely diabolical. There was no other way to describe it.

So far, all efforts at civility had only riled Duvall, so it had taken more then ten of their strongest men to drag him from the cruiser down to processing and then to lock-up. *Ten men.* Not children, not women, but the strongest bench pressers around on the force during their graveyard shift. How Cooper had gotten the man into the car in the first place was, in itself, a wonder, and they believed it had something to do with the pleading of the other two parties he'd come in with: a dark, beautiful woman with perfectly coiffed hair, and the big half-breed man known to be Duvall's sidekick.

Hissing how much he hated cops, Cooper especially, Duvall was kicking and tossing men around like pillows before someone finally aimed a gun squarely at his head. They promised to kill him without hesitation if he didn't cooperate. Only then had he let up, walking into the cell on his own while three officers with various broken bones had been rushed to county hospital.

In his six years on the force, Rodgers had never seen anything like it and he was glad he'd hung back, pretending to be answering phones when they took Duvall down.

Even now, the disgusted look Duvall was giving him as he leaned back against the wall of the narrow cell with his arms folded, set his teeth on edge.

Primitive, thought Rodgers, failing to find any other explanation for him.

"Breakfast," Rodgers said now, shivering in spite of himself. He stood waiting for the hurled words he knew would follow, seeing the sleek dark features, the black cowhide pants and jacket, the $500 hiking boots.

In the animal kingdom, Duvall would be a panther. Stealthy, dark, quick and dangerous. Even surrounded by bars and brick, Duvall, with his manicured moustache and Hollywood features, was, as Rodger's wife would say, "Drop Dead Gorgeous," and Rodgers marveled that evil could be so pretty.

"Get that mess out my face." Duvall threw his words past the cage like a ventriloquist,and Rodgers thought they sounded like one long hiss, coming at him from every side; the sound a snake makes before it strikes.

"Look, Man, I ain't the cook." Rodgers attempted a smile, but changed his mind. "Where you think you at? The House of Pancakes?"

He was fronting, feigning bravery, but Duvall shot him a look that made him back away shrugging. "This is illegal, you know," he started up again. "….the way y'all holding me like this, against my will… Don't that fool know who I am? I can open these bars with my bare hands and have my teeth on your throat before you can holler for back up. Tear out that jugular and chew it to pieces."

"I wouldn't doubt it. I'd hate to put you through the trouble though," Rodgers acquiesced.

"I got rights. I made bail. I don't have to talk to *nobody* if I don't want to."

"I don't have anything to do with it, Sir."

"Yeah."

"That's Coop, Man. Trippin' as usual."

"Yeah. Aiight."

"Remember that when you get back to the ward. Joe Rodgers ain't have a thing to do with this."

"I'ma remember aiight. Your boy better watch his back."

"I feel you."

"Ain't no steel bars in the Third Ward."

"True dat."

Lincoln looked away, dismissing him, and Rodgers shrugged, hearing the pronouncement that rang like a promise. He hoped Coop was still a praying man.

Rodgers edged over to the next cell as Lincoln sidled up to the bars, gripping the cool metal.

"Cooper?! Cooper! Where you at, Baby? You gotta go back to the wards sometime! You can't stay holed up in here forever!"

"And that's why you insist on threatening me?" Cooper had appeared from nowhere, his face worn, bleared with sleep. "Just 'cause you're from the wards doesn't mean you have a right to act ignorant."

"Open this cage 'fore I get Johnnie Cochran up in here. Give a brother a uniform and he starts trippin'."

"I'ma ask you one more time, Duvall."

"And I'ma tell you 'no' like I have been for the past two hours."

"All I'm asking is that you give her thirty minutes. That's all she needs."

"Thirty minutes? That's half my lifetime."

"Speaking of lifetimes, rumor has it you should be serving a couple of them consecutively right about now. You and that pretty sidekick that swears he's El Debarge."

"I don't know what you talking about, Man."

"No? You haven't heard the news?"

"What news?"

"Those last 'D.O.A.'s' from the Second Ward? The ones they found near The Hull? Next to the burning dumpster? Brains spread all over that new Lex with the Georgia license plates?"

"What about them?"

"They had your signature all over them. Just like the two before them. More ward dealers biting the dust, killed with the same weapon as all the others. Am I right about it?"

"You tripping. I don't know nothing about that." Duvall clicked his tongue, stroking Cooper with a gaze that began at his old brogans and worked itself up to his eyes. He licked his lips, and for some reason, his tongue, to Cooper, seemed unnaturally long. "But I do know about you," Lincoln said, and grinned, pacing each word. "I know all about you and that twelve-year-old girl in the back room of her daddy's Laundromat that day."

"Back room?"

"Don't tell me you don't remember, when you dream about it at least once a month."

"You crazy, Man. Loc, for real."

"Yeah. I'm loc. Like you were that day. Back when you was all of sixteen and qualified to do a nice bid on a charge of statutory rape."

"How did you...?" Cooper shrugged, choked back the beginnings of a chuckle. "She... I never knew, Man. She lied to me..."

"Yeah."

"That's the God's honest truth. She told me she was sixteen, and had the body to match."

"Yeah. We know."

Cooper raised his chin, cupped it with one hand. But Duvall wasn't finished.

"And what about that time in Salem?"

"Salem?"

Duvall grinned, showed perfect white teeth. "When you and your lil' college frat brothas got drunk and left that club? Luckies? Was it Luckies?"

"Luckies..." Trev repeated the name as if in a trance, his voice falling off.

"You was driving, wasn't you? An old Cutlass with white walls and walnut veneer, and an old eight-track that used to get stuck after the third song."

Coop shook his head now, swallowed hard.

Lincoln chuckled, but his eyes, like his voice, were stone cold and hard as cement. "You used to play the Dazz Band. Play Kool and the Gang and The Ohio Players, like you was crazy... In fact, you was playing 'Rollercoaster' that night y'all hit that ol' fool wandering around out there in the rain. Homeless as an alley stray and smelling like eight miles of bad road. You was fulla gin and juice. Dragged that old man's body a quarter-mile before you realized it. Thought you had a flat tire. But it was his body, wasn't it? Making the road suddenly get all bumpy..."

Cooper was coughing now, looking over his shoulder before he spoke. "He didn't die, Man. We did the right thing," he said as softly, as coolly as he could manage without prompting suspicion.

"Drunk driving? I don't think so."

"We called the ambulance when we knew. We got him some help soon as we saw him."

"Yeah. Guess it was too bad y'all didn't stay around to let Five-O smell that gin. Find that Mary Jane under the front seat. Y'all never told 'em that y'all were the ones who hit the drunk fool. Y'all lied to the paramedics. Said y'all found him that way."

"He didn't die though, did he? And that was the point. He *didn't* die."

"Nawl, Baby. Not then. He died four months later though. Got out of ICU, but the injuries y'all caused to his brain caught up with him, and that first time he took a drink, he had an aneurysm and died right there in the middle of the street. What was left of his brain just burst in his head."

Cooper backed away, squinting, then came closer. "What manner of evil...?" he said, disbelief standing in his eyes.

"The kind you don't wanna mess with." Duvall spat on the floor behind him, looked back at Coop, grinned through the bars. "What? You don't think I was with you that night? Who? I was inside of you, Cuz. Front and center. Now open this cage and let me out."

"I ain't scared of you, Duvall. I know whose power is greater."

"It ain't your power."

"Why it ain't? You know all about me, but you don't know nothing about that court appearance coming up in two weeks though, huhn? The one on those two possession charges."

"Get out my face, Man." Duvall gripped the bars tighter and concentrated, closed his eyes as though making a wish, or summoning some hidden strength.

"Give her just thirty minutes and I guarantee the judge will go favorable on you."

His eyes flew open, were aimed at Cooper so hard, for a moment he, too, glanced away. "How favorable?"

"Favorable enough for evidence to get lost, be misplaced in the shuffle." Cooper spoke softly now, seemed much shorter somehow under the harsh county lighting. He stood at least six-four in those soft-soled brogans; his haircut was parted in the middle and cropped close to his head, military style. His hands were as big as oven mitts, and Lincoln remembered how back in the day he had been a center for the ward's street basketball leagues. Had "balled" so well and so hard, brothas had wanted to shoot him after games. They'd chase him from the courts and beat him down in some back alley, tearing off that favorite jersey he always wore, chanting his name like an incantation they were trying to conjure up. "SuperCoop," they'd called him even then, and Linc remembered that even after all of that, he'd still had his pick of the prettiest girls. Was one of the few ward brothas who'd actually made it to college.

Linc sees it even now as he watches the big man's frightened eyes—19 and 82. The wards cooking under July heat so intense it roiled up like smoke from the blacktop to toast everything in sight. They all remembered those white recruiters in dark glasses creeping through the haze, carrying pocket-sized notepads and clipboards, the long white envelopes full of quiet money. They hung at the edges of the dilapidated courts, jotting stats in tiny scrawls, memorizing nicknames. Nodding, grinning, clapping brothas on the back. They never made promises to anybody outright. Just smiled a lot with Colgate teeth, dipped into their pockets for quarter snow cones sold in paper funnels.

Just before graduation from high school, Super-Coop was driving a used Cutlass with polished rims. Had earned enough points on the scholastic courts to make it through four years of paid-for university schooling.

Now he stood winking outside of the cell, those big hands hanging loosely at his sides, head tilted sideways as if he were standing at half-court again, attempting to measure the distance from floor to rim. "Evidence could get lost," he said again so quietly, Lincoln strained to hear. "Paperwork could get misplaced." He did not smile, and Linc saw that the first four buttons of his white oxford shirt were unbuttoned; his bare chest visible inside the white cloth was like a slice of roast beef between white bread.

It was a set-up if he ever saw one, and Lincoln growled low in his throat, backed away from the bars and threw himself down onto the empty bottom bunk. He sat with his haunches wide, feet splayed in a "V" as he watched a team of roaches clustering around what looked like an old bean in a filthy corner behind the filthy toilet. It stank worse than a porta-potty in the cell, and the stench of urine alone could make the eyes water.

Cooper drew closer to the bars, brows raised, mouth a hard line. "You gonna talk to her or what?"

"Sounds like blackmail, and you supposed to be a man of the cloth."

"Then we're even, 'cause you supposed to be the biggest devil to walk the earth since Capone."

"How you a man of God, and blackmailing folk?"

"How you the devil, and don't know how to get over?"

"You ever see the inside of a grave? Feel what it's like to lie in an airless box with the lid fastened tight? Maggots everywhere, Baby. Slick and white as heat..."

"Do you or don't you wanna deal?" Cooper held up the keys and Lincoln sighed, his nostrils burning from the odor drifting from the next cell over. Someone was getting rid of their breakfast already. Probably some vagabond full of dysentery and who knew what else.

"Aiight." He looked up. Grinned. "But whoever she is, she must have some *real* good stuff, got you tripping like *this*."

"Man, what you say?" Cooper opened the cage and grabbed at him roughly, but Lincoln was quick, slippery in the cool leather, and they fell hard against each other; two deer with locked horns. Rodgers and another bluecoat with a red beard came running and hovered close, pistols drawn just as Duvall heaved Cooper like a sack of potatoes to the other side of the tiny cell.

"Don't shoot him! Rodgers! Burke! Hold your fire!" Cooper could barely get the words out, his chest heaving from exertion. He pulled himself up painfully from the cold hard floor, marveling at the smaller man's unnatural strength, a bead of blood appearing in the corner of his mouth. Under two hundred-thirty pounds of pure brawn, his bones felt bruised, muscles pulled taut beneath the skin. Duvall at five feet eleven couldn't have weighed any more than one hundred-eight pounds.

Rodgers and Burke eased carefully into the cell, Burke attempting to cuff Lincoln on his own. But he shrugged the short man off, smoothed his clothes again. "Get off me, Fool; y'all trippin' in here."

Cooper leaned sideways in the open doorway, fighting to catch his breath, and Linc couldn't help but to admire his heart. Any brotha that could take a whupping that hard and still be bad enough to keep talking smack deserved his props.

"You just better watch your mouth about her. She's a lady. A Christian woman. Something you know nothing about."

"What she doing with you then?"

The question hung in the air.

Cooper frowned, pushed Lincoln past Rodgers, down the familiar corridor lined with battered file cabinets and empty water coolers, surveillance cameras poised like light fixtures in the ceiling.

"You just remember what I said."

From a ring heavy with keys, he selected one and opened a door on the right of the corridor. He waited as Lincoln stalked inside and sank into a chair, rubbing his wrist and the bare space where his $18,000 Rolex had been only hours before. It had been a birthday gift to himself, and Lincoln thought, they had better return it when this fiasco was over. Valuables disappeared all the time at the precinct, and if that diamond-studded trophy turned up missing, he'd spare no mercy. Both Super Cooper and the writing woman would die for sure.

Cooper was arranging chairs around the narrow conference table while Lincoln sat stroking his goatee, watching the keys that dangled from the preacher-cop's hip. Keys to what? Broom closets? Supply cabinets? More interrogation rooms? *A poor man's authority*, he thought.

"Just 'cause we both from the wards doesn't mean you know me." Duvall's words were snarled, tangled as fishing wire. "Educated niggaz always sizing folk up, thinking they can look at them and tell what they are."

"Don't flatter yourself, Prettyboy. Maybe I don't wanna know you. You ever thought of that?"

"You got a strange way of showing it."

"Matter of opinion."

"I'm not as ignorant as I look, Preacher. I know all about that lil' world you live in."

"What world?"

"You know. That place where y'all do all that praying and stuff…"

"Most outlaws do."

"My momma wasn't no outlaw." Linc cut his eyes sideways, watched him through peripheral vision.

"Do tell." Coop hung impatiently in the doorway, one eye partly swollen, a bruised hand thrust deep inside his pocket.

"I ain't telling you nothing."

"And now?"

"Now what?"

"What she think about you now? About the man you turned out to be?"

Linc closed his mouth. Sat as still as a stone. He still had not given an answer when Cooper left and reappeared minutes later with the only woman who had ever dared him to his face.

INTERVIEW

Her? Her? She's the one he wants me to talk to???

Chinere says that I never ever laugh, claims that most of the time she can't even remember what my smile looks like. But I'm laughing myself silly tonight, shaking my head at the irony of what's become one of the worst nights I've had in a long time.

This entire day in fact, had proved to be disastrous, what with this same woman screwing up an ambush that me and Ghost had been planning for six months, a screw-up that made us miss out on $50,000 apiece. And, to further add insult to injury, her lil' boyfriend up and arrested me on some trumped-up charges (it's a good thing he ain't find the floorboard), cuffing me all in the street on my own "block," like I'm some kinda sidewalk crackhead.

So I couldn't help myself. "Aw, nawl… This can't be happening!" I said out loud when I saw it was *her*. Again.

Chinere and Ghost got to leave after two hours on their own recognizance, but this preacher-fool's got me here until the sun comes up, and then wants me talk to this religious skirt he's probably "banging" behind some choir loft.

Five-O's got their paws on my $18,000 Rolex and now, here she is again, Miss Goody Two-Shoes, stepping up in my face talking about, "How do you do?"

I wanna tell her so bad how I do, but Cooper's standing here like some kind of guardian gladiator, looking for a reason to shoot me, and I ain't trying to bloody up one of my favorite outfits.

"I told you to watch your mouth, Man," he's saying with his hand lingering on the small of her back. He guided her to a chair and pulled it out, all the time watching the slide of my eyes.

Coop can watch all he wants, but ain't a brotha alive gonna stop me from checking out beauty like that, don't care if she's married to the pope.

Baby's got so much back, the long dress can't begin to hide it, and I'm thinking, if all the women at that big brick church look like her, then maybe I'm fishing from the wrong pond.

But I'm cool when I need to be, and to stop this big joker from breathing down my back, I rolled my eyes up to the ceiling and pretended that I ain't impressed with her looks at all.

"Don't tell me *she's* the one you want me to talk to?" I say, and that's when Mother Teresa leaned forward and offered me one of those pretty, but plain, hands. I play the role good now and just look at it, and Coop relaxes some, feeling that the threat is gone.

"Just answer her questions," he ordered, like he was somebody's daddy, and I'm trying real hard to pretend he ain't here, 'cause there's a part of me that wants to "smoke" both of 'em on general principle.

"This a joke, right?" I say.

"What joke? Just answer the questions."

"And if I don't want to?"

"I'll just take your trifling, no-job-having, player-pimp-wannabe-small-town-Capone behind back down to lock-up and hold you another week on disorderly conduct... And wait, did I mention 'assault on an officer'? Or maybe an attempted murder charge for pulling a weapon on this lovely woman?"

Preacher's showing off big-time now, even though his right eye looked like it was swollen; but I stood up and almost grabbed that collar, planning on doing the same thing to his left one. I wanna see what he's made of now that his boys ain't here to rescue him, but it's like she'd read my mind, because she jumped to her feet between us.

"Trevis. Don't." She said the big man's name with a sweetness that froze both of us in our tracks. I can't help thinking, it would be real nice for a woman like her, to call my name *that* way.

She touched a hand to all that thick hair that's spiraling over her shoulders, and when she smiled with those dazzling teeth, she had the deepest dimples I've ever seen. Her smile's so pretty, I couldn't help myself. I sat back down just because I'm hoping to see it again.

"I think I can handle it alone from here," she whisper-talked. "Please, Trevis."

"But, Sis, this man is violent. He's sinister. You don't understand."

"I can handle it," she's said like I ain't even here.

"You don't want me to sit here just in case?"

"In case of what? If the brotha were dangerous, he'd have shot me hours ago."

"Gabriella…"

"*Please*, Trev. We'll be fine. Leave us."

Is it my imagination or does the gun-toting preacher slam the door on his way out?

I sucked my teeth hard, trying with everything I have not to go ballistic up in here. One thing's for sure though. I'ma "deal with" Cooper if it's the last thing I do.

So her name's Gabriella, I'm thinking, turning it over in my head as she sat down again and pulls a small notepad and pen from her big leather purse.

She crossed her legs, covered this time by black silk cloth, and the skirt drapes across her ankles, falls almost down to those black, ballerina-looking shoes with tiny satin ribbons on the toes.

She looked up at me, and her eyes are tawny colored, light, like copper. There's no artificial coloring on her face either. No mascara, nothing. Just that brassy skin that's the same color as her eyes, and those thick lashes, spreading like a fan when she looks down at her pad.

"So…"

"So?"

"To what do I owe this harassment?" I asked, and Miss Miniver raised an eyebrow like she didn't get it.

"What do you mean?" she asked.

"What do I mean?" I echo.

"Yes," she insisted.

"Well, first you cut me off in traffic; then you send your boyfriend to come arrest me; and now you wanna make me the subject of some tabloid exposé…."

"Beg your pardon?" She's plays that dumb role very well.

"I can sue for this, Babygirl," I said, stroking my lips with a single finger in that seductive way that drives Chinere crazy.

"But you won't now, will you, Mister...?"

She fishes for my name, but I play her off. "That's irrelevant," I say instead. "What y'all want with me anyhow? I was cleared of all those old charges."

"Cleared? What old charges?"

"I didn't kill anybody."

"Oh?" She raised both eyebrows now, sat back in her chair like some kind of doctor making a prognosis. "Nobody says you killed anyone," she countered in an accent that, unless I'm imagining it, sounds faintly Third Ward.

"So what's this about then?"

"What do you think this is about?"

"How you mean, Babygirl? You called *me* in here. Now you wanna play innocent? Play me for some kinda joke?"

"I'm neither your baby nor your girl. My name is Gabriella."

"What is this about, Miss Gabriella?"

"What do you want this to be about?"

"I want it to be about you and your man letting me up outta here 'fore I call Johnnie Cochran, Al Sharpton and 'nem."

"And you think they'll come to your rescue?"

"Why not? My money may be dirty, but it's just as green as anybody else's."

She laughed to herself, started scribbling on her pad, and it's my cue that the game's begun.

"Gabrielle, huhn?" I sat back in my chair, striking one of my classic poses.

"Gabriella."

"Like the angel?"

"Yes. And you are...?" Her mind was quick, I saw, almost slick.

"Alexander."

"Uh-huhn?"

"Alexander Lincoln Duvall."

"Alexander. Like the great conqueror?"

"Yeah. More like High-John though."

"And Lincoln? Like the man who freed the slaves?"

"Somethin' like that."

"Yet you are in the business of promoting slavery."

"That depends on which side you're on, Babygirl."

"Meaning?"

"Meaning, to some I'm the greatest liberator there is, while to others I'm just like Pharaoh. Minus the chariots, of course."

"So you've been to Sunday School."

"You'd be surprised where I've been. I ain't totally ignorant, Miss Lady."

"I didn't say you were."

"So you see that I'm not just undeniably good-looking, but I'm smart too."

"You do flatter yourself, my brotha."

"Why not? It's true."

"Who are you, Mr. Duvall? I mean, really, aside from your very public persona?"

"Who am I?"

"That's the question, Sir."

"Can you handle the truth?"

"Try me and see."

"Well then, to some I'm God. To others, I'm the devil himself. The general consensus though, is that I'm invincible. Can walk on water. Leap tall buildings in a single bound. Folks in the wards swear I got power over everything in creation. Recognize, Babygirl. I thought you knew."

She cleared her throat. "Well. Alrighty then…" She scrawled on her pad again, and I swear she's suppressing giggles.

"Well, you asked."

"So I did."

"Let that be a lesson to you."

"Beg your pardon?"

"Be careful what you ask for."

She looked up then, facing me squarely—a contest of wills. Who can stare the longest without conceding? Whose power will ultimately prevail?

I loved her eyes then. Liked her heart, her courage. Neither one of us flinched the entire time. Not even Cooper had been able to hold his stare against mine.

"You ain't that scary for a church girl," I ventured, and she didn't answer. Just soaked me up, taking me in, and I gave her something to hold on to. I licked my lips, cocked my head and allowed my gaze to speak for me, like I do to those professional sistas in those high-rolling clubs Ghost drags me to sometimes on the weekends. Doctors. Attorneys. Professors. Executives. I love showing those women what my minimalist street-power can do to their educated minds, their Delta Sigma methodologies, their philosophical doxologies. It's all part of the game. Me making them think they're analyzing me, dissecting my criminal psyche, re-directing my "negative energies," as one very beautiful, very snobbish psychologist-sista had termed it just before I blew her mind. The best part is when they dive in head-first to "rescue" me from psychological ruin and sociopathic damnation, that's when I show them whose really in control. That's when they see that my power is greater than all their degrees, and money, and beauty and lofty reputations in the white world.

By the time I'm done getting 'em addicted to my brilliant flattery, my seemingly endless attention, my late-night booty calls, they're convinced they've met their soul mates. That's when I drop them and end everything without looking back or saying good-bye. I become unforgettable to them that way, because everyone knows that jilted women carry memories that last a lifetime. By stepping out of the picture, I allow their memories and fantasies to paint me up larger than life, so that any other man that comes after me will never be able to compare with the legend they think I am.

Ghost and I bet sometimes at how long it will take me to totally and thoroughly turn each one out, because one thing is certain: A rich, educated sista will beg for good loving and quality time the same as any sister from the wards, only she'll do it with a better vocabulary.

On an average night, I'll leave a club with so many numbers I can't always remember who I'm calling. Sometimes, I just go ahead and give 'em to Ghost so he can do the usual taste-test. Lemme know which ones are worth the time it takes to "do 'em."

What does it all mean? It means that Churchgirl is hardly ready to deal with somebody like me.

None of that stops me from toying with her though, from sitting across this table letting her feel just a sample of my force. I let her think she's actually reading me when I'm really letting her feel the extent of my desire. I want her to know I'm more man than she could ever handle, that I have an appetite that's as insatiable as the grave. An appetite that no one woman could ever fill.

It worked. She lowered her eyes at last, pretended to make more notations in her pad, and I can't help grinning in triumph. Still, I have to give her her props, 'cause she made me smile in spite of myself, and if there's one thing I hate to do, I hate to smile.

"Are we done?" I asked, trying hard to rearrange the frown I'm famous for.

"Well..." Her eyebrows lifted and fell.

"Just say it."

"I wanted to ask you for a more in-depth interview actually," she pressed, bearing down on her words, the pen curled in her hand.

"What about?"

"To be frank? I wanted to learn all about drug dealers," she said. "About what it's like to hustle crack in the wards in these days of high-tech gangsterism. And..."

"And?"

"Several of the largest dealers from the wards have been murdered recently in gangland-style slayings. Two dealers from Atlanta were murdered here just days ago, and I..."

"You assumed that I had something to do with 'em, that all these shootings are somehow related?"

"Yes. Well, no. What I mean is, you *look* like you could very well know something about it but sometimes, looks *are* deceiving, and it's not like I'm trying to say you had anything to do with those shootings specifically, but I've heard rumors that you are... I mean, that *you*, specifically, traffic in *the business* and have a working knowledge of..." She stopped to scratch her head, looked confused now, and I know it's 'cause I'm getting to her, making her lose focus. "What I mean to say is, I trust Minister, I mean *Detective* Cooper's referral."

"Minister Cooper?" I grinned, slid my eyes across her face, fold and unfold my hands. "And you trust *him?*"

"Yes. I do."

Now it's my turn to laugh, and it's obvious she doesn't like that at all.

"Did I say something funny?"

I shrugged. "So what, you trying to be a black Barbara Walters or something? You looking to earn a Pulitzer? Gunning for Oprah's job?"

"Maybe," she said, and inserted the tip of the Cross pen into her mouth. "What if I am?"

"At my expense though, huhn?"

"Everything will, of course, remain strictly confidential."

"I've heard that before."

"Not from me." Those dimples reappear and again, I can't help myself. I smiled too. Her game so far was smooth, airtight.

"Ah… So you're one of those cerebral sisters?" I said.

"Was that a yes or a no answer?"

"I didn't hear the question."

"Will you let me interview you for a story? Share your insights about the wards, about the murders, about what life is like for a dealer nowadays in that kind of environment?"

"What's in it for me?"

Her eyes fall, then rise from her pad. Her pen moved furiously across the lined paper. She's making me wait on purpose, trying to draw me in to her quiet energy.

"I'm offering a priceless gift."

"Priceless?"

"Yes."

"Everybody has a price, Babygirl."

"I don't."

"That remains to be seen."

"By whom?"

"What gift are you offering?"

"My friendship," she said and there are those dimples again.

"And you think it's worth that much?"

"More than that."

She's flirting now, teetering on the edge of trouble, and I know she *has* to be out of her mind. Sure, she's fine and all that, has the kind of lovely mind I'd love to tame for my own purposes. But who had time for all the drama? I was running an empire that was growing by the minute. I didn't have time for petty distractions.

Churchgirl was actually making a daring attempt to flirt. But flirting was "gaming" and that was my territory. Nobody was better at running it than yours truly, so why was she even trying to play with me? Didn't she know I lived the game every day? Game is what I sell. Game is what I depended on to keep me alive, so Babygirl was truly out of her league. She needed to stop playing before she got seriously hurt, ended up another prisoner of war trapped behind enemy lines.

I fixed my stare on her hard just then, trying to imagine this soft little lamb out there in my jungle, trying to understand my wolf world. In the wards, wolves killed sweet, innocent prey like her for sport. In my world, wolves attacked first and never asked any questions.

"Even if I agree to do this interview, I doubt if you really have the heart to," I was trying to tell her nicely, knowing she wouldn't last a day following me around in the wards.

"What are you saying?"

"I'm saying it's a bad idea. I've seen *60 Minutes, America's Most Wanted...*"

"So you're saying that you think I don't have the heart to do *what*?" Miss Miniver was mad-persistent.

"I'm saying you don't have the heart to journey down into hell to get my story, to experience me in all the fullness of my glory. That, Miss Lady, is gonna cost you much more than friendship."

"What then?" she pressed, eyebrows creased with anger. "What's it gonna cost me, since you know so much, Mr. Alexander Lincoln High-John Duvall?"

I shook my head, leaned across the table and put my scarred hand over hers. "Everything," I tell her. "It's gonna cost you everything."

She fell silent at last, staring at my hand clapped over hers. Behind her, the sun rose full and round and as orange as a basketball, cresting over the tops of the skyscrapers beyond.

Avoiding my eyes, she took her hand back, slowly, carefully, like a rabbit removing its head from a lion's mouth.

I smiled again, without meaning to, and we both know it's already too late. Her mind, like the wards, like the life of her preacher-boyfriend, already belonged to me.

CHAPTER SIX

Gabriella

I t's impossible for me to fully explain what actually happened to me that morning. All I know is that seeing Mr.-Thug-Life up close again in that cramped interrogation room, made me understand what Lucifer must've been like in person.

To his credit, with all his huffing and cynicism and restrained jealousy, Trevis *had* attempted to prepare me. "The man's a snake, so expect to be charmed," he warned as he opened the door to that airtight room.

"Charmed? Don't you think that's a bit extreme?" I asked, although what I meant was, *I know you're trying hard to impress me, to make up for your reckless intentions last night, but why'd you introduce me to him in the first place if you knew he was that dangerous? Handing him over like a gift of prey, a cat dropping a dead mouse at the feet of his master.*

Still, Trev was right. I knew it when I stepped into the room and found him sitting there, scowling and rubbing his wrist like a victim. He hardly looked like the same ruthless assassin that had attempted to murder me in cold blood just hours before. But he *was* something to behold—larger than life in that tiny room, recklessly bodacious, and flawlessly handsome.

Being celibate prepares you for anything. Learning to deny those ferocious biological urges of the physical body when it's screaming for sexual release catapults the mind to a level of self-control that is accomplished only through the divine. But Lincoln Duvall was not just any man. His shoulders and arms, the trunks of his thighs, were thick with muscle under that expensive leather he was wearing. A prisoner's body, Trevis would have called it. But there was something more beneath his surface, a rhythm that kept perfect timing with something lurking deep inside of me. Neither one of us spoke at first, and the only sound came from the large clock on the right wall.

Something about this man was in perfect sync with "that other me" that had been so raunchy, so scandalous, so ruthlessly promiscuous before my conversion, that only a baptism in Jesus' holy name, only a good burying of my old sinful nature under a watery grave, had been able to cleanse me from. From all the chaos that had once ruled my soul. I'd stumbled up out of that cleansing pool babbling in a heavenly language not even I could understand. Only then had I become the kind of honorable woman that those who knew me before no longer recognized.

But it wasn't that me that Lincoln was interested in seeing. He'd sat back in his chair, stroking his chin and training his eyes on me.

"You trying to win a Pulitzer at my expense?" he'd asked, his voice even and cool as a winter's breeze. He was smooth and easy. Lightning-fast, like a reptile, and at first it seemed impossible to not be taken in by that kind of genuine machismo. Duvall's magnetism demanded recognition, and combined with his gift of gab, razor-sharp wit and a voice that could keep me listening for hours; his was an aura that could prove deadly to any celibate woman.

But I'd had some experience with the powers of lust, had met that kind of mesmerizing pull before, and I knew exactly what to do; I prayed. Sat pretending to jot every detail and prayed hard that the Lord would inoculate me right then against his poison. I sensed he had the answers I needed, not just about the Third Ward's drug fields, but about the last murder of a man Trev had called Joker.

There were things Duvall could teach me. Things he'd never mention with Trevis hovering so close. But on his turf, within his own self-proclaimed territory, there was no telling what I'd discover. In the name of journalistic professionalism, I pushed past my giddiness and better judgment and asked him outright for his number. Business was business, and I had a job to do.

He responded with a smile, a sideways grin that hid his teeth. "You sure you can hang? It might cost you everything, Babygirl," he said, making promises with his eyes, just like a snake.

"May I contact you for a later discussion?"

"A later discussion?"

"Yes."

He shrugged, his eyes boring into me. Trevis had come back by then and he didn't like it at all, me propositioning his mortal enemy and Lincoln smiling at me like a lion pondering whether or not to spring.

Lincoln spoke at last, "947-7574." He nodded toward my notepad and watched as I wrote each number carefully. "That's my cell. My private line. Call me anytime after ten in the morning. I don't share that number with everybody and I expect you won't either."

"Thank you, Mr. Duvall. I'll be careful to respect your wishes," I said, but he had already dismissed me. Was already out of his chair and moving toward the door, not once looking back

It would be another month before I'd run into him again. Another month before I'd discover that the voice message on the wrong number he'd given me would never say anything more than, "The cellular customer you are trying to call, cannot be reached..."

"What else could you have expected from a snake?" Trev had said.

✝✝✝

There were no real streets in Heartford's Third Ward district. There were just three main arteries that led in and out of the sprawling housing project known as "The Wards," so to simplify things, folks just broke each portion into separate parts, naming them the First, Second (Deuce), and Third Wards (Trece), which was easily the worst.

The signs on the street posts had fallen down years before, and the various roads that snaked through the 1,500-resident complex were full of potholes. To visitors, the wards were a complicated maze. They pulled up beside Cruz's Bodega and got out scratching their heads at the clusters of forlorn buildings that seemed to be collapsing.

"Anybody here know a Mr. Boudrow Turner runs the satellite welfare office?" a social worker emerging from a state car holding a clipboard might ask women shucking black-eyes on a front stoop, or men drinking from the same Red Rover bottle under the awning of Biggerton Funerals, Inc.

The new mailmen, who changed every six months, because they got tired of being robbed by fourteen-year-old boys with old men's weapons, always got confused at first. Slipped SSI checks into the wrong door slots, left *JET* magazines with the wrong families.

But these were forgivable mistakes, since after awhile, the worn footpaths that snaked through the maze of tenements all looked alike. The buildings did too—sandstone high-rises with plywood nailed over hallway windows. Barracks-style, six families lived together with small squares of yard that had given up trying to grow grass.

Third Ward was the largest of the six low-income housing developments that the city of Heartford attempted to hide behind unfurling ribbons of new interstate and factories so large, ward residents could hear when their blast furnaces kicked on. But since the homicide rates within those three miles of dilapidated brick were much higher than anywhere else in the state, and since the media was always down there snapping photos of crime scenes to be shown only on the 11 p.m. news, Third Ward was impossible to hide and even harder to forget. No one at *The Heartford Chronicle* knew that better than Gabriella. She'd been born there in the early '60s, surviving its petty gang turf wars and the crack-cocaine explosion of the early '80s. Most of her classmates were too busy getting high or making it possible for everyone else to get high, to even notice when she quietly slipped off to Hofstra University in New York where she majored in communications on an academic scholarship.

Years before that, before she'd watched what appeared to be an entire generation wiped out by crack and the other vices that came with it—prostitution, thievery, bad-check-writing, assaults with deadly weapons—her nickname, "Bunny," had been honorably bestowed upon her by the late Mr. Holt Soup, the director of the ward's decrepit rec center. Having a ward nickname qualified her as a bona-fide home-girl, although the new-school flygirls who strutted the blocks now, glancing at her Acura during her official forays into the wards on various story assignments, detected no ward residue in the way she drove, dressed, or spoke. To them, Gabriella was just another not-to-be-trusted spy from the white world come to exploit their poverty.

No one seemed to notice that the Acura, turning into the maze of blocks with an insider's accuracy, never got lost. Only an insider could find the mini playgrounds and barbecue shacks or differentiate between the high-rises where the crackheads bartered their children and the duplexes where Miss Emma sold illegal icies and sweet potato pies. It was for this reason Gabriella figured she'd easily find *him*, the man who had looked right into her face and lied. If that didn't work, she'd simply look for his ride, a black Cadillac truck with flashy gold lettering and expensive Vogue tires. A man's hooptie in the wards represented more than his street worth and status. It was his home away from home, a symbol of his manhood, and men like Duvall were never too far away from their rides.

†††

It was close to noon under an autumn sky threatening rain, and two drives through the ward had yielded nothing. She'd dressed casually in a denim skirt suit and six-inch mules, her hair caught up high in a fancy horse tail. It was her street-diva look, the perfect bait for a hard-edged brotha bent on escaping her. Kirk Franklin rocked her speakers and she'd rolled up her windows to ignore the brothas who wolf-whistled from their corner perches and souped-up sedans. Some, she'd gone to school with. Others she'd met when she came down to cover other "hood stories."Able-bodied, job-less brothers mostly, calling, "S'up, Bunny? You looking good" or "Yo, Baby, lemme get five dollars 'til Saturday."

"It's gonna take more than five dollars to keep that rotten front tooth from falling out your head," she wanted to yell back at a tall brother they called "Tree" but changed her mind. She'd known Tree and his sisters since the third grade, and even with his alleged learning disability, Tree had a cussing vocabulary that Richard Pryor couldn't match.

Near a fire hydrant in front of Sneaker World, two men stood so close talking their foreheads seemed to be touching. One man was as big and dark as a Brahma bull, his bright red hat like a woolen rooster's comb that matched his red and black ski vest. The other man had the darting eyes, skeletal limbs, and slack, dirty clothing of a crackhead. Brahma-Bull reached into his pocket, came out with a knotted fist, and the men appeared to be giving "daps." Gabriella saw the exchange of paper and foil, watched Brahma shove the loose bills into his pocket.

Wiping his runny nose, the crackhead shivered with anticipation. Mission accomplished, he darted out into the street so quickly without looking that Gabriella swerved abruptly, slammed on her screeching brakes to avoid crushing him. Her heart was thumping as he put up the proverbial finger, declared her a female dog through furry teeth.

Brahma shook his head in quiet amusement as Gabriella swerved to the curb, caught his eye and waved him over. He was big but swift, stood outside her window in the time it took her to roll it down. "What you need, Miss Lady? You new on the block?"

"Sorta."

"Bed not be no narc." He spoke quickly, his lips not moving, like a ventriloquist, she thinks.

"I'm looking for Lincoln. He owes me," she told him..

She fronted hard, watching his eyes. But Brahma was unreadable. "Who dat?" He played along.

"Lincoln Duvall. Don't play me, Sweetie." She smiled harmlessly, but he shrugged, looked off into the street and the slow-streaming traffic.

"Never heard of him."

A red Beemer rolled past and he whistled to slow it down, swaggered toward it. Gabriella sighed, pulled off again. Finding Lincoln was harder than she'd imagined, but she refused to give up.

Driving through the first and second wards again yielded nothing more than blown kisses, probing eyes that followed her expensive tires. In Trece once more, she stopped at The CD Shack, bought the latest Hezekiah Walker from a flirty salesman who spoke through a haze of MoneyPower incense while trying to give her a complimentary bootleg Jay-Z cassette.

"No thanks. Not my kinda music," she said, waving it away politely. "Has Lincoln Duvall been by here lately?"

"*Linc*? Oh. So *that's* the kinda nigga you like to roll with?" The salesman was cuter than average, she thought as he frowned distastefully and shook his head in stark disappointment.

"Are you gonna tell me where to find Linc or not?"

"Not. Never heard of him," he told her, turning away to knock a pesty fly off a side shelf.

The gunmetal sky looked pregnant with rain as she pulled up near Cruz's Bodega. "I'm looking for Lincoln Duvall," she explained to three truants smoking blunts outside a laundry. "Y'all know where he stay? And why y'all ain't in school? It ain't Saturday. Declared your own holiday, huhn?"

It was a deliberate slackness of diction. A loosening of the tongue spoken in precise Third Ward patois. The truants vibed with it, drew closer to hear above her churning gospel.

"S'up, Miss Lady. You looking for *who*?" The one closest to her stepped forward like a spokesman, the blunt still in his mouth. His name was Smiley, and he was much shorter than the others, his head skewered with cigar-sized braids, his toothless grin like a retired prize-fighter's.

"Lincoln," she repeated. "Lincoln Duvall?" She tapped her brake lights, signalled for the jeep behind her to go around.

"*Loc* Linc? That's who you want?"

"Loc? Why he gotta be all that?"

"Cuz he is. You don't know?" Smiley shook his head pitifully, and the two boys behind him laughed with their shoulders, looked at each other as if sharing a private joke.

"Can see she ain't from around here," the boy wearing the black bomber jacket observed.

"I'll know if you tell me," Gabriella pressed, but Smiley's head wagged vigorously.

"I ain't saying nothing. Shoot…" He toked hard, swallowed every bit of the smoke. "That nigga crazy as a roach. Ask his dead momma. Nawl. Ask his psycho brother that's locked up over at Ainsley. Ask him how he got there…"

The other boys high-fived him for that one, but Gabriella frowned. "Ainsley? The mental hospital?"

"One and only."

"What's his brother doing there? I'm asking you, Lil Man…" Her timing was off, the delivery too late. They thought her a joke and moved off to the next corner, still laughing, scattering pigeons along the way. Autumn chill crept under the heavy denim skirt, but she wasn't sure if that's why she suddenly shivered.

It's been months since she'd been inside Mr. Cruz's Bodega, and now, aside from seeing the store's aging namesake, a cold Pepsi and a bag of hot pork rinds are her primary objectives.

"Skins" or "Chicharones," the locals still called them, and Mr. Cruz sold the kind she loved best.

"Ah… *Mi Chica… Bienvenido…*" Mr. Cruz looked up from his register and smiled, nudging his sliding spectacles back up onto his nose. A fat cat skulked in a corner near the loose produce, guarding against mice, and she nudged him gently with her toe, stooped down to ruffle his rangy fur.

"Pepsi…Y… *Chicharonnes, verdad…*?"

"*Si, Senor.*" Gabriella giggled, took a diet Pepsi from the dairy case. Mr. Cruz reached behind the counter for the largest bag of skins, tossed in a pack of Juicy Fruit chewing gum and two Slim Jims. He shook it all into a paper bag.

"No matter how long I stay away, you always remember, don't you?"

Mr. Cruz nodded, and his bashful smile under the dark handlebar moustache was the largest thing on his face. She dug into her purse for $5, but he waved it away. "You still no eat." With a quivering hand that reeked of onions and ammonia, he pinched her cheek.

"I do eat, Mr. Cruz. Just not all the time."

His eyes were rheumy, the whites blued with age. His hands always spoke first. "*Tiene ninos? No muchacho?*"

"Not married yet, Mr. Cruz. Only to Dios."

"*Su madre? Su hermanas?*"

"Momma's still Momma. My sisters are all well."

The conversations were always the same. It was the ritual itself that mattered. Tearing open the pack of gum, she held it out, waited for him to extract his usual piece. "I'm looking for someone, Mr. Cruz. Someone you may have seen around here."

"*Si?*"

"He sells drugs, Mr. Cruz."

"*Si?*" His eyebrows were as thick as caterpillars. He raised one, frowning.

"I ain't buying, don't worry." She giggled, patted his knotted knuckles. "It's for a story. I do need to talk to him though."

"*Son nombre?*"

"Lincoln Duvall. He…"

But Mr. Cruz put up his hand as if stopping traffic. "*Mucho Diablo,*" he said just as the phone rang behind him. She excused herself and walked outside. A lecture was imminent if she'd stayed, and Mr. Cruz rambled for hours if she'd let him. Back outside the rain had started. Gabrielle shivered, wished she'd worn her trench. Had she left it in the trunk? At least she'd remembered to bring her umbrella.

A milk truck rumbled by, its tires gnawing deeper holes in the cratered asphalt. When it passed, she realized she wasn't dreaming. She saw it clearly, the vacant hole, the missing space where her Acura was.

CHAPTER SEVEN

Lincoln

She was looking for *me*.

Word rang out in the wards like the midnight rumors of "narcs" outside a crackhouse.

By the time I'd showered and left Chinere's that morning and drove up into the east side, the wire had it buzzing. A tan Acura with downtown rims, Rudder had said, and she didn't look like the type who wanted "blow."

Dante called from the record shop. "Looked like a case worker for DCF," he told me.

"Like an ebony Avon lady," Smiley said, grinning. "Fine too. *Whew*, she was fine."

It didn't matter what she looked like, I didn't appreciate her doing that, hunting me down on *my* block like she was my woman. Showing up in my dreams like I actually cared about how deep her dimples were. It was more than a breach of street etiquette. It was more than disrespect. It was a code violation that deserved swift and immediate punishment, and there was no way around it. Business was business and I had to do something. I couldn't have my rep in question. Couldn't have women thinking I was so soft and easy they could just roll up on me when they got ready. I couldn't let niggaz know I was that common and predictable, that easy to find. Niggaz be setting up ambushes sho-nuff then. Picking me and my crew off like buzzards on a fence.

So I handled it the way I'd have handled any other female looking for trouble. I had her car "popped."

Gabriella

All that money I'd paid for it, and that high-tech alarm system hadn't made a peep.

My car was gone without a trace, like a VCR in an addict's apartment, and looking for it in the wards was like scouring for a needle in a haystack.

You'd have thought I would've known better, would've remembered that not even a police officer was safe alone in the Third Ward, let alone a spanking new Acura with a Bose system. Hadn't Momma always said it would happen? Didn't she always warn me about driving my car through there, because "Them dopeheads will steal that pretty car with you in it."

But as usual, I had to learn the hard way.

I hadn't been in the bodega more than five minutes, so I knew that whoever took my car was skilled at dismantling high-tech alarms. They knew exactly what they were doing, had probably been following me around for the past hour, but of course, nobody claimed to have seen anything. And even though Mr. Cruz called the police eight times in the space of an hour, they still hadn't shown up by the time the sky morphed into a dome of smoky darkness, clearing the streets so that everybody who had sense went home where they belonged.

Lightning winked high above the water tower near the Flatbush Avenue Bridge, and heavy clouds churned, lowering close. "A sign from the Virgin," Mr. Cruz said from behind his counter, crossing his chest, ranting about my fascination with "*la vida loca*."

Standing in the doorway, I watched the drunkards pour out of the alley across the street like spilled wine, felt the rising wind whipping my hair.

The storm seemed to have appeared out of nowhere, and there wasn't a Yellow Cab or a transit bus in sight. I'd left my cell phone in the car, so that was gone too. And though I'd called Trev's cell and left several messages on his voice mail at work and home, he hadn't responded to any of them. Did headquarters know anything about this? I couldn't help thinking, are the police purposely ignoring my calls?

There was still no sign of that black Escalade, and it was beginning to dawn on me that maybe Trev was right. Perhaps I *was* out of my league.

Rain began to drop slowly, like big sloppy kisses, taunting me. I sighed as Mr. Cruz yawned, thrust the hot, angry mug of Bustelo coffee across the counter, insisting I sit and wait out the storm with him. I shook my head, placed my purse strap onto my shoulder and bid him farewell.

By the looks of this sky, it could rain all day and into the night, and the only thing worse than the wards during the day, were the wards at night. Even the folks at *The Chronicle* knew that.

Back outside again, I scanned the deserted street for a bus stop, dug into my purse for loose change. Behind me, Mr. Cruz called, *"Mi Chica, Mi Chica,"* but it was too late. The rain had already baptized me. Above the store, the words of a jazz tune floated down from a third-floor window. "Every goodbye ain't gone," the heavy alto voice sang.

CHAPTER EIGHT

Lincoln

It was a two-bedroom on the north side of the Third Ward that I'd had fumigated, flushed of mice and roaches, and painted with a shimmering silver patina. The kitchenette was adjacent to what could be a dining room, and there was a black wraparound sofa that seated ten. In the living room were glass end tables, plush black carpet, and a big-screen TV tuned in to BET, Ghost's favorite station. There were three of these exact apartments in each section of the three wards, three of these mini way-stations that I pay $312 in rent for every month, although my name's not on any of the leases. Folks downtown at the city's housing authority knew better than to rent anything to me.

Years before, my momma, Lillian Duvall, had been a model tenant, always paying her rent on time, keeping her apartment clean of roaches, never turning her Mahalia Jackson records up high enough to disturb the neighbors. Momma had been one of those old-time, sanctified church ladies, hardworking, thrifty and quiet, except during *those* times we never talked about.

Her two boys though, were another story altogether, panhandling outside of package stores, shooting dice behind the pool hall, throwing bricks through factory windows, and when we were barely old enough to go to Juvie Hall, pulling pistols on mailmen.

My brother Joseph, whom everybody called "Runt," seemed kinda "touched" from the beginning, but I was particularly devious, full of grand schemes and illusions. The folks downtown had never forgotten the havoc I'd wreaked on more than a few neighborhood businesses. I scouted for dope fiends who held up candy stores and stole hubcaps off of customers' cars in grocery store parking lots. I delivered number slips for the street lottery, transported liquor for bootleggers, kicked dogs, stole bicycles and earned a reputation as a general nuisance. My main objective even then was making money, all I could, however I could.

Since the Heartford Housing Authority still kept a file of my earlier exploits, I paid female hustlers to fill out rental applications and sign leases. I moved in and paid the rent and utilities, furnished the three places with simple accommodations like curtains and microwaves, so that each apartment looked lived-in. And although neighbors complained to each other about the endless traffic that flowed through their hallways night and day, they never reported it to the head office. Not when I was always sending over groceries or buying their kids new sneakers or replacing the nets on the wards' rundown hoop courts.

The apartments have made my operations much easier to monitor, since each (they are all on the eighth floor) was a high-rise that looked down on every entrance and exit into the wards. Apartments on the eighth floor offered aerial views grander than any sidewalk surveillance Heartford narcs have managed to assemble so far. When I stood in front of my apartments' living room windows with my binoculars, surveying the cars and buildings that from up here looked like Monopoly icons scattered across a board, the entire ward opened up to me like the pieces of an intricate puzzle. It was for this very reason that I'd immediately spotted the gold Acura when it passed the community rec center and parked in front of Old Man Cruz's corner market.

✝✝✝

It was a typical afternoon in Trece, with Ghost packaging product for the distributors who'll be doing their pick-ups in the next few hours. He was behind schedule again, slipping in a bad way and hoping I don't notice. He was wearing the usual plastic gloves and beautician's cape. Looked like a mad scientist working on some outlawed experiment.

Ghost hummed as he carefully concentrated on the mound of rocky talc that resembled Epsom salt poured from a carton. There was enough "blow" here to buy a new Beemer. Enough for a good down payment on one of those ritzy houses miles and miles outside the wards where I owned mine, inside a new development of sprawling cul-de-sacs known as Rice Heights.

With a piece of squared plastic, Ghost scraped the powder into neat piles that he transfered into glassine bags. It was up to the intermediate dealers to break up the bags and mix the silky powder into vials of small hard nuggets of rock. The lower-level dealers then divided the coarse fragments into thumb-sized manila envelopes to be distributed on The Street.

Once upon a time, me and Ghost did it all. We'd started out as neighborhood lookouts before graduating to small-time corner merchants like Rudder, moving up into petty drop-offs and then onto larger circles of distribution that involved mixing crack, packaging it for sale, and running it for the higher level dealers in and around the immediate territories that bordered the wards. It had been through this latest phase of development that we'd done our greatest networking, building up our own clientele both in and outside of the wards, offering choice product and competitive prices with a polished degree of professionalism, until eventually, a lead courier for J.D. Hahn, one of the wealthiest drug suppliers in the northern tip of the East Coast, began to request our services by name.

Someone in Hahn's organization had finally realized that Heartford, Connecticut, with its budding, though underserved crack trade, and its pool of moneyed, crack-smoking insurance executives, was for them, virgin territory. Better still, enterprising young urban mavericks like me and Ghost were smart enough and daring enough to triple any investment they were willing to make.

Originally, it had been my idea to start soliciting contacts through Ghost's infamous cousins, many of whom were already secretly working for Hahn, laundering excess money throughout Manhattan in notoriously quiet and extremely Bohemian circles of wealth that included nightclubs, day spas, and franchises of lowly check-cashing places. Kinfolk or not, me and Ghost had to pay them top dollar to get cut into the more lucrative drug markets supplied by the expanding Cuban distributors from the West Coast.

It proved to be money well spent. The ample supplies of outside product had generated enough funds to propel us into an entirely new class of ruling power on The Block. Plans were drawn up, logistics were explored and equipment was purchased. A carefully chosen staff had to be hired. Spaces had to be rented. Heartford's Police Department's vice division was infiltrated and spies were bought; protectors were put in place. Unemployed brothas, fresh from the pen and eager to explore lucrative ways to feed their growing families, were tired of all the street money flowing in one direction. They signed on with me and Ghost as runners, watchers, foot soldiers, lab techs, and corner assassins, and made more money than they'd ever seen.

It had taken less than a year for us to outclass the wards' small-time nickel-and-dime local operations with larger guns, greater vision, and enough manpower to cause a street revolution. The old storefront, street-level dealers were much too dumb, much too slow, and much too disorganized to keep up with my organized plans. One by one, the majority of the ward's fractured drug territories fell into control of the new faction. They had no choice.

I watched as the residue of white powder rose, tickled Ghost's nose, and he sneezed, reaching for the goblet that fizzed with rum and Coke. Behind him, a freshly bought pizza with everything on it emitted the aroma of onions and pepperoni, as Simone, the latest addition to my Third-Ward harem, stood at the stove in a scant babydoll nightie, scraping egg from a smoking pan. I saw her looking toward the arrangement of armchairs lined in a crescent in front of the living room window. She sighed. "You ready to eat, Boo?" she called, but I was too busy tripping over what I was seeing through my binoculars. I rubbed my neck, fingering the blotch of red hickies Chinere had put there the night before, marking her territory. Outside, the rain was falling again in sheets, spattering against the paned glass. Looking at Simone suddenly made me sick, filled me with anger. "Simone. Go put some clothes on," I told her and she and Ghost looked at each other. Ghost shrugged. Simone looked confused.

Simone has the face and body of a video dancer. She was always walking around in scant lingerie. It was the only reason I let her up here. I made her strip when the mood suited me, made her parade around that way to service my male guests, as a way of hospitality. "This one's on the house," I'll tell 'em, but then those fools don't wanna go home afterward.

My mind was churning now, zeroing in on what's down there trapped in the rain. I put down my binoculars, clicked on my cell, tapping numbers.

"Yeah. I know. But don't hurt her," I said into the receiver. "I'll handle it myself."

Ghost looked up and winked, changed his voice into a slurred falsetto. "Miss Mary Poppins forgot her umbrella?" He laughed, knocked the rum back hard.

Chinere

It's close to eight on a Saturday morning when I finally hear his key in the front door, smell the Hennessy, the Armani aftershave, and something else that's following him around like a clue to a riddle I don't feel like guessing at this morning. It's hovering over the stove where I'm stirring cheese-eggs, trying hard to keep something in my stomach. Waves of nausea are rising and falling over me, sweat popping out all above my top lip.

Linc, as usual, ain't noticed nothing but what he's wanting right then. He don't see the big jars of multi-vitamins and iron on the counter, the tall glass of milk, which he knows I hate, on the table. He just shakes himself out that leather jacket and folds it carefully over a kitchen chair, cuz if he's careful about anything, it's those fancy clothes he can't seem to get enough of.

Before I can get to fussing and asking about why he ain't called and who he was with all night, he comes up behind me, folds his arms around my waist and starts tasting my neck.

"S'up, Baby... You miss me?" He touches my face with his thumb, kisses me lightly near my ear, and although I'm so mad that I can hardly speak, my heart pounds under my white shop smock.

"Get away from me, Boy," I tell him, only he knows I don't mean a word of it. I want to make him give back the key to my apartment, slap all that sweetness out of his mouth. But for the moment, I can't bring myself to do nuthin' but let him hold me like this, cradling me like his arms be the safest place in the world. I'm just so glad he found his way back from the street in one piece, back to me, to *us*, where he truly belongs.

"You love me?" he asks while I'm trying to scrape eggs onto a plate.

"Hmph. You ask *her* that too?" I say, and he knows I'm pouting now.

"I'm asking *you*," he insists, but that strange Gardenia scent overpowers everything, and accusation hangs over his head like a noose.

"Why you make me worry like this? What happened to you?"

"When?"

"I ain't talked to you since yesterday morning. I been calling and paging all night, and you ain't pick up the phone to tell me nothing. I didn't know what was going on, whether the cops had picked you up again and was holding you on bond or something. I called downtown but they wouldn't give me no information, talking 'bout I wasn't no attorney. I was worried sick until Imani said she saw you and Ghost driving past the shop last night, so I knew then you was okay."

I feel it then, his whole body stiffening up. "Cooper," he says, like there's a bad taste in his mouth. "That crazy fool's gonna pay. Locking me up for hours. Swears he's Serpico or somebody. But it's all good. He'll learn some manners by the time I'm done."

"Linc. They been talking in the shop too. Imani a 'nem. You know how they do."

"Talking? About what?"

"You know Imani's cousin, Rhea, who goes with crazy Buster, one of Spain's boys? Her baby's daddy?"

"Buster. Yeah. I know that fool. What about him?"

"Well, he told Rhea and she told Imani they was looking for you that night. Spain and 'nem. Heard they was driving all over Trece looking, only they couldn't find you. Couldn't find *us*, cuz we was all on lockdown."

"What Spain want with me?"

"Imani say they got a hit out on you and Ghost."

"Again?" I can hear it, the smile in his voice.

"Something about they had a car following you and Ghost while y'all was supposedly following Spain earlier that day. Guess they figured you and Ghost was about to jack him."

"That's what she said, huh?"

I nod, tell him everything Imani had told me.

"Imani said they was ready to do both of y'all, but then you switched up on 'em. Pulled over to the curb next to some church like you knew something. They thought somebody was following them, an ambush maybe. So they let it go. Went back later that night to find y'all."

Linc starts humming very gently. He moves his arms from around me finally, and stands there plucking at his goatee as I butter toast, slap it next to the eggs with two sausage links, then slide the whole thing in front of the chair where he always sits.

"Sit down, Boy. You bed not let this food get cold," I say like I'm still mad, and ain't scared, and everything's normal as usual. He plays along, but I can see by his eyes that his mind's moving a hundred miles a second.

"Nawl, you eat. I'm straight. That's your food."

"I ate already," I lie and he gives me a look that says he needs to get in touch with Ghost and won't be getting any sleep this morning.

He pulls out a kitchen chair, drops into it, and for some reason I can't easily figure, I stand over him and start spooning eggs into his mouth. Wiping his chin with a napkin, dicing his sausage into bite-sized pieces with his fork, I'm feeding him like he's my only baby and he's loving it, fixing his eyes on mine like a satisfied infant at his momma's breast. The only breast he'll ever need. I hold the glass to his lips, and he drinks long gulps of milk until it leaves a white froth on his moustache.

"Thank you, Baby," he whispers, looking up at me.

"Hush," I say, stroking his head, 'cuz I know this is the closest thing I'ma get from him that's an apology. I bring the plate to the sink and start washing the rest of the dishes.

He heaves a deep sigh, pulls out his cell, calls Ghost and tells him to get out of whoever's bed he's in and meet him at the salon at nine, in about an hour. He gets up then and comes behind me. "Here," he says, and when I look over my shoulder, he's handing me his pistol, his eyes already turned back to stone.

Linc and guns be as natural together as fire and smoke, and for a moment I remember the first real date we had. How he took me out in the fields behind the wards, to the illegal shooting ranges where all the thugs went to practice and show off their women. I can still see that strange glint in his eyes as he made me hold that big .357 and aim carefully at those homemade targets, a line of empty Heffenreffer bottles poised on a rickety fence. It was the first time he'd put his arms around me, helping me to hold the gun straight out in front of me. And when it exploded in my hands, bullets running across the field, he'd laughed at my bad aim.

Now he is handing me one of his favorite guns, knowing how well he had taught me to hit a target.

"I hate these things," I wanna tell him, but since I know he's already upset, I don't. I just take it from him, put it on the counter next to the little New Testament Bible I'd been reading that morning.

I go back to washing dishes, and it ain't long before his arms fold around me again. "So you waited up all night for me?"

The clock on the microwave reads 8:15, and I know I'm running late, need to call Imani and make sure she's on time, have her open the shop and start the furnace, knock the chill off the air.

"So who was she?" I ask him.

"Nobody you know," he answers, real short-like.

"And I'm supposed to be comforted by that?"

"Who I came home to?"

"Me."

"Where do I lay my head?"

"When you don't feel like driving home to that big empty house in the country? Right here. With me."

"Aiight then. Quit tripping on me."

"I ain't tripping."

"Gimme my sugar then."

He spins me around to face him, drags his fingers through my hair, messing up my fresh curls. He pauses to smell the strands. "You ever gonna let it grow out? Get it to hang right here," he pokes my collarbone, "…past your shoulders?"

"For what? It looks aiight now," I say, but I can tell he don't like that answer.

"What kinda hair oil you use?" he asks, frowning, as if he doesn't completely approve of my present choice.

"I don't know... Some of everything. Since when you cared?"

"Who says I do?"

"Do you?"

He takes a long time to answer. Then I realize he ain't planning to answer at all.

His gaze hovers around the room now, falls on the sink filled with freshly washed dishes, goes to the carefully wiped counters. He picks up the jars of vitamins and iron, holds them up toward the light.

"What's this?"

"Nuthin, Linc."

"Bed not be," he says and sets them back like he's not convinced. Then he's shrugging that jacket back on, nodding toward the pistol. "See you at the shop, and this time, don't forget your heat."

Trev

We've just left the morgue and the air is frigid, clouds crusted white, heavy with snow. When I asked Gabriella if she was sure about walking, suggested that we get in the jeep, fire up the heat and take a nice long drive through the country instead, she shook her head, her eyes full of deep inside reflection.

"I'd rather walk," she murmured solemnly, and I'm sure it was because she was still struggling to get the mangled image of Joker Red off her mind.

The sidewalk near Keney Park, lined with rows of skeletal red maples and thick-trunked white birch, was slippery with frost, so we crossed over the wide boulevard known as Delta Row and walked toward the Saks Outlet Mall and the crowds of Saturday folk who are on their way to the Civic Center Plaza for that first cup of coffee, bagels, and the daily newspaper.

Lines from coffee shops extended out the door, and the sidewalks were filled with closed-faced people who rushed past without smiling or acknowledging anyone. But that's nothing new, just typical Yankee charm in full effect. Bunny paused at the display window of Salvin's Shoes to admire rows of leather boots in every color imaginable, and I took that opportunity to reach for her gloved hand and squeezed it hard.

"You okay?" I asked, my breath fogged white. She shrugged, tightened the woolen scarf around her neck. "It's just odd to me…"

"What's odd?"

"How people can leave this earth so violently." She opened her purse, removed a Kleenex and pressed it against her nose. "It makes you wonder what an individual has done to deserve such mistreatment." She looked at me for an answer, waited for some profoundness.

I shook my head. "The question is, Bunny, what kind of individual would inflict such pain on another? Somebody's got to pay for that," I insisted and she looked away, raised her eyes toward the heavy white sky.

"C'mon," I said, pulling her along, and she took a few steps before stopping again to pause in front of Kensington's Jewelers, can't seem to tear her eyes away from the rows of gleaming solitaire engagement rings displayed in a case that's decorated with faux snowflakes. The prices of the diamonds, arranged in the order of value, ranged from $3,000 to $15,000.

"Wow, Trev. Look at *that* one," she gushed, pointing at a emerald-cut solitaire with a wide platinum band. She stepped close enough to press her hand against the icy plateglass.

I looked at the price and couldn't believe my eyes. "Eight thousand dollars for *one* ring? That's a down payment on a house! There's not that much love in the world." The words slipped out and she looked up as if I'd cursed my own momma. It was an awkward moment but she caught herself, tore her eyes away and walked on ahead. "Bunny, wait," I said, stepping fast to catch up with her. "I'm sorry. Let's go inside to look at it. See what else they have."

"For what?" She was looking directly at me, but I could tell she wasn't seeing me at all.

"Let's look to see if there's anything else you like."

Her eyes clouded then and she blinked hard, insulted.

"Bunny, did I say something wrong?"

"How much am I worth, Trev? Have you come up with a figure yet?"

"I'm sorry, Gabriella. I didn't mean it like that." I touched her chin, turned her face toward me. "Let's just look, alright?"

She pulled away frowning, talked to her feet. "What for, Trev?"

"Bunny..."

"How long are you gonna play games with my heart, Trev?"

I was speechless then, and she walked on, her face turned away from me. As if on cue, a wail of sirens cut into the awkwardness between us, and I saw the first cruiser making a U-turn in the middle of Governor Street and tearing back toward the north side, toward the wards. Simultaneously my beeper went off and she stopped walking to look back at me, her eyes unreadable now. We both knew the drill. She shrugged as I checked the number, made the obligatory call.

Down at precinct, Capt, sounding stressed, answered the call on the first ring. His voice was adamant. A massacre was going down in Deuce and they were calling every available detective. "Yes, Capt. I'm on my way, Sir."

I hung up but she still refused to look at me. "Bunny. Look, I have to..."

"I know. You'll call me later, right?"

"You know I have to do this."

"I know. Duty's calling."

"It's almost Halloween. You know how hell cuts up around this time."

"I know. Go. Be careful," she told me.

CHAPTER NINE

It's the quickest way in the wards to offer a challenge, to throw down the gauntlet, to declare war, so they go for it. Because as Linc had put it to his crew as they stood in the basement of Chinere's salon intricately planning and loading their weapons, stocking bullets, checking chambers, "I ain't about to start tiptoeing in my own house."

Now, the air that surrounds the Second Ward basketball courts is heavy with the threat of snow as the Escalade rolls over shards of broken glass and pulls up near a row of rickety benches that edge the perimeter of the courts. Large "D"s, for "Deuce," are spray-painted everywhere, along the ground and on the overflowing garbage cans kicked over on their sides, on the ancient metal poles that support the sagging basketball nets that have suffered through far too many "hang-time" sessions.

Under the smooth film of jagged ice, the blacktop is grimy, but that hasn't slowed the parade of kids that are swarming under both baskets now, eyes and arms raised toward the spiral of broken chain nets as they await the arrival of falling balls.

It's the usual Saturday morning social hour in The Deuce, so it seems that everybody and their mommas are out here playing ball: sweethearts and crackheads, two-bit hustlers working three-card-Monty, and boosters with their canvas sacks of department store designer wear.

It's the perfect place, the perfect time, for a show-down, Linc knows. Word will spread faster this way. And according to The Street's timing schedules, he figures it'll take all of thirty minutes before word gets back to

Spain that he and his crew are out here, on *his* turf. Another forty minutes will pass before Spain'll actually come up with a plan of attack and make his appearance.

With only forty minutes to plan, Spain's strategy will be weak and confused, watered down by the fact that his men, after their typical Friday night drug binging and skirt chasing, will have a hard time pulling themselves out of bed this early on a Saturday morning.

There's no doubt though that Spain *will* come. He's never been one to lose face at the onset of a challenge, and after all the years of running Deuce, Spain, at fifty-two years old, and with twelve street murders under his belt, isn't about to lose credibility to a pretty-boy from the Third Ward. This morning's festivities are slated to be the grandest showdown the wards have seen in years, and Linc has no problem assuming the starring role. They sit in the Escalade and watch the courts while the clock on the dashboard ticks down steadily. In the front driver's seat Ghost slumps low, looks over and gives Linc a knowing look.

"Soon," Linc promises, reaching for a toothpick. "Soon."

On the court nearest to the street, all except one of the ten-year-old boys playing twenty-one are dressed like snowmen. They're wearing hooded parkas and bomber coats, insulated jumpsuits and knit caps. The tenth boy is pitifully scrawny. He hunches against the sharp wind in a thin nylon jacket, the ratty sweater underneath it buttoned to the throat in an inadequate attempt to block the razor cold that slices through to his bones. "Creeper," they're calling him, as he claps his bare hands to stir heat, runs up and down the court in run-over Jordans to wait for the ball to fall in his direction.

"Jakari? Hector? Milani?" he pleads, arms held open, but the other boys are promptly ignoring him, have made a game of it. "Right here. Pass it. Pass it!" Creeper's waving frantically, shouting against the wind, but the other boys don't even look at him. His clothes are an instant cause for dismissal.

Under the leather bomber jacket, Linc's football jersey has been exchanged for a black Sean John sweatshirt with green piping, and over that, a heavy wool Pendleton. He's exchanged the Armani trousers and leather slip-ons for black FUBU jeans, black Air Jordans made for long distance running, and on his head, a black knit cap is pulled low across his brows. Ghost yawns and cuts the engine. The two men tap their holsters once more under their jackets and Linc, surveying the scene carefully, steps out first, a basketball wedged under his arm. He swaggers toward the second net, little boys scattering to let him through, and tosses a few perfect shots backward from a side angle. Three times the ball slips perfectly through the net, and Linc holds up Trece's three-fingered salute, stands mid-court to strike an exaggerated pose. The Tupac tune plays in his head.

"All Eyez On Me, Y'all," he sings loud enough for the love-struck teenagers macking to girls near the jungle-gyms to hear. His hand moves under his jacket, emerges with his .357, and he aims it hard at the sky, shoots it three times into the air. Trece was officially in effect. The bellowing sound splits the air like a cannon.

Linc loves theatrics. Crazy fool always needs to announce himself with a bang, Ghost, hanging out of the ride, with the door ajar, can't help thinking. He smirks at the scattering crowd, at his own quart bottle of Jamaican Rum he's holding sheathed in a brown bag. Raising the bottle courageously, he takes a long deep swig and grimaces. A last drink, he thinks, and belches deeply. No need to fool himself. The gauntlet has just dropped and they both know the odds. There are never any guarantees or absolutes. Both he and Linc could be dead by noon today and someone else would be driving the Escalade and rummaging through their pockets looking for loot. By nightfall, some other lover would be creeping into the bedrooms of their night-women, trying on their left-behind clothes, looking for all that spare cash Linc keeps stashed under the floorboards of his project apartments. What *is* certain is that Spain is as crazy as a roach on his good days and notoriously murderous on his bad, especially on his own turf. It all adds up to a recipe for a massacre.

Ghost swigs again, knowing the sudden boomeranging silence is all the warning they're likely to get. Looking around carefully, he pauses to savor the backdrop of battered tenements, the boarded windows and rickety fire escapes, the ancient brick triplexes marked with graffiti like war markings that spell out where they are and who it belongs to. The name "Spain" is written in large crooked letters everywhere. Now, Linc turns slowly in a circle, looking around, marking all the entrances in and out of the courts. A hush settles over the courts as Linc looks at his watch, at the one ragged boy with the distinctly familiar face, and the memories float to the surface; he and Runt again, standing on the courts in the brutal cold with newspaper stuffed into their All Stars while they wait for somebody to acknowledge them for once and shoot them the ball. So many cold days back then. So much hunger.

"Guess it's time I lived up to my name." It's Ghost, coming across the black ice now, scowling at the cold, at what he feels in the air. "This ain't nothing but a death wish, hanging out with ya non-human, Eskimo self." The rum has upset his coordination, and Ghost swears, fights, and fumbles with the zipper on his coat.

Linc dribbles through his legs, palms the ball with one hand while surveying the distance to the basket. "Quit crying. It ain't that bad."

"You a lie. Cold as a freezer out here. I'ma take this jumper and get stuck, freeze mid-air like an icicle." Ghost shivers as Linc throws him the ball. He manages, barely, to catch it, makes a weak jumper that misses the rim entirely. The rum dulls his reflexes, makes him cumbersome, off-balanced.

He groans as Linc shakes his head. "You pitiful," he observes, snatching the ball back and dribbling it hard against the black ice, leaping, twirling up against the backboard to sink the ball in backwards with a hard, over-handed thrust. He comes down on one foot like a ballerina, laughing, impressed by his own skills. "Now *that* was pretty, Boy. Linc, man, you still got it, Baby. You still a badddd boy."

The twelve Deuce men who call themselves The Twilight League, an unofficial basketball team of forty-something brothas, ex-junkies and convicts mostly, who meet on Saturday mornings in an effort to ward off old temptations and stay in shape, quit their huddle near the benches and draw closer, sensing blood in the air. They call out to the younger boys and command them to go home to their mommas, to "get out the devil's way." Curiosity though is greater than fear, and their warnings are promptly ignored. The little homies are too mesmerized by the height of Linc's last leap. Ghost dribbles the ball ward-style and sinks in three consecutive shots. He attempts a fourth dunk and misses the lay-up clumsily. Linc kisses his teeth. "Look at you. You getting soft, White Boy. Playing just like an old crackhead."

Ghost coughs into his fist and holds up his hands for the ball. "Flattery will get you nowhere."

Snow's likely to fall momentarily, but they decide on going full court anyway. Spinning, fronting, alley-ooping and jostling flesh against gravity. "Oohs" and "aahs" rise from the crowded sidelines. Around the perimeter of the courts, the neighborhood's best ballers gather like buzzards to watch the floor show. It's not every day that two court legends show up on their courts at the same time, and now they know that the hype Trece has put out regarding Duvall's and Ghost's basketball prowess, is well-earned, their skills above everything they'd heard or imagined. Even in jest, the two play like acrobats, their moves poetically expressive, their feet barely touching the ground. But the biggest question still hovers like a familiar over everything. "*Where is Spain?*"

"Linc. Check out five-o'clock." Ghost is grinning, pointing toward the fence at the newly arrived cluster of teenagers watching from the other side. They all wear new Jordans, skullcaps over their braids and blue team jackets. They're players for the Heartford High Vikings. NBA wannabes with bulging calf muscles, hungry eyes, and testosterone breath. Most of them are on Spain's payroll but work for Linc as double agents. They keep Linc current with Deuce's comings and goings, so there isn't too much that Spain does or plans to do that he doesn't know about. Linc fights back a grin. "Yeah. Here we go…"

As if on cue, a late-model white Lex with shiny whitewalls rolls over the shimmering ice. Dante, Cheese, Scooter, and Bo Peete, fall out of it with a cacophony of noise. Linc looks at his watch. They're right on time, a few minutes early even.

"Heads up." Ghost tosses the ball to Linc who catches it but tosses it right back to him.

"Hold up," he says and walks over to where the raggedy boy, Creeper, is buried three-deep in the sideline crowd. Linc takes off his jacket and drapes the heavy leather over the boy's gaunt shoulders. "You Tariq's son, ain't chu?"

Creeper shrugs. "Some say I am; some say I ain't."

"What cha momma say?"

"She say I am."

"And your daddy?"

"He dead. He don't say nothing now."

"But what you say?"

The boy looks down at his tattered sneakers, and Linc remembers that long, hot summer when "Riq," as they once called him, couldn't get enough of the boy's mother. Nicola, her name was. Riq was twenty-two and she was barely sixteen. Jail bait-beautiful, she was then. Iron-colored with dark, wavy hair, she could fill out a pair of Levi's like nobody in their building, and Linc had told Tariq it was too bad he hadn't seen her first. They'd had a son by then that Riq had never claimed, although the boy looked exactly like him. The child was barely four years old when Riq was gunned down in the street over some beef he'd had with another homie from Deuce. It had been one of those senseless, spontaneous murders, and Nicola had never gotten over it, had been drugging herself to death ever since. Linc sighs as the boy stares him down, chin raised, eyes shiny with rage. "You'se a hard, fatherless, lil' nigga, huhn? Here." He pushes five c-spots down deep into the boy's hand. "You Tariq's boy. Don't ever let *nobody* tell you otherwise."

Creeper nods. "What's this for?" He's dumbstruck, staring at the money.

"For you to go down to Muffin's on the Avenue and get yourself a coat and some boots. A hat and gloves too. When you finish, buy yourself something to eat. Save a lil' for a rainy day. And when you done, *don't* come back here. Stay away from the courts until tomorrow at least. And don't give your momma *nuthin*, 'cause we know what she gonna do with it."

It was public knowledge that Nicola is a fiend. Linc watches the boy turn the bills over in his chafed hands.

"You heard what I said?"

"Yeah."

"You straight?"

"I'm straight," says Creeper, his voice, his eyes, his smile so much like Tariq's it's eerie.

"Aiight then. Get gone. And if you come back here today, I'ma shoot you myself."

Creeper nods, starts to walk away, then pauses, looking back. "But my momma, she..."

"You tell Nicky, *Linc* says, if she even tries to sell your new stuff or take your money, I'ma come over there personally and put my foot in her..."

"Linc." A warning's in the tone that makes him look up, see Dante waiting, both hands in his pockets as the Vikings are unsnapping their team jackets, filling the blacktop. "Showtime," he says, his face grim.

"Yeah." Linc swallows hard, watches as Creeper ducks through a break in the fence and zigzags across the wide trash-strewn field that leads away from the tenements to the Avenue. "I'm coming."

Dante massages the knuckles of his cold cold hands, and Linc thinks he knows. He feels it too. Spain's closer than they know, plans on making his appearance when they least expect him. All along the fences the crowd is an uproar; barking like hounds, cheering what seems to them the onset of a celebrity match.

Linc walks apart from his men just in case, his eyes scanning the cheering spectators, seeing the sly way Ghost pauses mid-court with the ball to slide his thumb along the side of his nose. Dante keeps his hands in his pockets. Cheese stoops near the fence, pretending to lace his sneakers.

"Y'all ol' niggas fulla antifreeze. Bet most of y'all can't even go full court!" Nickel, a heavy-set boy wearing wire-framed glasses and premature gray dreads, calls from the sidelines, his laughter loud and outrageous.

It's a diversion, Linc knows. In moments, nobody will be laughing.

SMOKED

Lincoln

Ghost, Dante, Cheese, Bo Peete, Scooter, all look up from their stances nearby where they're leaning against the Escalade or standing against the icy blacktop, tossing the ball back and forth, toking joints, inhaling nicotine from Newport smoke so coolly their white breaths seem almost transparent, figments of smoke. These playas always make up the inner sanctum. Proven men who've looked the Grim Reaper in the face so many times they ain't afraid of him anymore. Still, the waiting is never easy and without looking at any of them, I already know what they thinking. They wondering if they'll ever get to see their crumb-snatchers again, or their mommas, or the fools back in Trece who owe them money. They're never too concerned about leaving their women. Females, for men like these, are like dirty clothes, expensively bought at first but then, easily discarded. They came and went like transit buses, late and loud and carrying all kinda drama.

Only Bo Peete looks unsettled, rubbing his forehead, rocking back and forth on his heels like he's trying hard not to tip over. I'll bet he's worried about that old dirty gun I've been begging him to get rid of, or get serviced at least. It's a sentimental attachment, he claims, an old Colt that belonged to his brother who is up at Rykers doing double life for two homicides, but the thing is filthy and archaic, its springs loose and clotted with dirt, the trigger capable of misfiring.

In our line of work faulty equipment can get you killed. We've all seen it too many times to count. "That ain't no luck charm," I'd told Peete, watching him kiss it, tuck it away next to his heart. "That's a death wish."

But Peete's as arrogant as an alley cat, and he'd rather die than admit he's making a mistake. He'd grunted at me like an old lifer who doesn't care about surviving death row, and tucked that piece of junk down into his pants like he was Marshall Dillon. If he gets his head blown off 'cause he's too dumb to listen, it won't be nobody's fault but his.

"And I ain't paying for your funeral," I'd already promised him.

Fat coins of snow are hitting the ground hard as rice. Past the courts, across the field and to the left, the interstate leading to I-84 roars with Saturday morning traffic. I look at my watch again, restless as a prom date. It was time to start the revolution, the overthrow of this occupying regime, and my men all knew what to do. Each has been specifically assigned to one of Spain's soldiers to mow down upon sight. Any extra bodies Spain brings along for reinforcements will be handled by the freelance shooters I've already paid who are standing right now along the sidelines of the courts, fifteen maniacal young dudes altogether with enough fire power to take on the mafia.

Up here in this central part of Connecticut, fifteen- and sixteen-year-old killers are rarely guaranteed a bed on death row, so Trece is overrun with plenty of high school assassins who have their own guns that they're anxious to use. Kids with old hearts who'll shoot they mommas if the price is right. 'Nere once asked if it bothers me that we use children to fight our wars, but my answer to her was simple, "Why re-create the wheel?"

✝✝✝

One of Cheese's long low whistles slices the air and Ghost, like the rest of us, looks toward the opening of the driveway. Ghost blows a kiss into his cell phone and slams it shut like a trap door. The crowd near the fences, like a flock of blackbirds, suddenly dismantles, women grabbing the hands of children, older men walking fast toward the other side of the courts to get out of the range of stray bullets.

Rifle in hand, Cheese is pointing with his trigger finger toward two Isuzu jeeps tearing over the frozen grass toward the slick blacktop, tires sliding and screeching, wheels careening directly toward me and Ghost like Ray Charles drunk-driving through a tornado. Three men apiece in each jeep, and all of them are Spain's lead soldiers. Rooster, Huck, J-Dean, Big Mo. Men I've known since forever, since before we had moustaches and rap sheets, since before we discovered little girls. Downing gin and juice in the graveyard behind the 7-Eleven, rolling spliffs in the bathrooms of Pierce Elementary. Seems a shame to have to kill all of them; seems a shame what the jungle does to a man.

Car doors slamming hard, and brothas in dark hoods and ski vests spilling out like combat soldiers, rifles lifting, barrels aiming dead at me.

"Linc!" Ghost hollers, tackling me to the frozen pavement just as the air around us ignites, bullets exploding like popcorn, lead raining everywhere like it's the Fourth of July. Ghost rolls on the ground like his clothes are on fire, his AK sputtering crazily, his teeth clenched, eyes blind with murder.

Bullets whizzing so close over my head it sounds like a swarm of bees crowding my ears, but my men are meeting the challenge, one by one picking off Spain's men so fast they never see it coming. I stoop low to the ground, gun popping, red wash staining the black ice where I'm aiming, and Spain's men fall over each other like dominos.

Smoke clears, and J-Dean, close to seven feet tall, is the only one still standing, barely, his big woolly Afro looking wild now like the top of a sycamore tree, his hand pressing his gut as intestines unravel through his fingers like roped sausage. He's staggering toward me, his mag aiming crookedly while he's clicking hard. Although his face is twisted in pain, my name is in his mouth like one long sigh as I aim and shoot simultaneously. I can't help smiling now, my teeth flashing whitely in his face, because it's my fire power that makes him slap at the back of his neck, my bullets tearing into his flesh so that he topples forward, crashes to his knees and stays that way, eyes open, neck ruptured wide as an avenue, the Mag still in his hand.

It's sheer pandemonium now, children screaming and ducking, women shrieking hysterically, praying out loud as seven bloody bodies lay along the ground like crushed worms. I'm on my feet moving through the crowd when I see the lookout standing on the fire escape signaling with his wide-armed gesture, giving the word that Spain is here, somewhere in the crowd.

All around me brothas are retching, throwing up, gasping for air, and only one face in the entire mix looks like he ain't the least bit sympathetic. Spain looks like Father Time in his marshmallow shoes and maxi leather coat, the dark tortoise-shell shades hiding those yellow crocodile eyes. His head turns cautiously like a marionette's, his eyes running smack into mine, and what happens next is automatic. I smile. He holds up his arm, fires at me once, twice and misses; tries for a third shot but changes his mind when I take off after him.

An old man running in orthopedic shoes is a pitiful thing to see, but Spain is faster than most, running hard for his life. He's leaping over trash cans, knocking people down, running alongside cars parked on the grass while the rest of my crew are running to our cars, piling into the Escalade and the

Lexus to get as far away from the pandemonium as they can because Five-O is coming.

I can hear the sirens wailing in the distance, see Ghost and Dante, hanging out the Escalade, calling me to come on and "forget that nigga," waving me back like they crazy. Up ahead though Spain is running much slower, that tan maxi coat splattered with blood, his head tripping hard now, 'cause his entire crew has been wiped out in seconds, and he can't remember where he's left his car.

He's running, but I ain't finished. Running, with his big belly and bad heart in those twenty-dollar marshmallow-kicks that he probably bought from Family Dollar.

I leap over two cars and catch him near a break in the parking lot fence, but since he's five-ten and weighs close to three-hundred pounds, we both knew there's no way he's gonna squeeze through that little hole. Behind me, Ghost and Dante are screaming my name, honking car horns like geese, but everything around me is moving in slow motion, and I can't stop now. The scent of blood is in the air.

Spain's wedged in that fence like a trapped animal, begging now and making deals, offering me a partnership, the largest cut of the profits. But I lift my boot and kick him so hard in the back of his head his shades fly off, his head snapping backward. A line of blood trickles down his chin like a single tear and I don't say a word. If he were a football, he'd have still been sailing, flying airborne above the courts, over this parking lot that's gonna be filled with cops in a matter of minutes.

I kick him again, harder this time, and this time his Glock, wedged up against the fence, flies from his hand, more blood spurting from his nose.

I edge closer. Smile beautifully. "S'up, Nigga? I heard you looking for me?" I say, just before I smash my fist into his grill.

"I ain't got no beef, Son. I swear. I come down here to talk, try to work something out. It's enough for all us. Can't see why we jes don't…"

Wearied with his con, I hit him again so hard he spits teeth, gasps for breath. My knuckles are throbbing as he finally manages to extricate himself from the fence, a fly who only thinks he's free from the spider's web.

"I don't understand why you and me, why we just can't…" He's putting up his hands, pleading, doing anything to buy himself time, but there ain't nothing else to say now as I land blow after blow to his face, his jaw, his gut. I watch him fold and stagger, struggle to straighten himself up again.

He's dizzy with pain, barely coherent, but he's gonna do all he can to dissuade me, all he can to postpone the inevitable.

"I'm old enough to be your father, Son. You... you was jes a boy when I started running... We can talk... We can figure out... "

His reasoning isn't working, and this time, when I send an uppercut to his jaw, he attempts to defend himself, throws a few mindless punches to let me know that it's on now, just the way I like it. He rushes at me head first, arms swinging like some kinda sissified windmill, and we go at it old school style. No guns, no shanks, no crew to take up for us. Just fist on fist on skin, the way it used to be.

Spain's cushy life has robbed him of his street skills, and I was wailing on him good, landing flurries of punches that dropped him to his knees, close enough for me to stomp that fat face of his into the ground. I lean over him then and pulled out my mag, lean hard with my foot on his wide, floppy neck. Spain blinks, flicks his tongue like he's going into a seizure, and his pupils dilate then disappear, the whites of his eyes filling up and taking over the space beneath his lids.

"A kingdom divided against itself cannot stand," he growls, although it's not Spain's voice at all. A voice decibels lower than anything human is talking and sounds gravely, like rocks shaken in a box, like there's hundreds of voices talking inside. Hundreds of men spilling out of him at once.

Any other man witnessing something this bizarre might cut loose and run away, drop his gun in fear, change his mind, but I don't have time for theatrics. I push the gat up against Spain's temple, count silently to ten, feel my heart pumping like it wants to burst.

"I oughta blow your monkey brains out. Splatter you all over this fence. But I'ma do you one better. You gonna do it yourself, Fatboy. You gonna get up from here and jump this fence, and run down the middle of that interstate right there. You gonna do exactly like I'm telling you and you 'bed not come back alive. You hear me, Fatboy?"

Ghost and Dante screech up then and leap out of the Escalade to drag me off of Spain just as he breaks free, runs in the direction of the highway like a madman, screaming, hearing voices.

"Why you ain't just shoot that fool?" Ghost and Dante steady fussing, steady shooting after him although it's too late. Ghost is dragging me into the Escalade like a hostage and then we tearing out of Deuce, both vehicles flying like bats out of hell.

"Look at that fool," says Cheese, pointing at Spain running zigzag toward the entrance of the freeway across from the parking lot just like I'd told him to. Running toward those speeding Subarus full of suburban housewives and Saturday factory workers listening to Rush Limbaugh on talk radio.

In the Escalade again, I lean back into my seat and close my eyes, seeing it like it's already happened. The news reports will say that a delirious man was fleeing what they will call a "ward riot." They'll say he ran onto the freeway heading south where he was run over by a semi-truck hauling holiday pumpkins. They'll say he died instantly, that his identification is being withheld pending the notification of his next of kin.

Ling

In Ghost's quiet bedroom now, I laid back on the bed and folded my hands behind my head. Closing my eyes, I needed something else besides blood to think on. It came to me easier this way; her face that day in the rain, soft, like a whisper in a room full of noise, like a quiet breeze at the edge of a tree-lined river, and I can't help remembering all those curls in the precinct room, their pomade smell that was like fruit, like the hard candy inside my momma's purse.

She'd called herself a writer, but if Churchgirl ever got the inside scoop of all that went down in Deuce this morning, she'd win herself a Pulitzer fa sho. Blood and guts flying everywhere. Men crying and shaking, cuz Hollywood never showed how it really was, what happened to gangstas when the shooting was over and they were holed up in the back room of somebody's hideaway apartment, patching up wounds and throwing up, 'cause they can't stop remembering shooting somebody's head off.

If only she could walk up in here now. In Ghost's hideout crib, we call The Bat Cave, 'cuz nobody but us knows where it is. Not his women, not even his momma, since there's times when 5-0 gets on one of they nigga-hunts, and they don't care if you innocent or guilty, they gonna shoot first and ask questions later. Times like these, when they'll be handing out murder raps like government condoms, a brotha like me only emerges with a team of lawyers, the kind that wear $15,000 suits and snort blow in their spare time, the kind that know how to convince judge and jury with so much game, even the guilty start believing they're innocent.

Yeah. Wonder what she'd say if she could see us now? If she could see that the gang's all here, except for Bo Peete. Spain's second man had capped that fool so hard, it took a whole minute before his brain figured out the rest of him was dead. Like a wrung chicken running through the barnyard without his dome. Guess we all knew it was coming. Peete was slipping in a bad way. Slipping like dying on that court was part of his original plan.

Man, Peete... Why you always had to be so hardheaded?

I told them all before we left headquarters, downstairs in the salon, "Carry at least three pistols on you. Check ya chambers and make sure they all full." They all knew the rules, knew without me having to say anything, but Peete swear he Sinatra. Just had to do it his way.

Showed up with that old rusty gun like he wanted to get smoked, and he did. Peete's dead, and we don't need no preacher to tell us what we already know. Ain't gonna be no rest for that brotha's soul. Ain't no heaven for thugs like us.

Yo, Peete, Playa, we ain't never gonna forget you, Baby.

We hid the cars, got to the Bat Cave soon as we could and did our usual pouring-out ceremony, Cheese and Scooter breaking down with their sensitive selves, crying like girls. Now Ghost, Dante, and the rest of 'em in there laying low. They in the living room, stretched out in front of Ghost's big screen, smoking blunts, drinking tonic, and getting mad-high, 'cuz after tomorrow won't be no time for none of that. If the procedure plays out tomorrow like it usually does, we all gonna be too busy talking to 5-0 about where we was today and who we were with, as soon as they can round us all up, that is. Them lil' assassins we left back there on the courts know not to utter a word about nothing, 'cause having to smoke one of them would be as easy as giving a nod. We know it; they know it; and they families know it.

Right now, there's nothing more important than the moment, and I can't help being glad to still be alive. I sit up on the edge of Ghost's bed and flick on the dim bedside light. Pulling out my wallet, I take out the card she gave me that day: a white card with raised blue letters and a black feathered pen in the left corner. I'd had a few blunts and a quart of Hef, so I was buzzing a lil', but I could still make out what it says. The name of her newspaper's on there first, and then her name and work phone number and extension. Her voicemail's next, and what's this? It looks like... yeah. Her cell.

I'm laughing at myself like I've lost my mind, shaking my head like it's all one big joke. The room sways, music from the living room swelling in the background, but I still punch in the numbers, wait, and then listen to that voice that's sweeter than anything heaven's ever made.

"Hello?"

"Hello. This Angelfied?"

INEBRIATED

Gabriella

Little boys who played with big guns were dangerous. I knew it at the very moment he called, his voice laboring like a man who was breathing under water.

"This Angelfied?" he asked, and it took a moment for me to process the word, the meanings he had bundled up and tied to it like string to a kite.

"Beg your pardon?" I said and stopped in the middle of chewing my apple, of savoring the solitude of early evening Saturday quiet. Holy quiet. Peaceful quiet. A man-less night when Trev had not called once from his shift, as if he'd been too busy to consider my thoughts, my worries, or was distracted elsewhere, drawn to something, to someone, other than me. So I spent the time reading my Bible instead.

"Angelfied," he said again, and this time, I swallowed hard. The voice, hypnotic, alluring, like wind-chime music, was definitely inebriated.

"You have the wrong number," I said and started to hang up, knowing that I should, that here was trouble I didn't need right now, trouble masquerading as one of the best feature stories I'd had in years.

But the voice coughed and sniffed, fought hard to maintain its composure, and I couldn't help myself. I felt sorry, afraid for him. Wanted to jump in right then and save him from himself.

"Gabriella, right?" He cleared his throat like he's embarrassed. A silken thread was woven into the fabric of his words. The voice like liquid black, like cool water washing over a hot stone, tickled the insides of my ears.

"*Yes*, this is Gabriella."

He coughed again, and it's obvious he's battling a cold, or worse yet, crying. "Worst thing in the world is a coward," he said, and then it all comes back—his face that day in the interrogation room. The dark, luminous complexion. Those ferocious panther-eyes.

Lincoln.

The realization startled me somehow, and suddenly I needed to be in motion. I got up from the kitchen chair where I'd been sipping tea and enjoying my fruit, appreciating the solace of the warm stove, the intermittent click of the wall clock, the soft flip of pages from the book of Ecclesiastes that was challenging me to look deep inside my heart. "Vanity of vanities, all is vanity and vexation of the spirit," Solomon had written.

But Lincoln was on the phone and nothing seemed ordinary or vain anymore.

I was carrying the apple and the cordless phone into my bedroom, snapping on the TV set, conscious of my own womanish reflection standing in front of my mahogany dresser, phone to my ear, silk nightgown draped over curves only a man could appreciate. The apple had lost its flavor and I tossed it into the wastebasket beside the bed, stretched across the plush comforter trying hard not to be flattered that he had remembered my name, thought to call me on a night that had suddenly began to feel... cold.

It was the wrong time to play games. Always the wrong time to play games.

"So," I ventured anyway.

"So," he countered.

"It's the Invisible Man."

"Wish I was… Especially now."

"Why?"

"Then I could walk through walls, slip into closed rooms and locked doors, leap tall buildings with a single bound."

"What then?"

"I'd find you at least. Tucked away like some pearl, hiding in a cleft of a rock."

"It's not about me."

"It could be. I want to be the melted butter on your toast." He laughed, his voice so sexy I pulled back from it. I hung up the phone abruptly and he called right back.

"Forgive me. I'm sorry."

"I don't play that game."

He laughed like a caress. "You used to, or you wouldn't be so good at it."

"Is there something you want?"

"Can you handle that answer?"

"'Bye, Lincoln. Please don't call me anymore."

"Whoa. I thought church girls were…charitable."

"Only when it counts."

"It always counts. Have you seen the news tonight?"

"The news?" Snatching the remote off my nightstand, I flipped to a local news channel, saw the swirls of blue light, the cruisers, yellow crime-tape, bluecoats milling everywhere. Reports of a riot in the second ward. Nine men gunned down altogether. A tenth man fleeing the scene in disorientation, ran onto the freeway behind the ball courts and was hit by a tractor trailer. He died instantly. No names have been released pending notification of next of kin. The screen flashed to a white-covered stretcher parked next to an ambulance, bluecoats around the orange trucks of the state highway clean-up crew. The image winked and cut to a city park filled with kids. The youngsters that looked from behind the barriers of yellow police tape were wide-eyed and giddy with excitement. A reporter held a mic up to what looked like a crackhead who hadn't eaten in three months.

"They w-was shooting l-like the W-Wild Wild West up in here," his white lips stammered. Behind him sprinkles of freshly falling snow gave the park a winter wonderland appearance.

"Because of the fatal accident on the highway, traffic is backed up to the last three exits," the announcer reported. "The driver of the truck is not being charged…"

So that's where Trev must be, I'm thought until Lincoln brought me back.

"Babygirl. Remember this. It's all about the acquisition of power. Either a man has it or he doesn't. If he doesn't, he has no choice but to run. And if he runs? Well then."

"Well then what?"

"Well then he deserves to die," he concluded, slurring his words.

Before I could ask what he meant by that, if that included himself, since he'd originally run from me for weeks before I'd found him, it was over. He hung up as suddenly as he'd called, and I couldn't help thinking he didn't sound anything like a man who could shoot two people dead and leave them alone in a parked car.

Lincoln was flirty, of course, like most men. Daring, sensual, perhaps a little delusional even. But a murderer? I wasn't so sure. After all, Trev didn't have absolute proof. He was going on some gut instinct. He could be absolutely mistaken, grasping at straws, looking for anyone to fit the bill. What, I wondered, did a murderer sound like anyway? Crazed? Delirious? Maniacal, of course. I doubted very seriously that he sounded anything like Lincoln Duvall.

CHAPTER TEN

It was one of the ugliest scenes in ward history. So much blood it was hard to tell if the children who were in the midst when it happened would ever be able to play on those courts again. The memories might not let them. He'd grown up in the wards and he understood how lethal the memories could be, how they came back like a boomerang some five, ten, even twenty years later to haunt you..

"Man…What a total waste," Trev said aloud to no one in particular, and Avis, his staff supervisor, slapped the hood of his department-issued parka over his own head, shivering from the depth of the cold and the brutality..

All around them dozens of bluecoats chewed gum, barked at the press and held back hysterical family members who kept breaking through the yellow tape demanding to see if it were so, if it were one of their own lying there dead.

Trev stooped where he stood, lifted a corner of the Medical Examiner's tarp and shook his head, recognizing yet another face. Handsome. Brick-colored. Couldn't be any older than twenty-five. His real name was Terrance; Trev knew that much. Trev had known both the boy's parents, had helped to guard the body of the boy's father and uncle when he was a Bluecoat called to a similar scene some ten years earlier. Ironic, it seemed. You would think they'd learn but they never did. The sins of the fathers kept passing down to their sons. It was insanity. All of it. The work of a madman.

"Cooper?" Avis and Douglas Brock, the department's PR officer, watched him tentatively, were poised to break past the blue wall serving as crowd control and get out of the cold, into a warm idling sedan. Avis' face was grim, unshaven. Brock's was as white as a ghost, ashen with resignation.

"Sir?"

"You knew these guys?"

"Yes. All of 'em, Sir."

"A pity." Avis' cobalt eyes pierced him, softened, then shifted quickly to check his watch. "We're headed back downtown. Looks like everything's in order here. Notifications will be made by morning. You, okay, Guy?"

Cooper shrugged, lost for words. He stared at the ground. "I'm fine, Sir. Thanks for your concern."

"You bet."

Trev watched the two men push through the crowd, wondered how long he could keep doing it, how long any man could put up with seeing such depravity, such deplorable acts of inhumanity. Avis had been on the force some twenty-five years. Trev didn't think he'd last that long. The only safety was in becoming desensitized to the horror, but once that occurred, he'd also lose the greater part of his humanity. How could he preach without caring about what happened to people? Times like these, pastoring didn't seem like such a far-fetched proposition.

Crowds, noise. It had been just that way when his father had been stabbed. Even then it seemed that the neighborhood kids would never let him and his brothers grieve in peace. Everybody wanted to know what had happened and no one wanted to go home. Nothing it seemed, had changed. It was the same old procedure. Once the evidence was carefully bagged and ticketed and the bodies unceremoniously removed, another crew would come and bag up what was left of the refuse. By then, the other detectives would have already finished infiltrating the crowd of bystanders, gathering fragments of stories, writing down names and numbers and addresses for future contacts. Night had fallen hours ago, but he'd already done his own preliminary investigation, heard the gist of what had gone down. Yet another turf war with a scene like the one months ago, before Joker even got to town. One of the biggest First Ward dealers, Skyy Johnson, along with two of his men, had been cut down savagely outside an illegal after-hours club. There had been no witnesses then, and not many sympathies either.

A tall, thin, hateful man with a lisp and an artificial blue glass eye, hence his name, Skyy, was hated by his own men even. No one had been too disturbed by the news of his murder and his growing empire had disintegrated on its own, an implosion of inside suspicion and greed. But *these* homicides had another flavor altogether, and the facts were conclusive. There had been a transfer of power and now Deuce would be under a different kind of leadership, more ruthless than anything it had ever seen. Trev considered the evidence he'd gathered, mulled over the obvious questions he always asked himself. Where had the shootings occurred? What events had played out just before they went down? Who had been murdered? And what were the names that kept coming up over and over again?

"Sureshot" from the Third Ward had showed up with his crew, some of the older fellas who still remembered Duvall by that old nickname, had told him. According to witnesses, by the time the real shooting had actually stopped, Duvall was seen running away from the court toward Spain who was cowering "like a female" near the parking-lot fence. The two fought hard, with Duvall getting the better of him, but then it was over. Linc's crew pulled him into a car and Spain took off running in the opposite direction toward the highway. *Nobody* had seen Duvall shoot anyone, yet there were eight corpses slated for the morgue that deserved some explanation. One of those bodies was one of Duvall's lead men, Bo Peete.

It wasn't a coincidence. Duvall was at the root of all of it, Trev felt for sure. Yet bringing it all to the surface was another thing altogether, and he'd have to proceed cautiously with what he knew. Duvall was a snake who knew things about *him*. Things he'd never told anyone, things that only God, the folk involved, and of course, the devil, would know.

Walking a bit from the commotion, Trev stepped into the doorway of an abandoned tenement and whipped out his cell. She answered on the first ring.

"Bunny?"

"Yes, Trevis."

"I'm sorry."

"About what?"

"Not calling. I know you've been waiting, worrying probably."

"Well…"

"It's been a busy night. Eight bodies are down here. Thugs, all of them."

"I saw the news."

"I think *he's* behind it." He lowered his voice, looked around, watched the swarms of bluecoats and EMTs drinking steaming coffee out of foam cups. "I was wrong to introduce you to that monster. It was a bad idea."

"Are we talking about the same man? Linc Duvall?"

"Who else?" Trev sneezed and stamped his cold feet, wiped at his runny nose with the back of his hand. His eyes were smarting from the cold, his breath frosted white. "He ain't human."

"Because...?"

"Bunny, he just ain't."

"In other words, all you have is circumstantial evidence."

"Dead bodies are not exactly circumstantial."

"True."

Trev dropped his voice even lower, his words strung together, like a hiss. "He can do things with his mind. Make men do things to each other, to themselves, simply by willing it. That's not the kind of thing you can prove in a courtroom"

"So you're saying it's a spiritual thing?"

"Exactly. But who's gonna believe that?"

"I see your point."

"I gotta get back to work."

"You picking me up for church tomorrow?"

"Sunday School. Bright and early."

"I'll be here."

"And, Bunny?"

"Yes?"

"About your ring..."

"Yes?"

He cleared his throat, paused. "It'll be soon, okay? Real soon."

She hung up then. She could no longer hold her breath.

ALONE

Gabriella

It's Monday morning just after dawn, and just outside my bedroom window, the sky is the gray-blue-magenta color I imagine the inside of the whale must've been like. I knew why I was sulking about Jonah this morning. I felt just like him, like the will of God seemed so hard to understand sometimes, so impossible to obey.

I had been with Trev all day yesterday after church. We'd sat together through Sunday School and morning worship, gone to dinner afterwards with a bunch of other singles at a bustling Chinese buffet and then sat alone in a booth in a crowded ice cream shop proclaiming our undying love for each other. All that time, and not once had I tried to tell him that Lincoln had not only called Saturday night, but that he'd picked me up in the rain a couple days before, had brought me all the way home without me having to give him my address. I could never admit to Trev that I'd actually been amused, that the man had given me a nickname he'd used with a certain audacity. "Angelfied," he'd called me, like he'd known me all my life.

Not one time had I mentioned any of this to Trev, although my reasoning had seemed justifiable at the time. I was a reporter. Lincoln was my subject, and our relationship was purely professional. Confidential. It would be over after my story ran. But this morning, and late last night, lying here alone in this cold bed with the dark walls closing in on me, I'd wrestled with the complexities of my own heart and wondered if that were the only reason I didn't want Trev to know. Was it just because I wanted the story anyway, even though Trev was against it, or was it because deep down, in the marrow of my bones, I genuinely liked how Lincoln made me *feel*? Was it because I actually liked his voice and, crazy as it sounded, liked what he reminded me of about my past? That in itself couldn't be so bad, could it? I mean, I *was* human, wasn't I?

The alarm clock blared and I leaned over to slap it quiet, gave thanks for the privilege of yet another day. Yet the loneliness didn't leave me. Trev had come right out and said it yesterday, that he wanted us to be married within the next two years, but why didn't I believe it? Did I really and truly trust him at this point? Did I believe he really loved me?

†††

The features department consisted of rows of desks equipped with computers and phones. On a table in the middle of the room, the largest newspapers from all over the country were stacked to be reviewed and examined, mulled over between coffee breaks. Across the corridor, just a few feet from my desk were the offices of our head editors, and beyond them, large, plush rooms filled with thick burgundy carpet and rows of file cabinets, small televisions tuned in to CNN at all times, a single desk covered by stacks of old newspapers.

"Geesh. Some weekend over in the wards, wasn't it?" Joshua Mackenzie, our sports editorial writer, was standing near the department's fax machine in shirtsleeves. He winked, thrusted his thumb, and following his aim, I saw the slew of higher-ranking reporters clamoring outside the middle office of Trish Weitzman. Sharks had smelled the blood. A huge story was in the works, and even though I'd been covering the wards off and on for the past five years, this opportunity for front-page glory would be given to some higher-ranking vigilante writer from some other department, no doubt.

"Seven murders, and the eighth smacks of conspiracy," Josh said. "Bloodlust. Gang feuding. Who knows what the deal is behind this one. One thing's for sure, it'll take more than a team of blood hounds to sniff it out. I guarantee it."

"Maybe, maybe not," I said, dropping into my chair and picking up the complimentary, in-house Sunday and Monday editions of *The Chronicle* that all features' writers find on their desks every morning. The headline, "Empires Fall As Drug Lords Die Like Dogs" glared at me.

"Die like dogs? This Is Tabloid-ism. It's juvenile and totally insulting. Who came up with this title? Don't they understand that these men were *people* first? Someone's son or brother or father who died?" Josh smirked at me from his own desk, sipped steaming tea from his favorite mug. "Like I always tell you, Gabby, it doesn't pay to crusade about the small stuff. In this business, it's about selling copy. What else is there?"

Small stuff? I shake my head, open the paper and am saddened by the mugshot photos of the slain men. Most, except for two, were in their late twenties and all had those same menacing sneers, eyes that held an open defiance. According to the article, all the men had prior run-ins with the law and had done time for things that involved narcotics, trafficking, distribution, possession of controlled substances. I fought back tears. I'd seen all these faces before in the small bodegas and barbecue pits, the miniature restaurants and record shops around Deuce. It was eerie, especially since Lincoln had chosen that night, of all nights, to call *me* out of the blue.

"Geesh, Gabby," Josh broke in between sips. "Those people never get tired of going to funerals, do they? Buncha animals, I tell you. The mayor'd do well to bundle up the whole lot of 'em and toss 'em in the brink. Throw away the key."

"And then what?"

"Well, then of course…"

"Hush, Mackenzie. There are stories behind these mugshots. Lives, okay?"

"I wouldn't doubt it."

"You already did."

CHAPTER ELEVEN

Chinere

The things that man gets himself into sometimes ain't fit for public disclosure. Me? I finally learned not to ask questions for answers I don't wanna hear. Like that Saturday he and Ghost and 'nem came running into the back door of the shop just as Imani and me were trying to close early.

Queen George, Neva and Bev-Lou, my other three stylists, were already gone, fearing the snowstorm the weatherman was predicting all day. So it was only me and Imani left, straightening up, getting the money ready for the night's deposit. Imani was ready to go by then, had her purse on her arm and was reaching for her coat when we heard all this commotion in the driveway around back. Tires were screeching, doors were flying open, and we could hear feet running downstairs to that club house of Lincoln's he calls his "Headquarters."

"What in the world?" I'd said, turning to look at myself in the full-length mirror, since my pants were getting harder and harder to zip up these days.

"Gurl, what they doing down there *now*?" Imani asked me, 'cuz we can hear somebody down there throwing up. Hear grown men crying like females. I keep a washer down there in a little room in the back where I do my towels and smocks, and before long we heard the vibrations as it knocked against the wall. Somebody was down there washing clothes, a heavy load at that, and none of it seemed right to us at all.

"*Lord have mercy.*".…," Imani started praying. She went to the back door, opened it quietly and started waving for me to come quick..

"I don't wanna know," I told her, while I was shaking, but Imani just wouldn't give up.

"You *gotta* see this!"

"See what?"

"Blood, Gurl."

"*Blood*?"

"It's *everywhere.*"

She was right. Blood was everywhere. Blood so dark it was black in places, dotting the back steps, smeared along the banister. I fell into a chair then, rocked keep myself steady, and Imani came and placed a hand on my shoulder. "You gonna be alright, 'Nere?"

"I don't know."

"Gurl, he ain't worth it."

"I know."

"You want me to stay?"

"I got this."

"You sure?"

"Go home, Imani. While you can."

I could hear it in her voice, a scream, like she was on the verge of hysteria, and for a moment, both of us are afraid to say or do anything. We stayed like that until I lost track of time, and then it was only the thick stench of bleach, from Linc and'nem scouring the hallway with it, that that brought me back to myself.

"Gurl, I'm glad Buster took my cousin and the baby out of town, up to Springfield to do some shopping this morning, 'cause there ain't no telling what them fools have done," Imani was saying as she hurried out the front door.

Imani was right and I knew it. That afternoon was all I've been able to think about since it happened four days ago. I was still thinking about it four days later when the door to my shop chimed and that fine-looking detective, the one that Linc hated worse than church, walked into the shop like he owned it. He held up a piece of paper.

"Can I help you, Officer?" Imani stopped rummaging her fingers through her customer's braids to look him up and down, her hands dripping conditioner. It was obvious she liked what she saw a tall, walnut-colored brotha who was cleanshaven, with a deep cleft in his chin and a military haircut. The kinda man that probably ate Wheaties for breakfast and did a hundred push-ups every morning.

Imani had two customers at the sink, and I was ust doing my first press and curl when the cop, trailed by four bluecoats, walked up to the sink and said, "I'm looking for Chinere Adams."

"That's me," I said, and he turned toward me suspiciously, looked around the shop carefully, like he expected Linc to jump out from nowhere and start firing on him. Our eyes met and he gave me that look, *I remember you, and I know what you know, so let's not play games*, look.

"I have a warrant to search this place," Mr. Big Stuff said.

"What for, Officer?"

"Weapons. Narcotics. I've got enough warrants to arrest folk for everything from conspiracy to commit murder to operating a drug factory..."

I folded my arms over my belly, cradled myself to keep from screaming, but he went on and on, reading from his papers, and when he held them up, I see it's not two or three, but several pages stapled together. They fluttered when he held them up, and the bluecoats standing around him, who all had their hands on their guns, looked spooked themselves. That's when I looked across the room and saw that Imani was trembling something terrible, her bottom lip quivering, because she was there that afternoon, because she saw all that blood that Linc never did took the time to explain.

"Look here, Mr. Officer..."

"Cooper. Detective Trevis Cooper."

"Whoever. Look. I don't have nuthin' to hide, so search what you want," I tell him, "but if you think y'all about to interfere with my business and harass our customers, then..."

"No, Ma'am," Mr. Big Stuff said, real polite-like,. He folded his hands behind his back like some kind of ax-murderer trying to convince me to come into the woods alone with him. He cocked his head like he was reading me for a weakness. "It's not our policy to interrupt legitimate businesses, so as long as you can prove that's all that's going on here, then you won't have any problem from us."

"Yeah. I heard that before."

"If you cooperate, things will go easier, Miss Adams."

"Cooperate?"

"If you could help us to…"

"*Help* you?"

"An innocent man from out of town was murdered a couple weeks ago. They found him and his friend, shot-up in his car. He didn't deserve to die. He came up from Atlanta to see his kid. They called him Joker Red in the wards, back in the day. He used to…"

"I don't know nuthin' about that."

"Are you sure?"

"Did I stutter?"

"Well, I'm sure you heard about the massacre that happened in Deuce last week?"

"The *what*?"

"Eight men were killed. One had been chased onto the freeway."

"He ran on his own, was the way I heard it. Nobody chased him anywhere."

"So you have heard about it?" Officer Friendly's eyes darted from corner to corner, space to space. His eyes made me nervous, made me take a deep breath to calm myself.

"I don't know nuthin'," I told him. "You can search if you want to."

I was glad then. Glad I'd left Linc's pistol in my car. It was registered to me anyway, certified and legal like Linc had insisted, but there was no telling what else he had stashed away in this place.

Queen George and Lou-Bev cut eyes at each other over their customers' heads, and Neva hummed awfully loud while she did a manicure.

"I'll be calling my lawyer," I said and Officer Friendly nodded.

"I would too if I were you," he told me.

I rolled my eyes at him. "I got rights. I'm a tax-paying citizen," I said, but Mr. Big didn't answer. He was too busy organizing those scary-looking bluecoats he brought in here. Had two checking this floor while he and two more drew guns and went downstairs to Linc's headquarters. Queen George snapped off the radio. Everybody in the shop was as nervous and quiet as church mice, and I knew we were all liable to lose some good customers over this when word got around. The one good thing was that Linc and 'nem wasn't here at the moment. They've been scarce since it all went down, and nary one of them attended Bo Peete's private funeral.

Linc would have a fit if he knew I was even trying to pray, but I couldn't help it. I closed my mouth and thought the words deep down in my heart.

Thank You, Lawd, that Linc ain't here…Thank you, Lawd, that Linc ain't here.

TEAMS AND TARGETS

Linc

It's a quarter to nine on a weekday morning and me and Ghost have a head fulla "chronic" and a ride fulla lil' homies who are supposed to be in school. We out here taking care of business instead, bumping to the vibes of Tupac while I drive and Ghost rides shot-gun, heading over to the shooting range at the far end of Trece near the riverbank, in a covert place not even the police can find.

Running a dynasty means nothing if power's not passed down to the next generation, so we training four more lil' homies today—TicToc, Ray-Ray, Lil G, and the latest protégé to catch my eye, Creeper. All four of these lil' brothas got mad leadership potential, but getting 'em prepared to be soldiers is gonna take some heavy-duty work, which is why we start out testing 'em first. We gave 'em all beepers the night before. Gave 'em a $50 bill, and told 'em what time we'd be picking 'em up and where we want them to be when we get there.

Only one of 'em, Creeper, who's in the fourth grade, *again*, seems worried about missing school. But that's to be expected, what with him being the youngest and all. Still, it ain't like his momma cares either way, and it ain't like she's got a telephone for the school to call her and report his absence. We all know what cemetery his daddy lives in, but that's the case with most of the lil' fellas down in the wards. They been orphans since the day they were born, and the way I see it, teaching these lil' cats how to survive among the fittest is a community service that deserves duplication.

Aside from Creeper, the rest of these lil' homies are all truants and delinquents, kids who'll slap their teachers, curse their mommas, and ain't afraid to fire on Five-O if we tell 'em to. In short, these kids aren't afraid to die for the cause. Any cause. A pair of new Jordans. A peanut butter sandwich smuggled out of the school cafeteria. But we have to put 'em through "the process" just the same. Gotta see how much heart they have. See how smart, how hungry, how quiet and dependable they gonna be when it counts.

The initial examination can't be simpler; We give 'em all different times, make 'em all wait for us at different check points while we checking out how punctual they gonna be, watching and reading 'em all the while. We checking out how they do things. Will they show up early or late at the checkpoint or slide in just in the nick of time? Do they have any of their other lil' homies hanging around talking about they wanna be down too, or do they know how to keep their mouths shut about secret things? Do they spend all the money we gave 'em in one night, or is that $50 still crisp in their hands? Are they where we told 'em to meet us or do they get the location all mixed up?

So far, only one's batting a thousand, and you can guess who that is. Yeah. My man, Creeper. Lil' man's standing there exactly where I told him to be, wearing that new coat and hat and "Timbs" that I bought him, with the beeper and the $50 still in his pocket. He's early too. Ten minutes at least, and alone. Just like I knew he'd be. The rest of 'em are another story altogether, and it's sixteen-year-old TicToc who's ten minutes late and fulla excuses. Left his beeper at his girl's house last night, he says, although Ghost thinks he lost it in a crap game.

Thirteen-year-old Lil G's got just $5 left to his name, eyes fulla "whett," while he's trying to work his way up to ask us for $5 more. Ray-Ray's got two of his homies flanking him when we pull up, talking about they "wanna sign up too," like we some kinda boy-scout recruiters, and then he's half a block away from where we told him to be. It's cool though, 'cause by the time we get finished grooming 'em, they gonna be sharper than the Secret Service and just as deadly. Trained sharpshooters, each one. Like me and Ghost was when we first started out. Like Ghost used to be before he started taking his own poison.

They have a fit when they see we going to the neighborhood dump, and all of 'em 'cept for Creeper, start up complaining like lil' girls.

"Y'all lil' niggas better kill all that noise 'fore I shoot one of you... Squawking in my ear like a buncha ghetto geese," Ghost growls, snapping his eyes closed, pulling his hood up over his head and sinking down in his seat. Ghost ain't never been a morning person, and since he been dipping into the product, his energy and productivity levels are slipping hard.

The homies suddenly fall silent though, 'cuz it looks like a wasteland of garbage back here, like some kinda illegal dumping ground by the river, which it is. Hills of plastic trash bags. Old refrigerators with the doors torn off. Bicycle parts everywhere, like disconnected skeletons, and the husks of burned-out cars with the windshields shot out. Rats back here are big as yard dogs, will chase you if you get in their way, and it smells back here too, like something's died and was left out to rot. It don't bother me at all though. I'm used to it. Know every inch of this ground like the back of my hand. The dump was the closest thing we had to a playground growing up, and me and Runt and all the other lil' cats made more memories down here than any of us can even remember now.

I'm driving so fast over this rugged terrain that these lil' homies in the backseat are thrown every which way. Gulls and pigeons are scattering like gnats in front of my tires, and the homies are loving the secrecy of it, but holding their hands over their noses to block out the smell.

"Yo, Cuz, like why we gotta come back here, Mr. D? It smells *bad*, yo. You don't smell that?" It's Lil' G, whose always fulla questions. Lil G who looks like a broke Ray-Jay, Brandi's kid brotha, and can pick any lock man's ever made.

We start breaking it all down to all of 'em, then as I pull up toward the range, we tell 'em one by one how they did on the pop test we just gave 'em. They go to pouting and denying it all at first, what with their pride being hurt, but then, like kids, they snap out of it suddenly, teasing each other, promising to do better, looking at Lil Creeper with that quiet gleam in their eyes.

Ray-Ray, with his giant, raggedy afro and weak stomach, is looking like he wants to retch in the backseat, and that's when I start in schooling 'em about how they gotta get used to denying what they feel and smell. A good hustler ain't got no feelings. Stink, blood, guts, death, *nothing* should bother them, I say.

"'Cuz the absence of the self is *total* liberation," Ghost cuts in.

"Yeah, Baby, like…that's Zen or something, huhn?" TicToc speaks up, tapping Ghost. "I be seeing that junk on TV. Like that king fu mess or something."

The other lil' homies think that's mad funny, but I'm glad we finally pulling up to my favorite place in the whole world. The place me and Runt used to run off to when things got mad crazy at home. I can see it from here even now just as plain as day: the two of us running hard and fast, tripping over bed springs and old tires jutting up from the ground. It was the only place in Trece that was far enough away not to hear her crying, not to hear her telling *him* she'd had enough. Only thing was, back then, evil was here too. Loaded guns, rusty shanks, bottles of half-used prescription pills and the worst evil of all: that old Ouija board in a box stuffed between rotten crates.

"Aw, junk, Linc. Look at this. A game and it's practically new. You wanna play?" Runt's crazy self would try anything. Get me to try it too.

He was tearing off the box-cover before I could stop him.

"Nawl, cuz…," I'm saying, shaking my head. "That junk look funny, Man. That's why you always getting in trouble in Sunday School. You ain't listen? You ain't hear teacher say that game be bad?"

Runt sticks out his bottom lip, looks back toward the wards where the tenements look like Greek ruins 'bout to fall down. "How teacher know? She don't live in no Third Ward. He up there beating upMomma now. That ain't bad?"

"Boy, you crazy."

"Watch me. Come over here, Linc."

"Watch you do what?"

"Call up something, somebody, to help Momma…"

"She got God. He gonna help her."

"When? Where that nigga at now?"

"Runt? Boy, you crazy!"

"Watch when I move this over this board. See it move? Help gonna come. You feel it? Whew. I do. Come over here, Fool, and feel this. Quit being so scared."

"But teacher say...."

"You feel that? Linc? Look, Stupid...Come feel this... Linc...Linc?"

"But teacher say..."

Memories sometimes fall on me heavy as cement, but like always, I shake 'em off quick, look ahead to see the range stretched out all around me. The smell ain't all that bad now, but the land loses all those crazy lumps and lies flat for miles. Ghost yawns, sits up and wipes the slob from his mouth, and I pull into that spot that's covered by trees and overgrowth so it's hard to know that anybody's back here. Dead tree stumps everywhere here, lined up ahead in rows, and all we gotta do is take those cases of empty glass bottles we got in the Escalade's cargo space and line up the bottles on the stumps one by one. The lil' homies gonna be here all week firing, holding they ears and shaking they stinging fingers, but when we done, they'll have better aim than most grown men in the wards, and the world will be their oyster.

I park and we get out and start unloading the bottles and the boxes of weapons. The lil' homies are oohing and ahhing as Ghost, cussing 'em like sailors, starts handing them their initial weapons of choice to start practicing with. 6.8 mm Remingtons, Bulgarian AK74s, 9mms with John Browning designs, SA58 Tactical Carbines.

My cell rings, and when I see it's 'Nere, I go ahead and answer it.

"Where you been? You better stay home and get some rest 'fore you catch a cold," she says, her voice sounding funny. I know it right away. She's talking in code just in case 5-0's monitoring the airwaves again.

"Stay home 'fore you catch a cold."

"Yeah. It's all good. I'ma do that," I say, so she knows I've caught on. That phrase was just one of the many codes we had worked out. It meant the boys in blue were looking for me and I needed to stay away for a while. I would. But first I had to put these wannabe gangstas through their first initiation. Give 'em something to fire on after we were done, get them to use their skills on some place, or someone that counted.

Ghost hands me a cold quart of Heffenreffer and I poured out a little on the ground for all the dead homies, then drained it dry. It came to me then in a flash, where to go and who to use. As soon as they were done goofing off and getting their aims straight, we'd handle it. Pick our weapons and ascend on our target carefully, skillfully.

Trev

It was getting harder and harder on his body, the fight to stay awake past 6 a.m.

After years and years of being on the force's graveyard shift, there were more and more mornings like these when he questioned why he still did it. Mornings when he'd punched out and driven home with one eye open, swerving toward home through the lower south side of Heartford like a town drunk. Just this morning he'd swerved into the left lane on Cosgrove and Newton, and it had only been grace and mercy teaming up that had kept that old woman driving that new Volvo from plowing into him head-on.

Now, he wrenched his keys from the back door, pushed his way into the kitchen, ignored the sink full of dirty dishes and staggered into the living room. The couch. If he could just make it to that warm and familiar oasis. Kicking off his uniform brogans, he collapsed backward onto the old sofa, its ratty brown tweed, worn down to the frame from all those mornings he'd never made it back to his bedroom, as comforting now as the breasts of any woman. His large framed body had molded the couch into another shape altogether, like the soft ticking inside of a favorite teddy bear that has been squeezed too tightly. He groped for the small decorator pillows, shoved them behind his head and squeezed his eyes closed.

The room's heavy quietness unnerved him somehow, and he sucked his teeth hard. He never could sleep with all that nothingness pressing into his ears, and he reached for the remote control, sucked his teeth when he saw it was not down in the cushions, but lying flat atop that old floor-model Zenith that was facing him on the other side of the room.

He pulled himself up, staggered toward the set, and heard the screech of tires too late. By the time he looked up and attempted to snatch down the shade, glass was exploding all around him. The two front room windows burst simultaneously. A mirror crashed from the wall to the floor and he covered his ears, diving into that old couch as the air above him rained lead.

Outside, the spraying continued as he reached for his gun, trapped up under him now. He twisted his body until he could reach the revolver and ease it safely from his shoulder holster. He'd be ready when they decided to kick in the door. Would fire first before their eyes got the chance to make out his body lying still as a stone against the faded plaid. But there were no footsteps outside on the hallway steps, no heavy thuds kicking away the chains on the front door. Just the squeal of tires and the scream of a siren as the car spun like a rocket in a half-circle and ricocheted up the block.

CHAPTER TWELVE

"**S**ee some ID," the guard snarls, like he's done almost every Thursday for the past two years. Trevis slaps his wallet on the desk and yawns, watches Mr. Security examine the mottled police-issued photo badge as though he's never seen it before.

"Detective Cooper. Heartford Police. Hmm. Who are you here to see?"

"Miss Sinclaire, please. Gabriella. City Features Department. Extension 610."

Security frowns his distaste, dials the extension with quiet reluctance, and Trevis ignores the urge to snatch his badge back. He straightens his tie instead. Mr. Security looks up and scowls. His cobalt uniform matches his eyes. He's wearing a badge and looks like a cop, although he's never been armed. The kind of man who'd probably failed trying to get accepted into the Heartford Police Academy. Now though he settles for intimidating folks with practiced stares. Only Trevis doesn't intimidate easily. After yesterday morning, anybody else would've left town, taken a permanent leave of absence, gotten as far away from Linc Duvall as they could have. But he's still here. Still standing in clear view, in the lobby of this Heartford conglomerate, for all the world to see.

"Miss Sinclaire will be right down." The guard hangs up, looks at his watch and opens the magazine again. Outside, past the sidewalk, blustery winds carry a sweep of oak leaves in a slow circuit through the immense parking lot. Trevis opens a disk of peppermint and slips it into his mouth. A dark-haired Italian with a beard, carrying a briefcase and wearing a black trench, approaches the desk. The guard looks up and smiles, asks who he's here to see. He hands Trench-coat a corridor pass and sends him upstairs without once asking for any identification.

Trev turns away in disgust. All that marching and sign-carrying in the '60s and black folks were still getting the back-door treatment. Only now, in corporate America, the disdain was bitterly quiet.

"Hi, Bighead... You've been waiting long?" She's appeared from out of nowhere it seems, nudging him playfully from behind. She's wearing a navy pin-striped skirt suit and burgundy pumps, her hair pulled back into a neat chignon, and he fights the urge to catch her up in his arms. He bends to kiss her cheek instead.

"I just got here," he says.

"Well, I'm on deadline, so there's no time to waste."

✝✝✝

The booths at Redman's are much too scarce for the heavy lunch crowds that gather here every day, but the island cuisine was well worth the wait. Curried goat, oxtails, beef patties and cocoa bread were all city favorites, and Gabriella felt long overdue for some rice and peas.

She orders goat and a virgin Daiquiri, shares one of Trevis' oxtails.

"You seem a little quiet today," she tells him, watching as he spears a forkful of white yam and mashes it into his rice. "Is everything okay?"

He shrugs, chews. "We had a near tragedy last night with one of our blue-coats. Officer Joe Rodgers. A good man. Hasn't been too long on the force. His house was shot up. One of his kids was hit. But they're all okay. They'll pull through it looks like."

"Oh my." She sighs sympathetically, leaning forward to hear more, but he averts his eyes, seeing it all again, his own front windows blown out like something out of a disaster movie, his neck still burning from the bite of sprayed glass that he'd opted to pick out himself with tweezers rather than to sit up in some emergency room. He'd never have reported it, would never have called for back-up, but obviously somebody had, and the Boys in Blue had converged on his lawn in minutes like a miniature army. The

Brotherhood of Blue was always quick to defend their own. That's when he learned that Joe's house had been hit as well.

"I didn't hear about it, but the reports must've come through our office," she observes. .

"It gets better."

"Uh-oh."

"I just got word from Capt last night. Big Brass downtown wants to see me."

"*You?*"

Trev shrugs. "Something to do with Internal Affairs."

"Uh-oh. So that's why you're dressed a little neater than usual?"

He nods, sips his sorrel punch. His eyes soak up her face. "I'm not surprised though. A lot of strange things have been going on lately. Like the way you've been wearing your hair this week."

"*My* hair?"

"I'm not looking at anyone else, Gabriella."

"What's wrong with my hair, Trevis?"

"I thought you just had it done. Weren't you complaining that you were in the beauty parlor just a couple Thursdays ago for hours?"

"Who's counting?"

"I was wondering why your hair is tied back. Why your curls are gone already? They usually last, what? At least three weeks?"

"Is this an investigation?"

"No."

She swallows the savory meat, watches as an elderly couple across the room share a brief kiss over glasses of Spumonti.

"My hair got wet. I got caught in a storm."

"So I heard in your phone message." He looks up, his face as still as a stone. She knows that look, the face he uses for interrogating criminals.

"Just say it, Trev."

"You just had to go down there, huhn? You just had to find him."

She reaches for her water glass and sips nervously. "It's my job, Trev. I had no other way to get in contact with him. I didn't know what else to do."

"So you went looking for him. Alone. Why didn't you tell me?"

The Daiquiri was tart, had too much lime, and she licked the froth around the edges of the straw, saw the hurt playing about his eyes.

"I'm never alone, Trev. God is always with me. I have to know that if I'm going to cover these kinds of stories."

"And did you find out anything more about him? Did he share his heart?" It was meant to be a sarcastic statement, so she laughs it off, but Trevis drops his fork, pushes his plate away frowning. He rubs the back of his neck.

"I found out he likes black." She feigns a smile. "He had it on again that day. Black coat. Black boots. Even his car was black. Does he ever wear any other color?"

Trev takes his time answering, swallows hard. "Never," he says finally, like it hurt. "He has other cars, of course. They're all black. A Mercedes. A Beemer. A Jag. I think he owns a Lex as well. "

"All those cars and he's living in the *wards*?"

Trev shrugs. "Duvall owns property the way Jordan owns sneakers. He's smarter than he looks, unlike the rest of these knuckleheads that are dying for nothing. Duvall's into investing. Trading. Stocks and bonds."

"How do you know?"

"We've been watching him for some time. So you see, you really don't know this man. You only think you do. Just like a woman, going by his looks."

"I never said anything about his looks, Trevis."

Trev balls up his napkin, throws it onto his plate. "Pretty don't mean a thing. He's *extremely* violent, strong as ten men. He ain't human."

"And you know because…?"

"I bumped heads with him, remember? That night at the station? He tossed me around like I was a piece of paper."

"Just say what you mean, Trev."

"Bunny, *before* the massacre in Deuce, Duvall was already rumored to have murdered at least six people that we know about, all rival dealers, although no one has actually been able to prove any of it. And that's strictly off the record."

"Do we have to talk about this right now?" She shakes her head, opens her purse and takes out a stick of lip gloss, applies it while looking into a small compact.

"He keeps a team of miniature assassins that he trains himself, and has most of the night crew on our force paid off." Trev sighs, his eyes rivet to his plate. "Everybody knows it, but nobody's brave enough to do anything about it."

"So what does it all mean, Trevis? You said before it's a spiritual thing."

"And you're still not afraid of him?"

"Do you want my honest answer?"

"Think, Bunny. A man who is *that* smart? *That* strong and *that* evil? A man who's constantly getting away with stuff? The things he knows? The things he says? You ever listen to how he talks? Kinda low and hard? Like a growling animal ... A man with rabies?"

"My goodness, Trev."

"He's possessed with devils, Bunny."

"But he didn't seem that way at all the last time I saw him, Trev. I mean, he was *kind*. Tender almost. He even gave me a ride."

"A ride!" Trev sighs and cups his forehead, his eyes clouding with hurt.

She reaches over then, strokes his hand. It wouldn't do to tell him that he'd had her car stolen. Trevis looks worried enough today. A tall waiter in a bright floral shirt comes with the check and Trev hands over his charge card, avoiding her eyes.

"I'm sorry, Trevis."

"I just wish you understood."

"What do I need to know?"

"He collects women, Bunny. He's got dozens of 'em, all over the wards. If you got involved with him, you'd just be part of a very large menagerie."

"That doesn't make him any different from any other *eligible* bachelor."

"Church girls, Gabriella. That's all he ever gets."

She is quiet, folding her napkin into miniature squares. He sits forward then, lowering his voice. "He uses these women to sex his boys, to run product, to mock the church. Catholics, Baptists, Methodists, Episcopalians, he doesn't discriminate. If church girls are getting turned out by him, one after another, what kind of message does that send to the wards? How do they feel about God, about faith, when they see women who were once some of the finest, most upstanding parishioners in their community, serving time in Duvall's house of horrors? What does that say to our young people? That nobody is living right? That evil is stronger than good? That the church is powerless?"

"It says that flesh is flesh, Trev, that's all."

"In other words, we have no choice but to sin?"

"No, but only God can help us not to," she insists, folding her arms, and he sits back in his chair, quietly exasperated. He nods toward the street. "I've got to get downtown and you have a story to write. If it's about Lincoln Duvall, I'm praying you reconsider."

"What'll you pray if it's already too late?"

DESK JOB

Gabriella

They gave me the news as soon as I stepped back into the office after lunch.

Trish Weitz, our lead editor, her pixie face saucy and cute under a new bobbed hairdo, dropped the news printouts on my desk, then patted my shoulder gently. An act of consolation.

She was leaning easily into my personal space, reeking of White Diamonds. "I bet he's still very shook up about it," she murmured, her lips glossed the pale orange of tangerines to match her woolen pantsuit, the chiffon scarf artfully draped around her throat. "How's he handling it? I hear the inside of his apartment is fairly wrecked, what with all the windows blown out and all. A real bummer, isn't it?"

"Beg your pardon?" I slid my purse under my desk, totally confused, and that's when she got it. Her mouth fell open at the horror of my ignorance.

"Oh no, Gabby."

"Trish, what is it?"

"Don't tell me you don't know?"

"About…?"

"Well, you know there's another pestilence invading the wards again. Vermin, it looks like. We're sending ecologists in to investigate. But the biggest news this morning is of course, the shooting. Your boyfriend's place. Oh my Gawd. Peter, Paul and Mary. It's a shame his apartment was fired on yesterday morning. Police suspect foul play. He's being investigated on charges of brutality. There are witnesses. You didn't catch the news? I can't believe he didn't tell you."

Fired on? A hand goes to my hip automatically, my head reeling. "I fell asleep before the news came on last night. I was just with Trevis, and he didn't mention anything about…"

"I suppose you haven't seen this either?" Trish squinted over her half-lensed reading specs and unfolded the thin newspaper, stabbing the twelve-inch article with a manicured nail: "Heartford Detective Accused Of Taking Law Into Own Hands. House Is Fired On In Retaliation."

The headline on the third page of *The Connecticut Courier*, one of our rival afternoon newspapers, screamed at me, but I was playing it cool. I picked up the paper, peering closely at his handsome mug. It's the usual police departmental head-shot file photo, this one taken almost twenty years before, just after Trev had graduated from the academy. He's unsmiling in his uniform blues. His hat sits low on his forehead and he's clean-shaven, alert, his eyes serious, almost menacing under those heavy brows in a typical ward stare. A "mess-with-me-and-I-will-shoot-you-in-a-heartbeat" stare. I sighed. This picture certainly didn't represent well to suburban audiences. Trev looked like an escaped convict in a police uniform.

Standing over my desk, Trish sipped from her paper cup of Folgers and watched my reaction carefully. She did the same thing during the Simpson trial, kept poking and prodding me, waiting for a comment.

"Any connection, you think?" she asked now.

"To…?"

"Duvall."

"Who?" I was playing along, doing all I could to keep a straight face.

"Lincoln Duvall. The big drug kingpin from the Third Ward?"

"Oh. Him. You know him?"

"Who doesn't? He fits right into your story, don't you think? I mean, if you're doing the research I'm sure his name keeps coming up. He's certainly one of *the* smartest, most grandiose bastards the wards have ever produced. Not only does he rule with an iron fist, but he does his research thoroughly. *And* he's gorgeous. Gawd is he ever! According to reliable sources, he runs a highly organized, well-oiled machine second to none in the area. Even *I* know that, Gabe."

I was forcing a smile, wondering what Trev was being subject to at this particular moment. "And you are suggesting...?"

"I'm suggesting that perhaps this guy's gotten wind of your story and is trying to hit you where it hurts most. He's probably heard that you and your preacher-guy are an item."

"That's one theory."

"And a darn good one. All the biggest dealers do that, you know. Keep tabs on what's going on down there."

I dropped into my chair then, shaking from the sheer drama of it all. Trev dodging bullets and withholding information. My Ivy-League, white-collar, $75,000-a-year-making suburban boss attempting to school me like she's some kind of Mafioso expert. "And you just happen to be an expert on ward gangster-protocol, right?" I asked her.

Trish frowned, obviously taken aback by my cynicism, but Amanda Tate, our switchboard operator, had suddenly appeared behind her and was beckoning hurriedly. "It's the mayor's office," she warned.

"Talk about being saved by the bell." Trish grinned reluctantly, squeezed my shoulder. "I'll let you off this time, Gurlie. But listen. If you need to talk? Please. You know where to find me. And hey. We're going to do this. We're *going* to get to the bottom of this story. So prepare yourself. Do whatever it takes."

She was clicking away again on those stacked heels, leaving me alone to read the article for myself.

I still couldn't believe I was the last to know. How could Trev play me like that? Tell me about everyone else's business but his own? As if I'd be more concerned about a Bluecoat than the man I'm supposedly marrying someday.

I read the badly written article three times, and was still trying to process all of it when my phone started ringing off the hook, both lines buzzing at once. My momma calls wondering if Trev is okay, and after her, an entire slew of in-house reporters who'd seen the article and gotten the word before I did. "Your Reverend Boyfriend," they called him.

"Is it really true?" they kept asking. "How is Your Reverend Boyfriend holding up?"

"Is that why Your Reverend Boyfriend didn't come into the newsroom as usual to pick you up today?"

"Who does he think is responsible?"

I logged onto my PC and instantaneously began pulling up files. Opening and closing them, transferring information from one document to the other. The file I'd started on the "dead dealers" story was growing steadily, but obviously, not fast enough. I'd given myself another month to have it ready for press, although seven interviews were finished so far. Seven interviews, not including the brief talk I'd had with Lincoln, and I haven't been able to scratch the surface of what's happening in the wards. Three high-level dealers killed in the past eight months, one of them from out of town, and no one seemed to know who was "doing them," or better yet, who was ordering the hits.

The screen wavered as I called up the file, watched the blurry letters wink into focus. So far I'd gotten two interviews from former addicts who had broken down the Third Ward's major drug dynasties for me so that I would know who the biggest players were. Lincoln, I was told, reigns at the top of the heap. There were the two interviews I'd had with officials at the Medical Examiners Office, both of whom were reluctant to let me read the victims' autopsy reports. There was the five-minute interview with the officer who had arrived at the scene first after the second murder and another interview from a teenager who was washing his car close by when it happened.

The similarities were unmistakable. The first dealer, a wealthy, young black male named Skyy, who had been quickly ascending the ranks of illegal power, had been killed in his car in the wards in an apparent drive-by. His face had been shot clean off, his girlfriend had said. Almost like Joker's, Trev's frat brother's and his cousin who'd driven up with him from Atlanta.

Three men, all drug dealers, murdered in the wards, in their cars.

I had cost him $50,000, Lincoln had said that first time he'd snatched my car door open with murder in his eyes. He'd been furious that day, as if I'd interrupted something big, and I'd never stopped to wonder what he could have been en route to; $50,000 was a lot of money. The only kind of person from the wards who even had access to that much cash was a drug dealer. Someone like Lincoln. Like Skyy. Like Joker or the one known as Spain, the latest casualty. But what did it all mean?

And now, Trev's apartment had been hit; but by whom? Who could be bold enough to open fire on a police officer's home? And why did Internal Affairs send for Trev specifically? Could it be true, what Trev said, that Lincoln had bought off half of the vice squad's night shift? Could his money have bought off the folks downtown in Internal Affairs as well?

"A man who would run deserves to die," Lincoln had called to inform me that night the last big ward dealer had run onto the highway and been killed. News reports said he'd been running when he was hit by a tractor trailer, but there had been no reports of anyone chasing him.

None of it made any sense to me. Trev had let me sit through lunch without saying a thing about his apartment being fired on, about the witch hunt they were probably subjecting him to at the station.

What if he *had* been killed? What if Trish was right? What if Lincoln was at the root of all this madness and Trev was being attacked behind some vendetta Lincoln had because he was trying to help me? Why couldn't he tell me? Why did there always have to be so many secrets between us? Trev was always waiting until I heard the news elsewhere first. Always waiting until the grapevine got to me first.

It was after five and still no word from Trev, so I called his cell phone, his home phone and got his voice message both times. It was a far-fetched attempt, but I phoned him at his job anyway, prepared to leave yet another message on his departmental voice mail. I stammered when Sergeant Jay Tervalon, picked up at his extension. "Good God, Sweetheart, haven't you heard?" he asked when he recognized my voice. For the second time today I swallowed my embarrassment and admitted that Trev hadn't told me a thing. Tervalon launched into his typical rantings, and when he was finally finished, I was speechless. Trevis, he'd said, had been reassigned pending further investigation and had been moved to a day shift. A cushy desk job with minimum responsibilities until things were settled once and for all. A position Trev, with his high-octane personality, would hate with a passion.

"Did he have to turn in his gun?" I asked and Tervalon coughed.

"Not yet," he said. "But soon, maybe."

†††

I try to reach Trev from the office one last time before I leave for Imani's. He's home at last, moping on the couch it sounds like. He picks up on the fourth ring, his voice low, guarded.

"Yeah?" he says.

"I know all about it, Trev. Tervalon told me. Why'd I have to hear it from him?"

He asks me to hold on, takes a while coming back, as if he'd needed to regroup, rehearses his words carefully.

"Guess you heard by now, huhn? There's another plague coming up from the river and overflowing the wards again. Must be the cold weather stirring things up. I heard folks been packing up their kids and leaving for a few days. Going to stay with relatives until things get back to normal. Whatever that means. Rats this time. They started in Deuce, near the warehouses down around the wharfs and they're running everywhere. The basements are crawling with them. It's like they're crawling out the river, breeding up and down its banks. TV news is saying they'll be in Trece in another twenty-four hours. Some things don't ever change. Seems like that river's been breeding calamity on the wards ever since I can remember."

"Maybe now folks will stop worshipping it, eating from it, smuggling drugs across it."

"Maybe."

"So why didn't you tell me about the shooting?"

"I didn't want you to worry. It's my problem. I'll work it out."

"That's selfish, Trevis. Inexcusable."

"Listen to the pot calling the kettle black." His sarcasm bit hard.

"Are you gonna tell me what happened downtown today?"

"You can see it on the news tonight like everybody else."

"Don't shut me out, Trev."

"What more do you need to know? The brass showed up in full force. Cameras rolling. Reporters from all the newspapers. Yours too, of course."

"Someone shot up your windows. Did you get a look at the assailants? Were there any other witnesses?"

"No." Trev sighs, like he wants to hang up. I could hear him flicking through channels; hear ESPN blaring.

"Could you at least explain to me what's going on?"

"I'm not sure myself, Bunny. Something about brutality charges." His voice trails off. He starts rambling about departmental proceedings, about protocol, about loyalty. Sentences clash, make no sense at all, details unfolding in pieces between coughs. Something about a room full of witnesses who claimed to have been attacked by him in the past. Two young boys, brothers, each no older than seventeen, claiming to be star witnesses. Claiming he'd been shaking them down for money. Touching them inappropriately. Accusing them of dealing drugs.

Trev falls silent. "I'm serious about my job. I'd never do anything like that." Bitterness curls his words like the fringes of dying leaves.

"I know, Trevis."

He rambles on again about lying folks who have come forward to claim they were there the night Duvall was pulled over and arrested. Folks who claimed they'd seen him beat Lincoln down in the street before bringing him into custody without proper evidence.

"Duvall's lawyer, some big shot, was there in his stead." Trev sighs. "He's filed charges against me. I could lose my job."

Outside his apartment a dog barks and he gets up from the couch, carrying the phone to the window. He isn't sure what to expect next. "Hold on while I get my gun," he murmured.

He comes back to the phone, shares more details. Another criminal, a booster who'd been in lock-up that night, had given a statement that Officer Joe Rodgers had been commanded by Trev to assist him in brutalizing

Duvall for his own pleasure, an act that Rodgers supposedly wanted no part of. Internal Affairs thought all of this led to the open attack on Rodgers' home and ultimately, the senseless shooting of his six-year-old daughter.

"No man who wears our badge should be responsible for any senseless act of violence against children, and Detective Trevis Cooper is no exception," Mayor Cochran had read from a prepared statement and now Trev recited it verbatim..

"The *mayor*, Trev?" My voice rises in shock.

"The mayor."

"In other words, if Duvall did order the hit on you and Rodgers, he's totally justified."

"Exactly."

"So what will you do now?"

"Pray," Trev says, and I can tell he's done, wants only to be left alone. "I won't give up until I find Joker's murderer. You can believe that," he promises.

✝✝✝

It's close to 6:00 by the time I hang up with Trev, just enough time to make my 6:30 salon appointment with Imani in the third ward.

Around my desk, the flow of activity hadn't ceased for a moment. Writers and editors were still in and out of Trish's office and phones were still ringing. I glanced at my watch, reached for my purse. After all that's happened today, I didn't feel like going to the wards. Not at night. Not when Trev and Lincoln have officially become mortal enemies and weather reports are forecasting a major snowstorm. I smoothed a palm over my head, stroked the wiry, flyaway strands. My hair was a mess, no doubt about it. If a major snow was coming, the salon could be closed for the next few days, and there was no telling when Imani would be able to reschedule me.

I sighed, reached for my coat. Drama not withstanding, getting my hair scrubbed and massaged by Imani's expert hands was absolutely crucial to my holistic well being at this very moment, and neither threat of snow nor bullet would keep me from it.

THE SHOPKEEPER'S MAN

Lincoln

Linc, Man, you must be slippin', 'cause the more you try to control this situation, the more it keeps slipping away from you... And now look; Mr. Elliot Ness ain't learned his lesson yet. Blew out every window in that fool's apartment but he still sends his woman down here to spy on me. How he gonna do that? Send a female to trap Linc Duvall? If that ain't the ultimate epitome of a punk.

That's what I'm thinking to myself when I look up and see *her*, of all people, sitting on the other side of the salon, staring me smack in the face *again*. And I'm wondering if it were possible that I'd dreamed her up, because she was all I kept thinking about last night. Touching 'Nere, but seeing her. Strategizing with the crew while her name flooded my mind again and again.

Now I shake my head, snatch my eyes and my mind back quick, 'cause I can't believe it at first, why her man would put somebody fine as her at risk. And even though I've built my business on my ability to trust, not what folks say, but what my eyes see and what my head says, I'm still sitting there, thinking, nawl. That ain't her. Can't be. 'Cause there shouldn't been no way she was able to get this close again without me knowing it.

I can't have that in my line of work, things, people, slipping up on me unexpected. People get killed that way. Smoked, graveyard dead. This ain't no game. This life and death out here, and one false move, like the one she made tonight, can be the deciding factor. And those the kinda folks she shoulda interviewed. The folk who tried it anyhow. Tested me to my face and found out what they'd heard about me was true after all; that killing for me comes real easy.

Things ain't been the same around here since "Elliot Ness" showed up with them toy cops of his, rummaging all up in my personal business, asking questions. I knew I shoulda broke his neck when I had the chance. Shoulda snapped his head clean off his shoulders and stomped what was left into the floor Rodney-King style.

Chinere's business took a big hit once word got out that 5-0 was here, but after a few days have passed, things are finally starting to pick up again. Only reason I'm here right now. After I had Creeper and 'nem do target-practice on his house, I figured Preacha-Cop wouldn't be showing up here no more. That's for Vice to worry about, and now that he'll be pushing paper on some east side Mayberry outpost, Super Cooper's the least of my worries.

But why he wanna send her instead?

✝✝✝

A salon fulla fine women up in here tonight, Chinere included, and for some reason, I can hardly take my eyes and my mind off of "Sister Angelfied," the bravest female I ever seen besides my momma.

My heart's pumping a hundred beats a second, and in these heavy boots, my feet won't be still. Nothing like this has ever happened to me before. Not to *me*, and I wish she would quit jabbing me with her holy voodoo. I get out my chair, go over to the PA system, and turn up the volume on the piped-in music from the radio station Chinere has on, but it still don't change a thing. Angelfied's got me as nervous as a junkie trying to "kick" cold turkey, and I can't keep my mind on the business at hand.

Ghost is looking at me like I've gone simple, 'cause it ain't making sense to him either. He feels it too, that strange vibe she's brought up in here. And even though she ain't saying a word to me, it's like something in her's pulling me in. Calling, whispering my name.

Ghost gets two chairs out the back room, and I set up that little folding table in our usual corner. He pulls out the books and we start our usual thing, adding up figures line by line, talking softly and trying to decide which of our nine distributors is pulling in the most profits and who needs to be replaced. I'm fighting hard to concentrate, but the figures keep swirling, look like they're breakdancing across the page.

"You cool, Baby? You see this?" Ghost, cold-sober for a change, looks concerned, presses down hard with his #2 pencil, pointing arrows at what I need to be focusing on.

"I'm straight," I lie, reaching for my Newports, but one drag sends me into a coughing fit. Ghost smirks, watches as Chinere comes over and taps my back, hands me one of her Evians like I'm some baby. "Quit that," I tell Chinere, but I'm really talking to *her*.

149

She's wrecking my flow, because I was *sure* I'd never see her face again. I was sure she understood how easily I could hurt her if I wanted to, especially after that last lesson. But she hasn't taken heed to nothing I've said or done, and that alone infuriates me. How's her man gonna feel when he sees her slumped over the wheel of her car, shot up like Bonnie, Clyde's woman?

Ghost leans over the table fighting a grin, cutting his eyes at Angelfied and then back at me. "You wanna do this later, D, 'cause you seem a little preoccupied?"

"Who? Not me. I'm cool. You the one tripping." I stand up again and stalk off, walk into the back storage room and pretend to be doing inventory.

Chinere has been on me about bringing a case of perm up to her stand to restock her shelves, getting them out the storeroom before the rats show up to gnaw through everything. I scrounge through boxes, reading labels, still coughing here and there. Since 5-0's been through here I gotta make sure things stay on the up and up. Gotta keep myself one step ahead of myself.

Dag. I drop a jar of conditioner on the floor and it cracks open, splatters all over the floor and all over my steel-toed boots. Chinere glances at me with one of her looks as I kneel down with the paper towels and clean up the mess. I'm tripping, I know. But any man would be if he were in my shoes. It was dangerous, for one thing, to be turned on by the very thing that could destroy you. And two, Babygirl, even with her hair half-done, is *beautiful*. And for three, she ain't scared of nothing, including dying, which looks like it's gonna end up happening real soon, since she insists on playing this game to the end.

Lastly, Honey's got game. I give her that. 'Cause she looks right into my face and plays me off so smooth, nobody but me and her and Ghost know what's going on. And Ghost can care less. He's got his eye on a female in a tight red mini he wants to get with, so it's just Chinere, with her feline instincts, who ain't comfortable at all. She's sensing something. But she knows how I roll with skirts, and has sense enough not to ask me about my business right now. 'Bed not. She knows I'd get her straight in a hurry up in here, so she ain't saying a word to me all the time I'm watching Miss Angelfied go from the sink to Imani's chair, to the dryer and back to the chair again. And when she's finally done-up all pretty, and sways her fine behind through the waiting room and out the front door, Chinere doesn't say a word when I get up too. Just sucks her teeth when I follow Miss Gabriella out into the parking lot.

"Ey," I'm saying, but she keeps walking, acts like she don't hear me, like she's not comfortable talking to me out here in the dark. Inside my jacket, my .38 presses hard against my ribs, tempting me, egging me on.

"Ey," I say again, getting angrier by the minute, 'cuz I can't believe I'm actually allowing her to "dis" me like this. Can't believe I'm still following her into the parking lot although it's absolutely necessary.

It's after nine now, and the cold night sky hangs like a black shroud over the ward, a few weak stars like tacks, pinning the blackness above the sky-line. She gets to her car, digs around in her purse for her keys, and I just stand there watching her with my hands in my pockets.

She can't find the keys and suddenly looks up at me with surprise, as if she didn't know I was standing there all this time. "Oh... Mr. Duvall," she says, then sucks her teeth like she's mad at me, like I hid her keys, like she does-n't know how much I hate to be ignored.

I ain't said a word yet. I'm just standing there feeling the cold iron digging into my side. Standing there thinking, if I "did her" right here, pulled the trigger and walked away, the salon would be swarming with 5-0 again in a matter of minutes, would probably make Chinere close things down for a while. Meanwhile, she still can't find her keys, and this time when she looks up and gives me this helpless look, she sees how mad I am and looks away from me quickly.

"Lincoln...," she starts, but I interrupt her, stepping closer without meaning to, folding my arms across my chest and unfolding them again to keep my hands still at my sides. My heart is pounding crazily, like it did the first time I took my first hit of "chronic," and a warm melty feeling flows into the tips of my fingers, fills my chest. Voodoo, I think. She's working some crazy conjure on me and I ain't having it.

"Lincoln..." Her voice is so soft, and I can't help it, I like the way she calls my name.

"I don't wanna hear it," I tell her.

"It's not what it looks like."

"It looks like your man's a punk."

"'Scuse me?"

"Sending you down here to take his bullet. What kinda man is that?"

"He did no such thing."

"What are you doing here? He sent you, didn't he? Sent you down here to spy on me? Get yourself killed?"

"That's not what happened," she's saying, but I'm trying hard not to hear that voice. I start in stroking my chin, getting angrier just thinking about it.

"Look," she starts.

"No, *you* look," I finish. "Don't you know how dangerous it is down here? Brothas fire first and ask questions later. And you're down here at night too?"

"Lincoln..."

"You didn't think they'd recognize your car?"

"I didn't know. I wasn't sure if..."

"What? Just 'cuz your man is weak enough to put you at risk, you don't care about yourself?"

She looks at me, startled, like something just touched her, and I shrug, look away from her. But it's too late. She'd recognized it the same time I did. We both saw it—that I actually cared about what happened to her.

She has no idea that this thing is much bigger now than either of us. She don't know that she's a potential security risk. She don't see all the armed brothas stationed around the salon right now ready to take out anybody at a second's notice. Some are sitting in their dark cars in this very lot watching us even now, and who knows who might have hurt her had I not come out here and escorted her to her car personally? They needed to see us together to ensure her safety. My presence lets them know that it's all good. That I'm aware, and in total control of this situation, since they all know who she is and what car she drives. They know her man has a vendetta against me and one of those ambitious brothas may have "did" her just to score points with me, to let me see how loyal they are to the cause. Of course she don't understand none of that.

You tripping hard, Man. Letting this female get to your head.

I'm fed up for real now, ready to go back to the shop, but when I turn to walk away, she starts up again with that voice.

"I came to get my hair done, Lincoln, that's all. Imani does my hair."

"Since when?"

"Since last year."

"I don't believe you."

"Ask her. Ask Chinere how long I've been coming down here."

I don't know what to do, so I cough, shake my head. "A hard head makes a soft tail, my momma used to always say. Some people only learn that way. The hard way. They don't know how to respect boundaries."

"I assure you this is not the case," she insists, looking at me like she needs for me to understand. Like it's important to her. Her eyes are too soft though, too pretty to stare into for long, so I look at the ground instead, kicking at the broken pavement like I'm ten years old again.

It takes me a couple seconds, but I'm finally able to shrug it off. I give her my hardest look then. The one my enemies still see in their dreams. "See though, when a brotha *finally* resorts to force, folks gonna swear he was being violent. Call him a monster. Even though he's tried his best to be a gentleman. Even though he gave the warning first."

She blinks quickly, sees for the first time how close we're standing, and it's like neither one of us are breathing.

"Are you threatening me again?" she asks, and although I'm furious, I can't help noticing it's here again: that sweet, fruity smell that emanates from her and conjures up Momma, so it's like she's standing here instead. Momma, not her, looking pretty under the streetlight with all that hair softly curling over her shoulders. Angelfied sighs like something's bothering her, tugs at her ear. With her hair all done up, she's irresistible. Her skin looks as soft as the satin lining of a coffin, and I can't help thinking how much I'd hate to see that pretty face splattered all over this parking lot.

"Are you threatening me, Lincoln?" she repeats.

"Looks that way."

"Why? What have I done to you?"

"Ask your man."

"I don't understand."

"Do I look like a joke to you?"

"Not at all."

"Why y'all trying to play me then?"

"Nobody's playing you."

Six rats as big as possums lumber from under a parked car and waddle toward the street. I pull out the .38 and point it carefully, show her how good my aim is. The gun cracks six times as loud as a firecracker and Angelfied jumps, calls on her God. The rats explode with squealing noises, entrails flying everywhere. I look at the gun, then back at her. I put it away, but she's shaking quietly, a hand over her mouth.

"You keep showing up," I tell her. "Everywhere I look, you're there. What you want with me? You trying to get with me? You wanna gimme some? Is that it?"

She gasps in shock, lowers those pretty eyes. My heart turns over again. "Well?" I press.

"It's not what you think, Lincoln."

"Well, what is it? 'Cuz I need to understand. You making me look bad. Making me look soft, like I can't handle my business."

"I'm sorry. I don't mean to interfere."

"What you expect from me though? You think things down here are supposed to change just for you? That I'm supposed to treat you different, jes 'cuz you fine?"

"I didn't say that." She presses her lips together and her eyes speak before she does. She's afraid, I can tell. Scared I might try to hurt her out here in the dark.

"Don't you know anybody else would've been dead by now? Or maimed at least. And here you are, coming and going like me and you got something going on."

"Lincoln."

"And your preacher-cop? He's only living 'cuz of you. But after tonight…"

"Look. I'm sorry, Lincoln. What else do you want me to say? I honestly didn't know you'd be here. I didn't come to spy on you. I just wanted my hair done. That's all." She touches her new hairdo, looks at me sideways. "I'd never intentionally disrespect you. I'd never invade your privacy."

"What you call this?"

"A coincidence?"

This chick is naïve, and I can't help it; I laugh then without meaning to, and she laughs too, showing me those pearly whites. Dimples. We both catch ourselves.

"Lincoln. You are what you are and I accept that. I'm not saying that I condone how you choose to live, but I respect your right to live as you please." She drops her eyes, plays with the strap of her purse, and her voice falls off.

I step closer, straining to hear what she's trying to say. "To be honest? On the way over here tonight, I was thinking that I'm just going to tell my editors the truth. That it's impossible for me to get this story unless I risk life and limb, and I can't do that. I don't want anyone else to get hurt. Trev especially. It's not his fault. No promotion, no story, is worth that to me."

"So you telling me you gonna drop all of this? Quit following me around? Stay out of my business?"

"Yes."

"Bet."

"What about Trevis? All those charges... Can you, would you...?"

"That depends on him. Call him off and I'll see what I can do."

"Ok."

"Aiight."

There was nowhere else for us to go with it now, so I look away from her, back toward the street where the cars swish past like floating fish. I've got an armed brotha stationed near the corner, set up with a lil' table like he's selling handbags and incense and oils. Inside the salon, three more brothas are poised at each end of the shop, reading magazines, eating junk food, watching the TV 'Nere keeps in the lobby as if they're waiting on a haircut. Another soldier is sitting outside on the front steps talking on his cell, rapping to some female no doubt, but watching the street carefully. Which is why I can't believe nobody alerted me that she was back down here again.

My men are fidgety now; I can feel it. They see I'm acting totally out of character. Fraternizing with the enemy. They don't understand what's up with me and her. I don't know myself. She sighs again, and I turn back to her as she finds her keys finally, moves toward her car.

"Good night and thank you," she murmurs.

"You're welcome."

She unlocks her door and I pull it open for her.

"Take care of yourself," she says.

"You do the same," I say, and before I can stop myself, I'm doing it. Have my hand on her shoulder, snatching her close for a kiss. My heart is pounding so loud I swear she can hear it, and her lips are sweet, much softer than I'd imagined they'd be. A virgin's lips, they feel like. Mmph. Indescribably delicious.

She freezes, shocked at my boldness before her lips part slowly and she kisses me back, tasting me before she catches herself, pulls away and gets into her car. I feel drunk with something I don't even understand, and I still can't believe I went there. Kissed my enemy.

She starts the engine without looking at me, her head lowered apologetically, shamefully, as she looks back toward the shop. I follow her eyes and we both see Chinere standing in the doorway watching us, one hand on the door jamb, the other hanging limply at her side, like she's posing for a Polaroid. Angelfied waves slowly as she pulls out of the lot and I head back toward the shop, signaling for my men to let her pass safely. The crew's tripping hard right about now but they got sense enough to keep their thoughts to themselves.

It's cold out here, and the heat inside the salon is turned up so it's warm and toasty, but I don't feel like seeing Chinere's hurt face right now, don't wanna hear Ghost nagging me about no numbers. I just go and sit in my car that's parked a few feet from the salon door obscured by somebody's old pick-up truck. I turn on some old-school Luther. Turn him on high enough to drown out the throbbing in my heart.

From here I can see her tail lights blink twice and then snap out as she turns the corner, heading home no doubt where it's safe and sound, toward the quiet west side. Toward her preacher-man and that world where somebody like me would never fit in at all.

Chinere

It's not like it never happened before; like she the first woman ever come up in my shop that he either been with or was trying to get with. All kinds of womens show up through these doors looking for Linc, and they all just as brazen as alley cats.

Can't say I ain't a lil' surprised at this one though, since she s'posed to be so different from the rest, her being one of Imani's favorite customers and all. I *never* expected it be a somebody like her this time, what with those grand, high and holy manners and that quiet, little, pouty mouth. A small-lipped mouth with perfect teeth that looks like it wants to shush folks. Long dresses and high-necked blouses, chile looks like a schoolteacher instead of a tramp, which is what she gonna end up looking like anyway by the time Linc gets through with her. They always do.

It's almost eleven by the time I hear him come back in, hear his keys in the door of the shop, see him stomping snow off his boots on the mat outside on the porch. Outside in the street, snow's falling hard as bricks in the ward, the cool white gleam prettying up all those grimy sidewalks and alleys strewn with trash. Nobody knows though how long this quiet's gonna last, what with all those rats running down here anytime now from Deuce.

The bell on the shop's front door chimes gentle as a crib mobile, and here he comes with his fine-looking self. Shows up just in time, like always. Like he the Black Ward Ranger and I'm Lil' Bo Peep, and he's here to save the day. Last time I saw him, he was all up in another woman's face, following her out the door like she a dog in heat and he was the fire department, so what he expect me to say, to feel now? *Especially* now.

He's carrying a bag of something that smells good, comes in and starts laying it all out on the counting table. I look to see what he's doing and he flashes me one of his rare, million dollar smiles. I look away from him. Want him to know he can't always buy me with his Hollywood teeth, but he struts past me and goes to my sink to wash his hands like he don't care either way. Like he don't care if I got an attitude and gonna do what he wants to anyway so ain't no use in us talking about it.

It's barbecue he's brought, and I'm glad 'cause I haven't eaten since noon. He arranges the food neatly, then looks up at me like a little boy who wants to be rewarded for doing a good deed. "So, what's up, Gurl? I can't get no love?"

"What you need mine for when you so busy running behind somebody else's?"

"What's wrong with you?" He's frowning, tearing into a piece of rib.

"You act like I ain't nobody. Chasing other women in my face, embarrassing me in my own shop. Did you have to *kiss* her, Linc?"

He licks the barbecue off his fingers and comes sidling up behind me now, wrapping his arms around my waist and turning me around to face him. The broom I'm holding clatters to the floor. "What's wrong with you?"

"Nothing."

"Why you tripping all of a sudden?" he asks, rubbing my chin with his thumb, like he's finally noticing how much my face is filling out. "It ain't never bothered you before. You know how I am."

I can see that look bleeding into his eyes and my heartbeat speeds up. I try to kiss him now, pull his head down so his lips touch mine, but he doesn't move, just stands there holding my face in his hands.

"Why you gaining all this weight all of a sudden? Why your face spreading like this?"

"Like what? My face ain't spreading."

"Lift up that smock," he tells me.

"For what, Linc?"

"I wanna see something."

"See what?"

"Uh-huhn. I thought so."

"Thought what?" I try to say, but I can't because he's just slapped the words back down my throat. He slaps me so hard I'm falling backward against the wall, seeing stars, but he ain't finished yet.

"You went on and did it, huhn? You went and got yaself knocked up after I told you not to."

"Please, Linc…" I am trying to explain but his second slap knocks me off my feet onto the floor. Blood spatters down the front of my white smock but he's still at it, kicking my hips and behind with those hard boots, boxing my ears until my face stings.

"Linc, don't… It's *your* child… It's *our* baby…"

But he's so mad he can hardly see straight. "What I tell you? What I tell you?" He snatches me up off the floor and knocks me back onto it. Picks me up again and slaps me around from sink to sink until I'm pinned backward, covering my face. He's hollering something I don't even understand now, knocking all the shampoos on the shelf over my head to the floor. I cover my head as he holds me down backward and he turns on the hot water while I'm kicking and screaming, trying to get free. The water burns my scalp, the pain shooting from my forehead down to my belly it seems. I'm sobbing like a little girl, my skin numb now in agony before he finally lets me up and walks away without looking back at me.

"Get up and eat this food so I can get you home," he says, and sits down at the table and finishes his barbecue.

Weather forecasts run across the TV screen, advertising all the places that will be closed tonight and tomorrow because of the snow, and Lincoln takes a Bic out of his back pocket and flicks it, lights up a Newport. He inhales deeply, exhales away from me, then looks at the cigarette. Finally, he dabs it out like he's disgusted, fixes his eyes on me pulling myself off the floor, picking up shampoo bottles. The back of my blouse under the smock is soaked clear through to my bra, and my scalp feels like it's on fire. I can't look at him directly, can't bear to see all that evil pooled in his eyes, but I drop into the chair across from him, open up the foil wrapping and force myself to eat a piece of overdone rib whose sauce seems much too spicy.

Linc belches, looks at his cigarette lighter, plays with its silvery flame adjuster.

"What you doing?" I ask him, but he don't answer. He flicks his lighter, turns it off and on. He changes its settings until the flames rise higher and higher. He's staring at the fire, its reflection dancing in his eyes. "How many has it been altogether?" he asks.

"Five, Linc. Five of our babies you made me get rid of."

"And you ain't learned yet?" He ain't hardly done with this. He never is. He takes his thumb now, inserts it into the flame and watches as the skin blackens, reddens, then bubbles and blisters. I look away from him but he ain't letting me go that easy.

"Look, 'Nere. See. What I tell you?"

"Stop, Linc. Please. Ain't you tripped enough for one night?"

He smiles with those movie star teeth. "That's what I do, Baby. I trip. That's my occupation."

"*Don't, Linc.* Please, stop it. For me. Not this time…" I look away, can't bear to watch much longer, but he's having himself a good time just watching himself burn. Smiling harder the longer his flesh stays in the flame, like he really don't seem to notice that I'm here. "'Nere. Look at this, Gurl. Wonder what it feels like when it gets down to the bone. Burns past all this muscle."

"Please, Lincoln. Stop it!" I get up then, and walk away from him, my nerves jumping in my neck.

"What is it gonna take to convince you, since you don't believe? Do I really need this thumb? Lemme think. What they use thumbs for anyway?" He's still on fire. Still smiling. Still looking from me to those flames.

"I'm convinced, Lincoln! Stop it!" He's got me screaming at last. Got me feeling like I can't take any more, would rather die instead.

"What? I can't hear you, Gurl."

"I'm convinced, okay?"

"Say it then."

"What, Lincoln? Say what? Put the lighter down. Please… For me…"

"Say what your momma and 'nem always telling you."

"Linc…"

"Say it!"

"Linc ain't 'human,' okay?! He… he's… a 'mad dog'! A 'maniac!'"

"Uh-huhn… I can't hear you though. Stop whispering now…"

"Lincoln's 'crazy'!'"

"How 'crazy'?"

"Too 'crazy' to have children! Too 'crazy' to…" I collapse at my own stall in my own chair, smelling his flesh mixed with the aroma of barbecue sauce and corn muffins. I'm crying uncontrollably now. Crying so hard my mascara's running, streaking black down my cheeks. And I'm thinking, they so right about him. They always been right.

Linc cuts off the flame at last and wraps a napkin around his badly burned thumb. He looks up at me, smiles that half-smile. His eyes are dark and shiny and beautiful. A black panther-man with sequins for eyes.

"Call the clinic. Kill it," he says real even like, like his baby growing inside of me ain't nothing but an ant or a roach crawling up a wall. Suddenly, his smile fades, and he looks away from me like he hates himself for saying it. He gets up quick then, like he scared he's gonna change his mind. He goes to the front of the shop and makes himself busy, starts pulling down the grate.

I'm hurting so bad now I can hardly talk, let alone look at him, so I don't hardly feel like telling him about those pitiful-looking men that came by the shop today. Two of 'em, looking all broke down, and asking for him by name, saying they had to see him, had to pay him in person. Only one I knew had one of those names ending with "Pete" like so many of these men in the wards. Q-Pete, his was, I think. The other man looked like something that crawled out from under a bridge.

Linc gets out the keys and I follow him to the door so he can lock up the shop that belongs to me. Following him thinking maybe things'll change tomorrow after he get himself some sleep, let me tuck him in and explain why it's so important for me to have our child this time, no matter how evil he says he is. I can see his face now in bed, his lips still as a stone, and me stroking his bare chest and whispering, "*Please*, Linc... *Please*..."

CHAPTER THIRTEEN

Gabriella

H e *kissed me and I still can't believe it.* Kissed me so good the memory of his taste still lingers on my lips even as I brush my hair up into a neat swirl and tie on a kerchief to keep it in place.

It's well past midnight in my bedroom, and the moon outside my window is a sharp sickle suspended above the firs. The "Witching Hour," some people called it, and on a night like this, I can understand why.

He'd *kissed* me. His hands were on my shoulders; his smell was in my nose; and before I could stop him, he was kissing me in a way I'd never been kissed by any man. Kissing me with such skill and passion, I didn't know what else to do but to kiss him back. At that very moment, I'd suddenly felt powerless, not because I had no power but because just then, I didn't *want* to be strong. It was the kind of chemistry that comes along only once in a lifetime. The kind so rare that throwing it away could mean closing the door to the possibilities of unspeakable pleasure. And pain. Yes, definitely pain. In the darkness of that cold lot, I was being lulled into a spell where my own passions were used against me.

The phone is ringing but I'm afraid to move, afraid to touch it. Outside, a low-flying plane makes whirling noises like some kind of strange bird, and the digital clock on my nightstand clicks.

The ringing stops, then starts up again. A shrill sound, like a small bomb that ignites beside the bed.

Don't answer it.

The notion presses on me heavily. Whoever's calling at this indecent hour is up to no good and I shouldn't answer it. Should wait for the voice mail to click on after the fourth ring and check it later, in the safety of daybreak when the rest of the world is alert and watching. But I'm fumbling in the dark instead, snatching up the cordless receiver, amazed at the sheer weight of my own need. The voice on the other end seems to hesitate before it quickly recovers, as if it hadn't expected to hear my voice so soon. "I'm not a monster," it says. "I think you, better than anybody, can show that. Can write it like it's supposed to be written."

A man's voice. Deep, extremely sensuous. It certainly isn't Trev's.

"Lincoln?"

"You know my voice."

"Do you know it's after three a.m.?"

"I know." He makes a low, soft sound like a chuckle. "I haven't been to sleep in five days so it's all the same to me; night, day, it don't really matter."

I'm quiet. Waiting, knowing he's stalling. Is he feeling what I feel? Is that why he cannot sleep, even after five days of total exhaustion?

My ears, for some reason, are beginning to roar. *What can he possibly want with me? We've already said everything that needed to be said.*

"I'm calling to apologize."

"For...?"

"Kissing you. I don't know what came over me and I didn't mean to disrespect you. I'm sorry. I was out of line."

The silence looms before I hear my own voice saying, "Apology accepted," although we both know that it wasn't all his fault. That I had allowed it. That I could have stopped it if I'd wanted to. I'm afraid to speak now, unable to remind him of any of that.

"I'm sorry too," I say at last.

"What for?"

"For allowing it."

"Is that what happened?"

I'm too ashamed to answer, but he knows that in itself is an indictment.

"I've been thinking," he continues. "I want *you* to write the story. If anybody can break it down, you can. I feel that. Trust my instincts. They gonna write something anyway, and I'd rather it come from you."

"Do you know what you're saying?"

"I never say what I don't mean."

"I'd write it honestly, Lincoln. If you'd trust me to let me do it. "

"I don't trust nobody, Baby."

"Oh?"

"But I think you'll do your best."

"Are you doing this to get next to me?"

"Yes."

I fumble then, taken aback by his directness. "Look," I fight back a yawn, "I'm not trying to play any games or lead you on. I'm in love with Jesus first and Detective Cooper second, and I'm not planning to hurt either of them. What happened tonight with us, in the lot, well…that was wrong and it won't happen again. "

"Do you have to use my name?" he asks, bringing things back to a business level, like he hadn't heard a word I'd just said.

"Maybe not. There could be ways around it."

"What would I have to do?"

"You'd have to open up to me, allow me to see who you are. See that world you live in."

"You ready for that? What if it's too much for you to handle, you being a church girl and all?" I can hear the smile in his voice.

"I'll decide what I can handle."

"Decisiveness. I like that in a woman." It's his turn to be quiet. "What do you want to know exactly?" he asks finally. "What do you need to see?"

"I need to understand what life is like as a dealer in the wards. I need to somehow be able to experience it with you."

"In other words, you wanna roll with the Big Dogs?"

"If you'd let me."

Behind him, the heavy voices of men rise and fall in rifts of laughter. Old music plays softly. Otis Redding is sitting on the dock of the bay.

"Where are you?" I ask.

"At The Skillet Black. Just outside the wards."

"I know it well."

"Can you meet me here in an hour?"

"At three-forty-nine in the morning?"

"I thought you wanted to see how I rolled?"

"I do."

"Now's your chance."

"But, Lincoln…"

"First thing you need to understand, Babygirl…"

"What's that?"

"If we gonna do this, it's gotta be *my* world, *my* way, and *my* time. This is who I am and what I do. I don't sleep when everybody else sleeps. I move in my own sphere. How else do you think I stay on top? This is all I do. Put in work. So if you wanna roll with me…"

"Okay, Lincoln. I'll see you in an hour."

"I'm counting the minutes."

"Okay."

"And, Babygirl? Leave that pretty ride of yours at home. I'll send a car to pick you up. Can you be ready in half an hour?"

"Yes, but…"

"See you then."

A resounding click and he's gone just like that, leaving me to step out of my blessed quietness into something I am totally unprepared for.

DREAMING

No one ever talked about this side of the business—the things reporters were willing to endure to get what they believed was a *good* story.

They could kill her easily and no one would know the difference, except that she's left a note in a place only Trev would know to look—inside the candy dish on the coffee table.

Words scrawled on the sheet of lineless stationery read, *"To meet L. Duvall at 3:49 a.m. for an interview at the Skillet Black. 13 Union Street, Heartford."*

No one has to tell her that this early morning rendezvous is completely out of order. Something the folks at Zion or even *The Chronicle*, for that matter, would never in a thousand years approve of. She, better than anyone, knew that she was putting herself in harm's way, stepping down into the kingdom of hell with the ward's worst thug, a man who was sending for her as if he were a ghetto Gotti and she were Lil' Kim. The only thing missing, she thinks, is the paparazzi.

Disconnecting the voice of her conscience, she watches herself move through the lobby and out the main entrance as if she is dreaming, an apparition moving past the glass walls and into the snow dressed like a runway model in the cream-colored wool coat and matching dress, the cream-colored hat and boots she believes will somehow neutralize the black she's sure Lincoln will have on.

†††

The late-model Lincoln, black of course, with two big dudes sucking on stogies in the front seat, has arrived ten minutes earlier than scheduled and is idling near the front lobby entrance, tinted windows throbbing with bass. All around her, snow is falling hard, layers the frozen ground and curbs like spilled grits she must step through carefully, afraid to fall down in her high-heeled boots.

"Sorry, Sweetie, 'D' don't do 'CPT,'" the pale driver says when she raises her eyebrows and points at her watch.

She keeps her mouth closed, watches herself moving outside of herself, away from the safe harbor of suburban civilization and the west side, away from anything that makes sense or has ever clearly defined her boundaries. She's stepping outside of where she believes God has securely placed His hedge, and nothing's making sense anymore. A year from now, her face could be printed on the back of a milk carton under the words, "Missing," and she'd have no one to blame but herself.

Everywhere the sole of thy feet shall tread have I given unto you... The verse from Deuteronomy unfolds in her mind, but she is not fooled. It is His word but He has not sent it just then. Not here and not now, she knows. God has not called her to tread here, into a strange car with strange men who will take her to who-knows-where. God did not operate indecently.

Everything He did was always in perfect order, and He would never put her in harm's way.

Just another writer's odyssey, she tells herself. She'll be back home before the sun crests above the pines outside her window and no one will know the difference.

I'll be back before the cock crows thrice, she insists to that part of herself that still needs to believe the lie, that has no desire to pull her back from the ledge.

RENDEZVOUS

"How you doing, Miss Lady?" The man in the front passenger seat gets out and holds open the back door for her. Tall and caramel-colored with a neat goatee, his handsome face seems eerily familiar. He smiles, tucks the hem of her pale coat into the car, and when he winks at her slyly, she places him at last. Yes. Dante. The man who ran the record shop in the Third Ward.

Dante shuts her into the warm car and the music ends abruptly. Door locks slide into place. The men put out their cigars but Gabriella still coughs. The driver apologizes profusely as if afraid that word of his poor manners could get back to Linc. He cracks the window to allow in fresh air, turns and nods over his shoulder.

Gabriella makes out a mulatto's face with wooly curls attempting to pass as dreads, gray-green, red-tinged eyes, like a cat on amphetamines. Like the man in the beauty parlor last night, she thinks when he smiles. Was that him? Yes, she thinks it was. She's almost sure of it.

"Miss Sinclaire?"

"Yes?"

"We've been sent by Mr. Duvall to take you to The Skillet and we intend to do that as expeditiously as possible. In the meantime, please make yourself comfortable. There's a bar back there with juice and crackers and cheese, and of course, French vanilla coffee made fresh by Dunkin' Donuts, compliments of Mr. Duvall."

"Thank you."

She nods, sits back quietly in her seat while the men stare ahead at the road without speaking.

Snow pelts the windows like grains of rice, leaving thin white streaks as it slides slowly down the glass, and she wonders if it bothers them at all, what Lincoln is doing, allowing her this special access into their secret world.

The roads will be treacherous soon, salted with ice, but the Lincoln is wide, deep and plush, owning the road. The tan interior boasts heated leather seats, lighted backseat mirrors and lamps, a small bar on which sit two bottles of chilled cranberry juice and a Thermos filled with coffee, no doubt. In a small compartment that folds out are packets of gourmet cheese and crackers, chocolate candy kisses, cellophane-wrapped butterscotch candy and linen napkins. A small color television, VCR and CD changer are combined into a single unit that's installed into the back console of the front seat and she marvels at all the extras. A custom-designed Lincoln, it must've cost a fortune.

Its engine breathes silently as the wide car maneuvers easily through the foamy streets.

Gabriella shuts her eyes, wonders if it's too late to pray for mercy.

✝✝✝

At The Skillet-Black, the parking lot is overrun with cars, trucks and motorcycles, huge semi trucks, their engines still running, drivers watching from inside the diner over cups of hot coffee and bratwurst sandwiches.

It's a place for the lonely, for middle-class and street types who hang out at this twenty-four-hour sit-down to exchange numbers and favors and hard-luck stories. It's more greasy spoon than diner, a hot-spot spilling over with gamblers, whores, bikers, salesmen, lonely housewives, truckers, and two-bit hustlers. White men wearing platinum wedding bands and straw-colored toupees as coarse as astro turf, lean across vinyl booths. Whores wearing indigo eye shadow and stiletto boots laced up to their thighs hover outside of men's rooms chewing Dentyne hard and fast.

From a distance, even in the snow, blue winking lights advertise daily specials in broad windows filmed by dust. Close-up, hand-painted signs advertise grits and hash. Catfish and fritters. Porkchops smothered in red-eye gravy.

It's not the kind of place he'd choose to eat or even to bring a woman, but it's the safest middle ground to meet potential clients, to close deals with outside suppliers who won't come near the wards. A place where even *she'd* be comfortable meeting him, even if it was at night. So Lincoln's there, standing with his hands in his pockets under the flapping awning, when the dark car pulls up.

He's wearing a black cashmere overcoat and a Bogart-brim, calf-skinned boots with thick squared toes. He's flanked by two armed men on either side of him. "Here we are," Driver says as Dante gets out, one hand inside his coat. Scanning the street both ways, he finally opens the back door.

The armed men part and Lincoln steps through, sliding into the backseat beside her and nodding as he stretches out his legs. The smell of his after-shave fills the car. Dante checks the street again, gets back into the car, and The Lincoln moves forward.

Beside him, Gabriella doesn't move. She can neither look at nor speak to him, even as he removes his hat and allows himself a close-up look at her, as if checking for holes.

Is he reading her for a weakness?

She sits frozen, a cornered sheep surrounded by wolves. Curls fall from under her hat and he eases off his leather gloves, lifts a tendril from her shoulders and twirls it around his finger. His own curly hair has been recently cut, the edges and sideburns perfectly shaped and rounded. Chinere's handiwork.

"Hey," she stammers nervously. "How are you?"

"I'm aiight. Just business as usual." He allows the beginnings of a smile to play about his lips. "So. Hanging with the Boogeyman, huhn?" he teases, his eyes full of mischief. "You scared? You think you can handle it?"

"I can handle anything."

"Oh? I've heard that before."

"Not from me."

He smiles beautifully then, his gaze piercing through her.

He's wearing some fragrance she cannot put her finger on. Something heavy, mannish, oriental almost. Mixed with his chemistry the scent is deliciously overpowering, and she realizes her mistake too late. She has underestimated him. Had not realized that in close quarters like this, in his natural habitat, he would be virtually impossible to resist. She doesn't know how long she can do it, sit there holding her breath.

He touches the collar of her coat with two fingers, fingering the top pearled button as her heart hammers beneath the soft wool.

"Angelfied," he whispers. "Stop shaking. I'm not gonna hurt you."

"Can I get that in writing?"

He laughs. "So what's up? You got something against black?" he asks softly, touching her collar again, his finger gently probing. She doesn't answer because she can't just then, sits still as a stone as waves of thought wash over her.

The thoughts, she suddenly realizes, are emanating from him. Those are not her wishes. She does not really need to feel his hands on her body. She doesn't really want to kiss him again, although his full lips under the perfectly shaped moustache do look succulent.

She crosses her legs, clasps her hands. She can barely contain herself and she knows he has brought with him these sharp currents of evil. She remembers what Trev said, that he can make people do things with his mind.

"Lincoln," she stammers. "I… I appreciate this opportunity," she manages finally, sounding like an election candidate, and he nods, clicks the CD changer. Babyface croons softly as the car moves in a smooth circuit toward the wards.

He faces her again, his eyes dark, a smoldering fire.

"What you see tonight? What you hear? It's a privilege I wouldn't trust to anyone else."

"I understand."

"Don't disappoint me."

She blinks, wonders what the price is for this prized knowledge.

"It won't be good for you if you do. You understand?"

"I understand." What else can she say?

He reaches into his side coat pocket, pulls out a pistol so small and dainty it doesn't look real. He gestures for her to take it and when she refuses, he thrusts it into her hands anyway.

"Hold it."

"I can't... I don't..."

"Look. It's a requirement if you gonna roll with me. You may need it. Especially on a night like this."

He turns away, facing the street again, and the issue is closed.

She watches his face. The sculpted profile stony and hard, like an Arabian mask carved from flawless mahogany, the three-carat diamond ear stud easily worth $10,000. His wasn't the face of a murderer. A prince maybe, a model, easily, but certainly not the countenance of a man who had spent the majority of his life in and out of reform schools and prisons.

"I'll do my best," she manages finally, hearing her words spoken outside of herself, and he nods, sits back and folds his hands, satisfied.

She lays the pistol across her lap, pulls the small pad and pencil from her coat pocket, but he shakes his head. "What you can't remember from memory, you don't print. Understand?"

"I understand."

"Aiight." He looks ahead at the dark space opening up on both sides of the narrowing street, opens his hands as if to measure it all. "Then welcome to *my* world, Babygirl. "

COSMOS

Gabriella

Trev would disown me if he saw me now—in the devil's backseat with him doing the driving and there's no telling where I'll end up. I shouldn't be here but it's too late for all that now, so I focus my eyes and stare out into the blackness, realizing I forgot to bring my cell phone. But who would I call if I needed to be rescued? Certainly not Trev, although nobody but a praying cop would even attempt to rescue me. If I prayed right now, would God hear me? Should He hear me? I wouldn't if I were God.

It's two hours to daybreak and the Third Ward is jumping off like a Saturday night in July instead of a Friday morning during the worst snowstorm of the year. So many folks coming and going it's like a pulsing beehive, a city inside of a city inside of a city.

"Like something straight out of New Jack City," I whisper and Lincoln, stroking his goatee, laughs at my naiveté. "This ain't exactly Hollywood," he assures me.

The huge Lincoln gleams like a chariot, cutting through the veil of snow as it turns a wide arc into the Third Ward and enters a world that's never seen before daylight. Everywhere there's noise, drama and people. Couples tangled against buildings and in doorways. Cabs double-parked in front of after-hours joints. The doors of pool halls and burger joints are flung open, pouring funk music into the street against the cascade of falling snow. On every corner, young men flanked by "chickenheads" in scant clothing, are perched like soldiers, their eyes watching the sliding cars that might pause at any moment to roll down their windows, signaling with the traditional ward sign of thumb and pinky extended, as if the purchaser is making a phone call.

Now the black Lincoln moves into their line of vision, and they freeze, halting whatever they'd been into. Linc taps the headrest of the driver sitting in front, and the Lincoln pulls up to the curb. The car docks just as a young girl wearing old men's sneakers and an ankle-length sweater rushes toward it. With her dark mascara and mocha lipstick, she looks all of eighteen, although in reality she can't be any more than twelve, thirteen at the most, Lincoln says.

Now she grinds her hips seductively. Strips off her sweater as she screams for Lincoln, flicking her tongue like a serpent, like a promise, toward the back seat and his head that's purposely turned away from the spectacle she's making of herself. Snow's swirling like confetti from the sky, but she's totally naked under the thin sweater, her breasts like dried figs, the rest of her amber body so gaunt with hunger, her hip bones protrude like dresser knobs. She almost reaches the car. Pummels the air like a mad woman striking away at nothing before one of the corner dealers snatches her backward by those long braids. Grabs a handful of the hair that looks like vines and slams her face down in the street.

I wince. Know that must've hurt. Half of her is covered with snow, but she seems oblivious to the cold. A second dealer kicks her away from the car with his heavy boots like she's a dog that's disobeyed her master. She's flicking her tongue at him too now like she doesn't feel a thing, and Lincoln yawns impatiently, looks at his watch. "Just the usual quitting-time drama," he explains nonchalantly when he sees the shock registered on my face.

One by one, the dealers leave their corners and come to clock out, each waiting until the other is done before approaching the Lincoln with the stealth of a cat. A few look well over thirty, but most are in their mid to late twenties. Cocky brothas dressed for the cold in dark knit hats and colorful ski gear. They say things like, "S'up, Baby? You know I handled it," or "Another day, another dollar."

Their eyes scan the back seat, acknowledging Linc, and scoping me like I'm just another piece of his harem. "They think you fine," Linc tells me, obviously amused, but I don't laugh at that. *What if one of these men came into Zion Apostolic on a Sunday morning and saw me singing with the choir? What explanation could I give then? And what if Trev, who knew every dealer in each of the three wards, found out? He'd report me to Pastor, declare I'd lost my mind for real.*

They're talking in typical Third Ward patois—guttural language peppered with hardcore slang, choice expletives and words of trade. *Icing. Jimmies. Spooling. Kicking the Noddies.* Beneath all of that is the usual small talk about cold weather and hot police. The latest Jay-Z joint. The chicken-head who's been trying to "game-'em" all night.

Driver takes a notebook from his breast pocket and makes checks next to each name as each man steps up, counts wads of bundled cash from his pockets into the gym bag that Dante holds open on his lap. The bundles are anywhere from one to four inches thick and bound with rubber bands. The sums for a day's work, anywhere from $4,000 to $13,000, stings my ears. It's hard to believe there's that much loose cash in the wards. When I ask Lincoln how that was possible, he takes awhile before he answers. "Somebody ain't paying their rent or furniture bill this month. Some BeBe kid won't be getting that new coat," he admits.

"And that doesn't bother you?"

He gives me a look as if I've just insulted him. "Why should it? That ain't my business."

There's a whole lot of money changing hands, and I can't help but notice that the dealers don't look too shabby themselves. According to Linc, they've got nice cars stashed somewhere close by until quitting time. Cars they've paid cash for to dealerships that specialize in servicing "street clientele." Their hiphop clothes and camouflage hunting suits, the $300 hiking boots and herringbone chains, aren't cheap at all.

"They're definitely doing aiight for themselves," Linc tells me, lighting a cigarette, looking at me and putting it out again. "I only hire the best of the best, and I treat 'em right. Keep 'em safe. In return, these brothas do some *serious* clocking. Got sistas out here too. It's called supply and demand."

"Women dealers, Lincoln?"

"Why not? They just as hard as the brothas. Some harder. Shoot you in a heartbeat. They like nice cars and fancy hairdos. Custom jewelry. Cell phones. You should see their cribs... Like something out of House and Ghetto." He looks at his watch again, shakes his head.

The tally-up is late again tonight, he explains. Earlier trouble with Vice the week before meant everybody had to lay low, wait past 2:00 a.m. to tally, when Vice finally pulled back. He signals at a burly woman crossing the street wearing pink curlers and a bathrobe under her winter coat. She's crossing the intersection near the package store, heading straight for the Lincoln, but the dealers leave their posts and alight on her with the swiftness of buzzards. They form an impenetrable wall around her, hands in their coats, eyes daring her, but the woman sees only the black car that's idling near the curb.

Linc nods. "She's aiight," he says, and Driver flashes his headlights, puts up his hand. The wall opens; the dealers part to let her through. The woman rushes directly to Linc, and he takes his time rolling down the window. "What can I do for you, Miz Johnson?"

"Mr. Lincoln..." She eyes me curiously, blinks, then finally averts her gaze back to Lincoln.

"I'm listening, Miz Johnson."

Her face is wet from snow or tears, it's hard to tell. She goes on and on about her oldest boy who just moved back home with her. Somebody named Q-Pete, who stole her toaster yesterday morning and took her sixteenth check out the mailbox before she could get downstairs to get it. She hadn't seen him since, and now, because she hadn't been able to make her payment arrangement, the gas company had shut off her heat. Her other kids had gone to bed hungry and one of her twins who had the "the sick-cell-disease" was bad-off sick again. Q-Pete hasn't been right since he got out of jail that first time, and now that he'd stolen her check, she wasn't sure what he…

She hasn't finished the story before Lincoln sighs, looks up in the rearview at his driver and flashes ten fingers two times. Dante checks one of the bundles and peels off twenty-hundreds. He passes it to Driver who passes it out the window to Q-Pete's momma. She bursts into tears and Lincoln frowns. She's crossing her bosom and blowing kisses but Linc shoos her away with his hand, looks away as she crosses the street again, disappearing between the tenements.

"That was kind, what you just did," I say, but he shrugs it off.

"They swear I'm the Welfare Commissioner."

The last of the men register their payments while Lincoln listens intently, watching the exchange of money the way a hunter eyes prey.

"Q-Pete," he says finally, when the last tally-up has walked off. "How much he owe?"

"Six hundred dollars," says Dante.

"Where's that Nigga?"

Driver calls out the window, asking the men if they've seen him, but they all shrug, anxious to get out of the cold, glad to have survived yet another night on the street. Nobody has seen Q-Pete.

"Check the East Side," Lincoln instructs and the Lincoln obeys, pulls away from the curb, turns the corner and runs smack into a beanpole of a man standing with two other men that look like sprung scarecrows.

"Mmph," Linc says. "Ain't *this* nothing."

Q-Pete's wearing a New York Yankees jacket and puffing on a cigarette. He's holding what looks like his momma's toaster under his arm, looks harried in all this snow, like he needs to shave, like he hasn't slept or had a bath in days.

"Look at what this fool's got on, cold as it is," Dante observes, but Lincoln tilts his head back like he's exasperated. Q-Pete looks up and sees us at last, looks as if he's deciding whether or not to run.

Lincoln yawns. "Shoot him," he orders matter-of-factly, as if he's asking for the time.

I look hard at him to see if he's joking, but he's staring straight ahead, as sober as a judge. Driver doesn't bother to get out. Just pulls alongside the men, rolls down the window and fires three shots from a silver handgun. The other two men scatter like roaches, but Q-Pete spurts blood from his mouth, drops the cigarette and topples backward against trash cans. The toaster clatters to the ground and breaks apart in the street. Red fingers of blood leak from the sidewalk to the curb. Dante and Driver look at each other, break out into guffaws and slap high-fives. Lincoln rolls down the window, hawks and spits far enough to hit his target.

Before I can process any of it, the Lincoln rolls up the street and out of the ward just like that.

"You ever seen a gangster's crib?" Lincoln asks as he hits the CD changer, switches to a track by Maxwell. I'm shivering uncontrollably now, but Lincoln laughs softly, slips an arm gently across the back of the seat, humming along with the song.

CHAPTER FOURTEEN

With all he was dealing with now, he'd had nothing else to lose. It was either now or later. Either he loved and wanted her or he didn't. Either he'd make her his wife or wait until someone else came into the church and snatched her up right before his eyes. He could only pray that he wasn't merely acting out of duress. Hoped that after he married her, he could make her as happy as she deserved to be. Whether or not he was really in love with her was not the real issue, he believed. He *did* love her, he knew. He just wasn't sure how much.

The fact that there were no real secrets between them anymore had a lot to do with it. He'd already tasted of her delicacies, back when he was a much weaker man, and knew that what he would be getting was better than good. That in itself was as perfect an incentive as any to go ahead with the marriage. Sure, it had been wrong of them to *go there* then but they'd learned from it and moved on from that. Now though, the mystery was over. He knew she had what it took to please him well, at least in *that* area, so what was he waiting for?

Even after that though, he had wasted so many years making excuses and seeing other women and changing the subject when she'd brought it up, and blaming her for all the failings in their relationship. He'd been imma-ture then. Arrogant. Afraid of the possibility that somewhere, there could be someone else still waiting in the wings for him, and that Gabriella was merely causing him to miss the opportunity to find her. The thrill of the chase had always been so important to his hunt for a wife and by sleeping with him before they'd married, it seemed that Gabriella had robbed him of that pleasure, killed the mystery of what she possessed at the very core of her womanhood. He'd never admitted it to her, but deep down, in the very recesses of his soul, he knew he wanted a wife who would never make the mistake of sleeping with him before marriage.

It was for that reason that he did call and date other sisters on the sly back then. Sanctified sisters who were all beautiful and smart and gifted and eligible. Women who could sing or cook or preach or teach at levels that seemed unearthly at times. But there had been no one anywhere who had been able to take Gabriella's place in his heart, and now he needed her in a way that he needed no one else. If anyone would stand in his corner with the entire world warring against him, it would be her. He was sure of it.

So he went to Beckworth's Jewelers, and without giving himself a chance to talk himself out of it, he'd bought the kind of stone she'd always wanted. A two-carat Marquis, as bright and clear as water.

She'd called to see how he'd fared after the press conference and he knew then, what he needed to do. He'd hung up and pulled himself together and went out and bought the ring. He'd gone to her place about 8, but she wasn't there, and when he made it back home, planning to call again and ask to see her, he fell asleep in his favorite place, on the couch. This morning though, he'd called her about 7, and she still hadn't answered. Now it was close to 1 p.m., and she still wasn't answering her phone.

His own phone was ringing, but when he picked it up, it was only his mother, obviously very distraught, at the other end.

"Trevie? Boy, get up. Don't sleep your life away, Sugar. Your cousin Petey done got himself shot up again, and poor Gertie's up at Heartford General, coming apart at the seams."

Aunt Gertie was easily his mother's favorite sister. The youngest girl in a family of fifteen siblings, Gertie always had the most troubles, beginning with her succession of deadbeat husbands and ending with her trifling oldest son, who now lay panting under white sheets, at the end of a hospital respirator.

His mother had blown on her hot tea, making her request as simple as possible: "Would you *please* get yourself up to that intensive care ward and see about making some negotiations with The Man Upstairs?

"And bring that Lil Bunny-Gurl with you. Everybody knows she can pray back the dead, and from what I heard about Petey this morning, she need to do it right away. According to Gertie, the boy's got one foot in the grave and the other on a banana peel."

"Aiight, Ma. I'm going. But I can't find Bunny."

"You can't *find her?*"

"She ain't answering her phone."

"In all this snow?"

"That's what I'm saying…"

"You call her at work?"

"She's not picking up there either. Her voicemail keeps coming on."

"Well now." He hears the way she catches her breath while considering the matter, bites her tongue to keep from saying the wrong thing. What she'll come up with won't be much better, but he waits for it anyhow.

"Truth be told, I guess if I wasn't your momma I wouldn't be standing too close to you either, all them bullets been following you lately…"

"I'll explain it all later, Ma."

"Mmm-hmm. That's what y'all always say. Nineteen and seventy-four your daddy goes and gets himself killed over soupbones and leaves me to deal with all of this mess alone."

"It's not that bad, Ma. Really. And please stop watching the news. Can't you knit a quilt or something?"

"Least the news lets me know what's going on. My own children don't tell me nothing…"

"Things aren't always the way they seem. Sometimes you just *look* wrong. It doesn't mean you are."

"And a speckled leopard just *looks like* a speckled leopard, don't he?"

"Thanks for the vote of confidence."

"Just get up to see your cousin before the undertaker beats you to it. I got one black dress and I sure ain't up to trudging through the snow to take it to the cleaners."

"I love you too, Ma."

"Bye, Baby. Remember. The sixth floor, ICU, and don't forget to bring flowers. You know how Gertie is."

✝✝✝

His mind is so much on the ring that's burning a hole in his pocket, and the woman he can't wait to give it to, that he forgets the flowers anyway. Pressing to the hospital in all this snow, after what he's been through this week, is sacrifice enough, especially since his aunt is allergic to flowers, and Petey never appreciates anything anyway.

If it wasn't for her, Petey would have been dead years ago, and even now, according to everyone but her, he still isn't worth a down payment on a ginger-snap cookie. At thirty-six, Petey's got nine children with six different mommas, and all of them are huddled around the sixth-floor waiting room. Trev pushes through the plastic chairs filled with bodies that are holding babies and reading magazines. Bodies that reek of everything from fried fish to Lanola Hair Cream, and finds his Aunt Gertie inside the specially equipped hospital room, touching her boy's toes at the foot of his bed.

"It don't look good, Trevie..." Aunt Gertie breaks down the minute she sees him. Points to Q-Pete's ashen face. "Why they have to shoot him down like this? Why they wanna kill *my* child?"

Trev looks hard at his battered cousin, shudders at all the blue that's seeping under his amber skin. "What a mess. It was bound to happen eventually, Auntie. I came as soon as I heard..." He's kissing her doughy cheek, wrapping his arms as far as they can reach around her wide waist, but Aunt Gertie is inconsolable. "I'll find out who did him, Auntie, and bring him in. You know I will."

"Why for? So he can shoot you too? You know that's what'll happen." She's pressing the rough paper towel against her red nose, dabbing at her eyes. "Everybody knows who did it, but bringing him in be another story altogether.

"Everybody knows my boy owed him money. And Petey ain't got the

sense God give a pickle no how. He knew Lincoln was crazy when he started running for him. What he think was gonna happen when he spent the
man's money?"

"Duvall *again*? *That's* who Petey was 'slinging' for?"

"Why he didn't just tell me though? That's what I can't understand... I'da
done my best to help him get up the money. I always have."

"Yes, Ma'am."

"Had it right in my hand, Trevie."

"Yes'm."

"I goes to find Lincoln myself that night. Tell him how Petey's been stealing out my house again. The boy puts two thousand dollars in my hand. *Two
thousand dollars*, then turns the corner and guns down my baby like he on
some kinda wild-life safari. Blood-money is what he give me, and he think
that's worth my boy's life?"

"No, Ma'am."

"I'ma give it back to him too. Let him know he can't buy everybody."

"Yes'm."

"And if my child dies? So help me I'ma see to it they put his behind *under*
the jail. So you tell Bunny for me, she better watch her back too. 'Cause
when the hatchet falls on that boy's peasy head, they *all* going down."

"*Bunny?*"

"That cute lil' thang you been toting on your arm for the past two years?
Don't weigh but a one-hundred-ten pounds and most of that's hair."

"Yes, Ma'am, but..."

"Bunny. The one whose daddy left her momma with all them girls? Got
them dimples like they cut into her face? Bunny. Ain't that what your momma
and them calls her?"

"Yes, Ma'am, but..."

"Saw her plain as day, Trevie, I'm trying to tell you. She with Lincoln last
night in the back of that boy's car when I comes to him."

"Nawl..You sure, Aunt Gertie?"

"Sitting up in that car just as brazen as a heifer. And I always thought she
was a do-right gurl. Much as she in and out that church."

"Yes, Ma'am."

"You gonna pray for your cousin right now, or do I need to raise up Reverend Ike?"

"Yes, Ma'am... Right now, Auntie."

He doesn't know how he manages to get through the prayer, but when he's done, he can't stay there any longer. His aunt's still crying, pulling those old Polaroids out of her purse like he's gone already, kissing Q-Pete's indigo face, but he has to leave somehow. Promising to check back in a few hours, he staggers back into the blinding corridor light and makes it out to the street. Outside the hospital, a parking ban has cleared the street, and he's glad he'd had the presence of mind to call out for the day, to park in the high-rise garage across from the hospital.

He starts the car and reaches for his cell phone, shivering in the growing twilight as the snow continues to drop by the handfuls. Gabriella's still not answering. He'll just have to drive through the snow to her condo and wait for her there. She'll probably just be getting in from work. He'll grab her and hug her and tell her how much he's missed her, and afterward, over coffee at her kitchen table, she'll explain it all clearly for him. Explain that Gertie's mistaken, that it wasn't her at all but someone who looked like her, in Lincoln's car, because she's had nothing to do with that devil since their talk about him.

Pulling out of the parking garage onto the main drag that's almost deserted now, he reaches into his coat and opens the small velvet box. The ring blazes like an ember, each facet a distinct spitfire, and he can't wait to pop the question, knows exactly what her answer will be.

Lincoln

They were always like that, females. Had so much mouth in public, but when they got with me alone, one-on-one behind closed doors, there wasn't a thing they could say. She's like that now. Quiet as a mouse as she snaps open her eyes and fights to wake herself up. Course I can't help smiling, rubbing it in, 'cause she hadn't realized she'd fallen asleep right on my shoulder, right in my arms, and now that she's waking up and seeing where she is, in the back of the Lincoln with *me*, of all people, I can see she ain't too happy about it.

Sun wants to break through the blanket of white that's been draped over the sky like a crime-scene tarp for hours now, but it just don't know how to. Snow's still falling hard, and it don't take a meteorologist to see this is one of the biggest storms the state's seen in years. Plow trucks everywhere. Schools and state agencies closed for the day. Vehicles breaking down or stalled all along the roads on the way up here and state troopers whizzing past, en route to some accident from some fool driving too fast. But Ghost can handle it easy. His daddy has folks from New Hampshire, so he grew up hanging out at lodges, trading skis like dime bags, and he's always joking that the only reason he loves 'cain' so much is 'cause there really is snow in his veins.

So he takes his time to get us there. Enjoys every bit of the messiness and sliding. Almost four inches on the ground now and there's no telling when it'll end, so it makes no sense for him to rush through it. Dante takes a call in the front seat and it's about the rats. Although a few did make it to Trece, the caller says, the snow's killing 'em all off, and there's hundreds of dead ones, frozen stiff in piles everywhere.

I can feel my body shutting down like the state of Connecticut in all this snow, craving rest. And I plan to climb into my king-sized bed just as soon as I can. *'Specially* now that I'ma have her next to me to keep warm. Chinere's called twice already but I ain't answering the page 'til I'm good and ready. She's still acting strange, trying to make me feel shamed about hitting her. Trying to get me to validate my feelings, is all she wants, but the girl's going too far lately, and I'ma have to deal with that soon enough. Show her what I always told her: "A brotha like me can't afford to love nobody."

"Where am I?"

Man, she fine. Looking up at me with those scared, pretty eyes like she swears I've kidnapped her. Holding her ransom or something.

"Windshire, Connecticut, Babygirl. Thirty-two miles away from Heart-ford," I say.

She sits forward like she can't believe it, touching her bare head because her hat's no longer there. Yeah, I took it off so I could play in all that hair while she slept, and it's like she suddenly feels naked without it. I couldn't help myself though. Got to touching it and next thing I'm twirling them curls like I bought and paid for 'em. Hair so soft and sweet-smelling and shiny, I'm wrapping it around and around my fist like I used to do Momma's. If I had one of those looms, I could make me a sweater. Have her cut it all off and be wearing a part of her when I'm cruising Da Block, shaking down niggaz.

Ghost ain't saying a word. Just drives in all this snow with his mouth hanging open like he's in a trance or something. To each his own, that's how he sees it. He knows I got enough women for every day of the month, so he probably thinks this just another flavor I'm itching to try. Caramel-strawberry or something. Ghost doesn't think one woman is any different from any other. Can't believe there can be one that affects you in a way that no one else has. But Dante's been married before and he knows otherwise. Keeps looking back at me like he don't blame me at all. Like he'd be playing in that hair too, if he were me, only maybe doing a lot more. Dante would've had her clothes off by now and be into some serious rhythm; only something about this woman's so different from all the others that a man has to be different in the way he approaches her. A slow mover, that's the way she is, the way she needs me to be.

My crib's an hour and a half from the wards, all back roads and pastures mostly. Only a few of my men know the way and that's how I likes it, because busters start tripping when they see you living too good and will do anything to mess that up. Connecticut's valleys so beautiful they look like something out of a Monet painting. Yeah. I read about him too. Monet. Chagall. Picasso. See those reprints every time I walk into those downtown banks to make my deposits. Got those big banana plants and those Monet or Rockwell reprints next to some water cooler, and it always makes me think about how folk ain't dying over money in those little all-American towns. Everything's lush and green and abundant in those portraits. Nothing like the ward's bullet-colored streets and dirty black snow and pissy hallways with some bum lounging in the corners. The kind of place you never wanna come home to. Rather stay in a detention farm up on some high purple hill than to come home to that prison ward they let you out of only to go to school. And then you'd better hurry back home, or they send police cruisers to follow you. Ward schools ain't designed to make no difference anyhow, 'cause they never showed you how to get out of there. Just how to come back and pretend you can read and hang out on some corner until you figure out how to rob and scheme and beat some fool out their little money.

Neither Momma nor Runt ever understood why I was always trying to get sent away from there. Momma just kept taking us to her preacher and telling him to dribble holy oil on our heads, but it never did much good.

"Your boys got more than a few ornery devils in them, Sister Duvall," he'd tell momma, but he never asked us where they all came from. Nobody but Runt and me knew it all started that day we found that old game buried in the dump down by the river.

Still, Momma tried her best. In the summers, while she was uptown cleaning houses and we were much too little to stay in the wards all day by ourselves, because she was afraid the welfare folks might come by snooping, or worse yet, they'd have let Daddy out early for good behavior or something, she'd send Runt and me to the library downtown for hours at a time, trying to make us read about some other family, about some other white world we'd never fit in. Both Runt and me did turn out to be very good readers, but Momma's ideas about us having a grand future, never turned out like she planned. Not when we had to come home to a fleet of cruisers parked in front of our building, and ambulances pulled up on the balding grass, cuz niggaz got ornery in the summer when they was hot and broke and got to slicing each other like Christmas hams.

Momma never understood that I'd rather be sent away to Juve than to stay there, that all those places, in addition to the steel doors, had plenty of what I could never get enough of; trees and books and plenty of green grass. Trees and green-green grass and a hard kinda quiet like there was down inside Trece's river bottom. The Chesterfield Reformatory, The Mason Douglas Detention Center, The Heartford Youth Institute for the Criminally Insane, they was all like second homes to me, like vacation spas, like summer resorts. I did long bids at all of 'em. Got to know 'em so well, brothas came to ask *me* what was on the menu each day; Mondays meant succotash and mashed potatoes at Mason Douglas. Chesterfield served footlong chicken dogs with those lil puffed potatoes that always tasted freezer burned. On every third Friday, Heartford Youth always gave us fruit cups, and on Sunday afternoons, we had my favorite, gingerbread cake with whipped cream. Although nobody's gingerbread ever tasted as good as Momma's.

"Home is where the heart is." I would use her own words, when she'd insisted on knowing why I could never stay out of trouble long enough to be home for the holidays at least...

"Home is where the heart is," she'd always tell Runt and me all those times we'd be running down to the river to hide or packing up to move from one apartment to the other, 'cause the man who she said was our daddy was always tripping hard. But this girl sitting beside me with her long dress and puppy-dog eyes wouldn't know a thing about any of that, about what it feels like to be chased and hunted like some kinda butterfly specimen somebody wants to keep in a glass jar. Closest she's ever probably come to knowing a criminal of my status was watching a rerun of *America's Most Wanted*. But maybe that's what intrigues me most about her and all the others. Maybe it's their innocence that seems so impossible to corrupt. Maybe it's that homemade wholesomeness that I keep trying to own for myself. Funny thing is, robbing them of their innocence never makes me feel any purer.

It's actually this long ride that I love most about getting to my crib. All these beautiful fields and meadows and trees gone skeletal now because the wind has snatched off leaves from branches and thrown them to the ground. At night, these sloping hills and churning roads always remind me of a spiraling staircase reaching up to the stars. And I like that, like to think I'm sitting just as high as the One they say made all of this. Me? I ain't convinced. I ain't never seen no proof of anybody bigger than myself, and until I do, I ain't believing in nobody but me. Life is what *I* made it, and that's the way it's always been.

We've been driving and driving and she didn't enjoy none of it, 'cause all she could do was sleep. "We almost home," I say as she sits up suddenly and looks around, pats her messy hair like she's embarrassed, tugs at her clothes.

"Home?" She squints, looks hard through the cloudy window glass. "I don't live anywhere near here. Oh my goodness... Where am I?"

"Home is where the heart is, Babygirl."

"The heart?" She shakes her head like she can't believe any of this and reaches for her purse, pulling out a mirror. She frowns into it, applies chapstick to her lips and reaches deeper into her bag for a piece of Big Red, offering me one.

"You acting like you expecting to get kissed," I say as she eases back into the seat with her hair all ruffled, watching my face like she's afraid I'll bite her.

"Am I being kidnapped?"

"Do you feel like a hostage?"

"Not really."

"Why you tripping on me then?" I touch her face and she lowers her eyes, startled, like she never expected I could go there. Be that gentle when I wanted to be.

"I didn't mean to insult you," she says, straightening her shoulders and sitting forward, away from me, trying to be a professional and see out the snow-covered windows. "What time is it? Oh my goodness. Work. I have to call my job. Trev. He'll be worried."

"You said you wanted my story."

"I do."

"I'm giving it to you."

She sighs, cups a hand over her eyes like she can't believe any of it. "Was I dreaming last night, or did y'all shoot a man?"

Ghost catches my eyes in the rearview mirror and I look at her, wink, press a finger to my lips.

"Another rule of The Street?" she asks.

I nod. "*Never* talk about what you *think* you've seen."

She's speechless as Ghost pulls up to my gate and punches in the alarm security code. The gates pull apart and swing out to let us through. They close again behind us as Babygirl just sits there, stunned.

"What's wrong?"

"Do you actually own all of this, Lincoln?"

"Is that so hard to believe?"

"Yes."

"Why?"

"You don't have a job…"

"If anybody asks, I just tell 'em I'm an investor. I 'specialize in commodities.'"

"What kind?"

"Stocks. Bonds. You name it. I got shares in internet companies and coffee house franchises. Nike. FUBU. Even breakfast cereal. I own a lil' of everything."

"A drug dealer who invests in the stock market." She shakes her head.

"I'd invest in a meatball if I thought I could make some money."

"I believe you."

"White boys do it all the time. Just ask Ghost."

"Ghost?"

"My man that's up front playing chauffeur. Boy's a genius when it comes to commodities. Among other things. His pops, his grandpops before him, always gambled big in the market, so of course he's taught me everything he knows. And since I just happen to have good instincts, I just keep on making money."

"You trying to convince me you bought all this with legal cash?"

"I've got the papers to prove it."

Ghost pulls into the gate and heads down the long lane that's already been plowed. The landscapers know to come automatically during a storm, so the circular driveway is cleared too, although new snow is still falling.

She's shocked. I can tell. Twisting around in her seat to see out the window, see all my land, my trees, like some kind of Ponderosa ranch. Ain't much to see though since the grounds are covered over with white, but Angelfied is still shaking her head.

"You aiight?" I ask her.

"My gosh, Lincoln. How much land is this?"

"Just fifteen acres."

"*Just* fifteen?"

Ghost pulls under the carport, grinning, and I get out and go around to open the door for her. I take her hand and don't let it go and she isn't comfortable with that, but understands when she sees my dogs come running at us from every direction.

Most folk keep one or two guard dogs, but I keep seven, well-trained Rottweilers up in front of the property, letting them patrol things. Each of them easily weighs over 160 pounds, and I gave three of 'em names to represent different parts of the wards that I'm fighting hard to control. My favorite dog is named Trece, of course. Out back there's the kennel with twenty more dogs, puppies mostly, that I'm breeding and training. Just another hustle I have that keeps my mind off of business when it needs to be.

Breeding dogs ain't a whole lot different than breeding men, Runt used to say when his mind was still good, except that dogs seem to have a lot more sense.

Now the four youngest pups, "Fee," "Fi," "Fo," and "Fum," are more than happy to see me. They run up, licking my hands but hang back from her like they supposed to, sniffing the air, feeling her out. She holds onto my arm like she's gonna pull it off, don't know what to expect from the dogs, and I go to teasing her. "See," I say. "You ain't so tough now, huhn?"

The closer we get to the front door though I can tell that she doesn't know which is worse, staying outside with the dogs or going inside with me.

"Who has the worst bite? You or them?" she asks me, standing outside the threshold, like she's afraid to go in.

"Only one way to find out," I tell her.

"What's that supposed to mean?"

"Just another level of this interview, that's all, right?"

"Right."

"Aiight then. C'mon in."

Inside the house, she zips down her boots first thing and leaves them near the door. Ghost and Dante take the car to the garages around back and we won't see them until I call for them. I've got the soundproofed guest house out back where they'll eat and crash until I call for 'em, so there's nobody here to distract us. Just the way I like it. By the time I get finished rocking what's under that beige dress, she'll be glad there are no witnesses.

She steps through the wide foyer, climbs three steps and wades into the first living room in her stocking feet, touching stuff.

"*Oh my.*"

"What?"

"Your home. It's… exquisite."

"Thank you."

"You didn't decorate all this yourself, I know?"

"Who else?"

"Chinere?"

"Nawl. That ain't her thing. Who do you think hooked up her shop?"

"*You?*"

"I took all kinds of correspondence courses when I was incarcerated. Got a couple certificates in interior and exterior design. I hired a professional though, to help me with all of this. Me and her together, we got it all hooked up. She did all the shopping; I just showed her what I wanted."

Angelfied looks over her shoulder at me, giving me that look, making me feel funny again. "Where'd you ever find purple leather?" she asks, looking at my careful arrangement of leather furniture, chrome tables and black art, all done up in a black and purple color scheme. Black and purple because it reminds me of my momma and, well, speaking of Momma…

"And who is *this* pretty lady? She looks so familiar to me."

Before I can respond to her first question, Angelfied's moved on to the next picture, is standing there holding the silver frame with both hands, seeing the ruffled collar and pretty face bare of artificial color. Hair's spilling out under that lacy veil of church hat that's draped over Momma's left eye, 'cause there always had to be some way to hide the bruises.

"Must be your momma. "

"How can you tell?"

"The smile. You have that same beautiful smile."

"Beautiful?"

"Yes."

"Nobody's ever told me that before. Nobody's ever said that anything about me was beautiful. But thank you. Yeah. That's Momma. Just before..." She notices that I don't finish my words, just takes the frame and sets it gently back in place where she found it.

"She's very lovely, Lincoln."

"Yeah."

"Looks very young too."

"She is... She was..." Her gaze slides toward and then away from me, as if she's changed her mind about something.

"She looks sanctified. No makeup. No jewelry."

"If that's what y'all call it."

She does something with her eyebrows. It's that same look she had at the salon when I couldn't stop coughing. She's waiting for an answer, and I guess now is as good a time as any to tell her all of what happened that day. But I don't want to. I don't like the way she keeps making me feel.

"Moms was just thirty-one in that picture. My brother, Runt, took that just before she died."

"She died? I'm sorry to hear that, Lincoln. *Really*. How old were you?"

"Sixteen. I was doing my first hard bid when it happened."

"Wow. I'm sorry."

"Me too."

She looks away from me, but I can tell she's calculating the numbers. Seeing that Momma was just fifteen when she had me. But I don't say anything else. Just head to the bar and pour myself some wine as she moves away, her fingers moving gently over sculptures, her eyes lingering on the large, elaborately framed Jacob Lawrences.

"Lawrence, huhn? These must've cost a fortune."

"Yeah. Worthy investments though. I love me some Lawrence. Brotha was tight. His work? Those smooth, curving lines...? They always seemed so... street, kinda. Urban. Like he'd a been the baddest subway graffiti artist in New York if he was out there on skid row or something. "

"Urban?"

"Yeah. His style's kinda funky to me."

"Funky?"

"Yeah. Like a man who don't care about nothing but his art. That's the city, ain't it? Tough and selfish?"

She smiles, moves away, looks inside the glass curio that I light up for her. She peers at my Tiffany crystal, my Mikao and Steuben figurines.

"Hmm…"

"Hmm? What's all that about?"

"I guess I'm impressed. That *does* happen every once in awhile, you know."

"See."

"See what?"

"I knew you would be. That's 'cause you swear everybody in the wards is ignorant and shiftless. Told you this ain't Hollywood. Everybody ain't shucking and tap dancing."

"I never said that."

"You didn't have to. Some of us can actually read and write, you know."

"You sure about that?" She was challenging me head up, one hand on her hip. I loved her sassiness. It turned something inside of me, made me want to cross the room right then and take myself a kiss.

"For your information, Miss Lady, there were some who actually thought I was college material. And I ain't talking about my 'balling' skills either. Don't have me testifying up in here, Babygirl. I'll take you to church, you ain't careful."

She's giggling, those dimples showing deep in her cheeks. "I'd *love* to see that."

She stops in front of an arrangement of flowers, touching the silk leaves, the carefully crafted petals.

"What's your favorite flower?" I ask, and she looks up, surprised. "Orchids," she says finally, looking away from me again, like she don't want me reading what's in her eyes.

"I figured that."

"Beg your pardon?"

"I just knew. Orchids. They exquisite and graceful. Rare. Costly too and real hard to get in these parts this time of year. Just like you, Babygirl."

She eyes me again like I just pinched her. "Are you trying to *get* me, Mr. Duvall?"

I sip, letting the question hang in the air. "Only if you want to get got."

She don't answer that. Just looks away quick again. "Look, do I get a house tour, or a lecture from Farmer's Almanac?"

"Whatever you want."

She's looking at a snapshot of me and Chinere posing in front of her old salon. Me standing there all hugged up on her, looking like a typical hustler; baseball cap turned backward, a baseball shirt opened to the navel to showcase my dukie medallion that's as big as a Spanish onion. I'm wearing Timbs with the laces untied, looking like an escapee from some Run DMC concert, and Chinere don't look much better.

"I see y'all been together a long time,"Angelfied offers, but I know not to step into that one. Me and Chinere ain't exactly "together," I'm thinking, but if you ask her, she'd come up with a different explanation altogether.

"You want a tour we can start with the kitchen," I say instead, 'cause I know she's got to be hungry as I am right about now, and my instincts tell me that Babygirl can cook.

A GANGSTER'S CRIB

He wants to see for himself if she can cook, and she knows it. Knows she's wrong for being there alone with him anyway in this immense house that looks like something out of *Lifestyles of the Rich and Notorious*. It's the kind of showplace Al Capone would've loved, a midnight-blue baby grand piano and enough rooms and luxury to please Donald Trump. Chandeliers in the foyers. Leather and crystal, chrome and silver, brass and jade and onyx. He has a thing for metals she sees, for varying textures in odd unconventional colors.

She notices fish tanks in every room, built into the walls like curios. In the living room, a tank the size of a small swimming pool is filled with baby sharks. His prize pets, he says, staring into the shimmering water, stroking the aqua-colored glass. Feeding them costs a small fortune, he admits, and she marvels how he can be so tender with fish and so harsh with humans.

The tour of the house, with him demonstrating, takes all of fifteen minutes, and she has yet to see the basement.

"I need to stop and call my job," she explains, still wearing her coat like she's afraid he'll try to rape her. "I need to call out. Say something."

It's an admission that she plans to stay there with him awhile, and he nods, giving her a look and pointing to a 1930s drug-store wall phone with a receiver that must be talked into like a microphone. He smirks while she fiddles with the knobs and dials senselessly, gives up finally and reaches for his cordless instead, her hands trembling.

At *The Chronicle*, Trish's voice sounds odd. Yes, she knows there's a blizzard outside, but there was also a shooting in the wards last night. Another dealer gunned down, it looked like. Or maybe even a gang banger. She's not sure if he's alive or dead, although at last count, news reports described him as being "critical." "Haven't you watched the news?" she quizzed, "Doesn't your cop boyfriend tell you anything?"

Gabriella can hear her nails tapping like nervous mice against her steel desk.

There aren't any gangs in the wards and there haven't been for years. She could tell her that if she wanted to be arrogant. Could explain that men like Lincoln were too selfish to allow their profits to be divided up amongst an entire gang. But she doesn't say a word. Feigns ignorance instead, pretends to be listening hard. Trish though, is relentless. Sure, it's snowing, but she doesn't want the trail to get too cold, does she? If the snow stopped and the roads cleared up, would Gabriella be coming in that evening at least? Gabriella says she doubts it and clicks off on Trish's whiney voice, thinking Zora was right. The black woman was the mule of the world and *The Chronicle* was determined to work her to the very bone.

She wants to call and check her own voice mail messages, but somehow can't bear to be reminded of what she has so irresponsibly left behind: God. Trev. God. Trev. God... God.... God...

Linc sits back on a leather divan, lights a cigar, takes a few hard drags, then puts it out. Drifts of cherrywood smoke hover, cloud-like over his head. Gabriella sighs, moves to the huge bow window that overlooks the back end of the property. Snow covers the gazebo and the wide, above-ground pool, the basketball court that's big enough to host a small tournament.

"Rest your coat?" he offers, and rises as she hands it over. He leaves the room with it and when he returns, she's pulled back the custom drapes to better enjoy the view. Thinks the whole thing is strangely surreal. Macabre. Him. Her. This house. His money. She wonders if murdered women have this same feeling before they are killed... Was this what it felt like? A cat and mouse game before the woman becomes his dinner?

He sees the way the dress hangs fluidly past her hips and wonders what she would look like in his Jacuzzi. He thinks of lighting the fireplace in his bedroom. "Brandy?" he asks, going behind the lacquer bar and uncorking a small decanter filled with a deep, salmon-colored liquid. He pours brandy into a goblet, raises it as if to toast her. Blows a kiss at her. A thug drinking apricot brandy. She shakes her head.

"I don't drink, Lincoln," she says, watching him sip.

"A Newport?"

"You know I don't smoke."

"Why not?"

"Because."

"Because what?" He stands behind the bar waiting, the goblet lifted to his mouth.

"Because I'm a good girl."

"You sure about that?"

"You don't believe me?"

He comes from behind the bar and perches on one of its three stools, draining the last of the brandy, seeing how easily she seems to fit into the quiet elegance of the room.

"Y'all religious girls all say the same things at first... Y'all must read from the same script."

"What are you trying to say, Lincoln?" She stops sifting through the dozens of jazz albums and CDs shelved near a state-of-the-art stereo system, and frowns at him defiantly, right hand hanging loosely near her hip.

"This *my* house, Baby. I ain't *trying* to say nuthin'."

"I guess what they say about you is correct as well."

"Which is?"

"That you like to hunt *easy* game. Like defenseless females and little boys trying to be juvenile delinquents. It stings and she knows it, but he smiles. She sees the muscle in his jaw twitch and lies still again.

"So you defenseless now? Or are you just determined to insult me."

"Neither."

"You don't like it when I deal with things on a theological level. Is that it?"

"Since when are you an expert on theology?"

"I'm not. I was just trying to determine *why* you kissed me that night."

"I don't remember it that way at all. In fact, I remember it being the other way around."

"How do you remember it?"

"I don't…," she said and going to the piano, drops the subject with a soft chord that makes them both chuckle.

"I see you have that disease most Christians are prone to."

"What disease?"

"Selective memory." He rises from the stool and drops down onto a loveseat, his eyes never leaving her.

She hits another chord hard, ventures a glance at him, and suddenly his smile is so pretty that she must look away from it. She shivers, goes to the window and watches a string of chipmunks scampering across the white lawn.

"Some might say your smile has a diabolical quality at times," she says without looking at him.

"Some might also say a *good* girl wouldn't be alone with me in this house."

She whirls around then, snatches up a pillow from the couch and without thinking, throws it at him playfully. He ducks, looks amused. "You one crazy chick, you know that?"

"Why should you get to be the only one to play crazy? That ain't fair." She throws another pillow at him, watches him duck.

"Look, Churchgirl. I'ma have to take you home; you bad for my rep *and* my ego."

"Hush, Lincoln. You ain't as bad as you think you are. You ain't as bad as me." She's giggling, throwing pillows.

"Aw, Man. Look at this… I gets no respect at all, huhn? Don't you know who I am? Don't you know I eat little girls like you for breakfast?"

She blushes, throws another pillow in response, and this time he ducks unsuccessfully as the pillow glances off his shoulder. He jumps to his feet, pretends to shadow-box her, then grabs her playfully around the waist. "Why you always challenging me? You're supposed to be scared. Don't you know that?" His face was close to hers, enough for her to read the softness that was beginning to seep into his eyes. He touched her chin, looked like he wanted to kiss her, but didn't.

"Turn me loose," she insists, her voice breaking. "I'm not scared of you."

"You should be." He is frowning. He kisses the tip of her nose on sheer impulse, releases her, watches as she backs away into a corner, arms wrapped around herself. She is shivering again.

He licks his lips, laughs, then goes back to the bar and pours more brandy. He sits down again on the loveseat, looking at the swirl of golden heat inside the glass, then back at her again.

With his jacket off, his arms look incredibly strong under the black cashmere turtleneck, she can't help notice. Why has she come here? It was all a bad mistake that was getting worse by the minute.

"Don't you think it's time we called a truce?" he asks, playing with the hairs under his chin.

"Who? You and me?"

"I don't see nobody else in here."

"A truce. Like a covenant sort of? An agreement?"

"Call it what you want."

She smoothes her bangs with the flat of her hand, shakes her head. "I don't make deals with the devil. Especially not on an empty stomach."

FOOD & FUN

The kitchen is a glare of wide open windows and sparkling chrome, new-age appliances, cabinet shelves stocked with everything from Spam to imported caviar.

He stands back to offer her free access, watching as she lets her fingertips dance across the bright cellophane encasing various kinds of crackers—Ritz and Triscuits, Cheese Nips and Saltines. Cans of minestrone soup, hearty chowders and gumbos, and beef stews in heavy glass jars afloat with carrots and potatoes are crowded among jars of vegetables and spices and bottled sauces, varieties of pickles, boxes and boxes of hot and cold cereals.

"This looks like the food pantry down at the county welfare," Gabriella observes. "Who are you expecting for dinner, Lincoln? The Third Ward basketball league?"

He cracks a grin. "Aiight. So you got jokes."

"How many kids do you have anyway?"

"Nawl. It ain't nothing like that. Better not be. Just the 'Hungry-Man's Syndrome,' I guess. Trauma resulting from all those years of never having what I wanted to eat."

"So now you're making up for it in a big way, huhn?" She tears open a paper cylinder of water crackers sprinkled with tiny sesame seeds, crunches down carefully, savoring the pungent garlic after-taste.

"Something like that."

The crackers are delicious, though dry, and as if reading her thoughts, he throws open his stainless steel refrigerator's double doors like a pair of French windows, rummages around on shelves and tosses several blocks of cheese on the counter. White, wine-soaked Colby. Extra-sharp cheddar layered with pimentos. A wheel of smoked muenster that's missing an entire wedge.

"Somebody likes cheese," Gabriella observes.

"Not really. It's just about being prepared for anything. Know what I'm saying?"

"That you're obsessively methodical?" She giggles, reaches for a hunk of cheese to hack off a neat slice.

"Speak English, Gurl." He eats a piece of her cheese, swallows a chunk without chewing.

"With you, everything has to be a science, that's all. Things have to always make sense."

"It's called life, Babygirl. See, the way I remember it, Momma was always having to turn off the stove in a hurry before she finished anything. She was always having to cut off everything and run for her life. You shoulda seen all those cakes and pies we had to leave half-baked in the oven. All that gingerbread that had to be thrown away... And those holiday dinners." He shakes his head, both palms flat on the marble counter. "All those Christmas hams and turkeys and chitlins gone to waste... So me and Runt? We got used to grabbing stuff we could eat on the run. A box of cereal. A handful of pickles."

"So that's why you're storing up everything you can?"

He shrugs. "Long as I don't eat it all myself though, right? Isn't that what's really important? To try to share what you have?"

"Is that what you do, Lincoln?"

"When the homies come over here with the munchies, yeah. Or if I see a kid hanging around the salon who looks like he hasn't had a meal since never, I just let 'em come in here and eat to their heart's content."

"It makes you feel good, huhn?"

"I don't feel nothing. I do it 'cause I'm supposed to. Because somebody should."

She positions herself on a leather stool in front of the gray laminated island in the middle of the kitchen, chews cheese, watching him.

"So..." he says finally, not trusting what he thinks her mind might be coming up with.

"So...," she says, cutting off another sliver of cheddar to share with him.

"You gonna cook us a real breakfast? Or am I expecting too much?" He stood with his back against the smooth-topped range, arms folded.

"Beg your pardon?"

"You know how y'all fine, educated sistas are... Got three degrees and can't find their way around a kitchen. Break a nail trying to open a box of grits. Need a manual to figure out how to turn on a stove."

"I ain't studying you, Boy."

He smiles teasingly as she waves a hand at him, gets up to inspect his top-of-the-line pot collection dangling from a ceiling rack. The Italian-tiled floor is slippery, cool to her stockinged feet.

"I brought one sista here who didn't even know how to turn on the oven.

Baby burned up a fifty-dollar roast. Can you imagine that? I mean a smooth-top ain't that hard to understand, Babygirl."

"And I suppose that's your idea of reverse psychology? Your ploy to get me to cook up some grand, Southern cuisine?"

"Did it work?"

She laughs, but reaches for the apron hanging near the sink. "Quit harassing me, Lincoln."

"I haven't done nothing to you. Yet." She meets his gaze as he licks his lips, lets his eyes travel the length of her. She snatches her eyes away quickly.

He's fighting to get the silly smile off his face and almost loses the battle. He can't help it. It does something to him, makes his insides turn over, to watch her feel her way around his kitchen. He pulls up a stool to see how easily she puts it all together, loves the sound of eggs being whisked, flour being beaten in a bowl, a woman's hands chopping stuff and mixing it all together, patting and forming homemade biscuits.

She looks up from the dough, hands white, offering her smile. "A penny for your thoughts," she tells him, when the silence lingers between them as heavy as a stone.

"A penny? That's all you offering? You know what's in my head is worth much more than that."

"What's in your head, Mr. Duvall?"

"You."

She lowers her eyes, turns toward the warming oven to begin the task of greasing a cookie sheet.

"You shouldn't ask questions you can't handle the answers to."

"I can handle anything I set my mind to."

"Is that right?"

"That's right."

A dab of flour spots her forehead. "Hold still," he says, getting up and taking her face into his hands. He wipes away the flour with a corner of a linen napkin, stands holding her face, drinking in the soft angles of her high cheekbones, moist pucker of her lips, flawless skin the color of raw honey. He's standing so close that she can hear his heartbeat. Or is it hers?

It's a dare, and she knows it. Who will move first? Who will turn away from the strain of emotions pulled taut as a rope?

If they stand this close a second longer, there will be no breakfast at all, so she steps back from him quickly, asks him to get a knife to slice the thickly slabbed bacon.

He's hesitating, floundering she can tell, as if he can't believe she'd had the power to turn away from the immense feeling of his passion. He regains his composure quickly, strokes his chin and tells her he hates butcher knives.

He slices the bacon anyway, makes neat, even cuts in the pink meat. She asks why he needs an aquarium in the kitchen anyhow, tells him funny jokes about those few times her daddy had taken her fishing. Talk turns to the memories of lost kinfolk and childhood promises. To her momma's kinfolk and her earliest memories of the saints over at Zion Apostolic.

Listening closely, he can hear what feels to him like loneliness hidden within the fabric of a carefully folded cloth. He's reminded of things he hasn't thought about in years; All those warm Sundays walking to morning services up on The Ave from the ward, with Runt on one end and their momma, holding both their hands, in the middle. He can still see that Sunday School class with the old heater and the squeaking chalkboard. The sloop of old widows' homemade hats upstairs in the sanctuary, and the wide, white-clad ushers standing guard against flies at the vestibule doors.

Somehow, she brings it all back.

He doesn't mean to crack a smile, but he can't help himself somehow. She can tell a story better than any *Def Comedy Jam* comic and is as funny as one of the homies on Da Block. She's got him using a butcher knife and wondering at his own blossoming strangeness, for he'd always thought himself incapable of those deep belly laughs that everybody else has always enjoyed without him.

Now he's laughing so hard at her in-house stories of what folks do around the altar when they're supposed to be praying, that his stomach hurts. He dabs the wetness from his eyes, spills his brandy, and she says, "good," and gives him a mug of hot cocoa instead.

"You a crazy, Gurl, you know that? How'd you get to be so funny?" he asks.

"How'd you become so easy to talk to?" she answers. "You're not the same Lincoln who was in the car last night."

Sitting on a stool near the warm oven, he looks up, her last comment feeling like a slap as he watches her spoon the skim off her cocoa. He shakes his head. "You just don't understand."

"What's to understand?"

"Me. I've done things. Things no normal man would ever wanna do." He looks down at the marble counter and swallows, tracing the swirling patterns of vein deep in the stone.

"Things like killing those other dealers?"

"Things like wanting to kill you."

"Except...?" She looks up at him, no trace of fear in her eyes.

"Except your God wouldn't let me."

There is no place else to go after such a statement but to laughter strong enough to release the tension. Nothing is making sense anymore.

"You like barbecue, Babygirl?" he changes up, watches the softness that envelopes her face, her hands, her pert breasts nestled in the empire-waisted dress. His mother had never approved of the girls he'd brought home; she complained about the way they dressed and talked. Their loudness and brash profanity. The way they clung to him in her kitchen with their sharp claws, navels exposed, breaths reeking of tobacco, of wine, even though they were barely eleven and twelve years old.

But she would've liked Angelfied right away, he knew. Would've asked about her momma. Her church. Her God.

Somehow, he could almost imagine her being here with him, like this, for always. He could see the large stone he'd put on her finger, and maybe even, her belly suddenly growing round as a globe under that princess dress. A normal family life.

Man, he thinks, suddenly clearing his throat and quickly smoothing his curls with the flat of his hand. He is tripping hard this morning. Thinking about his momma and weddings. About church folks and babies. He is only tormenting himself with things that would never happen for him. There is too much bad karma to collect on, too many bad things set to boomerang in his face at the right wrong time. Now, she is looking at him with that little-girl wonder that had a way of calming him, making him back away from the edge.

"I *love* barbecue," she confesses, looking right at him. "If it's done right."

"Yeah? Well, me too. I mean…"

Was he stuttering? Standing up against the sink, he takes his hands out of his pockets and puts them back in again. He wants to tell her how good she looks to him just now, standing barefoot at his stove, turning bacon. He wants to tell her how easy she makes things seem somehow… How relaxed he feels around her now.

"I don't know a ward brotha who don't love barbecue," he says instead, and looks down at his feet.

"But, Lincoln. When I was little, there was a man who made the *best* barbecue ever… Mr. Chauncey. Mr. C., we called him… That old man could…"

"Buck-toothed, hump-backed Mr. C. from the north side of Trece?"

"One and only." She laughs, sprinkling more salt and pepper into boiling water, grating Monterey into a bowl of hominy.

"What you know about Third Ward? About the north side, Churchgirl?"

He isn't laughing now, and she looks up, dimples reappearing as she smiles, tastes more cheese. "I was born there, Lincoln. You didn't know that?"

"*You?* Born in Trece? And I ain't never see you? I can't believe that."

"Believe it. You wouldn't have noticed me anyway. Not with all those fast little girls running around. We were a dime a dozen."

"So all this time I've been dealing with an original home-girl?"

"In the flesh. Which isn't good at all."

"I don't believe you."

"It's true."

"What building you lived in?"

"Fifth building, eighth floor. Third apartment on the right. Stayed there until I went away to college. Moms finally moved out that first year I was away, but before then, that was all I knew. Trece. I came back and she'd bought a lil' duplex over on Fairmont. So I never got a chance to say goodbye to anybody. Seems like peeps have been hating on me ever since. The sistas, really."

"Fine as you are, they'd hate you if you were still there. It has nothing to do with the fact that you left. Females are just like that sometimes. Catty."

If he wasn't so dark, his face would flush a plum-color, she thinks, because he's fighting hard not to start grinning again, feels like Beaver Cleaver has taken over his body.

"C'mon, Lincoln. What are you smirking about now?"

"I ain't smirking."

"You are too."

"It's just that I had a big crush on this lil' girl lived in that same building." He rubs his chin with a thumb, watching her.

"A crush?"

"In the worst way." He's smiling again, shaking his head.

"Was she cute?"

"Gorgeous. Reminded me of a lil' doll baby. She had a killer smile; dimples, a head fulla tawny hair. 'Course she hated my guts. Never gave me the time of day. Told me her momma said I was 'bad.'"

"Were you?"

He shrugs. "Who wasn't back then? I was an angel though compared to who I am now."

"The wards were a trip to live in, even back then. Remember all those crazy pestilences? Pigeons and toads and biting flies and armies of gnats coming out of the river like some kind of disaster movie? They'd make us stay inside with all the windows and doors closed for weeks. We couldn't even go to school."

"Yeah. Nobody understood it and nobody could control it. Nobody could do nothing but wait for it to pass. All those cameramen would come down there knocking on doors and taking pictures. Calling it 'a phenomenon.' 'A freak of nature.' My momma used to tell us they were signs of what the end of the world would be like. I didn't believe none of it."

"It's funny, isn't it, Lincoln? How kids flirt at that age?" She giggles, pours hominy into boiling water. "I didn't have brothers, so I never understood that little boys showed their affection by pestering you silly, pulling your hair, messing up your name."

"So what they called you?"

"Bunny. They said my ponytails looked like rabbit ears, I guess. "

"You serious?"

"Would I forget my own name?"

He shrugs as she goes to the stove, his eyes odd in the sparkling kitchen light.

"This one pickle-headed boy drove me *crazy*. Always yanking my pony-tails. Promising me he'd cut 'em off one day and sell 'em to the Koreans." She giggles, spearing forkfuls of bacon and turning them over.

"And you hated that, huhn?"

"Well, I just believed the boy was serious, 'cause he *was* bad, you hear me? Always stealing. Always into all kinds of mischief."

"Did you think he was cute at least?"

"Uh-huhn. We all did. Then he moved away, thank God. I never got the chance to say good-bye. I heard he got into some trouble and his momma had to move to another side of the ward."

"Is that how you heard it?" He stands up abruptly, busies himself setting the table.

Gabriella

Homefries with green peppers and onion. Spanish omelets. Cheese-grits. Slab-bacon, link sausage, homemade waffles and biscuits from scratch. By the time I pour Lincoln's third cup of cocoa, he can barely move, wants to know who taught me to cook so well.

"I'm a Sinclaire, Lincoln. That's all you need to know," I tell him, getting up and gathering the plates to take to the sink to start washing them; only he grabs my hand and pulls me back to my chair.

"All that cooking you just did, and you think I'ma let you wash a dish in my house?"

"Lincoln…"

"Hush now, Woman. That's what this dishwasher is for."

I'm protesting as usual, trying my best to help him out, but he won't hear of it.

"Just sit there and look pretty with your feet up," he insists as I watch him clear the table and load the dishwasher like a champ. He cleans the stove and counters, sweeps the floor, scouring the sink when he's done, and I wonder if it was his mother, or all those years of being institutionalized that have trained him to clean so thoroughly.

By the time he finishes loading the dishwasher and hits the start button, I can hardly keep my eyes open. Sit right there in his kitchen chair and fell asleep.

"Angelfied? Angel?"

It's a little after 10 a.m. when I feel his hand shaking me gently and pulling me up and onto my feet. "Look at you. You tired, Babygirl. I should've known you couldn't keep up."

"I'm okay. But I do need to use the…" He nods before I can finish, pulls me gently along behind him down a wide, carpeted corridor lined with contemporary artwork that leads up to a series of open doors on both sides. It feels strange, my hand tucked into his this way.

He stops before the first door as if waiting for me to choose. "Pick one," he tells me, and finally, releases my hand.

I peek into the first room to find a library filled with shelves of historical black books and videos and cassettes, two computers on two desks. Lush plants are everywhere, and a large high-tech telescope is aimed toward the open skylight built into the high ceiling. Somebody obviously has a great interest in astronomy.

Lincoln trails me from bookcase to bookcase, his hands folded behind his back. He has volumes of first-edition novels and anthologies, black autobiographies and shelves of poetry, all kinds of dictionaries and periodicals. A section of nothing but the latest magazines.

"I didn't know you were such an avid reader," I tell him, and he gives me a look that says, *there's a lot about me that you don't know.*

The next room has a gray rubber floor and is filled with all kinds of exercise equipment. From this room, a door opens into a sauna, another door leads to a large Jacuzzi, and still another door opens into a corridor that leads down into an immense space occupied by an inground pool. The smell of chlorine is sharp in the air.

"Amazing," I say as we stand looking out at the glistening water, and he shrugs nonchalantly. "I guess you have everything you always wanted."

"Almost everything," he says, and his eyes roam over me.

I look away quickly then. "You swim?" I ask.

"Every day," he says. "When I'm here, that is."

On the other side of the long hall is a mini theater complete with a large-screen television and rows of cushioned chairs. Two doors down are two spare bedrooms with full baths, and beside them, a small kitchenette leads back outside to an open deck. Just across the hall, a room free of furniture and embellishments has been painted a pristine white.

Outside, the snow is falling harder than ever; shows no signs of letting up.

The phone rings from somewhere down the hall, and Lincoln kisses his teeth, annoyed by the interruption. He excuses himself, telling me to make myself at home.

I move inside this bright white room where no drapes hang on the windows, and in the center of it, there isn't a couch or a loveseat, but an easel, of all things. Against the wall, a stack of painted canvases are covered over with a paint-smeared dropcloth, and the floor here is covered with paint-spattered industrial tile.

The smell of turpentine hovers faintly as I flip through the wide squares of canvas to gawk at the intricately painted images, each more bizarre than the first. Some of the images stop me dead in my tracks, make me want to peer more closely.

It's clear, even to my untrained eye, that the artist has a strong and decisive eye. I see wide, fluid lines, stark primary colors and mutilated bodies lying in various stages of unrest. Heads are decapitated, limbs floating above prostrate forms, bodies lying face down in dirt and on pavement, arms akimbo, legs splayed.

In one, a brown man in a blue uniform has a barbed wire through his nose while his mouth spits a linked chain of handcuffs. A shiny badge crests the middle of his forehead like a belly dancer's jewel. A red heart drips from his hand, the black hole where the heart once was, gaping wide open, pouring dark blue blood. The brown man looks exactly like Trevis.

My heart stammers. The easel. The easel. I must see what's on the easel, see what was the last thing he's painted.

I remove the old paint-smeared cloth to unveil a portrait of a two-faced woman with dimples that are nails, driven into her bronzed cheeks. One side of her face frowns bitterly, is hideous with blue-black bruises, the caramel skin caved in and distorted, as if she'd been beaten with a crowbar. The other side of her face wears an easy smile as smooth as Hershey's chocolate. Her eyes radiate white light. That side of the woman's face is pristinely beautiful.

Down the hallway, I hear a door open. I can feel him standing there in the doorway.

"The bathrooms are down here," he says.

There are three fancy bedrooms on the other side of this corridor, and I pick the last, biggest one toward the back of the house. It's a huge, beautiful space done up in various tones of blue—cobalts and slates and turquoises and teals. The walls are merely blueglass windows that look out on the most private section of the property, and there is a seating area positioned in front of yet another big-screen TV. A great blue marble desk faces the other end of the property, and on the other end of the canopied four-poster iron bed, a fireplace is already set to be lit.

No one has to tell me that this elegant room, layered in plush carpet and tapestry, is Lincoln's master bedroom, his spacious bathroom with its sunken whirlpool tub and built-in TV and VCR, that I decide to use.

He's at his desk, talking once more on the phone when I come out of the bathroom and sit on the edge of his bed. The faint odor of his cologne lingers here, near the column of fancy pillows, and I wonder what kind of cologne he is wearing that lasts all night and day like this?

He is talking into the phone but studying me, watching my face the way an artist studies blank canvas. His expression is pained almost, unreadable. Harmless, I think. He looks away from me, sighs into the phone.

The smell of his scent is intoxicating, beckoning me, and I curl the rest of my exhausted body onto his bed to inhale it better. This is much safer, isn't it? Sniffing his things instead of his physical person?

Folding my hands under my head, I realize how plush and comfortable his bed is, the velvety blankets, the downy pillows.

From his bed, the view is spectacular; I can see what looks like acres and acres of endless whiteness, the snow still falling, gathering in great sloping drifts among his cedars. Without meaning to, I close my eyes just for a second and think of snow-capped mountains, of little boys in bright red parkas throwing snowballs, of massive ice floes floating on blue artic waters and a beautiful barefoot woman standing at a stove in a veiled church hat saying, "Eat up now... Don't waste anything..."

CHAPTER FIFTEEN

Linc

She looked so natural, lying in my bed.

She must've felt real comfortable too, because she stayed like that for the next five hours, snoring lightly, holding my pillows like she didn't ever wanna leave. When I went to spread a blanket over her, I couldn't resist the urge to touch her hair again, to kiss her soft cheek, stroke her face with my thumbs, and she groaned in her sleep. I wondered if she was calling my name. I started tripping hard then. Couldn't help wondering if she was dreaming about what's been on my mind since she got here, about her and me sliding around on those silk sheets until the sun rises over the tops of my cedar trees.

I lit up the fireplace, put on some Miles Davis, got some Cold Duck out the fridge and took a long, hot shower, after which I shaved, put on my best cologne, and came into the bedroom wearing jeans and a wifebeater. The fire was burning nicely, brightening the room that was already growing dark. Outside, the snow is still falling hard, and I couldn't help wondering what the wards looked like right about now, about what 'Nere was doing and how swollen her face probably was. I sat on the edge of my bed, looking at this Angel-woman, thinking that no female had ever slept in my bed without offering herself totally to me. If she made it as far as my bed, that was it. I took what I wanted of her body and she got to keep what was left. That was all there was to it. That was the only way it had ever been. The fellas down at the guest house probably thought I was tearing it up right now, because why should this time be any different?

Sitting there, I was thinking of so many ways I wanted to undress her, to make her lose her religion like all the rest of them. Piece by piece, everything was coming off in my hands, but I couldn't do it just then somehow. Not yet anyway. It was all in biding my time. All in making her think it was accidental, her being here. Me taking her to bed. It's got to be her fault, her idea. So I got out my cleaning kit and started cleaning and oiling some old pistols I'd been meaning to get to. I was doing that for close to an hour, sitting in a chair across the room drinking Cold Duck and feeling real mellow when she finally coughed and sat bolt upright, like she was expecting Five-O to bust in on us.

"Oh my God, is the house on fire? Lord, where am I?"

The room was filled with the sweet aroma of apples and cedar, and Angelfied was tripping hard.

"You here."

"Here? Where is that?"

"With me. In my bed, Babygirl."

She fell silent then. Looked at me sitting in the glow of the firelight cleaning my .38 and shook her head like she couldn't believe it. She fell back onto the pillows, an arm folded behind her head, and stared at the ceiling while Natalie Cole and her daddy were crooning "Unforgettable." It was all too strange to try to fathom now. This house had never felt so peaceful to me, and I don't know when I'd ever felt so calm. It was like a scene from some movie I saw long ago, like *Beauty and the Beast*.

We stayed like that, in total silence, for thirty more minutes, the only sound being the soft swish of my rag against the smooth iron in my hands. Finally she turned over on her side, watching me as I put the gleaming gun back into its special box. Even from here I could see the way the blankets fit around those sharp curves of that killer body, but I knew how to wait, sat watching to see how she was gonna try to get out of this one. "What's next, Lincoln?" she asked.

"Whatever you want. Whatever you need."

She watched as I got up and put away the cleaning kit, then sat back in the same chair, legs folded, a finger pressed against my temples, watching her trip.

"You changed clothes," she observed.

"Yeah. Took a long hot shower. It felt good too."

"I know."

"You can too if you want."

"What?"

"Take one of those long tub soaks y'all females love."

"I don't think so."

"Why not?"

"It doesn't look right. Me being here with you as it is, then soaking in your tub."

"Whose gonna know the difference? Nobody's here but us. You snowed in with me until the morning, at least, and I've got plenty of clothes for you to put on. Stuff I buy for 'Nere that she never wears. She's got drawers of new stuff. Panties, nightgowns, housecoats and slippers. Brand-new, still got the tags."

"Sounds nice, but…"

"You can't be comfortable sleeping in that dress."

"Lincoln…"

"If I wanted to hurt you, I'd have done it by now."

Her eyes were weighing me. "But this feels so…"

"So what?"

"Wrong. Strange… Everything is just so…"

"Angelfied. Don't insult me. I won't hurt you, aiight?"

†††

When she emerged from the bathroom an hour later, smelling and looking all good, I tried hard not to stare at her. She'd used the spare toiletries I had given her and brushed her teeth and scrubbed her face and pinned all that hair up off her neck. Chinere's new ice-blue robe and slippers looked tailor-made on her, and underneath, she had on some kinda smock thing that looked like the long house dresses Momma used to wear. I glanced at her and all I could see was Momma, and then it took all I had not to stare at all that behind when she came into the theater where she found me kicked back, watching an old black-and-white Bogart classic.

She's terrified, I could tell, but I'd seen that before. Still, my own heart was thumping like a madman's, but I was playing it real cool as I looked up from my seat and smiled, then looked back at Lauren Bacall, although it's really Gabriella's pretty face I was seeing on the screen.

"Lincoln. I am *totally* tripping," she said, sitting three seats away from me, but I pretended not to hear her. I was too busy smelling her soft talcum smell. A smell that must've beenmixed with some kinda aphrodisiac, because it was driving me wild. She must keep a bottle in her purse. But I didn't say nothing to her about it, pretended not to notice it at all. "You hungry?" I asked. "'Cause I sho am."

"Well... What do you have?"

"Everything. You know that. Last I looked there was leftover pizza. Lunch meat and hotdogs. Wings too, courtesy of KFC."

"A bachelor's refrigerator." She smiled, touched a hand to her throat, a bundle of nerves, although I was determined to do whatever it took to relax her. I snatched up the remote and pause the movie.

"Yo, Bogie, you gonna have to wait, Playa. C'mon, Babygirl. I'ma hook you up real good."

Minutes later, we were back in the theater with plates of chicken wings and slaw. My heart was pounding so hard I could hardly keep my hands to myself, but I let her sit down first on the other side of the theater, drawing her robe close around her, crossing her legs. It was a big room. Much too big for her to be on one side while I'm on the other. She was surprised when I came and sat beside her, although not too close, and I was dropping napkins everywhere, trying hard to keep the desire out of my eyes. She was surprised that I'd changed up my seat, but my clumsiness made her start giggling. The more she giggled, the clumsier I got and now I was laughing too and dropping more things. Before it was over, I'd dropped two more wings and kicked over my can of Sprite.

She looked at me, her teeth showing. "You okay, Lincoln?"

"Nawl... And it's all your fault, Babygirl... See what you doing to me?"

We cleaned up the mess and I started the movie again and we ate and brought our plates back to the kitchen. Afterward, she snuggled back against the couch with a handful of grapes and I waited before coming in and dropping down again next to her, closer this time. She looked at me, sitting so close to her and aimed her eyes back at the screen. It almost seemed like she actually trusts me, like she knows I won't intentionally do anything to harm her.

"What are we watching anyway? Is that Bogart?"

"One and only."

"*Casablanca*, Lincoln? Don't tell me you're a romantic?"

"Yeah. I like to watch the old-school playas sometimes. But shhh… Don't tell nobody."

She laughed real soft-like. "Believe me, I ain't telling *nobody* about this…"

"You sure?" I asked.

"Positive."

"Then you won't have to tell this," I said, and wrapped an arm around her, pulling her into my arms. I squeezed her to me hard, holding her close, but I didn't kiss her lips, just her face. I just looked into those pretty eyes to see how afraid she was. She was watching me like she wanted to understand, like she was trying hard to read whatever she saw. She didn't push me away. Didn't look like she wanted to scream, so I kissed the tip of her nose, real gentle-like, kissed those soft eyebrows, the downy hair around the edges of her face. It was my chance now to do what I knew she wanted. What we both wanted. I started toying with the lace around her robe near that soft neck that's smelling so good. I wanna kiss that neck and peel that robe off and see what's underneath it. I wanna pick her up and carry her back to my bed where the fireplace was waiting and the covers were turned back. But somehow I couldn't move. I couldn't. And it's almost like things between us had gone to a totally different dimension that made us both freeze, unsure of what to do next.

That ain't never happened to me before, me holding a woman in my arms and not knowing what to do next.

But something about her, about her vulnerability, makes things different for me somehow, and I'm tripping, 'cuz hunter and prey don't usually see eye to eye. Her lips parted, like she wanted to say something, but she didn't. She's just watching me watching her, and the only thing that seemed to matter just then was the two of us being right there, together, in this world we were building, all by ourselves. I was wanting to make love to her so bad that I could taste it, but wanting to, needing to protect her suddenly became my main focus. I was speechless too, fighting with everything I had to protect her from the dog in me that, if she were any other woman, would have been all over her by now.

"Angel, you ain't the only one that's tripping," I finally admitted, my voice sounding all strange, like something's got me by the throat. I trace her pretty lips with a finger. "I don't understand this myself."

She nodded, obviously speechless and then tears were sliding quietly from her eyes.

"Ey. It's okay," I told her, not recognizing my own voice and the tenderness that's choked it all up. Suddenly she did something I was totally unprepared for. She sighed, and snuggled up under me even closer, holding on tight and closing her eyes.

Gabriella

It's close to 4 a.m. when I am awakened by the cacophony of barking dogs and open my eyes to see Lincoln standing at the window of his bedroom, peering out on his lawn from the shadowy fold of chintz drapes. The snow has finally stopped, leaving in its wake an ocean of glaring whiteness as far as the eyes can see.

"Is everything okay?" I whisper, but he places a finger to his own lips, gently shushing me, and turns back toward the racket that sounds as if it's coming from the kennel around the back of the property.

"Everything's fine, Babygirl. Go back to sleep," he urges.

By 6 a.m. though, he's shaking me awake again, telling me that it was morning already, and he had to get me home. I pass up his offers of frozen waffles and settle on a cup of brisk Colombian coffee instead. An hour later, Dante pulls the heated Lexus up to the carport and gets out, looking sheepishly toward where I'm standing in the doorway shivering from the freeze brought in from an arrogant northeastern wind. Shame burns my face, but at least I'm wearing my cream dress again, my heavy coat buttoned up to my neck. Lincoln comes out of the house and stands there, shrugging into his jacket. Standing by the open car door, Dante turns toward me, raising his chin in my direction. "How you doing, Miss Lady?"

"I'm doing."

"I see."

It's a double meaning and I look away from him, from the sneer he's not even trying to hide. Lincoln doesn't miss it. "What's that supposed to mean?" he cuts in territorially, his eyes challenging.

"Nothing, Cuz. Miss Lady just looks like she's cold, that's all."

Linc gives him a hard look. "You wanna be cold too?"

"Nawl, Man. I was just playing with her."

"Car's all warmed up for you, Babygirl," he says, looking at me. "You ready to hat up?"

He's standing outside the shelter of the carport door with his coat wide open, holding his pack of Newports in one hand, wearing a thick leather aviator jacket and combat boots, jeans. Everything, of course, is black. I suddenly realize he hasn't smoked at all the entire time I've been here, and now he looks at his smokes as if he isn't quite sure what to do with them. It's five degrees below zero, and unlike Dante, who's visibly trembling from the cold, his eyes still blurry with sleep, Lincoln doesn't flinch. He coughs though, looks back at me, and his eyes smile, although his lips and the rest of his face are as rigid as stone. Overhead, the sun is beginning to break through, a soft pearly light. Lincoln taps his watch and Dante reaches inside his heavy parka and pulls out a big black pistol. He hands it to Lincoln, who nods and slips it into his own jacket, cutting his eyes at me. He looks back at Dante. "I'll holler."

"You sure, D?" Dante asks, watching me. "Told you. I don't mind taking her home for you. I'm already here. It won't be no thang."

Lincoln touches my waist, his hand lingering possessively on the small of my back as he guides me to the passenger side of the car and opens the door to help me in. "Nawl. I got *this*," he says and Dante nods respectfully like he's realized he's pushed it too far already. He waves at me and starts walking, hunched down inside his jacket, back down the recently plowed driveway, past the garages, toward the guest house at the back of the property.

It's just after 7 a.m. by the time Lincoln pulls into the parking lot of my complex and insists on taking the elevator up with me, walking me to my door. He's quiet in the elevator, watching me as if he's trying hard to understand, and when we get off on the sixth floor and go to my door, he's standing there with both hands clasped behind his back as I fumble in my purse for my keys.

"Come in and have a cup of tea with me," I offer, but he shakes his head.

"That ain't my thing," he tells me. "I just wanted to make sure you got in safely."

"Well, I did, and thank you, Lincoln. For everything."

"The pleasure was mine," he says, and this time I pull him close and kiss his cheek.

"You one crazy church gurl though," he says, his eyes very serious.

"About last night…"

"Whatever happened between us stays between us, right?"

"Right."

"I won't tell if you won't." He touches my face, walks away toward the elevators.

✝✝✝

From my bedroom window I could see the dark sedan leaving the parking lot and heading back toward the main strip of shopping malls and morning rush-hour traffic. Back toward the wards, no doubt. The light on my answering machine is blinking incessantly, but I'm not ready yet to hear Trev's worried questions: "Where are you, Bunny? What's going on, Bunny? Are you okay, Bunny?"

Not even Trish with her frantic ruminations are on my mind as I run the tub full of hot-hot water and step into it to soak for as long as I can. For now, all that matters to me is where Lincoln is going.

ORCHIDS

Trevis

The funny thing is, when I park the jeep and step up into the lobby, the florist's truck is arriving at the same time. The sight of the stocky white boy dressed in delivery blues with grassy eyes that are tearing from the cold, cuts me to the quick. It's obvious he'd rather be elsewhere, doing something other than making deliveries in this weather, but he's here too, just like I am. He's pulling a cart behind him that's so loaded with flowers I don't bother to count how many. Who'd send so many flowers in this kind of weather? Somebody who doesn't have better things to do with his money or is trying to make an awfully strong statement.

"Cold as a grave out there," I say, since we're the only two guys standing in the lobby.

"You telling me?" He shakes his head, unfolding the crumpled paper from his pocket and mumbling her name to himself, presses Gabriella's buzzer hard. "I hope this broad's home. Jeez. Who'd wanna send orchids on a day like today anyway?"

It's happened to me dozens of times at too many crime scenes to count, the moment when unbelief metamorphs into shock so severe, that a single minute seems to stretch into an entire lifetime. The surreal feeling I'm experiencing now borders on the macabre as I listen to her voice, strained, exhausted, radiating over the intercom.

"Yes? May I help you?" Bunny sighs.

So she is alive. So she has decided to come home after all.

"Looking for a Miss Gabriella Sinclaire? Got a delivery for her," says Mr. Blueboy, scowling into the surveillance camera.

"A delivery?"

"That's what I said, Ma'am."

"What kind of delivery?"

"Flowers, Ma'am. From Avery Florists."

"Do you have to deliver them *right* now? I mean, can you come back tomorrow, same time?"

It was a strange request and one the driver wasn't trying to hear.

"Look, Lady. I've got a truckload of hothouse flowers down here, and I ain't leaving until somebody signs for 'em."

Her sigh is more than rude. More like disgusted as she clicks on the buzzer and rings him up, never realizing I'm standing right beside him.

✝✝✝

Orchids.

So many varieties she can barely find a place for all of them. Must be over $1,000 worth of flowers, and since she refuses to open the card in front of me to identify the sender, she's looking totally confused. Her hair is slapped back into a horsetail; her lips are dry and there are dark circles under those usually luminous eyes. More than anything though, she is refusing to even look at me, as if she doesn't have a clue about anything right now. As if she doesn't know why I'm even here or what I could be looking for, but would rather I'd just leave her to continue writing.

But I'm not leaving until I get answers. I'd sat in her parking lot from late yesterday afternoon until six this morning, a surveillance stakeout like so many of the others I've done for the force, and now, there was no way she was *not* going to tell me where she slept last night. It's almost two in the afternoon already, more snow threatening to fall again, and in her condo, the heat has been turned up to full blast, ward-style.

"Not to worry, Miss. It won't hurt these flowers none," the delivery man teases when she hands him his $5 tip and closes the door a little too quickly, moving around to arrange vases and knick-knacks, making room for those lush, exotic blooms. I don't say a thing, wait to see how long she's gonna feign indifference, although I can tell by the way her hands move, that she's scared of something.

"I've been calling," I say as she gulps Folgers from a huge mug without offering me any. She looks like an old woman, bent over her laptop in that little room she uses for an office, and that denim dress and wooly slippers remind me of Cinderella's "before" pictures. She's wrapped herself up in a chenille bedspread that loops and drags from chair to floor. Wrapped herself up like she's trying to knock a chill from deep inside her soul, but I pull up a chair anyway, wait for her to look at me.

"Gabriella. Didn't you hear me? I've been calling you. Waiting outside in your parking lot all night." Her fingers seem to fly, hands swooping down over the keyboard like two birds. Her back to me is an unreachable wall, and I can feel it. She wants me to leave, is afraid of the questions that are burning, dangling on the edge of my lips:

Where have you been, Bunny? Why can't you look at me? Don't you know what's in my pocket? You're going to be my wife, and you can't tell me who cares enough about you to send so many flowers?

I sit back in the chair, and the edges of the small velvet box in my pocket jab into my ribs.

"Did you check your messages?" I ask finally, when I realize she has no plans to discuss any of it.

"Not yet." She doesn't look at me.

"I called six times already."

"I'm sorry; I wasn't available… I was…working… Sort of."

"Working."

"That's what I said, Detective Cooper."

"On a story, you mean?"

"Yes, I was…" She clears her throat, reaches for her mug and gulps again, and I know now that Aunt Gert wasn't lying. "I was um…doing an interview."

"All night, Bunny?"

Her hands freeze on the keys, and the glance she tosses me over her shoulder is tense with anxiety.

"I asked you a question."

"And?"

"I'd like an answer. Please."

"What is this, some kind of interrogation, Detective?"

"Why, do you have something to hide?"

"What am I? Some kind of suspect now?"

"Are you?"

She's trembling as she attempts to resume typing but gives up, pushes away from her PC, gathering up her cup and blanket, and going into the living room. She flops down on the loveseat that faces the couch. Her cheek drops into the palm of her hand and she squeezes her eyes closed.

The leather makes a heavy sigh as I sit right beside her, smack in the middle of the couch. "What's going on, Bunny? You can tell me. Please. Tell me *something*."

"Trev, I..." She bites down hard on her bottom lip, shrugs.

"Who sent the flowers, Gabriella?"

"Do you have to ask?"

"Yes. Why won't you look at me?"

She tosses her head back to face me squarely, wetness gleaming in the corners of her eyes. "How is this now? I'm looking right at you, okay? Are you satisfied, Trevis?"

"I just wanna know who..."

"Yes, Trev, okay? Lincoln did. *He*... sent me the flowers. There. I said it."

"*Duvall* sent these flowers?"

"Yes, Trev."

"And you know that without reading the card?"

"Yes. I know."

Aunt Gert's drawn face, flushed with tears, flashes before me. "Why is he sending you flowers, Bunny?"

"Trev..."

"Why?"

She cups a hand over her mouth, and her sleeves dangle in the long sweater. "I saw him again, Trevis. I interviewed him, and we..."

"You what?"

"We were together last night."

"*Together?*"

"I went to his house, Trev."

"His *house?*"

"Yes. I spent the night."

There are times when everything you've always thought you wanted in life makes absolutely no sense at all. Times when you feel totally out of control, the world around you spinning wildly, broken, like a child's toy that has snapped from the end of its string. I'm like that now. Out there spinning, emotions flying everywhere, racing out of control. I can still see Duvall's face on that first night I pulled him over in the rain; the girlish features that made him have to fight extra hard anytime he'd gone to jail; the rage of a beast in his eyes, daring me, promising vengeance.

So he had triumphed after all. Discrediting my rep, shooting up my home, gunning down my favorite aunt's son, hadn't been enough. He'd slept with the only woman I'd finally been brave enough to marry, and there was nowhere to go with this now. Duvall had won.

Bunny drops her head, plays with her fingers like a little girl in a confessional booth, and there isn't a thing either of us can say now because she can tell, can see how my mind is turning in on itself. She looks up at me, wincing at the pain she has caused, and I feel like a man who is breaking down, caving in from the inside out.

"Don't hurt him, Trev," she whispers. "Please... just leave it alone."

"You tell me you've been with *him* all night and all you can feel for is *his* welfare?" I shake my head; it was just too unbelievable to be true. "I just left the hospital, Bunny. My cousin, Petey. Duvall shot him down like a dog. They called the family together. Called us all in to say our good-byes. He's not expected to make it through the night. And where do you think he'll spend eternity?"

"Trev."

I ball a fist, knock it against my own head. "*Duvall* did it, Bunny. My auntie, people in the street, they all say he did it. Said it was his car the shots came out of. So I'ma hunt down that outlaw."

"No, Trev."

"That monster you chose over me."

"Don't, Trev."

"And I'ma charge him with first-degree murder. I am going to, by all of the powers vested in me, put that demon-criminal *under* the jail."

I'm standing up and walking toward the door while she's steady denying everything, calling me back to her as if I can trust anything she says now.

"He didn't do it, Trev," she's insisting. "He didn't actually pull the trigger," she's pleading as if she's his momma and he's some kind of boy scout truant, caught with his hand in the cookie jar. Her phone rings, but whoever it is that's calling her doesn't matter to me at all now. Inside my jacket, the velvet case feels sharp as an arrow in my ribs. Her machine clicks on and her editor's nasally twang speaks in neat, brisk clips.

"A phenomenal start, Sinclaire. Larger than life, this guy is, isn't he? Did all this really happen? A great first draft so far. Continue on. Prize material here. Get back to me soon if you can. We've moved up the deadline. Can she run next week instead?"

I slam her door as hard as I can, ignoring the sound of her crying, of her whimpering my name. Whose name did she call last night? Whose arms did she use to console her then?

Outside, the snow is starting up again, staining my windshield. There's my beeper going off, ringing and ringing like crazy. She's begging me to come back to her, and she should. She's crying on my voice mail, begging me to forgive her. I snatch the beeper out of my coat to see the tangible proof of her agony, the number of times she's calling to beg me to come back to her, but when I look at the beeper, I see it was only Momma. Momma calling to give me the latest update from Aunt Gertie no doubt.

I'm afraid to answer it. Can't face any of that now. Not until I find Duvall. Not until I make him pay.

CHAPTER SIXTEEN

It's a night so bitterly cold on the Second Ward's north side that even the rats haven't bothered to make their usual nocturnal excursions to the dump. They lingered under the rusted machinery of junked cars, under hallway stairs that led to basement burrows and narrow dirt canals lined with newspaper and shreds of brown paper bags. Across the street from the funeral parlor, filthy snow has been plowed into ragged mounds stacked alongside the narrow curb, and the wind gusting in across the Connecticut River was strong enough to make a grown man lose his balance as he waited in line to see the heavily made-up corpse.

Still, they came in droves, in knots of shivering walkers and by the carful. The viewing line reached halfway around the block, stretching past the Delta Theater and Josey's all-night café. Wall-to-wall street-level hustlers with gold teeth and bright parkas were the main spectators, coming more out of stark curiosity, out of a chance to be a part of another of the ward's historical moments, than to pay respects to a man who had met his fate in what they thought was a most humiliating manner. He'd been hit by two cars and then dragged thirty feet by a tractor trailer carrying 600 pounds of frozen bagels.

Most had hated Spain and figured his time had been about up anyway. He'd gotten selfish and petty in his dealings with the lower-level "runners" who'd sold for him, had begun treating folks like peasants, throwing their wages on the ground and expecting them to bow down and pick them up, using their thirteen- and fourteen-year-old daughters to sex him up in the back of his Mercedes. Lately, it seemed, Spain had forgotten where he'd come from, and foolishly began giving his suppliers the hardest times when they sent their "gophers" to collect their fees.

It was time for a change. They all knew it, but most hadn't been willing for a Third Ward man like Duvall, though hated, though feared, though rich as any politician downtown, to be his successor. Duvall was much too violent, extremely unpredictable, and his psychological make-up was so complex, not even his own men understood all the things he did. Besides that, he had little patience for error, which meant that all of the laxity and blunders they'd gotten away with while "running" for Spain, would in no way be tolerated within Duvall's expanding regime. Not when Duvall employed assassins all over the wards who shot first and asked questions later.

There were rumors circulating that Duvall was in the process of setting up an office in a central location that overlooked the largest portion of Deuce's narcotics' marketplace. If that were true, it was a move that most of Deuce's smaller level dealers thought deserved to be contested, although they had no idea who would be crazy enough to try to stop it. They were hoping that Spain's kid brother, Tyree, who headed a band of renegade truants that packed pistols and worshipped Tupac, had the guts and the stamina to assume his brother's mantle. But now that Spain and his main crew were dead, there was no one willing to offer Tyree wise counsel, and the empire of the Second Ward, though it appeared to be his to claim, would not be an easy acquisition. Not as long as Duvall was alive.

Edward Perkins Sr., a short, mustard-colored man with a fade haircut under his undertaker's dark homburg, pushed aside the crowd and opened the door of the limo parked in front of the Perkins & Perkins Funeral Parlor. The festivities inside Room Two of the rundown funeral home had already started, and the body, all five feet and six inches of gaudy gangster, was already lying in state. It was time now for all eight of the little hooligans sprawled inside his limo smoking marijuana, to get out and join the rest of the mourning party. The door of the 1989 Cadillac limo had yawned open, the boys inside spilling out like roaches. Dark, slippery, and with exteriors as hard as shell, the boys, fourteen- and fifteen-year-olds mostly and barely moustached, shook the wrinkles out of their sweats and gathered around Tyree like bodyguards, surveying the crowd.

"Gaw-lee. Don't pee in your pants, Man," Tyree snarled at Perkins, balking at the older man's impatience. He bit the soggy end off a cigar and spat it out on the ice-slickened sidewalk. Perkins tapped the face of his watch and Tyree sprung into action. Basking in the admiration of the thronging crowd, Tyree absolutely loved the attention. With Spain gone, he was finally out from under his shadow and could now strut in the glory of his own blossoming bravado. It was an awakening he was proud of, an image he worked hard at improving.

"'Scuse me. Y'all gonna let us through or what?" Tyree, flanked by his boys, moved toward the building and made his way up the steps leading to the visitation room, shaking hands with everyone, nodding appropriately at the mumbled condolences. "Yeah. Thanks, y'all. Thanks for coming," he repeated, his jacket too big about the shoulders, but too short at the wrists. "Yeah. Yeah. I'm sorry, too. Yup. On the freeway of all places."

Scrawny, but well oiled, Tyree, a former bantam-weight champ in the ward's amateur boxing league, had a head shorn to baldness and long hairy arms like a spider's. He had a noticeable lisp, a second-grade reading level, and when he wasn't selling product or sparring at the gym, he spent hours kicking back with his homies, watching hiphop videos on BET. His sisters, a few holding small children on their laps, were already assembled before the cola-colored casket on cushioned chairs, their cheeks smeared with tears. They looked like kewpie dolls in their rayon black dresses and synthetic wigs, their thick braids sectioned into elaborate crowns and updos. Having reserved Tyree a chair in the front family row between the two oldest girls, they watched now as he broke through the milling mourners and knelt at Spain's bier, crossing himself like he'd seen gangsters do in the movies, touching Spain's frozen hands. The sisters had done it all already. Had gone ahead to the parlor like Mary Magdalenes and dressed Spain themselves in new underwear and socks, a powder-blue suit, a black silk tie, and a white carnation wilting already about the fringes.

Tyree leaned into the casket, saw that one of Spain's eyelids appeared to be partly open, the lanolin cream the Perkinses had used to give his face an even gleam, giving him a shimmery, feminine look. Tyree frowned. "Got my brovah up here looking like RuPaul," he whispered, wiping at the stiff cheeks with his thumbs. "Yeah. That's right. Close ya eyes Big Bruh, cuz I'ma take care of it for you. I'ma get that nigga if it's the last thing I do. "

He sat down between his sisters finally, wrapping his arm around the youngest one, Ticey, and seeing at last, the single arrangement of elaborate flowers big enough for a man to hide inside.

"That's all the flowers he got? Who sent them?" He pointed, and since Ticey was too busy sobbing, he waited for Merlean, the oldest, to reply.

"I don't know." Merlean snatched her nephew up and cradled him on her lap. "Read the card, Stupid."

It was a mean thing to say, but Tyree stood up anyway, interrupting two crackheads kneeling at Spain's feet. He reached through the lush ferns and silk ribbons to snatch off the card wedged deep inside. He handed it to Merlean, holding on to the back of her chair. "Read it then. What it say?"

"It say, 'Best Wishes From Lincoln Duvall.'" Merlean shivered, shook her head, but Tyree was already walking to the bier, was grabbing the flowers with both hands, was carrying them down the aisle. He disappeared down the steps and into the crowd where there'd be witnesses; mouths that would get the word back fast.

At the front doors, two winos held them open while he hurled the arrangement past the viewing line and into the street, spitting after it. "Linc Duvall? He going down! Y'all tell him I said so! Y'all tell that punk nigga Tyree said to watch his back!"

Applause and wolf whistles split the air, but first things were first. He'd get Spain squared away and then he'd take care of Duvall. Yeah. Then Duvall.

Gabriella

It wouldn't be long. The smooth, deliberate click of keys always brings me back to myself, I think as I gulp the first taste of angry coffee and allow its heat to permeate my throat, my mind. My fingers tremble like separate creatures unattached to my body, and I must remind myself that it's my fingers, not my heart, that dared to make it happen, to write the story the way it needed to be written. Paragraphs bloomed like zinnias on the white screen.

Should I write *all* of it? Could I? He had said I could, hadn't he? No, that wasn't it. He had said he trusted me. Said, if anybody could say it just right, I could. The computer's keys click and snap, egging me on until I write almost everything I've seen, push myself to see how far I can go, how much I can write without flinching. The truth is always stranger than fiction, but would our readers believe such a tale? Would my editors? How close can I get to the edge without falling off? If I did fall, who would be there to catch me? Would God, even after I had failed Him?

There was no denying what I'd seen in his basement that morning: the paintings. A death portrait of Trev shot through with barbed wire. But more importantly, the canvases had been streaked and swirled with carnival colors—the blues and reds and golds of the dead men's fancy outerwear. Joker's and his cousin. Lincoln's paintings had held all the grotesque images of carnage identical to the images in the crime scene photos Trev had shown me that day at the morgue. Images that had stayed in my mind and made me sick for days afterward. So sick I'd been forced to remember all of them distinctly, held the memories like carvings engraved sharply in my head.

The question then at the very core of his art, his soul's expression, was simple: How had Lincoln re-created each murder scene with such vivid and precise detail? Details that looked as if he had been there himself? Had he re-created the violence on canvas for his own pleasure? It was a question only he knew the answer to, a secret I could not dare add to this story.

INFIRMARY

The Mason Douglas Detention Center never went to sleep. It stayed up and open all night like a twenty-four-hour drugstore, bringing in transient inmates at all hours, shipping them out again. In the inky darkness, if Lincoln lay very still on his bunk, his fingers clamped like iron around the metal shank he'd fashioned out of a metal bolt broken from the bottom of a cafeteria chair, he could hear everything, and it was more imaginative, more violent, more sexual than anything HBO could ever produce. He lay very still on those nights, watching the water spots on the ceiling, created from the upper tier's flooding toilets, and listening for variations. Nuances. Strategies that could elevate his stronger self above the surrounding tyrannies. Regardless of what he did, thought, or said, though, the chaos always unfolded like clockwork, beginning with the scratching and clawing of the plump pipe rats that emerged from their tunnels and knocked over wastebaskets in the dark, rummaging for food or climbing up into bed with him if they detected even the slightest morsel or crumb on his mattress.

Mason Douglas wasn't the first detention facility he'd lived in, but after the numerous juvenile reformatories where he'd learned to do six months, one year, and eighteen-month bids relatively easily, it was certainly the worst place yet, a world where, at any time of the day or night, he could hear the sobbing prayers of the latest arrivals begging for mercy or death, whichever came faster. Every night there were gang rapes or suicides, and often both, simultaneously. There were "love groans" and lovers' games played among cellmates, card games played through the bars of adjacent cells. *American Idol* wannabes, who once thought themselves destined for Hollywood, howled the latest tunes in loud falsettos. Others read poetry or passages of scripture aloud by flashlight into the dimly lit corridors, as if warding off ghosts. Men cried like children for the children they'd lost. Cried over the lives they'd taken, the women who stopped writing, the mothers who no longer sent care-baskets or accepted collect calls. At Mason Douglas, men cursed God all day and every day. It was a hell on Earth. Purgatory. A holding place for those who sold themselves to the works of eternal darkness. In time, the daily misery and hopelessness bred in him a hatefulness that brought his psyche to a new level of darkness. It was here that Lincoln discovered his own hidden talents for devising indescribable evil. He became imaginative when it came to inflicting bodily pain on those who threatened him, discovered that bars of soap and D-batteries knotted into wet socks, when swung with force, could open a man's skull.

He lay very still on his narrow cot night after night, surrendering to the surrounding darkness and growing accustomed to the nature of bad things.

The more evil he devised and gave himself over to, the more became available to him. His obedience to the Master of Darkness was rewarded with a certain sophistication of his skills. He was granted a mind, if he concentrated very hard, that could slam doors, turn on faucets, flip the pages of books and move large objects, like chairs. Other prisoners saw it and laughed, called him a warlock, claimed he was possessed of the devil and learned to leave him alone. Before any of that though, they'd claimed he was already violent, a danger to society. The incident that landed him at Mason when he was just fourteen began with a fight inside the ward's one junior high school in which he'd broken a bottle over another boy's head. In the wards, it wasn't a unique method of defense. He'd been arrested though, but the charge they gave him, of attempted murder, seemed much too harsh for the act of self-defense. His opponent had been a seven-foot tall, 340-pound sixteen-year-old armed with a wrench.

Their mother, accompanied by Runt, had pleaded in court, paying what she could scrape up to a shifty downtown lawyer who never showed up. But the judge, reviewing Lincoln's extensive reform school records of petty larcenies and truancies, and believing Lincoln carried a very bad aura that could contaminate his brother, had sentenced him to Mason Douglas, a population filled with grown men who had life sentences. Men with ravaged minds who didn't care that he was fourteen. Gang rape was Mason's typical initiation and Lincoln had endured it like a soldier, never once crying out in pain. Seven men held him down the first time, eleven the second, and ten on the third attempt. He'd fought back like a mad man each time, but by the third attempt in one month, his anal cavity had been ripped so violently, he'd required emergency surgery. Guards had found him face down in his own fecal matter, hemorrhaging in his cell. On a fourth attempt, two months later, he'd managed to slice the throat of a lifer and lodge a fork in the eye of another man, blinding him permanently. Both men survived, but he was left alone after that. It was while he was at Mason, on his cot, in the dark, that guards came to bring him the message from the chaplain.

Something, he knew before they'd said it, had happened at home. Something so significant that they'd waited almost twenty-four hours before they'd broke the news to him. He'd remember that July night for as long as he lived. Relive it again and again in night sweats and daydreams; the sympathetic tones of the guards as they stopped at his cell just after midnight, the jangle of their keys while they told him to get up and put on a shirt and shoes because the chaplain wanted to see him downstairs. He remembered the oppressive heat of that night and the sharp stench of urine, underarm funk and cigarette smoke, wafting into the narrow tier corridors they'd passed through to get to the chaplain's basement office. A bald Polish man wearing a crooked priest's collar, Chaplain Wilinski had waved Lincoln into his cramped space of books and shelves, the backs of his hands mottled with liver spots.

"I'm afraid there's been a shooting," he'd said, taking off his specs and wiping them with a Kleenex from a box on his desk.

"A shooting?" Having refused the stooped man's offer of a chair, Lincoln swallowed, pressed his back against the wall, hoping it would hold him up. His father had all kinds of guns. Too many to count.

"Your parents are both dead," Chaplain said as Lincoln stared at nothing. There was no need to ask what had happened. He already knew, had seen it coming his whole life.

"And my brother, Runt?" he'd opened his mouth at last, petrified of what the old priest was not saying. The old priest who was rumored to "like boys," to offer dollars to those who would sit on his lap and let him touch them. Linc shrank back against the wall, hated the cunning in the bald man's eyes.

"Joseph is critical, Son. If he survives, he will be a vegetable."

"A *vegetable?*"

"If you'd like to come in and sit down, perhaps we can work something out."

But Linc knew all about the details of Mason Douglas' typical funeral procedures. He had nothing further to say to the shifty-eyed man with the speckled hands.

They allowed him one five-minute visit with his mother's body while he wore shackles and leg braces, leaning into the casket's paper lining before the funeral to see that someone had put rouge on her cheeks, scarlet on her lips.

"Take that off," he'd told the funeral director. "That don't look nothing like her."

It had been a welfare-funeral with a welfare-casket, cheap as Styrofoam, and a welfare-burial, in Pauper's Field. But on the altar at the church an hour before the viewing, there were so many flowers there was hardly room for the casket. She had been loved. Greatly loved. He wondered if she ever knew it.

"Don't worry, Momma, I'ma be back to get you soon as possible," he'd whispered, tears hard as glass on his cheeks while the guards stood watching. "I'ma get you out of this cheap thing. Put you somewhere nice, where there's trees. On the side of a hill, just like you wanted."

But his mother was smiling, her face finally at peace, her gloved hands clasped against her middle as if still praying. When he kissed her though, her skin was ice cold and as rigid as stone, like the man's heart who had done this to her. Lincoln had declined the opportunity to see what he had always longed for; his father's dead body lying there without any trace of God. "Cremate him," he told the welfare worker from jail. "He deserves to burn."

Gabriella

I haven't heard hide nor hair of Lincoln since I called to thank him for the flowers. "Welcome, Babygirl," was all he'd said into his cell, his voice sounding rushed, and brittle as rock. Just two words and that was it. It wasn't hard to understand. He was back in his element, had returned to Babylon, and what happened between us that night wasn't just history, it was a delusion that had never happened. There have been no more late-night phone calls. No more last-minute invites back out to that fantastical house. I have been left feeling ashamed, sinfully unworthy and completely abandoned. A verse from the 137th Psalm rings in my mind night and day: *How shall we sing the Lord's song in a strange land?*

"You oughta be glad to be rid of that temptation," my best friend, Pleasure, would have said had I told her all of what had happened. Pleasure, whom everyone calls, "Leasy," grew up with me in the wards and still has family there. She knows who Lincoln is, and knows I've been trying hard to get an interview with him, but since she'd have a fit if she even guessed how far things have gone with him, I'd found it in my best interest not to tell her.

Even with that, I refused to play the role of a hypocrite and perform in God's house after all I've done, so I called Pastor Starks and made a full confession, swallowed hard as he rebuked me lovingly but very sharply, reminding me of how risky and reproachful my adventure had been and how I had not only taken advantage of God's mercy, but had provoked Him to great jealousy.

"Nothing and nobody must ever be allowed to come between you and your God. That, Sis, is the highest form of idolatry," he'd said, promising to pray for me and telling me what I needed to do to restore my broken fellowship with my God. I agreed, took a few days off from work to shut myself up alone at home, fasting and praying, laying on my face before God as I sought His forgiveness. I'd cried for days, talking to God about everything until I felt it again, the comforting warmth of His presence overshadowing my broken spirit, renewing my strength.

Two weeks later I was back to my Christian duties, attending my usual Bible classes and prayer meetings, the choir rehearsals where Trev and I did everything we could to avoid each other. There was no question though that I had made my battle to remain celibate harder, opened a forbidden door into my soul that made my body crave every day for Lincoln. None of it made sense to me. What had I needed so badly that I'd risked my salvation, my career, my very life to spend the night with a man who might have killed people? Why didn't I want to believe it, even after I'd seen the paintings done with his own hand? One thing was certain. Lincoln had triggered impulses deep inside my flesh that I never knew existed. He had awakened a hunger so fierce in me I was afraid it would never go back to sleep. That's what lust was, an insatiable desire for the wrong thing, a craving that, even after you fed it, still left you feeling unsatisfied. Waking up to find myself cradled in his arms had been revelatory to me for all the wrong reasons. Why I'd done it, I wasn't sure. I knew only that there was something about the way it made me *feel* deep inside myself that made me want to go back for more, regardless of the cost. How could something so wrong feel so right?

Beside me now on the second pew of Zion choir loft, my cell phone vibrated from deep inside my purse, and I snatched it up greedily, stared with disappointment at the familiar arrangement of numbers. Just a bill collector. Trev wasn't in rehearsal tonight. He hadn't even tried to contact me since that last night he'd shown up to find a forest of orchids in my living room. He avoided me totally those two times I'd seen him at Sunday morning and evening services. Now it was Thursday again and I was beginning to believe that both he and Lincoln had completely forgotten me. Why did I still care?

Suddenly, the bench beside me in the alto section groaned, and Pleasure was sliding in like a batter leaving third base, careening in for a homerun. She had a new Coach purse dangling from her wrist and her hair was done up in some kind of French chignon thing.

"You late," I whispered, conscious of her cotton candy perfume, her buxom body clad in green mohair. Pleasure's always attempting to make a fashion statement, but what all that green was saying just then, I sure didn't know.

"You ain't nobody's pastor." Pleasure smoothed her skirt daintily, nudged me with an elbow. "Who died and left you in charge of the alto section?"

"Hush, Girl."

"I will, as soon as you tell me where you been for the past two weeks, not retuning nobody's phone calls."

"I been busy."

"With Jesus I hope?" Pleasure's carefully arched brows rose in suspicion.

"Quit talking to me, Pleasure. Emmaline's looking over here like we backsliding."

"Hmph. I *know* I ain't, so she can look all she wants. But I can't vouch for everybody." She giggled at that, but somehow it didn't seem so funny to me. A chorus of voices rose around us in a rousing rendition of "Balm in Gilead," and we joined in too. The finale ended in sharp applause, but I sat there frozen, the lyrics waltzing in my head. Pleasure was nudging me again. "Gurl, snap out of it. Your song's coming up next, and you better sing it right because I'm in *need* of fixing. You don't know the kind of day I had. Whew!" Pleasure went to fanning herself.

"How can I sing the Lord's song in a strange land, Pleasure?"

"*What?*" She frowned. "Oh, Lord, Bunny. Don't tell me you rented *Love Jones* again?"

"I can't do it right now, Pleasure. I'm not really focused and I refuse to be a phony."

Emmaline was definitely cutting her eyes at us now, motioning for the tenors to go over the last section of "Balm of Gilead" alone. Tears were welling up in my eyes.

"Hush that noise and get those notes ready," Pleasure said. "The devil's just riding you because the choir's concert is a month away and you're one of our strongest lead singers. He knows God's gonna use you."

"The devil doesn't have a thing to do with it."

Pleasure took a Kleenex out of her new purse, blew her nose gently, and sighed in exasperation. The sound of opening foyer doors drew both our eyes. Somebody was dragging in late and I knew instinctively that it was Trev. He sat in his usual seat just behind me with the other tenors without acknowledging my presence at all. There was no affectionate tap on my back, no reassuring squeeze of my shoulders, no soft "amen" or his usual, "Praise the Lord, My Sister." I closed my eyes and then opened them again, was trying really hard to focus on Emmaline, who was directing the sopranos on a note they kept losing. I sat stiffly, not once looking over my shoulder to smile at the man who claimed to love me

"You hear that, Bunny? Ooh they sound *bad*," Pleasure whispered.

Turning around in her own seat, she nodded at Trev, allowed him to shake her hand. "I heard about Pete and I've been praying. How's he doing?"

Trev shrugged. "He's pulling through finally. Thanks to the prayers of the *saints*." He'd said the last word like an accusation. I stood up suddenly then, heading toward the foyer and the coat rack.

"Sister Sinclaire?" Emmaline's voice hovered in the air after me. "We're going to begin your song in a few minutes. Will you please be back in time?"

"I don't think so, Sis. I think it's best that you use somebody else."

"I beg your pardon?"

"I don't feel good. I'm going home to lie down."

A stunned silence fell over the choir loft, but I kept on moving toward the foyer, toward the small alcove where the coats were hanging. Behind me, the vestibule's doors swung open and I knew without looking that it was Pleasure. I hadn't expected Trev.

"Running's not the answer." Trev sounded angry, but Pleasure cut him off with a look, pushed him gently back through the doors. "I got this, Preacher. Let me." Trev met her eyes with a reluctant glance but nodded. It was too late though. I'd slipped on my coat and was making my way toward the outside steps.

†††

"Open this door, Miss Thang, 'cause we *know* you're in there."

Half past nine in the evening, and Pleasure's voice was like a shard being scraped against rock. Grating, sharp and intrusive. Gabriella wasn't expecting anyone, thought she shouldn't even open the door, but the knocks came again. Two different sets this time, each as urgent as the other. On the other side of the door, Gabriella knuckled her eyes, exhaled deeply and knotted the robe's sash tighter around her waist . She released the locks, stepped back just as the door was pushed open, narrowly missing her bare toes.

"It's about time," Pleasure complained. Behind her, Sister Nicole Rodgers, Bible tucked under arm, wore a demure smile, her plaid topcoat buttoned all the way to the throat. She opened her arms, gave Gabriella a quick, tight squeeze, and both of them stepped evenly across the threshold.

"What's this, a missionary raid? How did y'all get up here on my floor without being rung up?"

"Beg your pardon?" Rodgers blinked. Pleasure looked insulted. "Since when are we doing protocol? Girlfriend, that was some *strong* seduction that made you get up and leave rehearsal last night. You were *tripping.*"

"I'm not tripping."

"You are too. And that's why we came by here. To chase the devil out."

Gabriella sighed heavily as Pleasure pushed her way into the large half-lit living room littered with notebooks, newspapers and dying orchids. Rodgers trailed behind closely, seeing the small lamp near the desktop turned on, the screen up and flooded with text. On the floor beside the swivel chair, a dictionary and thesaurus lay open, pages bent from recent use. Gabriella snapped on an overhead lamp, snatched a nest of crumbled Kleenex from the coffee table and tossed them into a wastebasket.

"All that tissue. Somebody's been crying it looks like."

"I'm working overtime, Pleasure. I got deadlines. The Lord understands that."

"Was the Lord the one you were crying over?"

"Don't start with me, Pleasure."

Frowning at the disarray, Pleasure slipped off her coat, draped it across the couch, and headed straight for the kitchen, Rodgers trailing close behind.

"Some folks don't have any manners," Gabriella observed, following both women dutifully into the kitchen. She went to the stove automatically, adjusted a narrow ribbon of flame under the percolator that was still warm. She reached high on a shelf for mugs, selected spoons from a utility drawer, saucers from the dish drainer. Rodgers peeled off her coat and arranged it on the back of her chair. She sat down and opened her Bible, removing a folded slip of paper wedged between the pages.

Pleasure opened the refrigerator. "Uh-uh, Girl. How old is that coffee? Don't be trying to pass off none of that yesterday stuff…" Her voice from inside the fridge was muffled, as if seeping out from a cave, and Gabriella rolled her eyes.

"I just made it two hours ago," she said to the wide behind wrapped in plaid that was almost as big as the stove itself. "Cream and sugar?" She was looking at Nicole Rodgers with her dark, sultry features and coal-colored hair feathered into perfect layers lying flat as wings against her ears. Nicole Rodgers, who'd been "saved" since high school and was still a virgin. Thirty-something, but didn't look a day over twenty. A registered nurse at the Third Ward's walk-in clinic, Nicole was small-breasted, high-waisted, and had the narrow hips of a sixteen-year-old prom queen. Her fingers polling the worn Bible's pages now were as long and beautiful as the rest of her, nails squared and shiny from a fresh manicure.

There'd been numerous times during Gabriella's years at Zion that she,

Nicole and Pleasure had had to visit sisters just this way, pulling them back from the pain inflicted by some eligible bachelor who'd professed to love them but then, when they saw something else they wanted instead, conveniently "changed their minds." It had been such a constant battle for all of the single and celibate women in their congregation, Pleasure and Nicole included, that they'd finally organized themselves into squads to handle missions such as these, pulling lonely sisters away from the ledge.

Now, Nicole nodded toward the stove, began opening the folded sheet of paper.

"I take mine black, Sis," she said of the coffee, and Gabriella met her gaze and remembered. Years before, Trev, admitting to being attracted to her, had secretly taken Nicole out for coffee after services a few times while he and Gabriella had supposedly been dating. Gabriella and Trev had almost broken up over it. Nicole had continued to call him for months afterward, and deep down, Gabriella knew it was only because somewhere, somehow, Trev was still quietly spurring her on. Gabriella had seen the way they still looked at each other, saw how easily his eyes found hers across a room. And now, she couldn't help thinking, Nicole was here to see how easily she could move back into Trev's life.

Pleasure was through with grasping at empty cartons. She popped a few old grapes into her mouth, and emerged with a bottle of Perrier water. "Girl, your shelves are as empty as Jacob's kettle. When's the last time you been to the store?" She untwisted the Perrier, dropped into a kitchen chair and closing her eyes, took a long grateful swallow.

"Look, ladies, it was nice of you to stop by, but I've got edits on a big story to finish, so if y'all don't mind, after you've had your coffee of course, I'd appreciate it if you could…"

"If we could *what?*" Pleasure was poised, ready for a battle, but Nicole gently cleared her throat as if to say, *let me.*

"What kind of story are you writing, Sis?" She noticed Gabriella grimacing, folding and unfolding her arms with her back against the refrigerator, anxious for them to leave.

"It's one of the biggest stories of my career actually."

"And probably the last," Pleasure interjected. Gabriella shot her a sharp look.

"What's it about?" Nicole pressed, clearly going somewhere with it.

"About drug dealers, Nicole. The street pharmaceutical merchants of the wards."

"The *what?*" Pleasure burst into laughter, but Nicole raised her eyebrows, as she added a single spoonful of sugar into her cup. "Funny you should say that."

Gabriella didn't respond. Turning back to the stove, she reached for an oven mitt and picked up the percolator, pouring carefully into the two cups. She slid one toward each of them and waited, knowing Pleasure was up to something.

"Nicky could've helped with your research, Miss Thang. You know she sees everything down at that clinic. In fact, something happened the other day that I thought you'd find interesting."

"Here we go."

"Tell her, Nicole. Bunny. You need to hear this, Sweetie."

"If this is about Lincoln Duvall…"

"It's not, actually." Nicole reached for a paper napkin and folded it, blotting her lips with it. "It's about the mother of his children."

"His *children*?"

Pleasure patted a chair. "Sit down, Bunny. And hush."

"I don't understand…," she started, but Nicole spread the page in front of her, smoothing them flat with the tips of her dainty fingers. "It's all confidential information of course, and I can lose my job if it ever got out that I shared it, but when I heard you were dealing with Mr. Duvall…"

"Excuse me, but I'm not *dealing with* anyone."

"That's not what Trev said, so listen good." Pleasure's voice was sharp. "The evidence is right here." She pointed.

"What evidence?"

"Lincoln Duvall's." Nicole fought off a yawn. "We have a file on him at the clinic. Over nine different women have come through there— *nine* that we've recorded that is—who have aborted this man's children."

"That has nothing to do with me."

"Pleasure picked up the handwritten list, handed it to her. There were nine names with various dates scribbled next to them, some dating back ten years. The most recent dates belonged to Chinere Jackson. Beside Chinere's name were numerous dates, some only months apart." Gabriella was quiet, her eyes devouring each name and date.

"This last woman, Chinere, came in just a few days ago as you see, but she left. She didn't follow through with it."

Gabriella shook her head, suddenly feeling lightheaded. She ran numbed fingers through her already tousled hair. "And you are telling me all of this because...?"

"Bunny." It was Pleasure's turn, and she tapped her wrist, summoning her full attention. "If he has gotten all of these ward women pregnant, it means he's had unprotected sex with them, and the instances of STD's and HIV-infected women in the wards is..." She groped for words.

"...is much too great for you to take that chance with him," Nicole finished for her.

The quiet fell and lay there. Gabriella could not bring herself to look at either of them.

Nicole picked up her cup, sipped tentatively. Pleasure stirred cream and sugar into the dark, angry brew, sipped, and then frowned at the cup disapprovingly.

"We haven't made love yet, Leasy."

"Yet?" The women's eyes met over the table.

"I could have. We had a chance to. I wanted to. I was in the wrong place at the wrong time and feeling very vulnerable. I might have done it too, except he wouldn't let me. He refused to take advantage of me in my moment of weakness even though I could tell he wanted to. As crazy as it sounds, he had more honor than Trev. Trev would've been all over me; I know it. Lincoln wouldn't though. It was like he was protecting me from himself."

"*Lincoln Duvall?* Why would he do that?" Nicole put down her cup.

"I don't know. It could've been God. He just wouldn't. So we talked instead."

"Talked?"

"Yes. He held me all night in his arms and we talked until I fell asleep… It wasn't sexual. It was…emotional. I don't know… Paternal almost…"

"What did you talk about?"

"Everything. About life, about death, about the wards… About what we wanted out of life. About God."

"Yes. About God. And the amazing thing was, I felt so safe with him."

"*Safe?*"

"You know, like protected… Like, if there was anything that tried to harm me, he wouldn't let it. Like he'd fight to the death to protect me. Almost like he's my guardian sent to protect me while I'm writing this dangerous story."

"Lord, help her." Pleasure rolled her eyes.

"And what's so ironic about all this is that as much as Trev *says* he loves me, and as long as we've been together, I've *never* felt that secure with him. Never. Trev never seems to be totally sure about us. It's like he's always keeping part of himself back from me, just in case." She trained her eyes on Nicole deliberately. Their eyes held. Nicole looked away first.

On the stove, the pot hissed and hiccupped, and Gabriella got up to take it off the burner.

Pleasure sighed. "Well, we all know that Mister Duvall, as handsome and rich and charming, and sexy as he is, is a very high-ranking servant of another kingdom, Bunny. So as much as he may care about you in his heart, you *know* he has to obey his real master."

"Yes. I know."

"Even if it means destroying you," Nicole interjected, tracing the patterns of yellow calla lilies strewn across her china saucer.

CHAPTER SEVENTEEN

Gabriella

It's just after 8 a.m. on a Wednesday morning at *The Chronicle*, and Trish meets me at my desk, her smile as easy as a Sunday morning. "Congratulations, Sinclaire," she says. "You've finally reached the big time, my dear."

"Beg your pardon?"

"Your story on the drug dealer, along with a few others of course, has been chosen as an in-house entry to represent the paper in the national Bloom Awards competition for the urban experience division. The higher-ups thought it would do well and I happen to agree. Yours was a unanimous selection. It was a job well done, Lady, and an honor that's long overdue. Congratulations. We're all happy for you."

She walks off, humming one of her favorite Steely Dan riffs as Mark Blake and Joe Cartier, the city desk's two top editors, stop at my desk on their way to yet another internal meeting, to shake my hand.

"We're *extremely* pleased," Blake says.

"Best news we've had around here in years," seconds Cartier.

"Can this really be happening? The *Bloom* Awards?" I ask, as Blake grins, claps my back. The national Bloom Awards, named for one of Connecticut's most innovative and revolutionary veteran journalists, Lary Bloom, was *the* most prestigious recognition a seasoned journalist could ever hope to earn in a lifetime. A nomination alone was enough to propel a writer into the higher circles of print media, and it was hard to believe Lincoln's exploits could create such a stir. Now Cartier touches my wrist. "It gets better," he says.

"Oh?"

"Polinski called down here for you last night after you'd left."

"*Polinski?* The publisher himself?"

"None other," Blake chimes in. "He wants to take you to lunch when you have time. He wants to talk promotion, a huge salary increase, of course. He's left a message on your voice mail. Make sure you return his call this morning."

"Yes, Sir, I will," I say, watching the two men head toward the elevators.

I sit down at my desk and take a deep, slow breath. Why did God love me so much? I'd never understand it. My story had not even hit the newsstands yet and already the in-house early version was creating a stir. It would be available to the public this coming Sunday, and I had to find a way to let Lincoln know it was coming out. Surely he'd want to read it. I owed him that much, didn't I?

Lincoln

Yeah. They've "upped" the contract on me. I heard the rumors they all putting out; Spain's baby brother and Skyy's old crew and about a dozen other small-time busters who wanna "up" their status out here by taking me out. That ain't nothing new though. Brothas been gunning for me since I stepped into this world. Ghost heard they upped the bounty to fifty gees this time, thinks it's gonna really happen. Say he gotta check with all his babies' mommas, make sure they keeping up all them insurance policies he made them get so all his kids have money for college when the time comes around. Dying don't bother me none, so I just laughed and said, "Just make sure they ain't in on the plot, 'cuz what they stand to gain with you gone is a lot better than what you giving 'em now."

That's the difference between Ghost and me. He ain't looking forward to dying, especially if it's gonna be a hard way, so he always looking around the corner for it, expecting it to show up at any moment. I seen the face of Brotha Death so many times, I'll just give him "daps" when he shows up. Tell him it's about time he showed up. I figure it'll happen when it happens, and when it does, I'm taking a dozen niggas out with me. It's that simple. When I go, we all going, and most of these ward busters don't wanna make that kinda sacrifice, even if it means taking me out once and for all. It's what I got over the rest of these fools. They all love living too much. Love the money and the women and the power of running things. But me? I know what it's like to have none of it, so I can take it or leave it either way. It ain't gonna change what I am or how I feel about being Lincoln. Lincoln gonna be Lincoln, even if I gotta die to do it, so I don't worry when the streets heat up, and niggas start gunning for me, and the game gets to its highest level. Seem like that's really when I start to get amped up and turned on. That's why we out here on The Block as usual. On the basketball courts of Trece in broad daylight, doing our thing as always and waiting for them busters to roll up on us.

✝✝✝

You'd think they was in Siberia, the way these lil' homies out here dancing around and shivering on the courts. All except for Creeper of course. He's chilling right next to me on these bleachers, lips quaking, eyes tearing, face red as blood, but Half Pint ain't complained yet. Not him. Not one time.

Yeah. I know it's cold. Seven below zero, the weatherman claims it is today. Like a morgue freezer out here this afternoon, though the sun's steady dangling over the blacktop. Sun's kicking-back up there, doing nothing, like an unemployed wino, when I take off my coat to prove a point. "It's mind over matter," I tell those lil' cats as I leave Creeper and step onto the court. Ghost tosses me the ball, grinning drunkenly as I make my usual seventy consecutive shots from the foul line.

"Linc, man, you crazy, Homes," Lil' G starts stuttering.

"Nawl. Y'all lil' Niggas just gotta learn how to suffer," I say, and snatch off his hat and toss it over the fence while the other lil' homies are cracking up. Ghost is having a ball watching me train 'em, 'cause they whining like sissies, talking 'bout they cold, can they please go sit in the jeep? Talking about their feet are frozen, their noses are frostbit and they swear they're gonna fall off. Everybody out here's got on heavy gear but me. They wearing parkas with thick hoods and heavy sweaters underneath. Timbs with three pairs of socks, long johns, thick hats and thinsulated gloves, and they the ones crying.

"That nigga ain't human," TicToc is saying about me after I make him run full court with Ghost who can stay out here all day, 'cause he drank half a pint of bourbon before we got here, and is anti-freezed to the gills. I go back to the bleachers and Creeper starts sneezing, coughing hard, like he's 'bout to keel over. Ghost dribbles up and tosses me the half-pint of bourbon from his back pocket, and I hand it to the lil' soldier sitting beside me. He takes a long, deep swig, gags, coughs even harder, and I want to pat him on the back, but that would only undo what I'm trying to teach him. I don't wanna embarrass him in front of his boys, so I just wait until he finishes, watch while he wipes his nose on the back of his coat sleeve and leans over to hawk on these frozen bleachers.

"You got that asthma too, huhn?" I say, and Lil' Homes shakes his head fast. "Nawl. I'm straight. I got this," he says, but I can tell he's lying. On the courts, TicToc tries to check Ghost but trips over those big boat feet of his. He falls flat out on the cold blacktop, holding his arm, rocking back and forth and talking bout he's hurt, he's gonna need X-rays. The rest of 'em are all laughing at that, calling him a punk, and that's when I see that pretty car ride past the courts real slow, like she's looking for me especially. Ghost is standing there with the ball against his hip, so he sees it too and whistles as the car slows and idles quietly near the fence. "Look like you being paged, Baby."

Lil' G and them all stop what they doing and switch over like clockwork, start going into their clothes, coming out with their "pieces" so fast they break they own timing records. I try real hard not to smile 'cuz these lil' soldiers have been trained too well. I don't want the lil' homies to see what that looks like, me smiling, so I get up from the bleachers and head toward her. "Hold ya fire. It's all good," I tell 'em, and they get disappointed when they see it's just a skirt, put their guns back like they upset.

"Who dat?" TicToc's asking Ghost. "She fine."

Creeper follows me almost to the fence, poking his lil' chest out like he's hard. "D. That's *you*, baby? That's one of your hoes?"

"Nawl. Not this one," I say and walk up to that pretty Acura that's bumping something that don't sound nothing like churchified music. It's jamming though, and I'ma tell her that when she stops looking all scared and rolls down the window. I knock on the glass, and she rolls down the window, trying to appear all serious, like she ain't came down here on purpose.

"S'up, Babygirl? You slumming? Creeping up on a brotha?"

"Where's your coat, Lincoln? It's *freezing* out here."

"I like it this way. Cold better than hot any day."

Her mouth drops open like she wants to say something, preach a lil' maybe, but changes her mind. Baby looks *real good*, though, and she knows it. Good enough to be seen on a brotha's arm, most definitely. Yeah. Her turn, next, I think, even though I promised myself I was gonna quit tripping with this and leave her alone for real.

"I was just passing through when I saw you," she says with that sexy voice.

"Just passing through The Trece, huhn? Just ended up on the third side for no reason at all?" I rub my chin, lick my lips real slow-like.

"Actually, I was hoping I'd see you, to tell you the story is running this week," she says, being real careful with her eyes.

"Yeah. I know," I tell her, sizing her up with one of my classic looks.

"No, you don't," Baby says, throwing it right back at me. She cuts those pretty eyes at me and my heart dips, like there's a moth caught in my chest. But I shake that off quick.

I can't help it. She makes me laugh for no reason, and I'm glad the lil' homies don't see me over here, "cheesing" on the sly. "Why you always gotta challenge me, Churchgirl? You know you outta ya league. Why you ain't home knitting a quilt or something? Somewhere baking cookies for the pope?"

"'Cuz I choose to be right here, Big Time. This *is* a free country."

"Is that right?"

"Right it is."

"Mmph. You talk a lil' game. I give you that. But don't fool yaself. According to The Street's epistemological standards, we both know you still outta ya league."

"By what evidence can you substantiate your claim?" She got me speechless on that one, and we both go to laughing.

"What you listening to, anyway? Driving up in here like you auditioning for *Soul Train*. Don't tell me you still backsliding?"

"What do you mean, 'still'?"

"That wasn't exactly no prayer meeting we was having the last time I saw you." She smirks, looks like she wants to smack me, but she don't. Just shakes her head, still trying to pretend she ain't as happy to see me as I am to see her. She looks embarrassed to be out here, but I can't help myself; I just like looking at her. She's got on a fur coat that's the same brown as her eyes, and a matching hat she's rocking down hard on one side. I can smell that perfume from here, and it's like time's standing still, and neither one of us wants to break this spell, this moment.

"What are you listening to?" I ask, catching myself, pulling my mind back.

"Hezekiah Walker. A gospel singer from New York."

"Hezekiah, like that Old Testament king?"

"I'm impressed, Lincoln."

"Yeah. But that's still a jacked-up name though, I'm sorry. His momma shoulda just put a paper monkey on his back and got it over with. Brotha's music be flowing though, huhn? I can get with some of this… Yeah. I like that cut. Brotha's rocking them NYC church beats hard, ain't he?" I start in busting a move of my own right there on the street, and she laughs, shaking her head at my craziness. She looks over her shoulder at the lil' homies taking turns at the foul line.

"You have these children out here suffering in these temperatures, Lincoln?"

"Children?"

"They look young to me."

"Nawl. They ain't children. They more like… protégés."

"Oh, really?"

"Really. They out here voluntarily. Say they wanna be soldiers, so I'm just getting 'em ready, that's all."

"You training those little boys to be gangsters, Lincoln?"

"It's gonna be awhile before they're qualified to call themselves OG's."

She shakes her head, and I can tell she's disappointed by my answer. But what did she expect? This is what I do. "Well, I was just driving past," she says "...so I'll let you get back to your...duties. And, Lincoln, you're gonna catch pneumonia out here without a coat."

"I'm fine, Angelfied."

"Please go put one on, Lincoln. For me at least."

"Aiight. Only for you."

"Thank you."

"You're welcome, Baby."

I shake my head, 'cause there it is, that urge to kiss her again, but she looks away from me quick, like she's embarrassed, and shifts the car from "Park" into "Drive."

"Take care yourself," she whispers, but I lean into the window and touch her face, playing with her hair that's falling from under her hat and down her shoulders. "How do you do that, Gurl?"

"What?"

"You the only somebody in ward history that *always* knows how to find me."

"Who said I was looking for you?"

"You don't have to say it. I can feel it."

"Oh?"

"Only 'cause I'm feeling the same thing."

She looks up at me, not saying a word this time, so I know it's okay to run it down for her, take my time to say what I know she wants to hear. Behind me I can hear the sound of the Escalade starting up. Ghost and the homies have climbed back up in it, got some Snoop pumping full blown, probably passing around what's left of that half- pint. I look back at her, thinking she looks like some kind of exotic African queen surrounded by all that fur. "I know you was wondering where I was... I know you was wondering if I was just playing you like all the others." I stoop down near her door, fold my arms against her window. She pretends the cold's not bothering her, but I can see that it is. I know she wants me to go around and slide up into the front seat next to her, but I don't.

She switches the heat onto full blast, looks at me like she expects me to be shivering too.

I don't though. I just stare at all that beauty.

"About that night, Lincoln…," she was trying to say. "I was terribly wrong. I was a terrible example to you. Please find it in your heart to forgive me. I…"

"That night was 'bugged,' Babygirl. Like nothing that ever happened with me and *any* woman. I been thinking about it ever since. I mean we didn't make love… Now *that* had me tripping… We spent the whole night talking about things I never told nobody. I know you saying it was like, an interview. Research for your article. But it felt strange, you know? Like we was supposed to be together. It felt nice. Real nice."

We sit quiet for a minute, me watching the cars that pass by like always.

"You didn't plan to ever call me again, huhn?" She was looking away from me again, waiting for my answer.

"Nawl. I didn't."

"Why not?"

"I figured you had all the research you needed. I was just gonna wait until you published the story. See how it turned out."

"That's not the real reason and you know it. Why, Lincoln? Why weren't you gonna call me?"

"You know why." I was frowning, I could feel it.

"Tell me." She leaned forward and turned down her music, watching me again closely with that little girl look in her eyes.

"You really think you can handle this, Angelfied?"

"Is that your final answer?"

"I didn't want to; I don't *want* to hurt you, aiight? There. I said it."

"Since when has that ever mattered to you? Hurting somebody?"

Her question catches me like an uppercut and I can't say a word, just stand there watching her watching me with those butterflies in my stomach. I never had this feeling before with any of the others and I don't like it. Thinking it must be what they say fear feels like. Like not being able to guess the wheres and the whys and the hows. Like my own game is trying to turn in on me and swallow up all my words.

I knew what I needed to do just then. I needed to get out of them thoughts real fast. Just get up and away from this pretty "conjure woman," as Dante be calling her, that's trying to work mojo on my will.

I snatch up one of her warm, soft hands then and kiss it, hold it hard against my cold cheek.

"Lincoln." She was calling me all soft-like but I didn't answer, was real careful not to look into those eyes.

"Leave it alone," I tell her. "Don't come back down here," I said, and walked away quick before she could say or do anything else.

I heard the sound of her window rolling up, but I was steady walking away, and when I looked back over my shoulder again, mad now 'cause I didn't understand why I kept dealing with her in the first place, she was gone, and I got the saddest feeling I might not ever see her again.

GANGSTER PARTIES

Ghost

We steppin' up in the door of Soldier's nightclub, an army of seven dressed like we just walked off a Sean John fashion runway and it's about to be "on" up in here. Linc and Cheese. Wizard. Dante, Scooter, Mink, and Myself. Three deep on each side and we're all fully strapped; Uzis, Mags, Nines and sawed-off shotties. D's in the middle of all us, wearing enough armor to hold off a whole gang of fools by himself if he has to. He might have to, what with the way things have been lately since we've been expanding our operations into Deuce, so there's no telling what might jump off in here tonight. What matters is, we came prepared for anything.

"Whatever comes we'll just handle it," D always says, rehearsing it again on the way over here tonight, even though we all can tell his mind's not really on business. He's been that way lately, ever since that choir girl's tripped into his life, and we'll all be glad when he finally "bumps that off" and gets over with it.

No one knows D better than me, and what I've seen is that if he's nothing else, he's a thinker, a strategist. "A masochist," my father calls him, although he himself, a brilliant pharmaceutical chemist, is dumb as a rock when it comes to understanding what it takes to survive out here. D saved my life more times than I can count back in Juvie Hall and later in the pen, and had he stayed in school and gone to college, or maybe enlisted with Uncle Sam and left the streets alone, he'd have been running some big-time conglomerate with the kind of brain and self-discipline he has. He's never been much of a talker, but he's certainly a reader. Linc'll read any and everything. He has all those hours in solitary to thank for that. Now he's busy laying out plans for the expansion of our operations, an endeavor he'll turn into a major empire with four equally strong heads at the top, and dozens of brothas underneath us equally clocking top dollars. He's got Cheese and Dante scheduled to take over the First Ward, now that Skyy's gone; and he wants me and Scooter to hold down Deuce, what with Spain finally out of the way. Trece is still the biggest money-maker, one he'd never trust solely to anyone else but himself, but D says soon the other two wards will be grossing just as much, and when they do, everybody in the community will reap the benefits. Money can buy any kind of talent, if the price is right, so Linc got the mayor's office to pull some strings, and he's hired some of the city's best metropolitan planners to put everything on paper for us. He's got the plans all written out, plans that include daycare centers, Laundromats, shopping centers and fast-food franchises. D wants to do a whole lot of private expansion right in the wards, so that the neighborhood is its own self-sustaining entity, a place no longer dependent on the whims of downtown's selfish corporations who are only interested in dropping a few crumbs for all these unemployed folk down here. Linc's vision is for everybody to be working legitimately and somehow it actually looks like that could happen.

"Downtown Heartford don't care nothing about poor people," Linc had said just a week ago, "so let's keep our money right here where it belongs."

The fact that drugs are the foundation of Linc's plans for economic development make our entire plan "morally bankrupt," my pops said, but to us, the entire thing is sheer ingenuity, our own version of pie-in-the-sky. Tonight then, coming to Soldier's was about all taking a break from business and having some pleasure for a change, all about stretching out, staking our claims and establishing propaganda, especially since it was our first public appearance since Spain's extermination.

Soldier was always crying about homies causing him to lose his liquor license, so all our heat's concealed under the latest street gear to hit Heartford. It's a bitterly cold night under a sky that's thick with stars, and I'm wearing chocolate for the occasion. Suede. A two-piece get-up with pockets everywhere, like the lil' homies be sporting on BET. A white cashmere turtleneck sets off these brown-and-white low-riding Timbs, so I'm "styling," but can still stomp a fool if I have to. It's a general unspoken rule among our crew—never wear anything you can't "scrap" in. Outside on the street tonight, lines of Caddies and Beemers and Lincolns and Lexuses are being watched over by Soldier's crazy valets, armed brothas dressed in riot gear who are known to park a car and then sit in it for an hour while they get high with their homies. It's a Saturday past midnight. Oldies Night at Soldier's, so I'm chewing my Big Red and swaying to the beats of Parliament and Funkadelic as the doors open wide and Soldier's three *ugly* bouncers, muscles bulging like turnips under their sweats, move the crowd back to let us through. Decorated in green-and-black camouflage to look like one of those Viet Cong jungles where Soldier, the club's namesake and owner, lost his right leg, Soldier's is one of the classiest and most deadly places in the city to party. Classy, so it's expensive enough to keep out the wards' riff-raff, but smart enough to let in the culture and style and dancing and music that makes the hood parties be bumping. The deadly part comes in with the gathering of the city's worst gangsters, who all have armed entourages and specially reserved booths. "Gentlemen Hustlers," as D calls them, who aren't above beefing publicly whenever the mood strikes them. Everybody from Old School Italian Mafioso to downtown politicians in wing-tipped shoes, comes up in here, because they've all got their hands in that one pot of gold that produces all the illegal wealth the wards are famous for.

All this smoke in here is making me cough and I double over, barking like a sissy. D looks at me with that veiled look he has, but he doesn't say a word.

He's been getting on me lately about all the product I've been consuming, watching how slow I am in my body, how I'm getting up later and later every morning, losing all kind of weight like I'm on a crash diet, and for now, he won't ask me what I think is really going on. He'll wait until I feel like talking about it.

Once we're all safely inside the club, fools, not wanting any part of D's legendary temper, start parting fast to let us through. You would think the President had just rolled up with his Secret Service, the way the city's fiercest brothas stop what they're doing to signify with butts of their heads, or just plain start giving us all "daps."

"S'up, Baby... S'up, Playa?" we take turns saying. "Hey now..."

The aromas of expensive perfumes and aftershaves, simmering gumbo and fried shrimp, hover close now, overriding the reefer and the cognac, and beside me, D moves like a general. Swaggering. Profiling. Swaying to the thick bass rhythms. It's dark as a cave in here, but D's wearing shades to hide eyes he wants to stay unreadable. One hand is deep in his pocket, like he's posing for the cover of *GQ*, or holding on to something he can pull out quick just in case niggas wanna start an uprising. Dante's looking real smooth in his off-white topcoat and pinstripe suit, but it's Linc who steals the show as usual. He's Armani all over tonight, down to his cologne. He's wearing black on black on black on black. Brothers around here never even knew there was such a thing as black diamonds until D started wearing them in his ear. Black-diamond cufflinks. Black-diamond watches. Nobody knows where he picked up that classic taste, being from the wards and all, but he works it hard just the same. Michael Jordan, Puffy Combs, and the rest of those paid brothers don't have a thing on D's style, and all the little homies on the corners are always trying so hard to look just like him.

Tonight, it's those new baggy trousers that flow smoothly when he walks. Trousers that match a custom-cut three-quarter jacket, vest, silk shirt, and calf-leather boots with the squared toes. Smooth. That's how we do it up in here. Not just us, but all the OG's up in Soldier's right about now are looking fly. That's cuz we ain't playing gangster. We the Original Article.

Voices hard and soft are singing our names like we're in some kind of parade. We move into the flow of the rhythm, the bass taking us over, but the name we hear most is always "Linc... Linc...," like a chant on some football field. Brothas mostly call him "D," but females love singing it. Love calling "Linc," like some kind of TV jingle. If you weren't a strong man it could make you jealous, the way the women swoon all around him, blowing kisses and grinding their hips, trying to step out of the crowds to touch him like he Jesus, like they'd think we'd let anybody get that close. Our crew's all used to it by now, so we don't bother to sweat the small stuff anymore. We were there when Linc was still making his reputation, and every last one of us knows that it was hard earned. So hard, none of us, except maybe Dante, have any problem letting him keep that title.

So while he's playing King Pin, we're watching every hand in the place. It's a necessary precaution, as Soldier's has more smoke and mirrors than a carnival fun house. Crystal moons revolving from the ceiling. Strobe lights winking off and on like fireflies. Pretty women in foxy furs sipping Moet at the bar while the dance floor is packed with gyrating bodies. DJ Moe-Driver is throwing down hard tonight, and even the barkeeps are bouncing, the waitresses doing spins with trays balanced on their shoulders. Moe-Driver spots us and throws his hands up, churning his fist in the air, cranking up his usual mic drama; "Awwwwwwwwww..... Sooky Sooky *now*," he groans into the mic like a man who's making love to a woman. "It's about to be on up in here! Ladies and gentlemen, looky looky what the cat's just drug in.... It's da big boys fa sho... Soldier's, give a holler for D-vall and Da Crew making it happen, Baby. Passing that paper. It's tender but it ain't hardly legal. Yo, D! Shake dat groove thang, Dawg. Cuz it's eighties night and brovahs behind the bar wanna get piz-aidddd....Holla if ya hear me, y'all!"

The whole room breaks into barking.

"*Hey....Ho.... Hey... Ho....*"

All that hoofing and stomping is coming from the dance floor where couples are busting the kinda moves that'll never be seen on *Soul Train*. House-party moves so original that the next day, once folks are sober again, they won't even remember how to do them. We've been drinking cognac all night and now I'm enjoying drooling over all this gyrating pulchritude that's waiting on me to reach out and grab it.

"Aw, yeah," I can hear Linc murmuring, cuz a fine honey in a slinky green dress has caught his eye and swivels around in her chair to check him out. He blows her a kiss and we keep moving, but now it's my turn to get my scope on. I pop a cigar into my mouth and blow a kiss at a fine Shortie in an electric-blue catsuit with faux mink around the cuffs.

"Shake it, Baby," I say, but it's Big Cheese who steps in front of me and taps her on the behind. She stops and slaps the daylights out of him. Her eyes are on me, so I wink at her.

"Watch it, Gurl. Shake it, but don't break it now," I tell her, and she tosses her weaved hair back behind her ear, flashes me the sexiest smile. Driver's switched up, starts playing Parliament's "Knee Deep," one of Linc's favorite old school jams, and the place explodes into the familiar bass line. Lincoln stops in his tracks as soon as he hears it, busts a move right where he stands. He grabs a young skirt away from her partner on the dance floor and starts showing her how we used to do it back in the day. Girlfriend's giggling cuz she knows he's straight tripping, but his moves are kinda fly the way he does it—one arm tucked behind his back, shoulders low like he's boxing Tyson. It's Old Skool, no doubt about it and she can flow with him.

"My boy, D. S'up, Nigga?" It's Lo-Rider, who claims he's Linc's cousin, yelling from over by the bar with his arm around two hard-looking skirts.

"I can't call it," Linc lies, raising his fist in salute while we stand around him like a wall, low key, formidable.

"Y'all coming to spend some cheddar? Planning to behave, I hope." Soldier, looking worried, has stepped up to greet us personally. The wall opens slightly, just enough for him to hold out his hand to Linc.

"S'up, Pimp?" he says.

"You, Playa," Linc says, and lets his little dance partner go back to her fuming partner. Linc clasps Soldier's hand, never taking his eyes off the room. "Her tab? Whatever she want tonight? I got it," he says, nodding toward the girl.

"Aiight now," Soldier says, and Linc gives Soldier three c-spots in advance, looks toward his usual booth. It's a peace offering, and Linc knows it. We all do. Soldier knows all the money we drop when we're here, but he also knows how many niggas are gunning for us, and my man doesn't want any trouble. A place can get shot up quick when Linc's on board, which is why Soldier's still standing there, gesturing with his eyes. We catch the clue, follow his eyes and see Spain's little brother and his little set on the other end of the room. It's obvious they see us too.

"D, man. No trouble tonight, okay, Baby? I mean, I just had the carpenters in last month. Just got the place put back together after it was shot up the last time."

But Linc only nods. "We cool," he says and smiles. "You know we got this."

Soldier ain't hardly convinced, but he nods like he's supposed to and walks away to clear his waitresses off the floor. It's the price he pays for running this kind of joint, and everybody knows he's got enough insurance on the place to rebuild three clubs. Linc slides into the booth first, Spain's old booth, and we all follow suit, making our public statement, taking our usual places around him. It's a spot where we can see everything, so it's not lost on us that Spain's baby brother isn't smiling at all but watching us hard across the room. It's obvious they've got beef, and already we see other hustlers leaving their tables, grabbing their women and moving toward the door. Gunfire is inevitable, but Linc doesn't move. Times like these is how he earns his reputation and we all know the routine.

It takes less than five minutes for the bullets to start firing at us, but Linc pushes us out of his way and walks calmly, directly into the line of fire. He's got guns in both hands and is firing back, clicking off chambers like a madman until he gets right up to their table and stands there, shooting up lil' homies like he's invincible. Bodies are falling everywhere, slumping down in their chairs, but he keeps at it until he's satisfied that no one else is moving. He'd have been insulted if any of us tried to help him, so we just stay where we are, guns drawn, handing him napkins to wipe the blood off his clothes. When he's done, he doesn't turn and walk out, but goes back calmly to our table and sits down and orders his usual sloe gin fizz, even as Mo-Driver has fled the stand, and sirens can be heard in the background over the wails of females.

Folks are diving over each other, running out of the club in sheer pandemonium, but Linc sits there and enjoys his drink, makes us enjoy ours also, timing it all perfectly. Finally, when he has drained his glass, he belches and says, "That was good, Baby," to Soldier and leaves twenty c-notes on the table. We walk out to the Escalade just as the cops are pulling up, but they don't say anything to us at all except, "Good night, Mr. Duvall. You boys have a pleasant evening."

With Super Cooper gone, there's nobody left to question all the blood that's running in rivulets down the center of Soldier's dance floor, and I can't help thinking, maybe D's right after all. Maybe this *is* a new day; maybe things *are* getting much easier for us after all.

Chapter Eighteen

Gabriella

E zekiel Polinksi holds the menu just under his nose and squints, looks over at me and then up at the waiter in the velvet jacket who is hovering close to the table to hear our selections. The restaurant is beyond elegant, a meeting place for the city's most powerful corporate power brokers, one of whom is sitting across from me at this very moment.

"Miss Sinclaire?" Polinksi says, and smiles patiently, his eyes a deep cerulean blue, his gray handlebar moustache giving him the appearance of a modern-day Mark Twain.

"The stuffed shrimp looks great. I think I'll have that," I say to the waiter who nods efficiently and looks at Polinski.

"I'll have the scrod, thank you. And to drink, a mocha cappuccino would be nice. Miss Sinclaire?"

"That sounds great. I'll have the same."

The waiter disappears with our menus, and Mr. Polinksi smiles again and loosens his red paisley tie that doesn't do a thing for the dark pinstriped suit he's wearing. Under the table my knees knock nervously. Mr. Polinksi is the editor-in-chief of *The Heartford Chronicle*, and an audience with him, in journalistic circles, is like being with the pope.

"I appreciate your willingness to lunch with me," he says, and my smile is tentative and polite as I unfold my napkin and spread it across my lap in an attempt to quiet my nerves.

"It's an honor, Sir, of course," I say, as Polinski reaches for the bread basket and offers it to me first. We each take a roll and part the doughy flesh simultaneously with our knives, breaking open the gold squares of butter, spreading them sparingly.

"You've been with *The Chronicle* for how many years, Miss Sinclaire?"

"Close to fifteen now."

"Very good. I've enjoyed your pieces over the years and have often thought it was a great thing that you were on our team, as opposed to the city's other papers."

"Thank you, Sir. I appreciate that."

Polinski raises an eyebrow, reaches for his water glass. "This last story though was certainly one of the best I've read in years, and I was wondering about the subject you portrayed so vividly. The man you chose to call 'Jonah,' for privacy purposes of course."

"Yes."

"I'm told that you're working on a three-part series involving this particular character?"

"Yes, Sir. I am."

"His initial introduction was so shocking, to say the least, that I'm wondering if many of our readers have missed the point of why we've chosen to highlight such a person. I'm wondering if we'll in fact discover a little more about his childhood and background. His family life and where he's been in the judicial system. I'm not just interested in understanding the villainous activity he's engaged in, fascinating though it is, but rather, I wonder how he's managed to arrive at this turning point in his life where he has determined to, might I say, 'rule the world'?" Polinski touches a napkin to his mouth. "I was, to say the least, *extremely* impressed by the way you presented his humanity, and I think if anyone can paint the full picture of this man's fall into the underworld, you can."

"Thank you, Sir."

"In that sense, his story can be redemptive."

"I agree, Sir."

"For you to go to such a dangerous level of reporting shows tenacity and courage, of course, but it also shows, in my own personal opinion, that somehow we at *The Chronicle* have made you feel excluded in some way, so that you felt the need to resort to desperate measures to gain recognition that you should have already received for your hard work and talent."

"I concur," I say, relaxing finally as our salads arrive and Polinski winks before forking his romaine lettuce.

"It goes without saying that here is a man who must trust you an awful lot, to expose himself so fully to you," he offers.

"Yes, Sir. 'Jonah' has risked a great deal himself, allowing me to share in his world, and his is just one of numerous stories in the wards that beg to be told."

Polinski smiles warmly, pats my hand, reaches for his bread, and no one needs to tell me that the worst is past. Polinski was building his case. He was preparing to make me an offer.

"It has always been my opinion that writers who are able to develop that kind of wide open rapport with their subjects must be given a greater range in which to expand and pass down such valuable skills," he says. "I was wondering if you'd ever considered writing for the paper on a more editorial level?"

Ghost

Look at him. Carrying around that newspaper like it's the Ten Commandments or something. All because *she* wrote the article. Just because *her* name's on it like some sort of government seal.

"Cane: Lessons In The Life Of A Street Pharmacist," the story's titled. Six full pages in all following a shadowy cartoon of a black man in a black suit, standing with his arms folded atop the Third Ward's tallest high-rise. I haven't read it 'cause it looks exploitive to me. Another piece of ghetto-fabulous sensationalism. But Linc has read it three times and calls it "brilliant." "Provocative." Thinks she took a complex subject and personalized it, simplified it for the ordinary squares who actually pay to read *The Chronicle*.

It's not making sense to me. Linc, tripping like this over one female when all the sweet young things in the wards would sell their breasts just to have one night with him. He can't walk into a pizza shop without some skirt trying to negotiate: *Can I call you sometime? You married yet? When's the last time you had a homecooked meal?*

"Nothing worse than a chasing female," Linc was always saying, balling up their numbers and tossing them out the car window. He had no respect for females that didn't respect themselves, which is why I can't understand why he is tripping so hard over some intellectual-type who's sold her soul to the establishment and is trying to sell his too. Chinere says it's because she looks so much like his mother, but I'm not convinced.

"You having an emotional episode?" I almost asked him when the story ran two days ago, but he'd never admit to it anyway, so why bother? Truth is, he and Chinere aren't doing too good since he met *her*, what with Nere wanting to have his kid and all. D handles his women, and I handle mine. That's always been our policy. But now as I sit up here behind the wheel of his Beemer, Homes is seriously interfering with my cash flow. I light up another spliff, swallowing that sweet grade-A smoke.

"C'mon, Yo. We gonna be late!" I'm honking the horn one more time, beckoning with my hands, and he gives me the finger straight up, laughs at my impatience. He's standing in the doorway of Dougie's Pawn and Porno Shop with that new semi-automatic he just bought wrapped up in an old blanket. Linc buys guns the way some cats buy shoes, but today his timing is all wrong. We're taking so long Villanova might think something's happened to us. Cuz is just standing there talking to Dougie like he's chillin' in the cut and doesn't have to be on the other side of town in less than five minutes. Usually it's the other way around. Usually Homes has to come get me out of places. But today, it being his mom's anniversary and all, I suppose he's trying to redirect somehow. Trying to work through those feelings that hit him every year around this time.

He's walking toward the car at last, grinning like his mind's bad. "Quit crying like a girl, Money. Villanova's got sense. He knows we'll be there," he tells me. He gets in the car at last, unwraps the blanket to stroke the rifle's smooth dark finish. "Pretty, ain't she?" he says, kissing it, and I can't help but agree. It's hard to believe we're gonna be late to pick up our weekly supply, because it's never happened before. Linc's never late. Rain. Snow. Traffic. Cops. It doesn't matter. In seven years, nothing and nobody has ever stopped him from being on time to get our product, so I know he's tripping hard. He has to be if he's dragging his feet to make money.

I turn the corners like I'm on my way to a fire, but Homes ain't noticing a thing. Sits there stroking the gun like it's a woman he wants to make love to, like he's heartsick and doesn't know what to do with himself. It's the best time to reason with him.

"I was thinking, Yo, you know, after we make this last sum…?"

"Yeah." He puts the gun under the seat, unfolds the article again. Stares at it.

"I'm thinking we oughta lay low for a while. You know, kick back some. Smell the coffee. Enjoy all our other investments and leave The Street drama to these lil' knuckleheads."

He folds the article up again, looks at me like I've lost my mind. "See that."

"What?"

"I told you."

"Told me what, Yo?"

"All that smoke's making you loco, Man. Got you thinking like a straight punk."

"How you figure?"

"All that time we done together in jail and you wait 'til now to turn female on me?"

"Go 'head, Man. I'm just saying."

"You just bugging. Give up Da Block? All this cheddar to be made out here? Man, gimme dat." He snatches my joint and flings it out the window; thinks he's funny, although I'm trying hard to make a point.

"D. I know there's mad loot to be made in the wards, but we gotta be smarter than Jordan, Man. Get out 'fore these lil' fools try to retire us both."

He tilts his head back, eyes me like he does when he's trying hard to concentrate or is hearing something for the first time. "What's on your mind, Playa? Just say it."

"I don't know, Man. It's just how I feel. That thing with Q-Pete?"

"What about it?"

"That fool almost died. That was a close call, D. You know it."

"No closer than all the others."

"Too close when that fool's cousin is crazy Cooper."

"And?"

"And, I heard he been down here again asking questions."

"I ain't surprised."

"I heard he looking for you personally."

"It ain't got nothing to do with his cousin. Trust."

"Is that why 'Nere's been tripping?"

"Part of it. The other part's got to do with that belly that's getting bigger by the day. But after today, that ought to be over with." He looks out the window, watching the pretty women crossing the street.

"You think she gonna really go through with it this time?"

"She better if she got good sense."

"It's that easy, huhn?"

Linc sucks his teeth, gets real quiet then, and when we get over to Villa-nova's, he doesn't come in to engage in the usual banter. Just sits in the Beemer holding the article like he's sulking, or thinking on his momma, or maybe his brotha, Runt. Maybe D is just tired of being tired. He might even be think-ing about Chinere, and that big argument they had last night about their baby. Maybe he's thinking on why the streets are looking much too quiet, even though check day's just around the corner. After awhile I come out of Villanova's with the goods wrapped up inside the duffle, and we head over toward our south side depot where we'll spend another hour breaking it down for distribution. I'm almost there when he jerks his thumb toward a florist shop just outside the ward, and says, "Hold up, Man. Pull over right here."

He gets out, goes inside and comes back with three separate sprays of flowers, and when we get to the south side, he shrugs, turning the flowers in his hands. "You know what day it is, Cuz?"

"Yeah… I know."

"Said I wanted to go and…"

I nod then, understanding perfectly. I was right the first time. It's his momma after all, and if he doesn't do it, if he don't honor her memory, who will? Surely not Runt.

"Enough said, D," I tell him.

"Yo." He raises his chin, lets me read his eyes. "Thanks, Man. On the real."

"We brothas, ain't we?"

"Always."

"Aiight then. Get gone. Handle ya business. I got it from here."

"You sure?"

"Holler when I see you." I pull over to the curb at the depot and lean over smiling, give him some "daps," then watch as he takes the wheel, drives mad slowly down the block while our security force stationed around the perimeter looks on. They all know what day it is.

Yeah. He's troubled big time today, so I'm glad I didn't bother mentioning what I'd heard about Skyy and Spain's peeps uniting just to take us out. Talking payback. *Hard* payback, although they still can't figure out how to breach the formidable wall we've built around our operations. Could be just another rumor though. New rumors spring up in the wards every day, and a man'd make himself crazy to believe all of them. For now, though, I'm just glad D's gone to clear his head. Pay his respects. And it's funny how that works. How even the most notorious, fiercest brothas on Da Block get soft as cream when it comes to their mothers. Guess we're all the same when it comes to that.

Miss Haney from the first floor can't stand me, but she's smiling anyway from her window as I walk up the steps toward the building. Miss Haney's borrowing money from Lincoln every other Friday to play her street numbers and has the nerve to look like she wants to call Five-O tonight. She knows it's "Setting-Up" night. Knows it's gonna be wall-to-wall traffic as soon as the sun goes down and nobody in this building's gonna get any real sleep tonight. But that's the price one pays when one chooses to live in the wards. It's always been that way. Always will be that way.

CHAPTER NINETEEN

Gabriella

Emails are flooding in from producers of evening news shows all over the city, and the folks at WKKK and WBLC Radio have already called me several times, trying to get me on the air to do interviews. There are rumors that Bountiful Publishing has called our editor-in-chief's office, asking if they thought I'd be interested in a book deal, and the folks at *The Chronicle* are doing all they can to see that it continues. I'd expected some reverberations from the story, some moments of fleeting fame and the usual outcry that perhaps the man I'd so vividly painted as my subject, would be seen as some sort of fictitious outgrowth of my imagination, a larger-than-life cartoon character who couldn't possibly possess all of the attributes I'd described. Lincoln was much too Black, much too smart, much too savvy and much too rich to have grown up in the wards. And he *was* fascinating. The way he thought, the things he said, were definitely original, and I'd managed to capture most of that. It seemed that everyone outside of the wards, from the folks at the corner laundromat to the men who peddled magazines to me downtown, were yearning to know just who this drug lord was. I knew it would be that way, so I'd fought hard at the onset, vowing not to let them see, much less publish the piece, unless Lincoln's identity could remain anonymous. Not that I was in agreement with his notorious lawlessness, but he still deserved the same liberty cops gave suspects when they chose to cooperate and lend pertinent information to their investigations. They didn't call it amnesty for nothing. Besides, I couldn't get the story any other way.

It was still ironic that Amanda Milan, who had come to the paper five years *after* I did, and is nowhere as experienced, did a piece last year about railroad fraud and got promoted to city travel editor with a salary that had increased by $1,000 a month. I'd been putting my life on the line for years and up until now, had gotten little more than a handshake and a plaque, an employee-of-the-month discount at the cafeteria downstairs.

It's two minutes to quitting time and the phone rings on my desk. I don't feel like answering it but I do, hoping it's Trev, who hasn't contacted me since that night. Trev, who I still can't believe has walked away from me so easily.

"City Desk. Gabriella Sinclaire speaking. May I help you?"

"There's another part to your story that was better left unpublished…that's why I didn't share it with you." The voice hesitates, waits for recognition.

"Lincoln?" Just when I was beginning to get over him.

"He is I and I is he," he says.

"And how are the two of you?" My heart stammers and I fight to ignore it, have had enough drama this week to last a lifetime.

"Still living. So I guess that's good, huhn?"

"That's very good."

"And while we're on the subject of good… Nice story, Miss Lady. I'm impressed. You made me look almost human. Thank you."

"You're welcome. So you *did* read it."

"Six times."

"And you liked?"

"It was thoroughly satisfying. I thought you handled the complex subject matter with a provocative degree of sophistication and intuitiveness."

"Did I?"

"Yes, you did. You like how I just put that, huhn?" There was a smile in his voice.

"You know I do."

"That's how brothas be kicking it on lockdown, sitting around with all that time on our hands, getting real deep and trying to find ways to show off their vocabularies."

"Jailhouse philosophizing, huhn?"

"Most definitely. But as I said, there's more."

"Like...?"

"I wanna see you again, if that's possible. I'd like to show you exactly what I can't say."

My breathing slows now, speeds up again. I wait, listening to my own heartbeat. "You want to see me?"

"Yes. If it's possible."

"But you told me to leave it alone. To stay away from..."

"This is strictly professional. I promise you."

"When?"

"Now."

"*Now*? As in..."

"As in I'm standing downstairs in your paper's lobby as we speak, looking at this bighead security cat who is warding off crime with his fountain pen."

I giggle at that. "Be nice, Lincoln. You don't want the man to get violent, do you?"

"And do what? Write me to death? Draw circles around my name or something?"

It's his turn to laugh, and he does. His laughter is a rare thing and I can't help appreciating the sound of it. "Quit harassing our employees, Mr. Duvall, and tell me what you had in mind."

"I've gotta make a run, and I wanted you to come with me."

"A run."

"Yeah. It's a nice lil' hike, but I promise not to keep you away too long."

I sigh, thinking how hard this day, this week has already been with just trying to get over him, the impressions he's left in my mind. Now I'd have to start all over, figure out where I was with this. Was I making our relationship bigger than it actually was? We were friends, weren't we? There could never be anything more than that, especially after what Nicole Rodgers had shared with me. A long quiet drive might do me some good after all. Meant the possibility of discovering yet another part to the puzzle that was Lincoln Duvall. "Is anyone gonna get shot along the way this time?" I ask.

"I don't plan on it."

"But I bet you're strapped, right?"

"Babygirl. Do you really wanna know the answer to that?"

"I don't think so."

"Aiight."

"I'll be down in two minutes."

"I'll be waiting," he says in a tone that has a double meaning.

ROADS AND REVELATIONS

Gabriella

He's driving a late-model black Benz and wearing a beautifully tailored black leather suit with a collarless white shirt beneath it. His hair is freshly cut, the braids gone, the sideburns and goatee carefully shaped. He's wearing shades that he takes off and folds as I enter the lobby, and it's hard to believe that this is Lincoln standing here. Lincoln, wearing white of all colors. The formality of his get-up makes me feel underdressed somehow, like I'm being escorted to a banquet sponsored by the United Negro College Fund. He's holding his cell phone in one hand, and the most beautiful spray of flowers in the other. He sees me and puts the phone away. His face softens, breaks into the semblance of a smile.

"Babygirl," he says, like a pronouncement, raising his chin in a very macho gesture, and something moves down in the marrow of my bones. "You looking fine, Gurl. As usual," he observes.

I touch my hair, look down at the thick wool coat that's as heavy as a blanket. "More flowers, Lincoln?" I say, fighting to push my mind past his words, his looks, the toxic cologne and fresh haircut, but especially the flowers. He doesn't answer. Just hands them over, kissing my cheek. It's a tender, awkward gesture, but I play along, fumble for words that will somehow dilute all the feelings crammed into this moment, but can find none. The security guard looks on as if expecting an altercation. He's fidgeting with his walkie-talkie, his blue eyes watching Lincoln's dark hands as if he knows they're capable of anything.

In the car, the earlier gleam departs from Lincoln's face. His brows are furrowed as he drives onto the interstate in a steady stream of fleeing traffic. Behind us, the hard edges of Heartford's skyline jut like broken glass under the flat plain of colorless sky. The Benz's ride is smooth and easy, the heated leather seats rocking and ebbing like a mobile waterbed.

"So," I say at last, looking at him.

"So," he parrots, looking back at me.

"I won't even ask where you're taking me," I offer, and he trains his eyes on the road again, his mind like it's light years away.

He looks at me. "Dang, Girl, you always smell *so* good. Mmph. That's the same smell you left in my house, huhn?"

"Did I?"

"I could smell it in my bed for days. What's it called?"

"Why?"

"I wanna buy myself a bottle. Keep it close, for when you're not around."

"In that case, I'm not telling."

He smiles then at the windshield. Nods, like he's hearing a voice whispering in his ear. "Cashmere Mist by Donna Karan. That's what it is."

"How'd you guess, Lincoln?"

"That's for me to know. So what's up with you? You worried? Think I'm taking you somewhere to kill you or something? Hide your body in my trunk?"

"Are you?"

"Guess you gonna have to wait and see, huhn?" He glances at my face, at my hands folded neatly in my lap. He chuckles to himself. "Church girls."

"Goodness though, Lincoln. You know I have to ask."

"About what?"

"How many cars do you have?"

He smiles at that, his fingers gripping the leather-encased wheel. "Too many I think sometimes, according to the insurance company."

"That's not a real answer."

"I think it is."

"Why then?"

"Why what?"

"Why so many cars? You can only drive one at a time."

He shrugs, gives me one of those flirting grins. "Because," he says finally. "I'm a man. I like cars. I like things."

"Things?"

"Yeah. Things. What else is there? Know what I'm saying?"

"Not really. Haven't you heard? A man's life doesn't consist in…"

"…the abundance of things he possesses," he finishes for me. "What shall it profit a man if he gains the world and loses his soul… You cannot serve God and mammon… Yeah, I've heard it all before. My momma use to say all that. Especially when we was on the run from *him*."

"Him?"

"The fool who made me." He scowls, leans forward and clicks on slow, jazzy music peppered with soft horns.

"Your father, you're saying?"

"If that's what you wanna call him."

"And that's why you like things?"

"My momma never had things, Babygirl. She never let us have 'em either."

"Why was that?"

"Because everything she got, he took from her. From us. So she was always afraid to have anything."

"I'm sorry."

"Including her life."

"Oh, Lincoln…"

"Yeah. But I ain't going out like that. You not writing this down, are you?"

"Not if you don't want me to."

He just shakes his head, looks at the pale landscape fleeing behind us. "Runt never believed her, but she always said he'd do it. Called herself trying to prepare us for it. But how can you prepare for something like *that?*"

"Like what?"

"Seeing your momma get murdered."

I'm at a loss for words, but he keeps on, like it's really troubling him. "Sometimes though? I be sitting there thinking about it. About *him* and how evil he was. A man like that never shoulda had a family. He shouldn't have had any children. You feel me? And then I start tripping, 'cuz like, I got his name. He was Lincoln Duvall. I'm Lincoln Duvall. I look just like him, like how he looked at this age. Same height, same color, same hairline and everything. I got ways just like him, Babygirl, and I'm thinking, maybe that's why I'm so ornery, why I be tripping so hard. I can't stop asking myself why he had to pass all that evil down to me." He shrugs again, his scarred hands clutching the steering wheel much too hard. "I be thinking and thinking so hard sometimes I can't even sleep. I be up for days straight. Weeks sometimes. Just thinking about it."

"Weeks without sleep? That's a lot of thinking…"

"Do you know what it's like to be in a trance you can't wake up from?" He stops, clicks over to another CD, slows the car a little. "The things I be doing sometimes, Babygirl? It's like it ain't even me. Like there's somebody evil inside of me pulling the strings."

"What's that like, Lincoln?"

"What? You playing psychologist today? Trying to read inside my head like they been trying to all my life?" He finds this funny.

"No… I just figured since we're talking…"

"Yeah, I know."

"I just want to understand, that's all."

"Why you need to understand *me*?"

"I just do."

"'Cause you like me more than you wanna admit, don't you? C'mon, say it. You think I'm cute. Reckless. Intriguing. You trying to save my soul, huhn?"

I popped him playfully. "Quit flattering yourself, Big Head."

"I'm serious. You like me 'cuz I'm a challenge, and I'm dangerous. Admit it. You love the fact that I'm ghetto-fabulous. I remind you of all the men you've ever loved. I take you back to your roots, don't I? I remind you of your daddy, huhn?"

"You been drinking?"

"You don't think I know, Babygirl? I'm crazy, not stupid."

"I never said you were either."

"That's 'cuz you too polite."

It's my turn to laugh now. "You are bugging, Mr. Duvall."

"See. If I was that preacher-cop, you'da been Mrs. Duvall by now, only I wouldn't be playing with your heart the way he does. Talking to you, then slipping up with other women."

"That has nothing to do with you, thank you."

"You know Chinere hated the article. Women kept bringing it into the shop, asking if it was about me."

"Did she even read it?"

"Before I did."

"And?"

"What she thinks ain't important."

"That bad, huhn?"

"I was just tripping about it, you know. Reading about myself, like I'm seeing somebody else for the first time."

"And what did you think about yourself?"

"That there was so much more than you wrote."

"Like?"

"I mean, just 'cuz a man's up against a wall and has to take somebody's life, don't mean he's crazy. Nobody looks at soldiers funny when they get back from wars, and they be sitting at they momma's table, eating milk and cookies, like they ain't never done nothing wrong."

"Have you taken a life before, Lincoln? Have you ever killed someone?" The question startles him. "Will it make a difference if I tell you?"

"Not really."

"I had to handle my business," he says after awhile.

"Because?"

"You sure ask a lot of questions."

"Tell me, Lincoln."

"Because I had to."

"Oh?"

"Murder isn't as hard as it sounds, Babygirl. I mean, you start out making your lil' girl get rid of your baby, you know? I was thirteen, fourteen years old, getting girls pregnant. I couldn't take care of no baby back then. Not then. And in the wards, seemed like the girls just lived to do that. Have some nigga's baby so they could dress it up and show it off like some kinda doll.

After that, they give the child to they momma to raise, and you stuck buying Pampers. I'da had about twenty kids by now, Babygirl, and I wasn't going out like that."

"But you made them."

"Only 'cause the girls be lying, saying they on the pill. Next thing you know, three of 'em say they having your baby at the same time. Be out there in the street, fighting over who loves you more."

"I'm listening."

"I'm not gonna read this in the paper tomorrow?"

"No, Lincoln. I'm just curious is all."

"Well, that's how it starts… You start out killing ya own, and from there, you get niggaz always wanting to try you, 'cause they heard you got rep, and they know that 'doing you' will make 'em a legend somehow. So nigga's start hunting a brotha. And a brotha starts strapping. And once them guns go to blazing, *somebody's* gonna die, so you still ain't sure if you did 'em or not, since everybody's shooting at the same time. You just know that violence gotta answer violence, and however they come, you gotta be prepared for it."

"So that's how it works."

"You from the wards. You know that's how it is. You got lil' cats, seven and eight years old, strapped hard. Them lil' niggaz can hit you straight between the eyes at twenty paces out, which means that by the time he runs up on you acting a fool, you *know* you gots to kill him."

"And you're okay with that?"

"I'ma do what it takes to survive, Babygirl. We at war." He shakes his head, looks unsettled somehow. "Still and all though sometimes I'm thinking that maybe there's a bigger reason behind all this living and dying business than what I'm seeing." He glances at his watch, sees that it's 4:45, and frowns. "It's too late for all that now though, huhn? Too late to be thinking about what should have been. How I could have changed things. Made things better somehow."

"It's never too late to allow Him to change us, Lincoln. Never."

"So you saying even a *murderer* can be forgiven? That all that crime can be washed away from his record like he never did it?"

"Even a murderer, Lincoln."

He is quiet for a long moment. Now he takes his eyes off the road and strokes my face with the back of his hand. Stunned, I drop my eyes, fold my hands in my lap.

"You're a *sweet* woman, you know that? Soft..."

I turn away from him, look out the window at the growing dark. "I guess it hasn't served me too well," I have to admit.

Linc lifts a hand from the wheel to turn my face back to his. "If I had myself together, I would never be afraid to commit to a woman like you."

"Alrighty then," I say, giggling nervously. His cologne is toxic, and for a minute I cannot speak, cannot breathe. I am suddenly struck by his choice of words, by what he has not said.

"It's deliberate, isn't it?"

"What is?"

"That you don't curse. I just realized that."

"Neither do you."

"I know why I don't. I'm sanctified. But you? I don't get it. I mean, you do everything else."

"It ain't necessary."

"And?"

"My tribute, I guess."

"To your mom?"

He nods, squints hard at the road. "She hated swearing. He swore at her all the time anyway. Couldn't ask for a cup of water without cussing. Without calling her out of her name."

"And that's why you don't do it?"

"That would be like desecrating her memory."

"I see."

"Do you really?" He was looking at me, his eyes strange, wanting me to understand, and I sigh, not sure that I do. I look out at the winding ribbon of freeway that stretches ahead, that seems endless from here. It's a cold day, the breaks of sky between buildings a hard ice-blue, and I'm glad I've worn my heaviest coat, the thermal suede gloves with the furry linings. Rush-hour traffic, heading toward the low-lying hamlets and middle-class villages of suburbia, blares, weaves in and out on every side, but Lincoln ignores the drama, keeps his own pace, his own lane. A huge tanker switches lanes abruptly and cuts in front of us, almost causing a collision, and he sucks his teeth, fighting hard not to give in to road rage, to the pistol I believe is tucked under his seat. Today he's a man on a mission.

"You feeling okay?" I ask.

"Today's special, Babygirl. Nobody can spoil this."

I lean back into the soft leather seat, and since I am finding it hard to believe what I'm seeing anyway, I close my eyes, allow the lull of motion to settle my nerves. This Lincoln is sensitive, easy, and nothing like the one whose life sells newspapers, the one who has a rap sheet that's five feet long. Times like these, it's hard to believe they're the same person. I open my eyes and look at him.

"I remind you of her, don't I?"

He is quiet for a while, his gaze aimed forward. "She had that same quiet way...that same loving sweetness... But we knew. We knew she didn't play and we knew that no matter what we were, and no matter how many times she dragged us down to that river in the middle of the night, she loved us."

"Lincoln."

"No matter what I did, she was never afraid of me. She could always see beyond all the crazy things I did, and her love... Her love was always greater than her fear."

He's quiet now, turns off the exit onto a curving circle that opens into a wide field of graves on the left and right sides of this narrow snow-covered road. The Spring Grove Cemetery. He snaps off the music, pulls through an elaborately designed wrought-iron gate. He drives past the neat veteran markers as square and uniform as infants' teeth, jutting through the snow. Maples, spruce, cherry oaks, sycamores, the trees here look as old as time itself. More and more monuments begin to crowd the space, the larger markers like elaborate sculptures stamped with names, dates.

Beneath a sloping hill where flat identical graves spell out the individual names of the Gervaccio family, he parks the car along the narrow rim of road-shoulder, draws a deep breath, looks at me. "I had her moved here from the city field where they put all the poor folk. She always liked the country. Always said she wanted a house on a hillside far away from the wards," he explains.

I'm glad I thought to wear my flat boots today. Glad the wind has a hard time getting past this heavy down coat. He takes more flowers from the back seat, takes my hand and pulls me gently up the steep incline. At an isolated spot, away from all the others, he stoops and brushes away snow before a huge monument of a woman holding an infant child in her arms. I linger back, watch as he clasps his hands, whispering softly as he carefully lays his flowers. The elaborate monument must've cost him a fortune. It's immense, stands almost ten feet tall. Peach-colored marble swirled with silvery flecks, a pitiful-faced cherub-woman in a flowing robe from which protrudes great angelic wings. The woman holds a swaddling infant in her arms, peers out on the cemetery with blank, lidless eyes.

"MOTHER," the stone says. "Leah Rebecca Duvall. 1949-1981."

His head is turned away from me but his shoulders are shuddering. He cups his hands over his face and holds them there. Is he crying? He's touching, stroking the smooth stone, lingering for close to fifteen minutes in the biting cold. Finally, when he turns to face me again, his lashes are wet. He waves me closer. "This my momma, Babygirl," he whispers hoarsely. "Come and meet my momma."

He watches as I lay the flowers he's given me beside his own. I am stooping beside him, arranging the beautiful orchids carefully around the smooth wide base of marble.

"Momma, *this* is Bunny, the one I was always running home telling you about. The one I said I was gonna marry one day. The one whose ponytails I loved to pull. "

CHAPTER TWENTY

Chinere

He arrives in just under thirty minutes. Shows up right when I'm starting to get mad and feeling like pulling outta here, 'cause he late and maybe 'cause it's a bad idea after all. I snap off Mary J., signal with a quick flash of my headlights, and he nods, looking around like he expecting to be bumrushed from some secret car fulla homies stashed somewhere in this parking lot, Al Capone style. He got a scary look that makes me wanna crack up in his face. A smile breaks at the corner of my mouth although I don't feel much like laughing. A smile that makes my lips feel heavy, like this new lipstick is suddenly too dark.

"Cordovan Silk," the lid says it is, but I rub most of it off onto a napkin, leave just enough so I ain't feeling totally naked.

He pulls up next to my car, pats himself as if checking for his gun, and finally, he gets out, walking up to my passenger door like John Wayne, watching me with those suspicious cop eyes. He ain't a bad-looking brotha at all when he's not in those pitiful narc clothes. Looks like a churchified Will Smith if you stare hard enough, only a shade darker, and without all those ears. He handsome I guess, in a rugged sort of way, but not my type, and nowhere as pretty as Linc. He almost looks normal with those faded jeans, leather jacket, and Air Jordans, although that old jeep he's driving definitely needs a good washing. I roll down the window, roll my eyes at him for showing up so late. He said fifteen minutes and here it was half an hour.

"Hi," he says and walks up closer to make sure nobody's kneeling down in the back seat. He's watching my eyes, seeing my hands holding onto the wheel. *Man, he scary,* I think. *Plus, he late, and I ain't got all day, so if he wanted to run an inspection, he shoulda showed up twenty minutes ago.*

"Hi yourself," I say, agitated, 'cause I'm scared out of my wits and he ain't making things no easier. Stepping up like he James Bond or somebody.

"You gonna stand there all day looking stupid or you gonna get in here before somebody see us?" I snap, and he doesn't like that, I can tell, but he just sighs, does something funny with his mouth and slips into the front seat beside me, careful-like. I pull off and he throws his hand up like he's at a rodeo riding one of them bucking broncos.

"Whoa, Girl, where you taking me? Stop this car now!"

He's already inside his jacket, reaching for his pistol, but I just shake my head, say, "Shut up, okay? Ain't nobody trying to hurt you. Y'all low-yellow brothas are all alike. Always thinking somebody wants you."

The muscles move in his jaw but he don't answer right away, just sits there seeing that I'm merely taking him across the street, into the opening of Griswold Park that's half full of cars even on this cold, sunny day.

"What are we going in here for?" He looks aggravated, but I don't care. *Somebody's* gotta help me deal with this and who better than him, seeing it's his woman that started all this in the first place? I park beside a white Volvo station wagon where a tall woman wearing a very silly-looking hat is taking a bunch of toddlers out of a back seat, telling them to hold hands.

"So what's up? I came like you asked." Mr. Five-O looks like he's sick of me already. Sitting there with both hands on his knees and his mouth twisted sideways.

"I'm just doing what you told me when you came into my shop that day searching with those Blue Coats. You gived me your card. You told me I could call you if I ever needed... *help.*"

"Where's Duvall? What kind of help you looking for? And why are you wearing shades in the shade?"

That's when I suck my teeth, lean forward and open my glove compartment with a key. I take out the yellow envelope, hand it to him and wait for him to open it and look over those three funny-looking pictures.

"And?" He looks totally confused. "What are these?"

"Pictures, Man. What else?"

"Pictures of what? I can't tell what these are." He wants to get out and walk back to his jeep, I can tell.

"Ain't you never heard of a sonogram?"

"Is that like a telegram?"

"It's my babies, Man. These from the ultrasound they gived me. They say I'm ten weeks along already."

"Ten weeks?"

"I'm pregnant, Fool, can't you tell? They say it's twins this time."

"Okay?" He still ain't getting it. Starts shaking his head. "Look. I don't get into people's personal business. You called and said you knew where I could find him. That's all I need to know. Where is he? I want Duvall."

"Doctor say it's twins, Preacher. *Two* babies. They Lincoln's. Both of 'em."

"And that's why you called me out here?"

"He told me to get rid of 'em, Linc did. Told me to make the appointment. Like I done all the others. So I did like he say, but when I got there…"

"Got where?"

"…when I went to the clinic, they told me they was two in there instead of one. So I'm crying and upset, thinking, how I'ma kill *two* of my babies at the same time? It just don't feel right to me. One was bad enough, you know?"

"Then just don't do it."

"They kept sending people in there to talk to me, like I was crazy for wanting to change my mind. They say it don't make me a bad person, killing a fetus. That sometimes love means doing something wrong to make everything else right. But how they know about what's wrong? They not the ones walking around feeling like they deserve to die. They not the ones wishing they know what they dead child coulda looked like, or remembering the death day year after year."

"And Duvall don't see it that way?"

"Killing ain't nuthin' to Linc but a business expense. He always killing up everything around him. He just get somebody else to do the dirty work."

I shake my head then. The water's seeping into my voice now, but I can't help it. This just too much for anybody to bear. And Barney Fife, as Linc calls him, is sitting there as dumb as a post, listening to me and shaking his head like he don't know what he's doing here with me. Inside this car, the windows getting all steamed up, but not so much that I can't see the two red birds tip out of a wide bush naked of flowers. They so pretty together. Playing tag in the air, wings moving so fast they like propellers. They fly high up onto the electrical wires and sit there like they untouchable, like they just waiting for something to happen.

"I wish I was like them. Wish I had me some wings," I say, but he don't answer at all. He just sitting there, seeing me look up at the birds, staring at 'em too like he seeing something he never seen before. Then he turn away again, go back to looking straight ahead through the windshield. Hard again, like a cop.

"Wings aren't the answer," he says, looking at me. "Take off the shades. Let me see your eyes."

"My eyes? They don't have nothing to do with this. "

"Take 'em off," he says, and then just leans over and takes them off himself.

He sucks his breath in quick, shakes his head like he disgusted. "*He* did that to you?"

"That ain't why I called you."

"I don't understand how you could just let him…" He was all set with his speech, ready to go on and on about what some women accept and what men like Linc deserve, but I put my hand up. After what happened at the clinic this morning, I can't take any more speeches.

"I called 'cause I needed for somebody to know. Just in case."

"Just in case?" His eyes go soft under those thick brows.

"Linc gone kill me when he find out. I know he is. He got them funny ways to make things happen before you realize it. Before you even know what you doing to yourself. He can kill you and never lay a hand to you. He got them *ways* to get things to happen. So *if* it happen… *when* it happen… there won't be no question about the whos and the whys. Even if he ain't the one to touch me."

Fife looking strange at me. "What kind of ways?"

"I can't explain. It's just that everybody think Runt the one crazy 'cause he shot they daddy that day. He pulled the trigger alright. But I know better than that. I know Linc the one willed it to happen. Linc made him do it without saying a word."

"How do you know that?"

"I just do. He can do that. I seen it before. I seen how he gets."

"How is that?"

I'm starting to shake now just talking about it. It ain't something I ever shared before with anybody, and I think he gonna know somehow. I'm thinking he can feel what I'm doing and where I am, even as I speak.

"Linc? He real different, Preacher. He ain't like regular folks. He *special*. Like he got magic powers or something."

"Magic powers…"

"He can do stuff with his mind."

"Like?"

"Move furniture, walk through locked doors, or make folks fall out on the floor sick. Linc? He walk across rooftops without nothing holding him up. I seen it. I seen him make a friendly dog attack a child. I seen him make two cars crash into each other, and when the police came, nobody knew what happened. The drivers didn't even know."

"But all of those can be coincidences… You do realize that?"

I get quiet then and Fife puts up his hand like he really don't believe me, or wanna hear any more about it.

"I was there that day they come running in downstairs, to the clubhouse, on the day those two mens from Atlanta was shot up. I heard 'em only 'cause Ghost was throwing up something bad, so Linc came upstairs to get my towels. Wasn't nobody in the shop that day but me."

"What else happened?"

"When I ask him why he want them, he say Ghost was throwing up, and then he gave me that look. Ghost always throw up when he shoot some-body. Then they was both gone, taking the jeep to the carwash, although Linc had just washed it the day before. I think it was blood splattered on it, but I never say nothing about it. I never tell Linc I know… Afterward, I hear Ghost fussing in the lot. They came back and parked under my window, where my chair is, and I heard them fussing. Linc saying it ain't his fault, and Ghost saying why Linc always have to shoot first and ask questions later..."

"And you never told the police this? You never gave a statement?"

"You crazy?"

"So you're just going to stay there, with that deranged man until he shoots you too? You're just gonna stay there, although he's beating on you and wants you to abort your children, until it happens to you?" Fife is looking at me with his mouth all open like he can't believe me.

"What else I'ma do?"

I can't help it then. I start crying like I ain't got good sense, wetting the front of my coat, and he leans over real careful-like, sighs like he don't understand none of it and pats my shoulder. Two quick pats that don't linger and that's it. He sits back and stretches his long legs in front of him.

We sit like that for a while then, me crying 'cause I can't help it and he locked in his own thoughts. The sky is starting to go purple up over the light poles. The pretty red birds launch up and fly away, leaving us alone. He hands me the pictures back and I put them back into the glove compartment, locking it back again carefully.

"He likes *her* a lot. They been together. I can tell," I say, but Fife don't answer. "They looking for him on The Street too, I heard," I try again, needing him to talk back somehow.

"It ain't the first time."

"This the biggest hit ever though. Fifty, they said."

"Fifty-thousand dollars?"

I nod. "That's what I heard. A lotta people gonna be gunning for him now. They gonna come up in the shop probably looking. But that ain't the way to find Linc."

"How then? Where *do* I find Duvall?" Fife is serious now, patting under his coat for a pad and a pen he probably carries with him everywhere.

"That's what I wanted to tell you," I say, and sigh, just sick and tired of everything. "Nobody finds Linc unless he wants to be found," I tell him, as he leans close with his pad, waiting to write. "And if he wants to be found, you better believe there's something else waiting on the other side."

The preacher looks like he thinking hard, but he ain't scared. He ain't scared at all.

"How then? How do I find him?"

"You don't," I tell him, and he nods like he really understands. "You let *him* find *you.*"

IN PUBLIC

Gabriella

It's almost dark by the time we leave the cemetery but Lincoln is driving much slower, engulfed in his own thoughts. Rush-hour traffic has abated somewhat, and through the Beemer's tinted windows, the night takes on a bluish-white tinge, boasts a surreal, almost mythical quality. The highway unfurls like separate streamers, winding and curving toward Heartford, and straightening out again.

Lincoln's growling stomach suddenly derails our separate trains of thought and I turn to him, seeing how the fall of streetlight softens his rigid profile. "I guess I'm not the only one who could use some dinner. Can we stop and get something to eat?" I ask, and the eyes that lock into mine are beautiful but sad, human for a change.

"You sure you want to be seen with me in public? It could be dangerous. *Very* dangerous."

"We're together now, Lincoln," I say, patting his arm. "Do I look scared to you?"

"You could be fronting." He smiles.

"What's my name, Mr. Duvall?"

"Angelfied."

"Try again, Big Time."

"Bunny?"

"Three strikes and you're out."

"Gabriella."

"Exactly. Do you know what that means?"

"It's the feminine form for Gabriel, right? That angel-dude carried the message to Mary."

"Right."

"It means 'Messenger.' I know that."

"What does it all mean though?"

He shook his head, swerving around a stalled bus. "Wish I knew. Been asking myself that since I met you."

"It means, never be afraid when you're with an angel, Lincoln. You'll always be protected."

✝✝✝

He hadn't wanted to stop, but he did so just for me. He didn't remember the last time he'd sat down to eat a full meal and told me, kept suggesting restaurants inside the wards.

"There's a whole world outside the wards, Lincoln," I told him. "And besides, it's time you went along with my agenda for a change."

I suggested Caribbean food and he grinned, admitted he loved himself some curried goat. He allowed me to take him to Redman's, but only on one condition—that he pay for everything. We got to Redman's, on the west side, and it took him all of ten minutes to get out of the car. He was stalling, I could tell, digging inside the glove compartment looking for things, tugging around under his clothes, making sure his guns were accessible.

"Mr. Duvall?"

"Yes, Babygirl."

"If I didn't know how invincible you were, I'd seriously believe you were scared to death of going into this place with me."

He went to frowning then. "I'm not afraid of *anything*," he says, looking right at me like I'd insulted him. He finally got out the car then, came around and opened my door, but when we stepped up inside the place, waiting with the normal folk for an available table, he became so fidgety I wondered if he had held up the place before. I wouldn't have been surprised if he had. We sat near my favorite corner, a table for two in a space filled with laughing couples. Island music blared, and the aromas of stewing callaloo and thyme and ginger, was intoxicating, strong as any elixir. Lincoln helped me with my coat and then sat there uneasily, eyes shifting everywhere, clouded with suspicion. He seemed fascinated by the mannerisms of the white customers around us, seemed jumpy and put off by the sudden bursts of loud jarring laughter, the heavy clink of silverware, an infant's piercing yowls.

"You okay, Lincoln?" I sat forward, touching his hand.

"Fine," he said, lacing his fingers on the table, but I could tell he wasn't. He didn't even look at his menu.

"What would you like to eat?" the waitress in her colorful calypso outfit asked him, flirting with her fake eyelashes, her skirt short enough to showcase beautiful but thick thighs.

"Just gimme me what she's having," he said, ignoring her thighs, and looking up at me with the helplessness of a little boy left alone in kindergarten for the first time. I ordered two plates of goat and rice and peas. Fried plantains. Cocoa bread. Lincoln loved the food, said he never knew such a place existed on this side of town.

"So this was y'all spot, huh? You and Fife's?" he asked, almost spilling his water.

"How'd you know that?" I smiled demurely, hoping to take his edge off.

"That's y'all old table." He pointed exactly at it, and I smirked, giggled into my virgin pina colada.

"Who told you?"

"Nobody. I just know. It just comes to me like that sometimes. Like a voice in my head."

"You've always had that gift?"

"Ever since Runt and me found that game at the dump and started playing with it. A Ouija board, I later found out it was. Seems like I been strange and crazy ever since. I tried to tell Runt. We shoulda *never* have touched that thing."

The waitress came and brought a basket of warm coconut cookies, bending low enough to give Lincoln a direct view of her ample bosom. He looked too but dismissed her nonchalantly, passing me the basket.

"Did you know about your mother? I mean, before it happened?"

"I knew how and where. Just didn't know when."

"That must've been a terrible burden to carry. You were young, weren't you?"

"Fourteen."

"How can a fourteen-year-old prevent something like that from happening?"

"They can't. All they can do is make sure they not around to see it when it goes down."

He was looking at the table, shaking his head. "All that hiding we did at the river and it happened anyway. 'Deliverance always comes out of hiding,' she used to say. I never knew what she meant. Still don't." He forced a hard smile.

"Let me see your hand," I say, taking his right hand into mine, turning it over to look at the marbled brown skin, examining the rivulets of keloids and scars.

"Ugly, huhn? I know it. Women always tripping on these hands, asking me what happened..."

"You don't like crowds, do you, Lincoln?" I couldn't look at his troubled eyes, said it as softly, as easily as I could.

"I don't know these people. What they might do... I don't fit in here and they know it. I hate how they be staring at me."

I looked around, saw nothing but happy patrons enjoying their own moments, oblivious to this fine dark man who was feeling the need to shield himself from himself.

"Nobody's looking at you, Lincoln. There's nothing for you to worry about."

He licked his beautiful lips, furrowing his brows; he said nothing.

"I was the same way when I had to leave the wards to go to college. I was so used to that fishbowl mentality that for the first two years at school, I kept wanting to quit and go back home, insulate myself from having to deal with society, with white people, with the establishment. I was totally unprepared for any of it."

"Quit psychoanalyzing me, Babygirl. Just know I'm a man, aiight? A man who ain't afraid to go anywhere on this earth."

I giggled at his seriousness. "You'll come to church with me then? Be my special guest?" I ask, and he bursts into laughter at the very thought of it. Laughs like it's the craziest thing he's ever heard.

EXILE

"It's Saturday morning, Bunny, and you're not here. I miss you. I miss our time together. Whatever you've done? Look, it doesn't matter to me now. I still love you and I want us to be together. Can we talk? *Please*, Bunny. Call me." He hung up the phone just before the message beep ended the call and stared out of his newly installed living room window into the flicker of falling snow. It was half past nine in the morning and he wondered, as he had so many times for the past few weeks, where she could be. Once upon a time he knew her so well, knew her habits, her friends, her life patterns. This morning, though, she was a complete stranger to him, he thought. They hadn't talked since she'd stayed the night with Duvall, and the loneliness that filled his tiny three rooms seemed like more than he could bear.

He sat on the couch, cupped his head in his hands and listened hard to the stunning rhythms of silence, the whisper of flakes against panes, of creaking pipes, and the droning hum of network television. Where could she be? Why hadn't she called back? Didn't she know how bad this was hurting him? It was bad enough that she'd wronged him, but the very fact that she hadn't even attempted to contact him, hurt him more than anything. It was like she had thrown him away.

Why are you doing this to me, Bunny? Why are you doing this to us?

He snatched up the remote and flicked idly through the channels. He hadn't realized the basic cable channels had so much to offer, and now, with the Mayberry job and so much time on his hands, when he wasn't praying or studying his Bible he found himself wrestling with an inordinate amount of idle time. And loneliness. Loneliness so stark, it gnawed at him. He settled the channel on a fishing program and leaned back against the sunken couch cushions. It wasn't all her fault, and he knew it. She had tried so hard once, so many times, to give all that he'd asked for, and even what he wasn't entitled to. He'd said he wanted a wife who could cook, and she'd cooked for him, everything from Southern cuisine to Mexicali. He'd said he needed a wife who could listen, and she spent hours listening to his gripes about the force, about his crazy family, about church politics and what he wanted from God for his ministry. He'd said he wanted a beautiful woman who kept herself up, and she bought Tae Bo tapes and exercised, stayed at the beauty parlor, wore some of the baddest clothes a sanctified sister could get away with, and still he'd put her off and made excuses, snuck around and courted other sisters on the sly, just to make sure there was nothing else out there to miss out on.

Gabriella had heard all of the rumors but stayed with him anyhow. She'd loved him long before he'd gotten himself into the church, back when he was still in college and they'd started dating off and on. And even afterward, when he gave up chasing all women and turned celibate, in those early days of his conversion when he was prone to weakness and sexual "slip-ups," she still came to him and allowed him to "humble her" for his own pleasure. They made love in secret, in out-of-the-way places where motel rooms were cheap dives and the sex lasted for hours. He admitted that although he was in love with her, he could never fully respect a woman he could sleep with without benefit of marriage and who didn't want to serve his God. Eventually, she too started attending services at Zion, and when she gave up sin and surrendered totally to the Lord, even then, she was weak for him, and he knew it.

He could see them both now, sitting across from each other in Pastor Starks' office, heads bowed, ashamed to even look at each other as they made confession about what they had done together. Again. It had been so hard for a while to get a grip. It was like her body called out to him, begging him to touch her. There was the time Starks had silenced them both from doing anything in the church, the time she'd missed her "cycle" for a few months and she thought she was carrying his child. He was almost sure he'd loved her then, but afterward, after the sting of shame had passed and there was no real child to hold them together, just stress that had made her cycle irregular, he hadn't even mentioned getting married. The groan that escaped from his lips now came from somewhere deep inside of him. He had been so wrong so many times. There were so many memories between them, so much water under the bridge, and now it seemed, she was the one throwing it all away. Ironically, he couldn't blame her.

Someone knocked, and he jumped, startled. He looked at his watch.

Hoped. Prayed. Thought perhaps she too was feeling the loss, was missing their Saturday morning ritual and was coming by to talk to him. He jumped up, snatched the tangle of debris off the coffee table and tossed it behind the couch. The apartment was like a rat's nest of clutter but he opened the door anyway, stepped back in amazement when he saw not Gabriella, but Bluecoat Joe Rodgers standing there in civilian clothes: A baseball cap and denim jacket, tan khakis and black brogans. Joe lowered his voice and gestured down toward the inside of his coat. "S'up, Coop? I got *that* for you, what you had asked me to get. You sent word by Oliver? He told me and I came as soon as I could."

Trev looked puzzled but then remembered quickly. He nodded, waving Joe inside after looking both ways down the hallway to make sure he hadn't been followed.

"'Scuse the place, Man, and make yourself to home. You know I don't drink, but I got Pepsi."

"Yeah," Joe said, stepping past the threshold. "You know me. I'll take a can of anything."

Joe was looking around at the rangy furniture, the dusty tables, the walls riddled with bulletholes. "Man, Coop, your woman don't mind your place looking like this?" He plopped into a chair as Trev disappeared into the tiny kitchenette, emerging seconds later with a six-pack of Pepsi and an unopened bag of pretzels.

"My woman? We, I mean she... She ain't been over in awhile."

Joe nodded. "I don't blame you. It ain't safe since the shooting, huhn?" He watched as Trev arranged everything neatly on the coffee table in front of them and took a can for himself, snapping it open. "Same way with us," Joe said, not waiting for Trev to answer. "We had to move since they fired on our place. Wife won't stay there. Kids still having nightmares."

"Yeah." Trev pointed at his chest, looking at the floor. "You know I was *real* sorry to hear what had happened to your baby girl. I was coming up to the hospital, Man. Wanted to call, send a card or *something*, but Capt said I'd be terminated if I even tried, said I'd just put your family in harm's way again."

"Coop, Man. It's aiight. I *heard*. I understood."

"And your daughter is doing...?"

"She fine. Got some scars, but doc says she's still young enough for the skin to cover itself. Other than the nightmares, she alright. Since we in a new place and all."

"Man," said Trev. "Unbelievable."

They both drank long and deep, looking at the TV. Joe belched into his fist, smirking. "Pepsi and pretzels for breakfast. Guess we both pitiful. You ain't got no grits and eggs? No hotlink sausage up in this piece?"

"Nawl, Joe. Wish I did. But it sure is good to see a familiar face. Feel like a fly in the buttermilk out there in Mayberry where they got me now." Trev sighed, flicked off a spider crawling up the side of the table.

Joe pulled his eyes from the screen. "Yeah. We heard. Klan territory, they saying. You got my sympathies, for real."

"Well, thanks, Man. Appreciate that. But I'm alright though. Getting used to it now."

Joe polished off his first soda and reached for a second, popping it open. "Can't say you ain't been missed downtown though, Coop. Straight up. Lotta folks still upset about it. Waiting to see what the union'll do." Trev made a sarcastic face and Joe took a long gulp, belched again. "Everybody knows it wasn't fair, and even the hoes come up in the station asking for you—to borrow money as usual. They know you a good man. Got the Lord with you and all that."

Trev attempted a smile. "Is that right? Even the hoes? As hard as I was on them?" Trev picked up his can, but didn't drink, held the coldness in his hand, remembering.

Joe opened the bag of pretzels and withdrew a handful. "So they got you isolated and surrounded now, huhn? Making sure you not a threat to nothing or nobody."

"But myself." Trev leaned deeper into the couch, looking up at the ceiling. "I can't lie though. I miss Vice, Man. Miss the wards, and all those poor folks in crisis."

Joe shook his head. "I know. All those years of being out there? All those cases you solved? The criminals you've locked up. That's all you know." He shrugged, reached for more pretzels, devoured them in seconds. "It just don't make sense to me, that all this happened 'cause you arrested Duvall that night. I mean, why him? What makes him so special?"

"I been asking myself the same thing, Man. It was a routine arrest. The kind I made every night. Guess something went wrong though."

"What went wrong is Duvall having so much 'back' inside precinct, that's what. The kind of money I heard he spreads around? That nigga's got some of everybody in his pocket."

"Yeah. I know. I've still been doing my own investigations on the sly. Making calls, doing interviews on the 'down low.' I'm putting together my own case, and the things I'm finding out about Duvall and all of the illegal dealings he's got going on with the big men downtown?" Trev wags his head in consternation. "It would actually blow your mind, Man."

Rodgers shrugged. "Hey, I believe you, Coop. Ain't been no real arrests in the wards since you left either, although there's been plenty of shooting."

"Turf wars?"

"Yup. A bunch of young homies got shot up at Soldier's a few weeks ago. Spain's little brother and his crew. Bunch of wannabe gangsters. Rumor says it was Duvall making his usual statement, but you know they're not gonna follow it up."

"Murders?"

"Almost. Close calls."

"Somebody's praying for that man."

"Must be. Meanwhile, all of your old cases have been reassigned."

"Figured that. But to who, Man?"

"To cats who could care less about avenging some dead poor man's murder. All they care about is a pension, and with all this talk going on at city hall about budget cuts and layoffs, the last thing on their minds is dead niggas in the morgue. I know you were hunting Joker Red's killers down hard, Coop. Those of us from 'round the way? We all knew him. Knew he was caught up in the life, but he ain't deserved to get smoked like that. The sad thing is, the way things are going, the truth probably will never come out. And you *know* they not worried about what happened to Spain."

"Yeah. Guess not."

"So don't trip no more about it, Coop. Man, just go on."

"It ain't that simple, Joe."

"It's gonna have to be, Man. Just go on." Joe stood up then, zipped down his jacket and removing a large manila file, dropped it on the table.

"Make sure I get this back intact, Man. You know they'll fire a brotha quick for doing this."

"Enough said."

Trev picked up the worn folder thick with paperwork, saw Duvall's name, and followed Joe to the door. He put out his hand. "Thanks, Man. I'ma remember this. I won't mess you up."

Joe put his hand on the knob, pulled the door open slowly. "Look here, Coop. The way I see it? We gotta find a way to get this fool off the street, Man. I was scared at first, you know it. Wasn't no way I wanted a part of a man who walks arm-in-arm with the devil. But that crazy Nigga shot my house up. Coulda killed us all over nothing. He caused my little girl some *pain*. I ain't no Christian man like you, Coop. If that Nigga run up on me or my family again, I'ma bust a cap in him without hesitating. He'll be just another mad dog put out of his misery. You figure me, Man?"

"Yeah, Joe. I figure you."

Long after Joe Rodgers pulled off in his old Dodge Caravan, Trev couldn't help remembering the day they'd searched Duvall's girlfriend's salon. It had already been too late by then. The place had been scoured clean, Duvall's downstairs clubhouse reeking of bleach. They hadn't found a drop of blood anywhere, but the sharp stench of bleach, to Trev, was evidence enough that Duvall was hiding something.

"Deeds done in the dark have to surface in the light sooner or later," he said aloud to himself, reaching for the file before changing his mind and picking up the phone instead.

His mind was just too biased then, just too full of resentment toward a man who was becoming an obsession to him. He wasn't thinking clearly or objectively. He needed to step back from the obvious, needed to free himself from the preoccupation of Gabriella and Lincoln Duvall, for now at least. He sighed then, realizing he knew just how to do that.

He turned down the television volume, pressed the seven numbers and was relieved when she picked up on the second ring.

"Sister Rodgers? Hi. Minister Cooper here. I was wondering if you had plans around lunchtime today?"

RITES

It's one of those special moments when he'd been able to get them all together in the same place at the same time, Creeper, Lil G, TicToc and Ray-Ray. Dante, Cheese, and of course, Ghost, who was looking paler than usual in the meager winter sunlight. It's a warm thirty degrees outside in their covert place inside the dump near the river, but Ghost is shivering and holding his side, hacking into dead weeds entwined between the spokes of an old bicycle skeleton. Lincoln is sitting up high on the hood of the Escalade to watch the proceedings unfold, legs in thick denim splayed wide, a black knitted cap pulled low on his forehead and his shearling coat open to a flirty breeze. The river's just a mile away, and its familiar scent smothers the stench of the stinking dump, he thinks.

He's growing a beard that makes him look older and more settled, but it doesn't hide the smirk playing about his lips now as he watches the homies preparing to line up behind the marker, totally unaware of what they were getting ready to do. They'll each take turns shooting at the target poised on their partner's shoulder at thirty paces out. If they miss the sixteen-ounce glass bottles that Dante will set on each of their shoulders in turns, there will be a death on their hands and a murder rap to contend with. But Lincoln isn't worried. He wouldn't have approved this final rite of passage until he himself was sure the boys were expert marksmen, capable of firing under pressure, capable of denying their own personal feelings of sentiment or hesitation. He and Dante and Cheese and Ghost have trained so many of the ward's sharpshooters so well that most of them went on to become career criminals. He employs them to guard 'Nere's shop and his other substation apartments around the wards. He pays them extremely well, and they reward him with excellent service, hanging out on top of roofs and in hallways like sinister secret service agents, guarding the wards in cars with tinted windows, their presence as undetectable as carbon monoxide. The selfless loyalty of his leaders, of Ghost, and Cheese, and Dante, who had only recently become questionable in these latter days, had been crucial in establishing his power and plans in the wards, but the utter devotion of these latest trainees, he observes, was just as admirable. Among this last bunch of recruits were some definite stars, and Creeper has, by far, the greatest leadership potential he's seen in years.

Lincoln lights a Newport, takes a few drags and makes perfect rings with the smoke. It's an effort to hold on to a habit that is fast beginning to disgust him. He pretends it doesn't bother him and squints through the smoke at Ghost fighting to stand up straight before changing his mind and doubling over to hack again. Linc grimaces, flicks the Newport onto the frozen ground. "Ghost, Man, you turning green, Partner. Told you about letting those corner crackheads whistle on your jimmy. "

Cheese and Dante, both toking on spliffs the size of cigars, laugh at the commentary while they organize the boys into formation, carrying the crates of glass bottles from the Escalade's cargo space. "You look like bad jewelry," Cheese tells Ghost, giving Dante a high-five to bear witness, but Lincoln shakes his head at their frivolity, turns his attention back to the mission in progress. There was no time for joking and carelessness. He could feel the vibes every day now as he drove through Trece and now, especially, through Deuce, seeing the distilled hatred in the eyes of the hustlers who resented the way he'd shot up Spain's little brother. But what else could he have done? The little punk had no fear and was bent on revenge, and even though he and his crew were novices to the wisdom of street wars, the boy was ambitious and persistent. Cocky too, as were most prizefighters. Linc only wished he'd smoked them all when he'd had the chance. But he hadn't, and that in itself wasn't like him at all. His association with the angel-woman was making him soft, he surmised, and more than that, he thought she was working some kind of prayer-conjure on him.

An all-out turf war was inevitable, and no one had to tell him that as soon as those lil' busters got well enough, they'd be back to retaliate. Somebody was probably somewhere right now, planning their revenge, and he knew they were totally justified. There was no way around it. The attempts would come as long as he stayed on top, and the best he could do was to continue to prepare himself and his soldiers for the coming violence. Looking out at all of them now, he knew they wouldn't all survive to see another year. There were always casualties on both sides, and the funniest thing was that the ones who died were never the ones you expected to lose so soon. He himself could very well be the first victim.

He'd been thinking hard on it, and had planned to make an appointment with his attorney to get some paperwork written up just in case. It never paid to leave things to chance, and looking out over the men who had accompanied him from the first street corners when they were still hiding their product in the bottoms of their sneakers, to this new and highest echelon of power, he still wasn't convinced that they were totally trustworthy. Lil' G knelt to tuck his laces back into his Jordans, and Linc watched as Dante ambled close enough to nudge him, whispering, then clapping him on his back.

Secrets, Linc thought, watching them. Dante always had to be watched. Now Dante, as if reading his thoughts, spun around suddenly and looked Linc directly in his eyes. He smiled easily. Linc did nothing.

"Y'all lil' broke niggas quit joshing and listen up," Dante barked, clapping his hands, snatching TicToc by his elbow and leading him to the marked place where he made him face them all, shoulders square, eyes forward.

"What's up, Dante? What y'all fixin' to do?" Lil' G, always quick to sense drama, didn't like the looks of things. He sauntered over to Lincoln. He was shaking. "What up, Mistah D? Y'all 'bout to kill us now or what?"

TicToc's eyes were beginning to sparkle like crystal. He was biting down hard on his tongue.

"That's up to you, Homie." Lincoln slid off the hood and walked over to the steamer trunk that stood open on the ground, filled with a cache of weapons. He picked out a .38, stroking its barrel tenderly. Dante was grinning, telling TicToc to hold his arms straight out like a cross.

"Y'all 'bout to crucify us?" Ray-Ray's eyes were round as dimes, his mouth wide open.

Cheese sucked his teeth, reared back and slapped the back of Ray-Ray's head so hard his hat flew off. "Shut up, Punk. You ain't got the sense God gave a pickle."

Cheese handed Dante one of the sixteen-ounce glass bottles as Ghost leaned back against the Escalade, his eyes closed.

"Linc?" said Dante, "you care to demonstrate for these lil' girl scouts?"

Dante placed the bottle on his own shoulder, dangerously close to his ear, and held his arms out like a telephone pole.

"Creeper?" Linc said, and when the boy looked his way, the bottle exploded.

Dante grinned, brushed fragments of glass from his collar. The younger boys stood gaping in awe. They'd never even seen him take aim.

"Well, soldiers, what y'all think?" Dante was looking at them.

"I think that was *pretty*," said TicToc at last, breaking the silence. "But I don't wanna try it. That's way too close for me, Cuz."

"True dat," agreed Lil' G. "Homes never saw it coming. But what if we…? I mean, what if one of us misses?" He gave Linc a pleading look. Creeper, like Ray-Ray, said nothing, stood looking at the ground.

"Just don't miss," Linc said.

"Aiight. Enough with the stalling. Who wants to go first?" Cheese asked.

When no one answered, Dante laughed. "No volunteers? Y'all all faggots? We gonna have to pick somebody out?"

"Me." Creeper spoke up finally, holding out his arms. "I'll go first."

But Linc cut in. "*I'll* go first," he said, handing Creeper the gun and walking up to where Dante had just stood. He held out his arms, fighting back a grin. "One thing before y'all start," he said, looking directly at Creeper. "If y'all shoot me in my head, I'ma have to kill you."

CRIMINALS

Trevis

There's a note on my desk when I come in for my morning shift; Captain Finney from Heartford's Vice Squad needs me to come to a meeting downtown at 5:30 this afternoon, on the eighteenth floor of the

Hilton Building. I arrive at 5:15, still in my uniform, to find an empty floor and an open conference room. Inside the plush suite is a room full of velvet highbacked chairs, a conference table, and some of the most powerful men in the city: a councilman, two lawyers, a community activist and the president of the Mutual Life Bank. Captain Finney, in civilian attire, looks more like a tourist than downtown brass, and right next to him, with his hand curled around a fountain pen, is Duvall, in what looks like a $5,000 suit.

Duvall reeks money, just like his partner, the white-looking brotha sitting beside him with the Gucci shades on, and when he sees me, he gives me a look, like he wants to spit and laugh at the same time. He settles for a toothless half-smile, although his eyes locked on me gleam with hate. Capt nods when I open the door to the boardroom and step inside, closing it, and a chair at the helm of the table is empty, waiting for me. "Thanks for coming, Coop," he says, and his eyes shift to Duvall, whose two bodyguards are standing in a corner of the room, both suited up, standing at attention and watching everything. Just in case.

Directly across from Duvall, in his clean pinstripes and monogrammed cufflinks, is Horatio Canton, one of the slickest, highest-paid criminal defense lawyers on the East Coast. With his sleek, dark hair and suave persona, Canton's the Pat Riley of big-city attorneys, a gangster's lawyer with a rep as questionable as the clients he services. In all my years on the force, I've never seen any of his clients get convicted, even though we all knew they were guilty as sin.

I sit down and he won't look at me at all. He writes something on a legal pad and slides it to Duvall who reads it, nods and puts his eyes back on me, like he's tallying me up.

Capt clears his throat, has that rabbit-look in his eyes. "I'll make this quick," he promises as all eyes fall on me, and there's the sense that I've interrupted something big, that whatever I'm there for will only take a few minutes, so there's no need to drag it out.

"Trevis, Mr. Duvall is here with his attorney, Mr. Canton, claiming that you've continued to harass him, although he's tried very hard to cooperate with our investigations."

"Beg your pardon, Sir?"

"The case in question? The one involving the two Atlanta gentlemen who were murdered back in…"

"Yes, Sir?"

"You were told to drop the investigation and turn your evidence over to your superior officer. You were reassigned in the interim, were you not?"

"Yes, Sir, I did. I was, Capt, but…"

"Mr. Duvall here says you searched his fiancée's place of business, *without* a proper warrant, and that you promised to continue to be in touch with her. He demands that you drop the harassment or he will bring a civil suit against the city, against you personally, and against me as well."

"A civil suit? Against *us*?"

"Exactly."

"But the man *is* a liar and a murderer, Capt. He's running cocaine all over the wards, and there's evidence that…"

Capt brings his fist down on the table hard, still avoiding eye contact with me. "I've assured these gentlemen that such measures won't be necessary since the matter will be resolved in a most quiet and expeditious manner."

"But, Sir, with all due respect, this man is a deviant and a leech. As long as we allow him to stay in power, the streets of the wards will run with blood. We cannot afford to justify…"

"Do I make myself clear, Detective?"

"Yes, Sir."

"The last thing this city needs is another scandal involving the force. I won't allow it. Not as long as I am in charge. Is that understood?"

"Yes, Sir."

"Very good. Now, I trust that you can find your way out?"

"Yes, Sir." I stand up then, and with Duvall and his men watching my every move, I leave quietly and head for the nearest restroom.

†††

Could this really be happening? Could Joker's death be my first unsolved homicide? The irony of it enrages me, and I go inside the bathroom and punch the wall so hard my knuckles bleed. I stick my bleeding hand under the faucet and let the cold water run at full force, still seeing Duvall's reptilian eyes, his men standing back against the wall with their hands inside their pockets, poised for violence.

None of it was making any sense at all. First Gabriella, and now this? It was too much, just too much for one man to accept at one time. I went into a stall to relieve myself and was coming out just as the bathroom door yawned open. Suddenly he's standing there facing me, stopped dead in his tracks, as surprised to see me as I am to see him. Duvall. Alone, strutting in here with his shiny shoes, and looking at me like he's just seen a roach he wants to crush. My heart starts beating like crazy, so I go to the sink and wash my hands a second time, hoping the water will calm me, will help me to be rational somehow.

Help me, Lord, please… Keep me from hurting this man.

He's standing there with his hands hanging loose at his sides, like they do in those old *Wild Wild West* duels. Standing there like he can draw a pistol any moment, shoot me right between the eyes. "How's your girlfriend?" he says, his eyes gleaming like a cat's. It's a dare, and I know it, the lowest blow he could ever throw, and I know it's an invitation to get myself hurt."

"She's fine. I'll tell her you asked," I say, barely able to get the words out, but Duvall's not hardly finished. He folds his hands in front of himself, grins that half-moon smile like a choir boy.

"Yeah. 'Cause the last time I seen her, well, she wasn't doing so good."

"She's fine."

"I told her I could fix that. That I had something that could make her feel *real* good."

The sink's automatic faucet stopped suddenly, left me standing there with wet hands. I was shaking so badly I could hardly maintain my composure, walked toward the automatic blow dryer toward Duvall, wringing my hands, thinking the way I was trained to in the Academy, about all of the possibilities facing me now. I could kill him easily or he could kill me. We were both armed, no doubt about it. We were both quick on the draw and sure-shots once we took aim. I held my hands under the dryer, praying, thinking as fast as I could. If I took him out now, his boys would take me out later. They were probably just outside the door even now. If he took me out, what then? What would he do to Bunny if I wasn't there to warn her, to stop her? Who would ever get to the bottom of Joker's murder? Regardless of what Capt had said, I still had to know. I *needed* to know.

"Leave her alone, Duvall. She's mine." I step away from the dryer, facing him head-on.

"Ain't no papers on her." He made a step closer, raising his chin. "She's free to choose who she wants."

"'No papers?' She ain't no Rottweiler. She's a woman of honor. I told you that."

"Why you trying to play her then?"

"Play her?"

"Quit fronting, Preacher. She know about that other girl. The one in the choir? The one whose house you been slipping off to after hours, claiming y'all doing missionary work?"

"Who?"

"Yeah. Look at you. Standing there like a punk, fixing to lie."

"I don't have to lie to you, Devil. I don't have to prove a thing."

"But you'll lie to her though, won't you?"

"You sick, Man, you know that?"

"I'm sick, but you the one won't say nothing about all that time you still spending with that fine dark sister. What's her name? Rodgers. Yeah. Nicky Rodgers. When you gonna tell her about that? Or you just gonna break her heart again like you been doing for the past five years?"

"What you know about having a heart? You ain't even human."

"That hasn't stopped her from falling in love with me."

"*Love?* You better get out my face, Son."

"Or what? What you gonna do if I don't?"

"Get outta my face, Duvall."

"The boys in blue ain't here now, Preacher. Ain't no bars. No cameras, so who you gonna call?"

"Move, Man."

"It's just you and me. Man to man, straight up, Baby. Lemme see now. Lemme see how bad you is." He steps to me now, anxious to swing, so it's on. We grab for each other at the same time and the room tilts, is thrown into utter chaos as we crash against walls, banging flesh against porcelain and steel, against concrete floor. I land a punch to his jaw, to his gut and he doesn't flinch, keeps coming hard, pounding into me like a machine let loose. We go at it good, me landing punches against his head as he answers me pound for pound. My whole body's throbbing with pain and before I know it, he's got me floored like a girl, pinned into a corner. That's when his boys bust in as if on cue, pulling guns, and I know it's time to meet my Maker when I hear the chambers start to click.

"Move, D," one of them says. "Lemme smoke this Nigga now and get it over with."

He would've too, had that snub nose pressed against my nose, but Duvall says, "Nawl," and lets me go. He stands up, straightening his suit and touching the spot of blood at the corner of his forehead. He looks down at me on the floor, kicking me hard in my ribs. "Nawl. Don't kill this fool. This punk's got some serious reaping to do. He's gonna live to see, what they call that? Yeah. 'Divine retribution.'"

CHAPTER TWENTY-ONE

At the bottom end of the quiet cul-de-sac, at the entrance to the seemingly abandoned property obscured by a stand of red oak, the Escalade pulls through the gate, flicks its high beams off and on three times, and slides quietly into the darkened parking lot. It's a community of old storefront businesses and two-family houses, of postage-stamp lawns and elderly neighbors who go to bed by seven and never peek past their closed blinds at the organized lawlessness that's going on quietly just down their street. The brick building is covered with withered vines from the ivy that scales it in the summer. Too small to be a school but too big to be a church, the building is bathed in moonlight only. The outside motion lights once installed high on poles have all been shot out, but the watchers with their walkie-talkies and high-powered scoped rifles are nearby, in their usual stations, on the roof of this boarded structure that was once both soap factory and warehouse, and at the entrance to the barricaded doors and windows. Pinpricks of flame from the watchers' cigarettes and stogies glow like cats' eyes in the gloom.

The Escalade, not pulsating with its usual hiphop, as not to disturb the sleeping neighborhood, pulls around to the side of the building and drives straight through the huge overhead doors that have suddenly scrolled up in anticipation of its arrival. Once inside, the doors close quickly, and Lincoln, Ghost, Dante, Scooter, and Cheese file out like soldiers, moving as a single unit toward the helm of the bustling operations. Once the warehouse had employed 250 full-time workers who mixed vats of lye and fragrance and cut the cooled soap into bars. Now the vats and machines are replaced by a number of miniature labs, but the loading dock is still there. The two separate floors are now divided into smaller spaces manned by more armed watchers and street chemists in painter's white jumpsuits. The chemists, wearing plastic gloves, sweat now under dangling ceiling lights where they stand at long industrial tables mixing ingredients and manufacturing the talc-like white powder into jagged nuggets of rock cocaine.

The white-haired Italian who limps out of a side office and approaches them now, leaning on his cane, looks too old, too short, too pale, to be Ghost's uncle, but he smiles, extends his hand and looks at Lincoln first for clarification, clapping his shoulder. He ignores Ghost totally, waves all four of them into his smoky office and turns the volume low on the transistor radio blaring staticky Christmas tunes. Two more old men sitting at a table look up from worn notebooks lined with handwritten numbers and close them promptly. They grunt at the interruption, eyes aimed warily at Ghost as he bids his friends to take seats, reaches into a tall file cabinet against the wall for Dixie cups, and pours them all shots of good Scotch. "Once more, you, Giovanni, have exceeded my expectations," Ghost's uncle says in a lilting accent as the men all raise their cups, toss their whiskey back easily.

Ghost smiles, refills each cup. "Things are in place as you asked, Unc. We've already rented the apartments in the Second Ward. Two for now as you requested. My man, here," he gestures at Linc, "has already lined up nine good carriers. Proven men. All we need now is the staking. A word from you all to our distributor and we're there."

The second of the two old men, Salvatore Piscopini, snaps open his notebook and traces columns with an ink-smeared finger. He nods reluctantly. "It fits," he admits and Ghost's uncle leans forward on his stick, puts on his reading glasses to see better. He looks up at his nephew, then at Lincoln. "The dead moolie. He died on the interstate like a runaway deer crossing the road. Did any of you have anything to do with this?"

"Nothing." Dante speaks up too fast, and Salvatore sneers at him, glances at Ralphie Stokes, the stout man in the old blue suit sitting beside him.

"Who is to run this second territory now?" Ralphie asks and all eyes fall on

Lincoln. "Is it safe to move in just yet? We hear there is a younger brother. We hear he has much heart."

"Piece of cake," Linc says. "Not for you to worry about. I have someone very capable in mind," he adds, looking at Dante, who raises his chin nonchalantly like it didn't matter either way.

Piscopini jabs his thumb toward Dante. "So, it is he then? The Bigmouth?"

The room gives in to the lingering silence, waiting for his answer, and under the table, Linc knows Dante is tapping his feet slowly, methodically.

"No," he says at last, as the tapping stops suddenly. "Ghost is the man for that job."

"Giovanni?" Ghost's uncle frowns, looks at his nephew's pale hands folded on the table.

Linc nods. "Dante and Cheese must wait until the next phase which will involve the acquisition of the First Ward. They'll run that together in co-capacity, seeing it's the largest of the wards."

But Dante is visibly upset. "Wait!" He gulps his second shot of Scotch, staring at Lincoln. "Why?"

"Because I said so." Linc glares back, his mouth rigid as stone.

"For how long though, Man? I mean, it's been almost five years already."

"For as long as it takes."

"I don't understand why it's always gotta be us that's waiting."

"Shut up, Man." Cheese nudges him, but Dante isn't finished. "I don't understand, Cuz. Why is it *you* gotta always call the shots."

But Ghost's father claps his hands. "You moolies, take that home. Take it elsewhere, eh? The Street, no? Tonight, we here for business. We celebrate now; we fight later." He nods to Ghost who refills everyone's cup the third time. "For now, we rejoice for the Second Phase. The Third will come soon. We will welcome it then. We will welcome you all aboard."

TRESPASS

Ghost

Blood's in the air.

I can tell by the way D's looking as we finish the last of the Scotch and leave Uncle Lou's. Dark. Closed. It's a face that's shut up against light, like a trap door; the way I've seen him look in prison just before they've had to pull him off of somebody. The way I've seen him look before we'd go out on our drive-by "expeditions" back in the early days. It's the face D gets when his mind is made up to inflict damage, and I don't feel sorry for Dante at all.

Everybody knows he wouldn't have anything, wouldn't be anybody, if it wasn't for D bailing him out of jail all those times, paying our own uptown lawyer to handle his cases, teaching him everything he knows about the business of buying and moving product and letting him run the record store we own in Trece, just so he can get those management and accounting skills D insisted he needed. When Dante came to work for us, everything he owned was in a brown paper bag, and he was living in the ward's hallways. Man smelled like a billy goat and had run up a tab with Da Block's dealers, so he was hiding out on the DL, begging schoolchildren for spare change. Now the man's got two nice cars, money in the bank, a condo in the south of Heartford, and he's paying for his oldest daughter to go to college. He would still be in the gutter if it wasn't for D, so for him to "show out" like that amongst men of Uncle Lou's and Salvatore's and Ralphie's caliber, was a slap in the face. Treason. I knew it; Cheese knew it; D knew it. Everybody knew it except for Dante.

D isn't the only one who's troubled by this trespass. Cheese is quiet, the anger and distaste burning in his eyes, and I can see the expressions on the faces of Salvatore and Ralphie as they shake our hands and wave us off. They've never liked Dante, even if his name is one of theirs, and, on a night like tonight, it's almost as if they've expected this all along.

It's clear they don't like the way he spoke out tonight, pushing against D publicly that way. Back in Sicily, men died for less offenses, and they know that if D doesn't handle it, the next time the breach'll be worse. What Dante did represented a breach of respect and order, and the consensus is mutual; D *must* deal with the offense.

We pile into the Caddy, head back to the Third Ward, and as soon as we enter its main artery that's bustling with the usual drama, D gives me that look, says to me, "Pull over." I park the Caddy near the curb and automatically, Cheese and I get out, awaiting the show. In the front seat, D turns and looks at Dante who's sitting in the back, as quiet as a church mouse now. He's saying something that neither Cheese nor I can hear, and we can tell the way Dante's holding his head, the way he's explaining with his hands, that he's apologizing. Trying real hard to fix it.

Cheese, who's six feet four inches, and known for his jacked-up smile, hence his name, pulls out his Newports, hands me one, and we both light up, our backs pressed against the Escalade, although I know nicotine is the last thing my body needs these days. The doors open. D's first, and he gets out and takes off his jacket and leaves it in the jeep. Dante gets out too on the other side, much more slowly, and he's still trying to apologize when D hauls off and knocks the words right out of his mouth. The crowd that minutes before has been busy buying and selling rock, stops what it's doing to stare. Ward folks know not to get too close when D's having one of his "fits," but they make sure they don't miss this historic moment.

D takes off the three guns he's wearing and insists that Dante do the same. Dante obeys, although he's begging for mercy, insisting he doesn't want to fight. "I'ma be fair," D tells him. "I'ma give you a chance to be king. Handle this man to man," he offers, but it's obvious Dante doesn't want the challenge. "May the best man win," D says with that psychotic grin on his face.

"I'm sorry, Linc. I was high, Man; you know I'd never intentionally disrespect..."

D doesn't wait until he finishes. He swings on Dante again and again, beats the man up and down the street, past the hoes and the boosters and the crackheads and the crap shooters, into the pool hall and out again. D knocks him into a parked car, kicks him back up the street where Cheese and I are just finishing our smokes. Dante's crying like a girl, can barely stand up when D drags him back to the Escalade and slams him into the front passenger seat. He's sprawled there like a rag doll, thick black scarf knotted askew at his throat, swollen lips bleeding all over everything. Close to 100 folk are standing on the curb and in the street, laughing and mocking and enjoying the spectacle, bearing witness to Dante's shame.

But D isn't quite finished. Cheese and I jump into the back seat and D makes a wide U-turn, screeching out of the wards, back the way we'd come in. He heads for the highway, looking at Dante sobbing like a baby with his bloody clothes half torn off. He's still apologizing, one of his eyes swollen shut, and D says, "So you wanna be, king, huhn, Baby?"

"No, not me," Dante cries.

"I wanna show you something," D says, setting the childproof locks on all our doors so they only open from the outside. He slows the jeep just before the I-84 on-ramp leading to the highway as Dante starts pleading with him to "*Please let me out. Please let me out.*"

"Y'all got your seatbelts on?" D checks with me and Cheese.

"Do your thing, Baby," we tell him, and he does.

"You wanna lead, huhn? But can you do *this?*" D says to Dante, and unknotting the wool scarf that's barely hanging from his neck, he takes it off and ties it around his own face like a blindfold, covering his eyes. He leans forward then, churns up his Busta Rhymes, and drives onto the highway ramp at full speed while Dante claws at the door, trying to get out.

In the back seat, Cheese and I look at each other and shake our heads. Nothing D does surprises either one of us anymore, so we just go with the flow, rock to the music, watch D drive all the way to New Britton and back to the wards again in perfect formation. It's a lesson D's made sure Dante will never forget, which means that he won't kill him this time. Dante's got a missing front tooth to help him to remember, and a whole new way of looking at the world. But he still walked away with his life, and to Salvatore and Ralphie, that's still letting him off too easy. Even a fool knows that anybody capable of running the wards the way D does has got to have some qualities that ain't exactly human, like driving blind in the dark, so if Dante doesn't know that by now, well then he deserves to be dead.

CHURCHING

The altar was empty, the sinners prayed for and baptized, the sermon preached, so that by 2:10, when Elder Starks concluded his benediction with a hearty "Amen," the 400-member congregation turned collectively to embrace whoever was standing closest to them and proceeded toward the exit signs. From her place in the alto section of the choir stand, Gabriella, overcome with more hugs than she could manage, giggled, hugged back until her own arms were tired. She then proceeded toward the doors also, certain that who she thought she'd seen come in just before the choir got up to sing their second selection was probably a figment of her own imagination.

She had been back in the swing of things two weeks already, ever since Pleasure and Rodgers had stopped by to "pray her back," and on a morning like this, she'd felt more like herself than ever before. Dahlia had insisted she lead "Forgiven," and the passion and power in which she had sung the song had broke folks down to weeping in their seats. It was her life she was singing about. Hers was a song the angels couldn't sing. She felt the touch on her elbow and turned, already knowing who it was.

"Sister Gabby? Your song was off the hook this morning! On the real!"

She'd been wrong again. It wasn't Trev but Tierre Johnson, one of the choir's youngest tenors. At twenty-two, he was a new convert with a voice like a superstar, anxious to serve, and still bubbling over at times in the language of The Street.

"Thanks, Sweetie. You pray for me, hear?" she told him, accepting his bear hug. The boy was as tall as an NBA player and as brawny as a wrestler, but gentle and tenderhearted, one of the best things to happen to Zion Apostolic in a long time. Behind Tierre, the rest of the tenors were filing out, all except for Trev. She saw him clearly, his robe zipped down and flapping open, his attention riveted to the tall, dark female whose hand he was shaking much longer than necessary. Nicole.

Gabriella pressed her lips together tightly, turned and walked down off the platform and out of the choir loft, shaking hands along the way. Folks from the pulpit were bubbling over with praises about her choir solo, saying how much the song had encouraged them, and she thanked them all humbly, offered the glory back to the One who had allowed it and continued slowly down the aisle. She drew closer toward the back, sure now that what she saw was a mirage, but as she neared the very last row near the center aisle crowded with bodies, she saw that she had not been wrong.

He was still sitting there alone, one leg crossed over the other, a finger to his temple, as though musing. She couldn't help it. She saw him and stumbled in her high heels.

"Oh my *goodness*, it's a ghost!"

He almost smiled at that, stood up then and reached out his arms, as if to break her fall. "You okay?"

She regained her balance and shook his hand instead, saw how serious he looked, how uncomfortable and out of place he seemed to be there. But he was there, and he had stayed.

He wore a white ace bandage on his right hand, a white shirt and a black pinstriped suit. Black boots, his collar open to the throat. The large two-carat black-diamond earring in his right ear had been replaced by a much smaller stone, a black onyx, and she was amazed at how conservative he looked.

"S'up, Babygirl? Told you I wasn't scared."

"I can't believe my eyes," she gushed, touching a hand to her mussed hair. "I can't believe *you* are here."

"Why not?"

"I just can't."

"Stranger things have been happening lately."

"Yeah. Tell me about it."

"But *dang*, Girl, you can blow." He was staring in amazement.

"To Him be the glory, Lincoln."

"Where you learn to sing like that?"

"It's a gift."

"Must be. You could sell some records with that voice."

"I'd rather not."

They stood awkwardly looking at each other while he shifted from foot to foot like a little boy, looking down at his feet. He looked up at her. "So that's how you see me, huhn?"

"What do you mean, Lincoln?"

"A ghost."

"Well, I…"

"A ghost comes from a dead person, right?"

"Right."

He chuckled, then looked down at the floor again. Speechless.

Gabriella unzipped her robe, took it off and folded it over a pew, not sure where to go from there. He looked and smelled so good standing there, and old feelings stirred, pulling her like a magnet toward him. She was relieved when old Mother Thompson, weight supported on a walking stick, limped over and stood right in front of them. Her eyes, magnified by thick spectacles, were riveted on Lincoln.

"The Lord *shole* do answer prayer." She was rocking back on her heels to gauge the full length of him.

"Ma'am?" Lincoln raised his brows, looked at Gabriella for clarification or help.

"We been praying a long time for you, Son. Waiting for this day when you stepped back in here like you got some sense." She jabbed his side with a gnarled finger, grinning, her hat sliding down over her ear.

"You don't remember me, do you? Mother Thompson? I used to come by the house and pray with your momma. Get her to the hospital when he gone upside her head." Mother's jaws were pudgy, hanging low like a bulldog's. Her face seemed too big for the curly gray wig under her hat, but her eyes were very very kind.

"Yes, Ma'am," said Lincoln, obviously embarrassed, and because he knew no other way to respond.

"She was a *good* woman though. Loved the Lord and stayed faithful to the last. And we done just like we promised her. Prayed for the both of you day and night. The Lord let me know before he took me outta here, that I would see this day." She raised her hands to the ceiling and worshipped. Gabriella closed her own eyes, swayed approvingly. Lincoln was speechless, staring at both of them, until Mother Thompson opened her arms.

"Come here, Baby," she said, hugging him to her. "You done found your way home at last, ain't you? Welcome home. Welcome."

She turned him loose then, turned and hugged Gabriella for good measure, then pushed off for the door.

"Wow!" Gabriella said, looking at him. "That was the weirdest thing."

"Tell me about it." He was visibly shaken, she could tell, brows furrowed in confusion.

"Your mother was a member here, Lincoln? You were raised up at Zion? All this time and you never told me?"

"You never asked."

"What else is there about you that I need to know? That you haven't told me?"

"Nothing, Babygirl. Lemme get out of here before somebody else comes over and tries to baptize me again, and then I'd have to tell them that I did that already right here. Both me and Runt. Momma made us." He held out his hand to reveal slips of torn-off paper.

"What are those?"

"Phone numbers." He was smirking, trying hard to keep a straight face. "I made some new friends, I guess. Three sisters and two brothas. They want to call me for prayer, see if I want to have Bible study, come back for another service.

"I told them I had a friend already here. That whatever I needed, she'd be the one to get it for me. She the only one I would trust with my soul."

"And?"

"And, they still made me take their numbers." He chuckled.

CHAPTER TWENTY-TWO

He's still wearing the ace bandage on his right hand, his two middle fingers taped together. When she asks what happened, he shakes his head nonchalantly, focuses ahead on the traffic. "You don't wanna know. Just business as usual," he tells her and leaves it at that.

All around them sirens seem to be going off everywhere tonight, ambulances and police cruisers rushing past toward the wards, but Linc seems oblivious to it all. He can block out anything when his mind's on something else, she notices, and tonight, he seems especially troubled. They drive for over an hour outside of Heartford, and she thinks that the majority of their time together is spent in transit, riding from one place to another. She wonders if it's intentional, if the lull of the motion does something for him. "You like to ride, don't you?" she ventures.

"When I was little that's all I had to look forward to. Leaving the dirty wards and driving out real far to all those places I never been before. Detention centers. Halfway houses. Prisons. Funny thing is, those places were much worse than the wards ever were."

"Really?" He looks hard at her as if she doesn't have a clue.

†††

After an hour and fifteen minutes, the highway narrows and he takes an exit toward a cluster of hills speckled by small farms and meandering white fields. He drives up higher and higher toward blue-green mountains, more farms and miniature gas stations appearing sporadically along two-lane roads too narrow for passing. Finally, the land levels out and the air grows cooler, fills with the scent of roasting hickory. Small clusters of A-framed homes appear, chimneys roiling smoke, and each development of houses grows more and more modern. School crossing signs and traffic lights multiply on both sides of the street heralding strip malls and fast-food restaurants. Signs for Arthur A. Baxter Community College point north and Lincoln takes the turn, follows signs that lead to The Ainsley Rehabilitation Center.

"Where are you taking me this time?" Gabriella wants to ask but doesn't, waits quietly as he pulls into the crowded parking garage adjacent to The Ainsley Rehabilitation Center and pays the attendant. He parks, lets the car idle quietly, and turns to her. "Listen, we don't have to do this, aiight? If you're uncomfortable with it, I can turn this car around and take you back. I knew you were curious, and I wanted, *needed* you to meet him. Figured it might help you to understand… Help your stories and all…"

"Meet who? Understand who?"

"My brother." He looks away from her, looks down at the keys in his hand as if trying to decide another way to explain. "We're very close," he says finally. "It's important to me that he sees me, that he knows he'll always have somebody to look out for him. *Somebody* to make sure he never feels alone." He looks up at her, meaning more than he can bring himself to say, she thinks.

"It's fine with me, Lincoln. Really. I'd love to meet your brother."

"Runt," he explains as they stand at the front visitors' window signing themselves in, "…is kinda strange, Babygirl. Where the bullet went in? He's lost some functioning of the brain there. He understands most things though. I just hope he don't scare you," he says.

"I'm sure it'll be fine, Lincoln. Long as you're there, I'll be okay."

They take the elevator up eight floors, walk through several corridors with glossy floors and double doors, staff in white uniforms posted like sentries behind locked doors and sliding glass windows. A facility divided into sterile wards.

"Guess he went from one ward to another, huhn?" says Lincoln, playing with one of her curls, watching the way her heavy coat drapes around her curves. In the elevator, he grabs for her hand, squeezes it and lets it go, watching the color flood into her face. He wants to steal a kiss. Just take it, whether she wants him to or not, but he decides against it. He wants her memories of him to be easy, not tinged with regret.

On a ward called Chelsea South, Lincoln stops before a window and flashes his visitor's badge. "Two for Joseph Duvall," he says. Gabriella looks past the wavy glass partition at the oversized orderlies manning desks and phones, the neat racks of charts and files, the shelves of medications.

"What are you thinking?" Lincoln's watching her, loving her eyes and the way the loose strands of hair fall in a perfect curve across her brows.

"I'm thinking this is a very *nice* place," she says. "Very clean. Well-organized, it looks like."

"Yeah. It's a hundred times better than that county-run facility where they had him before." Lincoln looks up at the posted visiting hours, hands clasped behind his back as he remembers. "It was filthy there, and they never gave him his medication. He just sat in a corner all day and played with his fingers. Tripping hard, calling for me and Momma day and night, they said. Never getting no sleep."

"That's sad, Lincoln."

"Yeah. Runt ain't deserve *that*. What happened to him, he had nothing to do with. That was between *him* and my momma. But *he* was like that. Always wanting everybody else to suffer 'cause *he* was miserable. Hateful to the end." He coughs into his fist, unzips his suede jacket. "But this here's a private facility. It's much cleaner, the food's better and the staff is more professional. I put him in here five years ago and I can see the difference. He loves it here, never tries to leave or cries for me to take him with me, like before."

"That's beautiful, Lincoln. It looks *very* expensive though."

He shrugs. "Costs me ten thousand dollars a month, plus extras."

"Ten thousand dollars?"

He nods. "I couldn't do it without hustling. Every time I even think about leaving the life, I think about my brother. That's blood, you know? He's all I got left, so if he ain't happy, I ain't happy. Know what I'm saying?"

"And if something should happen to you out there?" He doesn't answer, reaches for a pamphlet on a rack with dozens of others and rifles through the pages.

"Lincoln. I know you heard me. What about it? I mean, what if something should happen to *you?*"

He closes the pamphlet and sees her eyes, sees the fear and the knowing down deep in the center of the orbs. "Who would care? Much as folks hate me? Long as *somebody* can come by from time to time to let Runt know he still matters… That's all that's important to me now. That's what I want *you* to remember, aiight?"

"You're wrong, Lincoln."

"About what?"

"*I* care."

"Why?"

"I just do."

"Since when? Since when you started worrying about what happens to me?"

She looks away then, studies the intricate patterns in the thick gray carpet. She backs away from him and stands closer to the waiting room door, fiddles with the snap on her purse.

"All I'm saying is, it's an important consideration. With all of your dreams and your planning have you ever considered the possibility of you…not being alive anymore?"

"I'm not as dumb as I look, Babygirl." He looks amused. "I'm heavily insured, Angelfied."

"Are you?"

"Course. I told you, I've got substantial holdings. I've set up a trust for Runt just in case, so if anything happens to me he'll be better off than he is right now… Set to stay here for life."

"Okay."

"Okay?"

"Okay."

"And your name again, Sir?" The orderly parts the glass window to interrupt, leaning forward to scrawl on a clipboard. Linc reaches to show his driver's license, but the staffer shakes his head, buzzes them right in. The ward they enter is full of zombies that walk, watch TV, and hover near the sealed windows looking out over the fenced parking lot. Lincoln nudges her toward a large waiting area where visitors sit playing chess and watching a big-screen TV. He takes her coat, hangs it on a nearby coat rack, and they sit on a plaid couch to watch reruns of *Laverne and Shirley*. Minutes later, a door opens on the left and in walks a beautiful dark man in a bathrobe and blue jeans, brand-new sneakers glistening white on his feet, an old stack of playing cards in his hand.

His is the halting gait of a man who is bitterly afflicted, a dragging of the right foot, as if pulling a load that is much too heavy. He is starkly attractive, but the eyes that dance and leap above the straggly beard are those of one who is plainly insane and wrought with unrest. Aside from his curly Afro, pudgy form and stooped posture, he is the spitting image of Lincoln, and Gabriella claps a hand over her mouth, sits forward in amazement.

"S'up, Baby?" Linc smiles, rises to embrace his larger self, and the man squeals like a toddler, touches Lincoln's hair, his clothes, his pockets.

"You bring me something, Linc? What chu got?" The speech is slurred, slowed with effort.

"I see you got the sneakers I sent." He points down. "They look real sporty, Man. Look real good on you."

But Runt is consumed with the effort of patting his brother's pockets, his eyes as dull as flint. "What chu bring me, Linc? You always bring something."

"Her," Lincoln says and drapes his arm around her shoulder. "I brought someone special to meet you."

Runt turns then, noticing for the first time that they are not alone, and Gabriella extends her hand, has trouble believing her eyes. "Hello, Joseph. I'm Gabriella."

"Who, dat, Linc? Mommy? Mommy? You got peppermint? Butterscotch?" He smiles, points to her purse, and his words seem unmanageable, although he's smiling, his teeth not beautiful like Lincoln's but chipped and mishapen.

"Linc? Ask Mommy. She got peppermint in her purse?" He opens his mouth, wags his tongue to receive candy and Linc lowers his eyes, pats his back as if to calm him.

"Nawl, Man. Runt, Momma's gone; remember? That's Bunny. 'Member, Bunny? Say 'hi' to Bunny, Man."

"Bunny? *Yeah*. Linc love Bunny. Linc chase Bunny every day."

Runt inches closer then, reaches out to touch her curls, and she stands still as a rock, holding her breath, watching as he brings the strand of hair under his nose and inhales. "Mommy," he pleads. "You brought me some candy in your purse?"

DEATH WISHES

Chinere

The phone rings in the shop and Imani picks it up. She looks over at me sitting in my chair with nary a customer in sight and sighs. "Yeah. She here," Imani says. Then, "Chinere. Phone. It's the clinic."

"I got it," I say, and when the hincty-sounding nurse asks if I'm still coming in tomorrow afternoon for the "procedure," I say, "Yeah. I plan to."

"No liquids after midnight..." Miss Nurse starts in reading down that long checklist of do's and don'ts before surgery and I suck my teeth, want to tell her, "Lady, I know that list better than you do. Got it memorized by heart." But it won't do no good. She still gotta read it and I still gotta listen. Gotta obey they rules if I'ma let the clinic "do it" for free.

I set the phone down finally and Imani starts whistling over her customer's hair, twirling bangs with her hot-comb and cutting her eyes at me like she do every time this happens. It's been almost two weeks since I seen Linc, since them boys got shot up at Soldier's, and the rumor is that he's taking up with that church girl again, like I'm surprised at that. I just sit here and pretend I don't miss him, although my cell phone ain't rang in days. Linc's the only one that really calls anyway. He don't like me talking to a whole lotta folk about nothing at all, interrupting us, so mostly it's just him and Momma a and 'nem that I expect to call me.

Imani's customer's wearing a red vinyl pant suit that's so loud I can hear it talking, but she tips her real good anyway and leaves, primping and preening because of how pretty her hair's turned out. Business for 'Mani's finally picking up again after all the rumors have slowed business down for all of us. Folks saying we selling drugs up in here, which we ain't, and many of my best customers done quit coming altogether, telling me, long as Linc and his fellas hanging around with them guns, they not ever coming back. So aside from a wash or two, I ain't hardly making no money these days.

"You going through with it tomorrow anyway, huhn?" Imani's upset. I can hear it in her voice, even over the water she's running in the sink to rinse the sticky perm out of her combs.

I pretend I don't see the way she's looking at me. "I might as well, Gurl," I tell her. "He had a fit when I cancelled my appointment and didn't go through with it two weeks ago. He found out and beat me like I stole something. You know how bad his temper is."

"I know you crazy for putting up with it." Imani purses her lips. "I don't care how much money he gives you or how good he is in bed, ain't *no* man worth all that."

That's when I pick up a magazine and start flipping through it. I won't do it this time. I can't let her see me crying. Imani looks up from the towels she's folding. "Look at you. I know you wanna cry."

"Cry? What for? What I'ma do with *two* babies when he ain't even here to help me raise *one*?"

"So. Our mommas did it for generations. You not the first or the last black woman to raise your children alone."

"Don't start with me, 'Mani."

"Them twins ain't asked to be here, 'Nere."

"Well, they ain't here. Not yet at least."

Imani kisses her teeth hard at that one, looks at me like I'm crazy, suds all over her hands. "When you gonna stop lying to yourself?" she fusses, and walks off to stack all those plastic curlers back into their proper bins. She don't even wanna hear what I got to say anymore. Guess she's heard it all too many times. I sit in my chair flipping pages, then look outside past that glass front door, seeing how slow the folks seem to be moving in the streets, like they underwater almost. Seem like everything going in slow motion, like a tape that's warped and 'bout to get itself tangled up.

Cold outside today, with the smell of snow in the air, and those teenaged boys are still playing catch football in the street while those fast-tailed gals steady flirting on the sidelines, doing those nasty drill team maneuvers that are just an excuse to shake they behinds. Too cold for all that, but they shaking 'em hard, got they hands on they hips and singing too. Singing about stuff that woulda made Momma slap the taste out of my mouth when I was they age. Back then I was the kinda nice little church girl that would've watched but never danced in public. Woulda sang along under my breath though. Woulda wished I was one of them nasty girls the boys wanted to touch. Back then, pretty bad boys like Lincoln would've never even looked at me, and now I'm thinking, maybe that's why I be trying so hard to hold onto him.

It's funny how life is though; how a woman like Imani gets more men to come sniffing in here after her than anybody I ever seen, and it's not that she looks all that special, but she sure acts like she is, and makes them treat her that way too.

She was a daddy's girl, that's probably why, and any man don't treat her good as her daddy used to when he was living, she don't even bother with. "I ain't throwing good after bad," she always saying.

'Mani's short and brown and sturdily built; ample shelf of bosom, but all hips and butt mostly, like her Alabama kinfolk. Her eyes are a little too far apart, fish-like, and her nose is like a fist on her face. She ain't exactly what you'd call pretty, but nice as she keeps herself, you hardly ever notice. Most of the time she wears wigs into the shop; Flips and Afros and Pageboys she orders special from catalogues. Today she's wearing something long and silky and auburn—her countess wig, she calls it. She snatches it off now, along with the stocking cap that's underneath it, and smoothes her own real hair down flat with the palm of her hand.

Imani ties a kerchief on her head and looks around for her purse. Outside the afternoon was already giving way to darkness. "I need to catch the bank before it closes," Imani is saying, looking at me. "You'll sweep up for me, 'Nere? I gotta get outta here."

"Go on," I tell her. "What else I got to do?"

†††

It's lonely in the shop with nobody here, so I turn on the lights and the TV and get the broom. *The Ricki Lake Show* is on and I turn the channel right away. I can't take seeing no more baby-momma-drama, not now especially, and not since Ricki Lake has one of the most racist talk shows on TV. I know she gonna have a buncha the worst black men on that she can find, so I watch Judge Mathis instead while I sweep. Think it's so beautiful how he can combine his street smarts with the law books and sum up folks' foolishness in a way everybody can understand and relate to. Besides all that, he's nice to look at, can make you laugh without trying too, and reminds me of my uncle Marcus in Detroit, who's got more street sense than anybody I know. Besides Linc of course.

Seems like my whole life is spent here, in this shop, cleaning up after folk from can to can't. Just that little bit of exercise makes me tired, it seems, and it feels like I ain't got the energy to do nothing but drop back into this chair and watch Mr. Mathis scold these folks for coming in his courtroom being trifling. I sit and sit, even though it's dark outside and I haven't locked the doors yet. If Linc showed up now he'd be fussing about me being careless and not taking precautions, even though his watchers are out there right now in the front, watching everybody that comes and goes through these doors. I close my eyes for a minute, trying hard not to think about what tomorrow's gonna bring, and that's when I feel it—a ripple in my belly, like a mosquito skimming through water. I sit up straight, think maybe it's that split pea soup I had for lunch, but it happens again, and I know for sure it ain't no soup, but it's our children, trying to let me know they in there. I cup my belly, squeeze my eyes even tighter, and the flutters go on like that for the next five minutes, making the water run down my face until the collar of my smock gets all soggy.

I'd have sat blubbering for the next two hours, only the bell to the shop starts ringing, and I look up to see the pizza man walking in with a delivery.

"A large sausage with extra cheese?" he says, looking around, and I shake my head, think maybe it was Linc what sent him, Linc thinking about me, about our children after all.

"I didn't order no pizza," I tell him, wondering how he got past all those men outside with guns.

"This the address they gave me," he say, with that smart tone in his voice, like he don't know who I am. Like he don't know I'm Linc Duvall's woman, and can cause him to catch a major beat down if he ain't careful.

"Well, what's the phone number in here?" Mr. Smart Mouth asks. "Somebody called from this number."

"From 722-3620?"

"I don't know. Lemme see," he says and puts down the pizza and reaches into his pocket.

NEWS

The night air is cool but not frigid when Trev pulls into the driveway of the vinyl-sided house Nicole still shares with her aging parents and parks. Her mother, frowning, answers the door wearing pink curlers and bedroom slippers, a house dress spotted with tiny pink butterflies. Her father, bearded and bi-focaled, sits in his armchair reading the sports page. He looks up at Trev in his neat white dress shirt and dark slacks and grunts, says nothing, even as Trev sits across from him and inquires about his health, the weather, the state of the black body-politic in Washington.

"Nicky'll be right down," Mrs. Rodgers explains, sitting on the couch to finish watching the news. She lifts a steaming cup from its saucer and blows into her tea. "She just got a call, poor thing. A tragedy across town tonight. It seems a client of hers from the clinic was gunned down in cold blood over nothing. She was just twenty-five years old."

"Sad." Trev closes his eyes, mumbles a silent prayer for the woman's family, whoever, wherever, they are. It never stops, it seems. Someone was always falling prey to someone else's hatefulness, and for once he is relieved not to have to rush to the scene to inspect the remains and gather statements from eyewitnesses. He'd done it for years. Had been in the mix of every major drama that went down in the wards. Tonight though, he sits with his hands in his lap and thinks of Gabriella. Of why she still hasn't returned his calls or says no more than five words to him at church these days. It seems tragic that they aren't together tonight, and he doesn't want to believe it's the only reason he is at Nicole's. Nicole, who never pushes him about commitment or seeks validation of his feelings. Nicole, who is tall and svelte and lovely and dedicated to the Lord, but is not, in any way, Bunny.

Heels clack on the stairs and Nicole, still in her white clinic smock, appears at the bottom of the landing, her face streaked with dried tears. "Did my mother tell you?" she asks, smoothing her ruffled hair back and away from her face with the back of her hand. She presses a Kleenex against her nose, blows hard. "Did she tell you about Chinere?"

"*Chinere?*"

"Yes."

"What about her?"

"She was murdered… They found her in her shop tonight. Just like she always said they would." Nicole bows her head, dabbing gently at her eyes again. "Trev? Where are you going?"

He was up and out of the chair, pulling at the door before he realized it. He had only two urgent thoughts pressed on his mind; where was Bunny and was she still dealing with Duvall?

"I'll be back," he tells Nicole. "I need some air."

✝✝✝

He calls Gabriella from his cell six times before he reached home, and each time got her voice mail. He drives past her condo, but her car wasn't there. He calls Pleasure, who hadn't heard from her since the night before, and finally her mother, who didn't have a clue where she was and hadn't spoken to her in days. Finally, he heads back to his own place, shivering at the possibilities and driving slowly, avoiding the long way around the other side of the avenue that dipped down into the wards. Things would be ugly for her if she was still in some way connected to Duvall. The fact that he'd showed up at one of Zion's Sunday morning services recently, was a telling sign, when he'd sat coolly toward the back, his eyes trained on Gabriella through most of the service. But afterward Pleasure had told Trev that Bunny had been just as shocked by Duvall's appearance as he himself had been.

"She promises she's not in a relationship with the man," Pleasure had said. "It's you and Nicole who need to define the boundaries of your relationship."

†††

Back at his apartment again, Trev checked his voice mail, left a message for Bluecoat Rodgers to call him, and headed straight for the coffee table. The file Joe had given him weeks before sat untouched since that night, beneath a mound of mail, but he sat down now on the couch with it, took a long deep breath and began the arduous process of trying to understand the man he believed *looked* to be responsible for such a terrible crime, which made it all the more suspicious to him. All those years in Vice and he could count the number of times he'd actually cried over anybody. He'd been deeply saddened time and time again and moved to despair more times than he could count, but there was only one time that he had cried. Just that once, that he could recall; six small children had burned up in a fire set by their own mother during one of her crack binges, and the tragedy of that scene had been beyond gruesome. They were all crying that night; the firefighters and the narcs, the drug dealers and the EMTs. He'd sat alone inside his cruiser and wept silently into his hands, wishing somehow, that he'd known, wanting somehow to make things alright again.

Tonight though, the tears for Chinere were different. They burned, stung his eyes. She had seemed so alive, so sassy, so full of purpose the last time he'd seen her. He kept seeing her pretty face wet with tears, the caramel skin and jeweled eyes that gleamed when she spoke about Duvall as if he were her god. She hadn't wanted to abort any more of their children. Reaching out to Trev must've been her attempt to escape what she must've known was inevitable.

"If anything happens to me," she'd told him unequivocally, "you'll know why."

But now as Trev cracked open the dusty file stained with Duvall's name and history and secrets, he wasn't sure that he had committed the murder. He'd know more when Joe Rodgers called him back, but for now he thought it was just too cut and dried, too neat and predictable for something Duvall was in on.

✝✝✝

Inside Duvall's battered file, the pages were worn and mildewed, yellowed with age, its width almost as thick as a small phone book. There had been petty arrests early on, juvenile occasions of truancy and shoplifting and loitering after dark. He'd done short stints in detention centers and youth camps, in a few teen halfway houses. But the real story of Lincoln Duvall began at the tender age of fourteen when he went into Mason for what looked like an assault charge that had been upgraded to attempted murder. From the age of fifteen on, the arrests became numerous and more violent, the majority dealing with violent assaults, attempted murders, and drug charges; possessions with intent to sell, operating a drug factory; interstate trafficking. Duvall's was a career that had extended into every level of drug operations, and the higher up he got it seemed, the more charges he had managed to walk away from.

The earliest mug-shots of him showed a young, angry boy with silky curls and scant traces of fine hair above his top lip. He'd had the eyes of a dove at first, wide open and honest, as transparent as glass. His later shots though looked like posters from an FBI most-wanted wish list; menacing eyes void of light beneath heavy brows notched with scars, lips slightly parted in a wolf-like snarl. He reminded Trev of a lion, fierce, fearless and majestically beautiful. Folded within the arrest reports were a series of report cards and handwritten support letters from educators, teachers mostly, a gym coach, a guidance counselor, elementary school principals, all of whom were from different schools and all of whom had written glowing testimonials of Duvall's exemplary behavior and exceptional IQ scores.

"Lincoln excels in all areas of academic performance, an amazing feat considering his chronic absenteeism and unstable living arrangements," a

Mr. Vin Mahoney, vice principal of Langely Elementary School had written.

"Lincoln has a brilliant mind that deserves careful cultivation," Mrs. Agnes T. Jaroz, a sixth-grade history teacher at the Hooker School, had written.

For an hour Trev sifted through and poured over the file, finally stumbling across the stack of handwritten letters, ten in all, bound by a single rubber band and signed by a Mrs. Lincoln Duvall, Sr.

Arranging these all carefully by date, Trev read through them in chronological order, deciphering the neat, but child-like, handwriting:

"*Dear Mr Police Captain,*" they all began. "*I be Lincoln Jr.'s momma. Please take care of my boy in you jail. He has a tender heart and alway says he prayers.*"

"*Dear Mr Police Captain. I be Junior's momma. Please take care of my boy in you jail. He don't like to fight and have a good heart. He say he want to be preacher when he grow up. Please do not let him be hurt. He still say he prayers.*"

The letters spoke of Duvall's merits from a motherly perception; his ability to read passages of the Bible before he'd started school and his knack for painting "the most beautiful sunsets."

The last of the ten letters was torn and faded in places. At the very bottom, someone had printed "subject deceased" in small red letters.

"*Dear Mr. Police Captain,*" it began. "*I be Junior's momma. He never write no more. He get hurt in that place and they bring he to the hospilla. He doctor say he almose lost all he blood and die. He say he don't think god want let he be one of he preachers. Junior say he too bad for god now. Can you tell me do he still say he prayers?*"

The letters are revelatory, ringing with a hint of desperation, and somehow Trev cannot help seeing that once upon a time, there was another Lincoln who, according to his mother, hated violence and yearned for the tranquil lifestyle of a priest. How one went from priest to thug was in itself, an odyssey, Trev imagined, and he wondered about all the times Duvall had scorned him. Wondered if he had been in fact envious of a vocation he himself felt born to but had never been able to fulfill. The shrill of his phone stirred him now, jarring him back to the present. He was hoping it was Bunny, praying she'd return his call, but it was only Bluecoat Rodgers, informing him of what he already knew. Chinere *was* dead, but the details of the homicide were sketchy. They were looking for Duvall, as he was a prime suspect.

No one had seen him or any of his vehicles anywhere near the shop in days, but his men were outside at their usual stations, and the fact that someone had gotten past them to execute such a horrific hit was in itself a feat of daring and intrigue. The consensus down at precinct was unanimous; it had to be an inside job, although it wasn't likely that Duvall had ordered the hit.

There were rumors though, Joe had reported. A big hit was out on Duvall himself, and with his camp in chaos the way it was, Rodgers said, with his crew scattered about trying to figure out what had happened to Chinere right under their noses, Duvall himself, and whoever was with him, could easily become, on a night like this, an easy target.

"Word is, another hit's set to go down tonight," Joe says. "His enemies have collaborated and I'm told they've been planning this for some time."

"I've got to check one more place, but I think Bunny's with *him*, Joe; I can feel it." Trev sighs into the receiver.

"So *you're* going to find her then? With *him?*" Joe asks anyway, although he ready knows the answer.

Chapter Twenty-Three

Trevis

I hang up with Joe and call *The Chronicle*, but I get Bunny's voice mail, the sound of her recorded voice so unfamiliar to me now. I leave a message for her to call me, but I still call the paper again, ask for the city desk directly this time.

A woman snatches up the phone on the first ring. "City desk, Trish Weitzman speaking."

"Trish? Trev Cooper, Gabriella's fiancé."

"Why, yes? And how are you?"

"I've been better, but thanks for asking. I'm looking for Gabriella. She's not answering her phone. Is she still there or has she left for the day?"

"Let's see." Trish shoots her words off fast, like gunshots. "I haven't seen her at her desk for the past few hours, but she must still be in the building, because her car was parked out front when I came in from supper. Would you like me to leave a message for her?"

"Yes, please. I need her to call me right away."

"Will do."

"Thank you."

She hangs up and I know my instincts were correct. She *is* with him. She is in mortal danger.

FRIENDS

Lincoln

In the elevator again, after we leave from Runt, Angelfied hits me with her purse, playing, making me look at her. "What's wrong with you?" she wants to know. "Are you sulking, Lincoln?"

"Listen at you, sounding like a college girl. Why I gotta be *sulking?* Why I can't just be tripping, 'cuz my brotha acted like a complete fool tonight?"

"He couldn't help it."

"He didn't try."

"It wasn't that bad."

"It wasn't that good."

We standing toe to toe then, so close, I swear I'm 'bout to snatch me some of that good sugar, don't care what *she* say about her religion and all that, but the elevator doors open on our floor, and all these refugee-looking folks come pouring in as we step off. The moment's lost, but I'm starting to feel better about the whole thing, even though Runt showed his behind something terrible in front of her. We step out from under the hospital breezeway and into the night, and Babygirl's pulling on my arm, making me look at her again, and that's hard to do without getting turned on, 'cuz she looks so good to me right about now.

My heart's doing something crazy, flipping and diving like it's never done before, and I can't blame Runt for tripping over her. A woman this fine can cause a man to have a serious chemical reaction, which I'm thinking must be what is happening to me right now.

"Look at me, Lincoln. It's alright. I *enjoyed* the visit with your brother and I'd love to go with you to see him again."

"*Really?*"

"Really."

I shake my head, not sure what to say about anything. Runt had cut up badly in front of her, flicking his tongue and dancing, acting like he wanted to take her to bed. A lesser woman would've been shocked, insulted, might have run out of there, but Angelfied didn't trip. In fact, she smiled, seemed more tickled than anything, and I knew then that she probably *did* understand, knew I was more embarrassed than she was. I had got on Runt hard and made him apologize, told the staff they needed to increase his medication, and when I was leaving, he did something he hadn't done in a long time; he grabbed me around my neck and begged to go with me.

"I don't know what got into him tonight though. He never acts like that," I told her as we stood on the edge of the street, waiting for cars to pass.

"Do you think it was my perfume?" Angelfied asks, and I can't help myself, I have to go there.

"Could be," I say, trying hard to look serious. "Lemme check," I say, and before she can stop me, I pull her close and take a good whiff of that neck, letting my lips graze that silky amber skin. "*Mmm...*" I say. "That smells *nice*."

Angelfied looks like she doesn't know if she wants to kiss me or slap me, but before she can decide, I step back, move away from her fast. "Yeah. It was the perfume. Had to be."

"Look, Lincoln..."

"What's it called? It's different. Not what you usually wear. But I love it. It smells... *nice*."

"Don't be smelling me," she threatens in her best ward accent, and I can see that look in her eyes that she's been trying so hard to hide. She likes me and she knows it. I'm getting to her just like she's getting to me. So we're even.

✝✝✝

The air is cool but nice tonight. Just above forty degrees, so it feels like spring compared to the other cold nights we've had lately. Over our heads, the sky's loaded with stars. Not like it looks over the wards, with all those factory fumes clogging up the view of where Momma always said heaven was. Angelfied's wearing a beautiful coat that's the color of a tangerine, brown fur at the collar and cuffs, a hat and gloves to match, and it's hard to believe she could be cold with all that on, although she's shivering beside me.

"You cold?" I ask her as we walk across the street of this lil' college town that's so clean and neat it looks like something out of a Norman Rockwell painting. Small pretty town, small friendly folks. Not a black face in sight for miles, but she seems okay with it; looks like she's liking all of this, being here with me, in this strange little place.

"I'm not cold," she protests in her feisty way, and I stick my hands in my pockets to keep from putting my arm around her.

"Why you shivering then?"

She don't answer and I think I know why. It's still early, just a little after six, and the streets are full of people, crossing the intersections, streaming in and out of all those mini malls, window shopping, stopping at those outside stands where they're selling all kinds of gourmet coffee and fried dough. The air smells sweet, like a carnival, and it brings back memories of those days we used to bike up to the east side and take the ferry to the Rivers' Edge Amusement Park.

She looks up at me. "Nice up here, isn't it?"

"Yeah. A lil' *too* quiet though. I need to hear some sirens. See some drama."

"Let's go set a dumpster on fire," she offers, and we laugh softly, watching the traffic lights changing from green to red and back to green again. I'm expecting Wally and Beaver Cleaver to come pedaling by on bikes at any moment.

"It's such a nice night for walking though, Lincoln. Do you have to get right back?"

"Why? You hungry?"

"A little."

"Aiight. We can go back to Trece, on the south side. There's a lil' place that makes the best barbecue."

"Do we have to?"

"What chu mean, Babygirl?"

"Why do we have to always go back *there?* To the wards? There's a world outside Trece, Lincoln."

"I ain't scared of it either."

"Prove it. Let's go right there to eat. To that little bistro."

"Ain't no black folks in there, Angelfied."

"Does it matter? Black, white, people are just people, Lincoln. And these folks up here are genuinely friendly. They don't care about what color we are."

Looking around at the smiling faces that are walking past us, I have to contend that she's right. Before I know it, she's pulling me along, and we're sitting at some corner table in a small restaurant that smells like baking bread. I order a meatball hero and some chili-cheese fries, a tall soda. Some kinda blueberry cake thing with ice cream on top. Angelfied orders a Caesar salad with grilled chicken diced up in it, sparkling water, fruit salad for dessert.

"So that's how you keep that fine body," I say, but she acts like she don't hear a word.

"How's your sandwich?" she asks.

"It's the bomb. Wanna bite?"

"No, thank you." She wipes her mouth real dainty-like with her napkin, sips her water slowly, and I can't help it. I'm watching those pretty lips chew and smile, remembering how good that neck smelled.

"Here we go. You got me up in here tripping *again*. Look at me. I'm turning into a Buppie. Next thing I'ma be ordering mocha cappuccinos and eating horse-divers with my pinky finger pointed out."

She cracks up at that, laughs until she has to cough. I hand her the glass of water.

"You are a *trip*," she says when she can finally talk again.

"You make me this way."

She looks serious then, looks down at the table real bashful-like, like she used to look when we were little.

"Did I say something wrong?" I ask her.

She looks up at me, smiles just a little. "Do you still feel like walking?"

WALKING

Gabriella

It's beautiful out here tonight. Warm, with just a hint of wind, and the stars are twinkling like all of these plaza lights strung up everywhere. Christmas will be here soon, and the "Sale" signs are blazing in store windows, some even blinking off and on like neon lights. We're half a mile down from Baxter College and the influence is everywhere—Baxter sweatshirt and pendant stores on every corner, Baxter sports equipment rental places. So many different kinds of quaint little shops and boutiques that sell everything from books to collectibles, pretzels, pets, teddy bears and of course, lingerie. People in heavy ski jackets and parkas are milling on sidewalks and sitting at outdoor cafes, lined up outside of movie houses and clustered around sidewalk musicians strumming guitars and working violins to produce a funky Flower Child kind of music. Nobody is paying us any mind, and when I look at Lincoln, swaggering beside me in his dark suede, his face has relaxed finally; looks much calmer than I've ever seen it. We walk and window shop for blocks and blocks, and it all looks the same—overpriced sweaters, insulated boots, Christmas mugs and all kinds of stuffed animals, handpainted dolls.

At one shop Lincoln disappears and emerges minutes later with the prettiest black porcelain doll I've ever seen. She's the color of burnt cinnamon and her hair is caught up in a fancy chignon. Tiny curls frame her large, Bambi-like eyes, and she's dressed in a white, hand-embroidered frock with a lace peignoir over top. On her feet are shiny black shoes, carefully hand sewn, and I'm afraid to know how much he's paid for this delicate piece of work. When he isn't looking, I find the small hidden tag, and practically fall out when I see he paid $385 dollars for it. "Here," Lincoln says softly, like a little boy, thrusting her into my arms.

"For *me?*"

"For you."

"She's *exquisitely* beautiful, Lincoln. Thank you. But why? I mean…"

"I was walking around up here once by myself and I saw her. She looked just like you. I knew I had to bring you here. I wanted to give you just a lil' something to remember me by, just in case," he explains.

"Just in case? Are you going somewhere?"

"Probably," he says, his eyes strange.

We walk some more, further away from the maddening crowd, and the trees lining the streets are skeletal, bare branches long and spindly as arms stretching toward us. Three sets of cobbled steps lead up to a quiet courtyard that looks down over the plaza ablaze with lights and movement, and here we stop. A wall of aged brick offers a beautiful view of this collegiate city tucked inside the northern hills of Connecticut. Lincoln gets there first, places his palms flat against the frozen bricks, staring out at the world as if there's so much on his mind. I hang back at first, watching him, seeing how harmless, how small, how terribly normal he looks away from his usual environment. He could pass for a banker now, an artist maybe, or even an architect, standing there as if deciding the breadth and scope of the universe's design. He looks like anything but what he is. He turns to look back at me, and his eyes are loaded with emotion.

His cell phone rings suddenly, the fourth time since we've been together, but he ignores it as he has previously, sucking his teeth and snapping it off this time without even looking to see who's calling. He folds it and puts it away in his pocket. Sighs, looks back at the sky lights sprinkled in front of him.

"It feels funny. Walking the street and nobody gunning for me or trying to run me over. Nobody looking at me funny or begging for credit." He shrugs, looks over at me. "Babygirl. You ever seen the view from here? Look at it. All those oceanic colors swirling together like the inside of a well. I could paint it so many ways. Make it say a thousand words."

"Yes. It *is* beautiful." I wrap my arms around myself, swaying gently. "I used to come up here all the time to do research at the college. Come here to eat my lunch sometimes. Just sit and think. I always thought it was so pretty up here. I've seen it many times."

"You never seen it standing next to me. Come here."

I'm not sure what he means, but I know he won't take no for an answer. I walk up and stand beside him to look, to see what he sees.

"What do *you* see, Lincoln?" I ask.

"The future."

"What's there?"

"*You*…" His voice sounds funny and he blinks, looks down at me. His look scares me. It's the same look he had in his house that night when he held me and we talked into the wee hours. It's the same look he had when I pulled up near the b-ball courts that day and surprised him. The look he had in the cemetery when he brought me to his mother's grave to re-introduce us. No man has ever looked at me *that way* before. I wondered if any ever would again.

"I can't believe you didn't tell me you were a twin. An identical one at that," I say and jab at him playfully, an effort to rescue myself from the tension of wanting him, of understanding and feeling what he is trying so hard to tell me.

Lincoln senses my need for a distraction and accommodates it, playing along.

"You the investigating journalist. You supposed to know," he teases, shadow boxing with me lightly, laughing and letting me get in a few soft punches. "Uh-oh. Look at you. You got good hands, Gurl. Speed. Precision. Tenacity. I can tell you from the wards."

"Don't be trying to butter me up, Mr. Duvall. What else do I need to know about you?"

"Well, they say I'm crazy as a bedbug," he says, ducking.

"I *know* that."

"And… I never eat all my vegetables," he says and pretends to rain on me with a flurry of make-believe punches, his hands moving so fast I can hardly see them.

"And I'ma probably die young." He stops and starts to tickle me, and we both giggle as I collapse hysterically against the wall.

"Aiight, Lincoln. Quit it, now. I give… I give…You win."

He backs away from me, smiling, arms folded, then steps to me again.

"But I ain't so bad, am I? I mean, don't I have *some* redeemable qualities?"

"*Some*," I agree.

"So what we need to be discussing then, is what a bad influence *you* are on *me*."

"Beg your pardon?"

"How you been on this holy campaign to corrupt me. Get me saved or something."

"I'm sorry," I say. "It's not my fault."

He looks serious then, moving so close our toes are touching. He strokes my face with the back of his hand. Blinks, looking at me.

"I just wanted you to know I ain't been the same since you came into my life. You got me *tripping*, Babygirl. I can't deny it."

I felt his hands then, taking off my hat, playing with my curls. "I'm thinking about stuff that never mattered before. I'm feeling things I didn't even know I could feel." He licks his lips, attempts a smile. "Funny how I always seem to learn stuff too late. But at least I know it was possible for me, that if we had more time, I could really make things happen for us. That alone gives me a great consolation. Lets me know I ain't that strange after all."

Now's the time I need to stop him, to walk away and never look back. I close my eyes in the cool darkness, summoning my strength, but I don't move. Not because I can't, but because I don't want to just then. He shakes his head. His voice is soft, close to my ear. "I used to *love* this hair when I was little. I was always grabbing them pigtails... Wanting to touch 'em... I could never get enough."

"I remember," I whisper back, and his hands move, rest on my shoulders.

"I used to tell my momma, 'I'ma marry her, Momma. I'ma marry that Bunny girl.'" He shakes his head, seeing it. "She used to laugh and gimme those big soft hugs. 'I believe you will, Lincoln,' she used to say. 'Ask what your heart desires...'"

"We were kids, Lincoln. Just babies back then."

"But we grown now, and you came back. My Bunny came back to *me*. It's like magic, huhn? Like we supposed to live happily ever after."

We laugh gently at that, but then his voice gets serious again. "I never thought it though. I never believed you would find your way back to a somebody like me."

He's ready to kiss me but I pull away from him, step back to the wall, watching the world pass below us.

"You ever been in love, Babygirl?"

His question, like his voice behind me, startles me, and I can hardly breathe. My heart is pounding as if I'd run laps, and I'm wrong. *So* wrong, and I know it.

"*Love*? I don't know, Lincoln. I thought I was once. But I don't know now. Real love doesn't die, does it? It doesn't change."

"It changes you though, right?"

"I guess. Some people say that you never stop loving a person; you just learn to live without them."

"That's deep."

"What made you ask such a question?"

He tucks his hands deep into his pockets, pulls his head back to count the stars. "I thought I could love Chinere. I wanted to. I tried *real* hard too, to love her."

"And?"

"She slept with my boy, Ghost. Could be carrying his baby right now for all I know. After that, it was just like I had no more use for her. I never could respect her after that. You know?"

"Ghost? The light-skinned brotha?"

He nods. "And they were together more than once. That's what *really* bothers me. She don't know I know though. But I always know. I just get these feelings about things sometimes, and when I asked him if it was true, he admitted it. But I ain't blame him none. A dog's gonna be a dog; that's just the way it is. We done shared so many of the same women back in the day. But 'Nere? I just thought she was different. I thanked Ghost for letting me see the light of what she was. But it be real hard dealing with her sometimes..."

"Hard?"

"More like impossible. Seems like I can't get no relief unless I'm going upside her head, which I told myself I'd never do to any female. *'Specially* after what happened to my mother. But I always find myself hitting her. Hurting her. Then I feel all bad afterward, 'cuz it's like she just brings out the worst in me."

It's quiet now, neither one of us saying anything.

"So you're a lot like your father?"

"I guess I am. She the only woman I ever hit though. Not that it's justified. I mean, I got a real mean streak, Angelfied. I'll admit to that. You wouldn't recognize me at my worst. And the last time, I beat her *so* bad..." He squeezed my shoulder. "It was ugly, what I did to her." He gulped a deep breath, his voice falling off. "I gotta let her go before I kill her. I can't keep playing around with it." He laughs a low, hard sound. "Man, I can't believe I'm telling you all this..."

"It's alright, Lincoln."

"I'm the same man, but y'all bring out two different sides of me. 'Nere? She brings out the worst. That monster that's just like *him*. But you, Babygirl?

You bring out the best in me. You keep taking me to levels I've never been and there are times when I can actually believe I don't have to go back to what I was. There's no greater gift than that, is there?"

"Yes, Lincoln, there is," I say, and this time, I touch his cheek, let him read the seriousness in my eyes. "Lincoln, friends don't let friends die without Jesus. *Please* think about that. It's not too late."

CHAPTER TWENTY-FOUR

Lincoln

It seems strange to me, this entire night. Like something's gnawing at me hard, but I don't know what it is. I keep thinking about Momma, though, and how I knew that night when they showed up at my cell to take me down to Chaplain's, that the end had finally come for her. I keep remembering how they said it was a whole lot of her blood everywhere, and that's what killed her. Not all those bullets in her head, but all that blood that kept running out of her; so much, it seeped through the floorboards, through the ceiling of the Johnsons' who lived downstairs right below us.

They say Mrs. Johnson was cleaning chicken at her kitchen sink when she looked up and saw all that blood splattering right down onto her kitchen table. It's a good thing she saw it when she did, else nobody would've went upstairs and found Runt in time. And it always makes me think of the Bible story Momma once told us, about the man who almost got away with killing his own brother, but then his blood cried out and told on him. I keep thinking about it all the way home; all that blood they say Momma lost, and it seems the more I try to shake 'em, the more the thoughts keep on coming.

✝✝✝

Ainsley's a beautiful metropolis, more villa than city; historical college buildings sprawled everywhere, all up and down the street; red brick with the ivy climbing, and dozens of miniature squares with park benches and ice-covered fountains, dense woods flowing all the way back toward the interstate. There are plenty of little motels and inns up and down the block, but I don't even mention it, 'cause I know she ain't going for *that*. Not now at least. Not with me. We just walk and talk about some of everything. About her sisters and her momma and why her daddy never bothered to come to her graduation from college. I keep looking at Angelfied, at how pretty, how wholesome she looks when she's laughing. The more I look, the more I don't wanna leave her, and the more I hate leaving this world we're making for ourselves in this little country town where nobody's looking at us funny or wanting to shoot my head off.

Eventually I start getting antsy again, feel that tug pulling me back toward the wards, and Babygirl looks up at me like she knows, her eyes glowing soft and warm. It takes everything I have not to kiss her, so I try to wrap her up in my arms instead, try to hold onto her, keep her close to my heart. But she sighs and pushes at my chest. "Please... don't," she says, like her conscience is working double-time on her. "I can't go there anymore."

I look at her and she looks at me.

"Things don't have to be this way, Lincoln," she tells me.

"Yeah... I could get all the kisses I wanted to if I was saved and we got married, huhn?"

"Exactly."

✝✝✝

In the car, on the way home, Angelfied leans her head back against the seat and closes her eyes. I think she's asleep until she starts humming in that soft way she has. It's a song I've heard before, a song Momma used to sing to us all those times she'd had to put us to sleep, chasing away the nightmares. I look over at her, pick up her soft, lotion-scented hand and squeeze it. I kiss it, think it's so amazing, how calm, how at peace, she makes me feel. "What chu singing, Girl?"

"By the Rivers of Babylon...where we sat down...we wept when we remembered Zion..."

"Amazing. Momma used to sing that all the time."

"Joseph thought I was her. Why is that, Lincoln?"

"You like a reincarnation of her spirit, Babygirl. It's funny, ain't it? The past. It seems like the more I try to move away from it, the more it keeps popping up to haunt me."

I reach up into the sun-visor over my head, take down the white envelope and hand it to her. She looks at me, an eyebrow raised, but opens the envelope and finds the folded note and the two keys inside. "Read it when you get home," I tell her. "It's for your eyes only."

"But what is it?"

"Keys to my safety deposit box at Webster Bank on the south side. You'll find a longer letter with further instructions in there."

"A *letter*? What kind of instructions?"

"A letter and instructions for everything I don't know how to say. Don't worry, it's nothing illegal or anything like that."

"But, Lincoln." She presses her lips together, trying hard to understand, but I put a hand to my lips and shush her quietly. "*Please*, Babygirl. Do it for me, okay?"

"Okay," she promises, exactly as I knew she would.

TROUBLE

Gabriella

On the way home I fall asleep, and when we are back in Heartford again, he wakes me up, his smile odd.

"What's so funny?" I ask.

"You. You snoring."

"*Me?* I don't snore."

"I didn't know if I should wait 'til spring to wake you up or what."

I swat at him playfully, can tell by the time we cross over the Langely Parkway near the rows of factories overlooking the wards, that Lincoln's back into his ward mode again and gearing up for something. He grows quiet in the silty blackness, driving faster than he usually does, and starts looking at his watch, watching his rearview mirror and bopping his head slowly to that hard gangsta rap that he keeps down low for my sake, even though it's all instrumental music, no words at all. It's the kinda hard-driving bass rhythm that thugs use to get themselves "amped" to do some damage, he'd told me before, when were at his house that day. And it's obvious something's in the air, yet he won't check the messages on his cell phone to find out exactly what's going on.

"Lincoln. Is everything okay?" I ask, and he gives me that look. "Just business as usual, Babygirl," he says, looks at the beautiful doll I'm still cradling in my lap and forces a smile.

But when he turns the corner that leads onto the long avenue near my job, his smile suddenly vanishes. He bites down hard on his bottom lip, contemplating something.

"Make sure you call me sooner the next time you visit Joseph. I'll pick up some butterscotch and some…"

I'm talking but Lincoln isn't paying the least bit of attention. He's looking forward, down the other end of the street at the cars parked near the lot just outside our employee gate.

"What's wrong, Lincoln?"

"Nothing. Just another Nine-Eleven."

"What's that?"

"Trouble," he says, patting under his clothes and up under his seat.

"Trouble?"

He looks at me, and his eyes have changed that fast, his face darkening, as hard as brick. "Look, Babygirl. I want you to do something for me. I want you to trust me, okay? I would never do anything to hurt you. Remember that."

"Yes, Lincoln, but…"

"Do exactly as I say, and don't look back. I'll explain it all later, *if* I get a chance to."

"But, Lincoln…"

"Listen to me. When you get to your car, I want you to get in and lock the doors immediately. I want you to drive away as fast as you can without drawing attention to yourself and I don't want you to look back. When I walk you to your car, *stay* in front of me. I'll be covering you from behind. Don't look at *nobody* else, no matter what happens."

"But, Lincoln…"

"You hear me?"

"Yes."

"*Don't* go home."

"What?"

"Your girlfriend, the fat one?"

"Pleasure?"

"Yes. Go to *her* house and wait until I call you." He fumbles under his coat, pulls out his phone and hands it to me. "Put this in your purse. *Don't* go home and *don't* leave her house."

"Lincoln…"

"If you don't hear from me by tomorrow morning, call your boy, preacher-cop, and tell him exactly what I'm telling you. He'll know what to do."

"Okay."

"Aiight. You got the envelope?"

"Yes."

"Good. Now here, take this." He clicks and adjusts it before handing me a tiny silver pistol that's so small it looks fake, almost hides in the palm of my hand.

"Lincoln, I can't. A *gun?*" My heart is pounding; everything's happening so fast I can barely think.

"Put it in your pocket, Angelfied. It's loaded and set to fire. All you gotta do is aim and pull the trigger. If anybody even *attempts* to come near you, I want you to fire first and ask questions later."

"Lincoln."

"Just do it."

I have no intentions of using the pistol, but to settle his mind, I take it anyway. The Beemer cruises slowly down the block and now I can see my own car parked exactly where I'd left it. Two other late-model cars, windows tinted, are parked on the other side of the street, idling quietly, and Lincoln sees them but pretends he doesn't, looks straight ahead, talks without moving his lips.

"Remember what I said, Babygirl. Remember the safe deposit box at Webster's."

He slows at the corner near the huge sandstone building that houses *The Chronicle* and looks over at me. "You ready?"

"Okay, Lincoln."

"Get your keys ready."

He pulls up directly behind my car now and parks and pats under his coat in a slick motion so fast it's easy to miss. He gets out first, walks around to my side and opens my door, walking me toward my car. Suddenly there are men standing around both of us. One on either side, but I do as he has said and don't look at either one of them. I smell them though; they reek of marijuana and nicotine and alcohol and fried chicken. Gangsta rap thumps from the back speakers of both cars.

"S'up, nigga? Looks like you 'bout to go see the bottom of that river you love so much. Where ya boys now?" The voice is young but hard, anxious for confrontation, but Linc doesn't flinch.

"Let her go," Linc tells them, standing directly in front of me, arms hanging loosely at his sides like a challenge. Outgunned and outmanned and he's still commanding his enemies. "Y'all gone do this, then do it right. She ain't got nothing to do with this. *I* got what you want."

The men look at each other. In the two cars, more men sit watching, shotties leaning out, small-caliber pistols aiming directly at both of us. The men look very young. thirteen, fourteen, no more than sixteen.

"Nawl, Punk. We gone do both of y'all right here and right now. This for Spain and Tyree. For Skyy and Dante, nigga. Catfish gonna be chewing up that pretty face of yours by this time tomorrow. Too bad your momma won't be around to try to identify you."

"*Dante.*" Linc cups a hand to his chin.

"That's right. Recognize, Nigga."

Both boys go under their heavy coats, but Lincoln raises his chin to both of them, cool as a cucumber. "Y'all do that here y'all won't even make it out this neighborhood, Fool. Security's in that building watching us right now. See that man in the lobby sitting behind that desk? See them cameras up on those poles? They already got y'all plates.

"And Babygirl here? This Super Cooper's woman. He's Five-O with some *serious* connections. And you know that fool is crazy. Anything happen to her, y'all nickel-and-diming lil' niggas be put *under* the jail. So let Babygirl go and we can do this easy," he says calmly, looking at me, nodding for me to get into my car. "Y'all let her go, I'll just get in the car with y'all and we roll up outta here easy. Take me where y'all want then; do what y'all gotta do."

The keys shake in my hand as I click the door open, my hands hesitating on the lock. The air is charged, pulses with a heat that cuts through the cold night air like a laser. Another voice, low, rumbly, sounds disgusted. "This punk-nigga always trying to be a hero. Think he still the number one 'OG.' But it's over, D. You might as well forget it, Baby."

"Aiight then." Lincoln's so calm now it's eerie. He tugs at my curls, then nudges my arm, pushing me ahead of him. "Get in, Babygirl," he says evenly. "It's all good."

I get in the car, lock the door and pull off fast, the tears streaming down my face.

He'd told me not to look back, to drive straight to Pleasure's as fast as I can. But I can't help it. I look in my rearview mirror and see Lincoln and the two boys walking slowly toward the first car. I see Lincoln looking down the road toward me like he's saying good-bye. He gets into the back seat then and the men get in beside him, one on each side. The car screeches off going ninety miles an hour it seems, up the other end of the street.

Ghost

Dead fools never see it coming, which is why they end up that way.

But Linc wasn't a fool. Never had been, never would be, which meant that if he chose to die, it was because he'd wanted to, plain and simple. It's hard to believe though that in the end, D would have chosen the path of least resistance, but that's exactly what he did. The things he did before he left that day alone to see his brother showed me that he knew, or at least had a feeling that something was up, but he never questioned me or hinted around. Just armed himself stronger than usual, and stayed away from the wards. Guess he figured if he had to go, he'd leave the only way he knew how; like a man.

They came to me with the plan last year and I'd vetoed it of course, at first. By then we were all making mad loot, and my uncle and his antique crew of Sicilian OGs liked things just the way they were. They thought D with his plans and investments, his commercial properties, custom-built cars and Technicolor dreams, was brilliant. Who would've believed that although I never had the discipline to actually carry out what I'd been taught, I was the one who'd taught D everything he knew about navigating in my father's world.

Pops always said had he lived in another era, D would've been an emperor. But to the majority of our crew, he was just an average brotha from the wards who didn't deserve to get any higher than the rest of us, which was why Dante believed we owed it to ourselves to set the record straight once and for all.

"All us is mens and all us is created equal," was how Cheese, with his sixth-grade education, had put it.

Still and all, any affront against D was an attack against my own financial livelihood, especially since D was the one who drew out all our plans and devised all our strategies. D was responsible for all our expansions, for our credible working relationships with all the local, top-level distributors. He knew how to bargain the best product for the least money and had a reputation for fairness that kept opening the doors for us to expand into other markets, should he ever choose to get into heroin or fencing or black market artillery. D though had opted to cultivate his own brainchild. He was happiest building right in the wards, watching little people make big money, making sure they had places to spend it. Since none of the rest of us had much patience for details and bottom lines, D did the hiring and firing and training of our close to fifty employees, and the system he had implemented worked like clockwork. He had a schedule and a payroll, an incentive bonus plan, and a method of street career advancement that had brothas climbing over each other, begging to become a part of our enterprise.

Still, somehow, dissension continued to rise in our upper ranks.

Dante kept saying he was tired of playing third fiddle, that D was a glory hog, that he was selfish and grandiose and kept pulling away all our women.

Killing Linc hadn't mattered to Cheese either way. Business was business in the wards and he liked the noble way Dante had put it: "It's D's turn to suffer the fate of all great hustlers."

None of us, of course, could bring ourselves to do it, so we got the ones who we knew were young enough and smart enough to get away with it. We picked out the ones we knew D had trained personally. We didn't tell Creeper, of course, but TicToc and Lil' G woulda shot they own mommas for $10,000 each, and that's exactly what we agreed to pay them. Nobody had figured on Chinere being a part of the equation, but with me and her still kicking it from time to time and with her becoming suspicious of some of the things we were trying to plan, Dante figured she was a high security risk and enlisted one of Tyree's boys to deliver more than a pizza. I'd agreed, but only after she'd told me she thought the babies she was carrying were almost 100 percent D's.

By that time, we'd already sat down with the wounded Tyree and his boys, a few of whom were older and had worked for Spain, and were determined to get Linc back for all that time they'd spent in the hospital. We'd all sat down and figured out how we'd divide the ward territories into mini-outposts and split the profits among all of us. When word got back to Uncle Lou about what we were up to, he threatened to quit supplying us. He called me a pompous crackhead and said he'd give our new order six months before we all killed each other.

Pops didn't trust anybody but Linc. He felt the Moolies in the wards were too dumb and too selfish to run such a sophisticated operation as smoothly as D had. He cautioned that all the politicians and lawyers and rogue cops D had been paying off for years would pull out once he'd been eliminated and that the feds would come in and shut us all down in a matter of months. So I lied to him, told him we had abandoned the idea, and hoped that when the word finally came to him of D's untimely demise, he'd have a change of heart and would give us a chance to prove we could in fact run things with a number of separate heads instead of the one, like D had done.

"Anything with more than one head is a monster," I've heard it said, but we were determined to prove that more heads were better than one any day.

†††

On a warm night like tonight, the air holds the promise of a short winter, but it's hard to tell. The wards are swarming with cops tonight, in and around 'Nere's shop, peeking around corners, stopping cars, knocking on doors to ask questions, so Cheese, Dante, Scooter and the rest of us are all here, kicking it at my east side hide-out. I've broken away and come here, to my bedroom, alone, pulling myself away from the festivities to wait for the phone call and turn on the nightly news, see if it might run there first.

"Third Ward King Pin gunned down in ongoing turf battle," the small headlines will probably read in the back of tomorrow's newspaper, but tomorrow hasn't gotten here yet.

I'm just waiting for this phone call from our mission-crew to give the all-clear before I can even begin to celebrate. Lil' G and his homies have been gone close to an hour already, and nobody's called in to tell us anything. The delay's got me feeling unsettled somehow, although I know such things take time, and anybody who has the guts to "do" Linc, deserves to take as much time as they need. Dante's bought shrimp and champagne, and Cheese has brought in a whole vanload of hoes, but sick as I've been feeling lately, I'm not in the mood for being with any woman right now. On the other side of this bedroom door, the music's pumping and the apartment's full of smoke, but it seems foolish to be celebrating D's murder without a body to show for it first.

Dante knocks on the bedroom door where I'm sprawled across the bed feeling nauseous, sick to my stomach and weakened by what is becoming an ongoing and chronic battle with diarrhea. He's swigging from an almost empty bottle of champagne, dressed in one of his best suits, creamy-white, with a matching brim and shoes, and his newfound power makes him look smarter, more sophisticated than he actually is.

"Ding-dong that nigga's *dead*," he starts singing, but I'm not in the mood to laugh. Too much time has passed since we've sent them out, and the longer we wait, the more I'm beginning to wonder if something has gone wrong.

"What's wrong with you, G? You missing the party, in here all alone acting paranoid." Dante slaps my head, teasing. "Did they call yet? You hear anything?" he asks and I can hardly answer; keep my face smashed against the pillows.

"Not yet."

"Well, don't worry, Gray Boy. It won't be long."

"Then I'll wait 'til it's official, if you don't mind."

Dante thinks it's hilarious, that I'm so somber and serious at what is to him, a joyous occasion. If only we could trade places; if only he could experience how terrible this diarrhea is.

He claps his hands, cuts a few dance steps. "That nigga ain't Indiana Jones. He trained them lil' assassins hisself, so you *know* he's got to be somewhere dead. Ain't no doubt about that."

"We'll see," I say, as he sits uninvited on the edge of the bed, runs his fingers over my head, and leans down to kiss my cheeks, Godfather style.

"Man, get away from me with all of that prison-passion," I say, pushing his drunk self off of me. He lumbers to his feet then, doubled over with laughter as he holds the bottle of champagne over my head and pours, dousing me good. I'm sputtering and gasping like a sidewalk preacher, trying to get up to swing on him as hard as I can, only the door suddenly bursts open and the room becomes flooded with Bluecoats, guns blazing, voices hollering for us to "get down," to put our hands where they can see them. In the living room, the music has stopped suddenly, and amidst the pandemonium of hoes screaming and breaking glass, there's the sound of gunshots, of bodies being thrown against walls. Dante's so drunk he bucks and kicks, throws off the three officers who are trying to restrain him.

"Get off me, Man! I'm the H.N.I.C.," he's hollering, reaching into his pocket for his wallet, his photo ID where he's got pictures of his kids, his daughter who's going to college.

"Put your hands down, Baby!" I holler, trying to get to him. "Let them see your hands, Fool!"

But it's too late. The first Bluecoat opens fire so fast Dante's chest peels open like a grape. "Wait," I say, trying to put up my hands, but the hands of the second Bluecoat react before his brain does and the force of the bullets lift me up and off my feet, throwing me back into what feels like a hole full of jagged glass.

I wish I could tell him for myself. Say, Yo, D. You was right, Baby. Grim Reaper ain't nowhere as bad as he think he is.

BUSINESS AS USUAL

Trevis

"I just wanted you to know, somebody's praying for that fool."

Bluecoat Rodgers' voice was low, barely audible in the receiver. In the background, the static of walkie-talkies and police radios crackled.

"Every last one of his crew was wiped out last night, Man. All those cats were mowed down by Vice like the Boston Massacre in that apartment," he hissed.

"And Duvall?"

"I dispatched two cruisers to the west side like you asked, and we just happened to spot the car he was in and stopped it, brought 'em all down here."

"That's miraculous."

"You telling me?" Rodgers stopped to take a short puff on his cigarette, exhaled. "They had him in the back seat, victim-style. Lil' punks so young they didn't have moustaches or drivers' licenses. No telling where they were taking him, but it's obvious what they were getting ready to do to him."

"Business as usual, huhn?"

"Yup. They've all been transferred out to Juve Hall for now. The oldest was only fifteen. Them lil' cats were armed like mafiosos."

"I believe it. So *he's* okay then?"

"Looks that way, although they've got him on a special watch. D.A.'s office doesn't want him to hang himself or get smoked before they can get him to do some 'fessing. Rumor has it he's agreed to talk, but only if they reinstate *you* back down here, put you back on that same ol' third-shift ward beat you so famous for."

"*Duvall* did that for *me?*"

"That's the way I heard it, Coop. And you know he's got leverage. The things he knows, the crimes he's rumored to have been involved with? He knows enough to put himself and a heap of other folks away for a very long time."

"True dat. No wonder Capt called and says he wants to see me first thing Monday morning. Said it was very good news. Now ain't *that* something."

"Stranger things have happened around here. So how's your girl? You find her? Y'all working things out?" On the other end Rodgers yawned, sipped tepid coffee.

"I ran smack into her that night I called you. She was driving down the street like a bat out of hell and I followed her to her girlfriend's house. We've been talking since then. Who knows where it'll go from here, but at least I know for sure now that she's the one I love. Scared as I was of losing her for real, I'm *never* gonna let her get away from me again. You can believe that."

"I don't blame you, Coop."

"And, Rodgers? Next time you see Duvall? Tell him for me, will you? Tell him I'm praying hard for him." Trev paused, cleared his throat. "Tell him, tell him I said, 'thank you.'"

Gabriella

Sometimes, the worst kind of pain we can ever experience happens when we are turned over to the power of our own will and the consequences of our own choices.

How close have we all come to the brink of destroying our own selves had not the High God pulled us back from the brink of our own insanity?

Such times warrant that we should acknowledge how good He is, even though we don't often deserve it or choose not to acknowledge His presence in our lives.

It seems that people like Lincoln, who have survived life beyond the breaking point, understand that most of all.

✝✝✝

Who would've ever thought that I'd be living on this beautiful fifteen-acre property, in a wedding-cake of a house that has been duly signed over to me?

Who would've thought that I'd become a senior editor at *The Chronicle*, where every day, I make sure the sufferings of those who are forgotten are kept always before us?

Who would've thought that Lincoln would've lived after that frightening last night I saw him, lived to be transferred out of state where he's doing ten to twenty, even though he's made full confessions about all of his illegal activities, about his part in Skyy's and Spain's murders, and about a whole lot of other crimes he's confessed to that they didn't even know about?

Genuine repentance is brutally honest, so when Lincoln wanted to come clean, he wrote to tell me everything. He'd wanted his conscience, like his record, to be changed, to become spotless before God, and he's working on that every day now, carrying on his mother's wishes to live an honest life at last, studying to be the preacher he'd always wanted to be, and painting landscapes of mountains and valleys and hills of falling snow...

The End

ABOUT THE AUTHOR

A native of Hartford, Connecticut, Cindy Brown Austin is a forty-one-year-old award-winning journalist who attended Saint Joseph College in West Hartford. Cindy made her mark as a columnist and cover-story writer for *Northeast*, the Sunday magazine of *The Hartford Courant*, New England's oldest continuously published newspaper. Cindy's writing has garnered numerous awards from the Society of Professional Journalists. She has written for *Reader's Digest*, *Essence* and *Priority!* magazines, and has received an honorary degree from Capital Community College. Cindy is a Connecticut Commission on the Arts recipient fellow and a past $1000 finalist in *Ebony* magazine's Gertrude Johnson Literary Writing Contest. A licensed minister of the Apostolic faith, Cindy is a public relations specialist who lectures extensively across the country teaching writing workshops and sharing the word of God. She has been a feature subject in several publications, among them, *The New York Times*, and was named by *The Hartford Courant* as one of the region's rising stars. Married for twenty-five years, Cindy is a mother of four grown daughters. She presently resides in Windsor, CT where she is hard at work at her next novel, "Oracle." Prayer, Cindy says, is one of her favorite hobbies.

Cindy's web pages are: MY SPACE: http://www.myspace.com/98458231
YAHOO: http://profiles.yahoo.com/cindawriter007
AOL: http://hometown.aol.com/canaan007/

SNEAK PREVIEW! EXCERPT FROM

A Love So Deep

BY SUZETTA PERKINS

COMING SOON FROM STREBOR BOOKS

Prologue

I t was early fall, and weeping willows bowed to sun-baked lawns while giant redwoods spanked the skies, casting a lazy-like setting about the Bay Area. Maple trees were adorned with leaves of gold and reddish brown while squirrels scampered up twisted branches in preparation of the winter months that lay ahead. It was an enchanting feeling—a movie-set backdrop. The summer was coming to an end, but its remnants were still very evident.

It was five in the morning when Charlie Ford, Dexter Brown, Bobby Fuller, with Graham Peters bringing up the rear, strode onto the Berkeley Pier, carrying tackle boxes, bait, chairs, and insulated coffee mugs filled with steaming coffee. The sun was not due to come up for another hour. The calm and peacefulness the water yielded was just right for the few fish that might nibble on their hooks.

Not much talk passed between the four men. This was to be a short trip— a two-hour excursion to help lift the spirits of a friend. Then it would be back to Bobby's house for his wife's hot, homemade biscuits with honey oozing from their sides along with a plate of soft-scrambled eggs, a couple pounds of bacon, and fresh brewed coffee to wash it all down. If they were fortunate to catch a few fish in the process, that would be alright, too.

Their poles were extended, lines laying in wait, birds chirping signaling the day to begin. An hour passed, and the sun rose like a yellow monster ready to devour the city. Its reflection illuminated the water a little at a time as it rose over the Oakland and Berkeley Hills to sneak a peek at the four men.

"Something's biting," Charlie yelled, reeling in a three-pound halibut. "Hey now, I got me a fish for dinner."

"Who you gonna get to clean and cook it for you?" Dexter chimed in. "See, I've got me a woman that'll clean my fish, fry it up in a great big pan, and serve it on a platter with homemade potato salad, collard greens, and hush puppies."

"But you don't have no fish for your woman to fry," Charlie countered, letting out a great big howl and slapping Bobby with a high-five.

"I wouldn't eat the fish from the bay anyway. Heard there might be mercury in the water," Dexter said. "These puny little bass and halibut out in this water are just for sport—test your skills."

"Amanda!" Graham shouted, jumping into the water, causing the other men to gasp out loud in alarm. Graham gasped for air, his arms flailing around like he was cheering on his favorite offensive end, Jerry Rice of the Oakland Raiders.

"My God, Graham. What's gotten into you? What are you doing?" Charlie shouted at the top of his lungs, ditching his pole and jumping in. Graham could not swim.

Dexter and Bobby threw down their poles and ran to the water's edge. Sixty-two- year-old Charlie was the only one in the bunch who could swim, and he was giving it his all in the cold, murky water to save the life of his best friend.

Three feet out into the water, Charlie's muscular arms grabbed onto Graham, pulling him up. Bubbles came out of Graham's mouth. Charlie gave him a quick glance while paddling back to shore.

Anxious faces looked down at Charlie as he neared the shore. Dexter and Bobby extended their arms as far and pulled him onto the bank.

Graham's body trembled as he stood facing the group. His wet clothing stuck to him like Saran Wrap. His teeth clinked together in rapid succession, making a chattering sound. Bobby took off his jacket and placed it around Graham's shoulders.

Graham appeared tired and worn as he stared back at the alarmed men who were unable to utter a word. He looked at each one individually—Charlie, Dexter, and Bobby—then shut his eyes, clasping his hands over his face. He let out a sigh and his shoulders slumped with the weight of his grief. Amanda's death had sapped the life straight out of him.

"What's wrong with you, Graham?" Charlie shouted out of fear. You could have drowned out there? Talk to me."

"Stop it, Charlie," Dexter cut in. "I know you're still hurting," he said, turning to Graham. "It's gonna take some time, but you hang in there, buddy. It'll be alright after awhile."

"Manda, Manda, Manda," Graham moaned over and over again, his tears flowing like a busted fire hydrant. He fell to his knees, shaking his head, unashamed of his outburst. Life didn't seem worth living now that Amanda was gone. Charlie held onto him. His crying was so uncontrollable that his body shook violently as if he had been injected with a thousand volts of electricity.

"It's gonna be alright, man." Charlie hugged and squeezed his best friend. "If I could, I'd bring Amanda back, but that is not humanly possible. I loved Amanda, too. I wish I could somehow drain the pain from you, but for now, you'll have to trust that I'll be there for you."

"I can't go on without my beloved Amanda," Graham wailed.

Charlie, Dexter, and Bobby sat down on the bank next to Graham and wiped tears away from their own eyes.

Chapter 1

She was everywhere. Everywhere Graham turned and in everything he touched, she was there. Her reflection peered back at him when he looked in the mirror. She was a glimmer of light on a distant ocean. He felt her hand graze his while placing the oversized pillow on her favorite spot on the sofa. On the day he'd gone fishing, there she was in all her radiant beauty, staring back at him through the ripples in the water, and he had jumped in to try and save her.

♥♥♥

It was almost two months to the day since had Amanda died. Graham had not ventured out of the house except for the day he'd gone fishing with his buddies. He sat home day in and day out waiting for Amanda to return so they could resume their life together. But with the passing of time, his obsession left him scraping the bottom of loneliness.

Today was going to be a new day, Graham promised himself. Self-pity had its place, but now he was ready to rise from its shadow. As he lay on the couch trying to make good on that promise, he was suddenly twenty again—a young man recently come to the Bay Area from St. Louis to follow a dream.

♥♥♥

Graham's best friend, Charlie Ford, had arrived in the Bay Area a year earlier. Charlie's Uncle Roscoe, or Roc as he preferred to be called, had migrated to California after the war, finding work at the Naval Air Station in Alameda. Uncle Roc had invited Charlie to come out West after high school.

Graham and Charlie went way back. They met at junior high school. Charlie was one year older and seven inches taller than Graham, although Graham swore he was six feet tall when he had his Sunday-go-to-meeting shoes on. Charlie had coal-black, wavy hair that appeared an iridescent blue depending on the light. Graham had a thick crown of self-made waves with the help of a little Murray's hair pomade and a stocking cap. They were a pair. You'd rarely see one without the other. And yes, they could turn the charm on and were not accustomed to being without a girl wrapped in each arm.

Graham and Charlie played football in high school and were the main ingredient in a singing group they formed. Now Graham found himself in the Bay Area by way of Southern Pacific Railways with a shoebox filled with all his worldly possessions under his arm. Graham's mother, Eula Mae Perry Peters, had died suddenly of a brain aneurism, one short year after his father died. So Graham set off to see the world, leaving his two younger sisters behind with his Aunt Rubye to care for them.

It was Graham's first week in Oakland. The city was all abuzz—a little like St. Louis, except that there were more jobs for Negroes and maybe a chance to strike it rich. Striking it rich didn't seem to be a likely event in Graham's immediate future unless he accidentally fell into it, but he did like the feel of the place he now called home.

Charlie subletted a small room from his Uncle Roc and asked Graham to stay with him until he got on his feet. There would be no problem with Graham getting a job. Hire notices were posted all over the black community. Everyone was looking for young, strong Negro men to work in the Naval shipyard, lifting heavy cargo.

But this was the weekend, and Graham was ready to see the sights. It had been a long, tedious ride on the train. The bright lights of the San Francisco Bay were a wonderful welcome mat for a young kid a long way from home.

"Come on Graham," Charlie shouted. "The show's gonna start in about an hour. Man, you and me will be back in business in no time—all the babes we want."

"Church, Charlie? You've gotta be kidding. All of those clubs we passed on the way in. I'm sure we can find some good-looking girls there. I'm ready to unwind a little, kick up my heels."

"Relax, Graham. They say if you want a real woman, go to the church house. There's a convention going on at this big church up on Market Street that's about three blocks away and in walking distance. My man, Curtis MacArthur, swore up and down that there's gonna be a lot of babes at the convention. They come from far and wide. Graham, man, you can take your pick—short ones, tall ones, skinny ones, fat if you like, but there's enough to go around for seconds, thirds if you want. There's gonna be good music, eating and even a little preaching, but this is the place to be if you want the cream of the crop."

"Charlie, you are crazy. You should have been a car salesman. Anyway, I don't have anything to wear."

"That's no problem. Uncle Roc got plenty of suits. They might be a tad bit too big, but they'll do for tonight." Charlie laughed and hit Graham on the back. "You're my buddy, and we're a team. Now what kinda friend would I be strolling with a fine babe on my arm and my best friend sitting back in the room all by himself?"

"You don't want me to answer that...?"

"Go on, tell me."

"What makes you so sure any of these girls are gonna even look at you? They're lookin' for preachers so they can become first ladies. No slick, jive-talking, unrepentant, tall, dreamy-eyed, dark-haired boy without an ounce of salvation got half a chance."

"I was counting on that tall, dreamy-eyed, dark-haired boy to do the trick." They both laughed until it hurt.

"You're right," Graham continued, "we are a pair, but you run on tonight. I'll catch you in church another time."

"Suit yourself, buddy. You're gonna wish you were there. And don't let me have to tell you I told you so."

"Get on and get out of here. I might take a walk later."

"Gonna try and sneak a peek, eh?"

"Catch you later."

Graham sat in the room contemplating life—what he was going to do tonight and then tomorrow. An hour had passed since Charlie left. It seemed the whole neighborhood had evaporated into the night—a hushed quiet that made Graham a bit wary. He jumped up and went to the window, but only the stars and the moon dared to stare back at him, the moon illuminating his face in the windowpane.

Graham grabbed his jacket off the chair and headed out the door. He wasn't sure where he was going, but he knew he needed to get out of that noiseless house—maybe hear a little music, ahh maybe some preaching, but he wanted to be where there was life and a little reminder of home.

He headed west passing a few couples out strolling. Then he noticed the cars—so many lined the street. He continued another block, and the cars—Buicks, Packards, and Fords, inhabited every available space on either side of the street. Yeah, he would own one of them one day. Then he heard it, felt it reverberate throughout his body. It reminded him of thunder, cymbals crashing. Yes, someone was having a good time, and it didn't sound like the blues they were playing back at Slim's in St. Louis.

As Graham neared the big church on Market Street, a flurry of activity surrounded it. The building seemed to sway on its cinderblocks, careful not to empty its precious cargo from inside. It was 10 p.m., and although there seemed to be a lot going on inside the church, there was a lot happening outside as well. Small circles of young people milled about holding conversations. Suddenly, Graham was converged upon by a sea of purple and white choir robes which dutifully stretched into a single line waiting to march into the sanctuary. Graham looked around, but Charlie was nowhere to be found.

As Graham inched closer, a beautiful girl in her late teens emerged from the fellowship hall. She was about Graham's height, give or take an inch. She wore the prettiest white silk suit and a white pill-box hat with a bow made of lace attached to the front. The ends of her hair were turned up in a shoulder-length flip that accentuated her nutmeg-colored skin. But it was the nut-brown legs that made Graham come from his hiding place. Graham stumbled over a workhorse that had been placed over an open manhole. He regained his composure and followed her right into church.

He'd forgotten for a moment that he was not dressed appropriately, but that didn't matter. Charlie was right; "the crème de la crème" resided here. Someone called "Amanda," and the girl with the nut-brown legs, waved her hand. What a pretty name. Graham would have to move closer if he was going to say anything to her at all. She looked his way and then quickly away, bobbing her head to the music as the choir marched in. She looked his way again, and Graham locked upon her gaze and didn't let go.

She seemed shy in a girlish sort of way, but Graham forged ahead. He pushed closer to her, the crowd unyielding until he was within an inch from touching her nose.

"Hi, Amanda," he said above the noise.

She sneered at him, wrinkling up her nose.

"Who are you, and how do you know my name?" Amanda Carter demanded.

"That's a secret," he said, even more mesmerized by her beauty. "My name is Graham." He extended his hand. "I'm going to be a preacher one day."

Graham saw the puzzled look on her face. "What does that have to do with me?" she retorted, leaving his hand in mid-air.

"Well...I. Would you like to go outside and talk for a few minutes?"

Amanda cocked her head back hesitating before she spoke. Her eyes cut a path down the length of his body and rested on his wrinkled khaki pants and blue peacoat that had doubled as a pillow on his trek to the West.

"Sure, why not," she said nonchalantly. "You seem harmless enough, but after this choir sings. They are so good."

Oh, if Charlie could see him now. Graham could tell Ms. Amanda liked the attention he was giving her, although she pretended she didn't. When the choir had finished singing, they quietly went outside. They made small talk, but Graham was transfixed by her beauty (eyes the color of ripe olives embedded in an oval, nutmeg-colored face) and those beautiful nut-brown legs that he wished he could wrap his own around. Actually, he wanted to reach out and touch her, maybe place a kiss on those fine chiseled lips of hers that smelled of sweet berries when he got close enough to catch a whiff.

There was something about Amanda that was different—unlike those other girls who stumbled over themselves vying for the chance to be his lady. Graham Peters became a different person that night—his heart ached for Amanda Carter, a girl he had just met. If given half a chance, he would cherish her until the end of time.